TEMPTING EVIL

TEMPTING EVIL

A NOVEL OF SUSPENSE

ALLISON BRENNAN

THORNDIKE
WINDSOR
PARAGON

This Large Print edition is published by Thorndike Press, Waterville, Maine, USA and by BBC Audiobooks Ltd, Bath, England.
Thorndike Press, a part of Gale, Cengage Learning.
Copyright © 2008 by Allison Brennan.
The moral right of the author has been asserted.
The Prison Break Trilogy.

The text of this Large Print edition is unabridged.
Other aspects of the book may vary from the original edition.
Set in 16 pt. Plantin.
Printed on permanent paper.

LIBRARY OF CONGRESS CATALOGING-IN-PUBLICATION DATA

Brennan, Allison.
    Tempting evil : a novel of suspense / by Allison Brennan.
        p. cm. — (The prison break trilogy) (Thorndike Press large print basic)
    ISBN-13: 978-1-4104-0549-4 (alk. paper)
    ISBN-10: 1-4104-0549-4 (alk. paper)
    1. Women novelists — Fiction. 2. Montana — Fiction. 3. Blizzards — Fiction. 4. Large type books. I. Title.
    PS3602.R4495T46 2008
    813'.6—dc22   2008017965

BRITISH LIBRARY CATALOGUING-IN-PUBLICATION DATA AVAILABLE

Published in 2008 in the U.S. by arrangement with The Ballantine Publishing Group, a division of Random House, Inc.
Published in 2009 in the U.K. by arrangement with Little, Brown Book Group.

U.K. Hardcover: 978 1 408 41341 8 (Windsor Large Print)
U.K. Softcover: 978 1 408 41342 5 (Paragon Large Print)

Printed in the United States of America
1 2 3 4 5 6 7 12 11 10 09 08

For my grandpas, Milton Turner and
Karl Hoffman.
Both men of few words and big hearts.

ACKNOWLEDGMENTS

I am grateful to the many people who helped with the research of this book to make the story as authentic as possible. Any errors are mine alone.

Dorothy Stout, volunteer with the Beaverhead County Museum, who helped me understand the geography and history of the county and Centennial Valley in particular; Jenna Petersen, aka Jess Michaels, who had the "key" to the story when I was stumped; Mike Anderson with California Custom Trailer & Power Rides; Caroline at Squaw Valley Ski Resort; Steven Dupre with the Sacramento FBI Field Office; and especially Lerrina Collins with the Elk Lake Resort in Montana, who went above and beyond in sharing her experience of living in the beautiful Centennial Valley.

My husband, my mom, and my kids all stepped up to the plate once again to give me more time to write when my deadline loomed; my editor Charlotte Herscher who always sees the big picture before I do; the incredible people at Ballantine who do so much more than I can mention in a page; and my agent, Kim Whalen, who says she loves everything I write, even the messy first drafts.

I hope you'll enjoy this story as much as I loved writing it. Please visit my website, www.allisonbrennan.com, to learn more about the ideas behind *Tempting Evil* and the rest of the Prison Break trilogy, to sign up for my newsletter, or how to visit me at MySpace.

PROLOGUE

Eighteen months ago

"I should have killed the bitch when I had the chance."

Aaron Doherty wanted to tell Linc to shut up. Instead, he ignored him. No confrontations until he was ready. He wasn't about to blow his only chance.

It was almost time.

August was the only time San Quentin State Prison lost its dank, musty drenched-dog odor. The hot, stagnant salty air couldn't mask the foul stench of old urine and sweat, but at least Aaron wasn't cold.

"Shit, Doherty, put the fucking book down."

He didn't respond. *Don't let him goad you.* He turned the page, wishing brick rather than bars separated the cells.

"I can't believe you're reading that crap. She's a bigger fucking bitch than her sister. You should have heard her on the stand.

9

Like I hunted down Trix! We could have worked it out. We would have, if it wasn't for her."

"You killed her husband and son." Aaron hadn't meant to say anything, but Linc was pissing him off.

"I *told* you how it was. I didn't mean to kill the kid. I have a kid of my own, I don't hurt kids. It's not like I'm a damn pervert like Monroe."

"Shut the fuck up!" Monroe shouted from the cell on the other side of Linc.

The buzzer rang loud in the prison, the announcement for dinner. Like trained rats, they lined up by their cell doors and waited for the electronic lock to be released.

Aaron's heart raced. *The time had come!*

Aaron walked behind Linc along the catwalk. He didn't look any of the other prisoners in the eye. They shuffled along, sweating, not talking. The slop they served was barely edible, but it was food and missing a meal was worse than eating the crap, so they stayed in order.

The shiv passed up through the line and landed in Aaron's hand. He'd had to call in favors and pay off a half-dozen people to set this up. What they'd do for a few smokes. They'd heard the rumor of a new directive coming down, that the prison authority was going to ban smoking. Everyone was hoarding, and Aaron had the best stash for now — he hid his allotment because he didn't smoke, couldn't stand the stuff.

Aaron hid the sharp, deadly, handmade wood shiv up his shirt. He waited for the signal. *Calm.*

It happened just as they were carrying their trays from the line to the table.

"Don't touch me, faggot!"

The ruckus came from across the room. Aaron didn't look, didn't comment, as he walked by Linc, tray balanced on one hand, and jammed the shiv just below Linc's sternum.

Aaron kept walking.

He learned later that he'd pierced Linc's lung. That was why the bastard couldn't scream.

No one noticed Linc lying there on the floor until after the confrontation on the far side of the dining hall had dissipated.

Then chaos.

By that time, Aaron was eating four tables away, mentally composing a letter to his one true love, a letter he would never write, much less mail.

Dearest Joanna:
Tonight I killed Lincoln Barnes for you.

11

He was a vile man, trash, and I am saddened that his brutality hurt you.

Tonight, justice was served. In the name of love, I killed for you. You deserve nothing less.

We can't be together now, but I have at least one more appeal. Maybe you'll visit me. I love you and I miss you.

Love Always,
Aaron

ONE

Twenty-four hours ago
Aaron Doherty caressed the worn, full-page picture he'd cut from a magazine article more than a year ago.

Joanna.

His love was beautiful: blonde hair woven with gold, large, round chocolate eyes, and two deep dimples that he suspected revealed themselves even when she wasn't smiling. He couldn't wait to touch her, her smooth, fair skin, skim his fingers over her red lips, kiss her.

Joanna's beauty was just part of her attraction. She was the only woman in the world who truly understood him. And when they finally met in the flesh for the first time, she'd know instantly that Aaron was her true love.

Just like he knew when he first saw her picture two years ago. When he read her

13

books. When he learned everything about her.

When he killed for her.

They were soul mates. Every word she wrote, she crafted for him. Every story she told, she told just for him. Like in *Act Naturally.*

He pulled the battered book from his backpack. He'd stolen it from a library last week, shortly after the quake and their escape. It had physically pained him to leave all his Joanna Sutton books behind in his cell, but he didn't have a choice. The earthquake had hit when his cell block inmates were on the exercise yard at San Quentin State Prison. He'd been standing alone thinking (of course) about Joanna. Doug Chapman was only a couple of feet away sneaking a smoke — much easier when it was so cold you could see your breath — and then the ground shook. Aaron had lived in California for years, but never realized how loud earthquakes were when you were at the epicenter. He and Doug saw the breach in the wall and they went over it as soon as they could move. No looking back, no stopping when the guards shouted. Aaron watched one of his fellow prisoners, a cold bastard named Theodore Glenn, kill one of the injured guards. Still, he kept going.

Aaron knew immediately where he was headed. Montana. To be with Joanna.

He'd taken three of her paperback novels from the library because they didn't have the security sensors in the spine and he could easily hide them in his jacket. He wished he had more.

He opened it to one of the many underlined passages. He'd read the book twice since the escape last week. It made this time moving from one filthy motel room to another more bearable.

She swung her legs just enough to make the porch swing move, then tucked them beneath her, the easy rocking of the old chair comforting her. Was Garrett thinking of her? Thinking of her over thousands of miles, in the desert, serving his country. Being the hero she'd always known he could be.

Grace took the newspaper article from her pocket. It was worn and torn from being carried everywhere, but she couldn't bear to part with it. Front-page headline: Hometown Hero Saves Three in Bombing.

She stared at the vast openness that was her home as tears clouded her vision. Her hand absently rested on the small swell of her stomach. How could she tell him over the phone about this new life they had created? Over e-mail? How could she act like everything was the same when her entire world had changed overnight?

"Come home safe, Garrett."

Garrett and Grace lived happily-ever-after, and so would Aaron and Joanna. She was thinking of him right now, he could feel it. Wondering when he was going to come for her. She'd recognize that he was her hero as soon as she saw him. She'd kiss him, touch him, love him. She'd stay with him forever.

I'm almost there, Joanna.

His dick hardened and he shifted uncomfortably in the motel's torn vinyl chair. He shoved his hand down his pants to alleviate the discomfort, but it only made his hard-on worse and he groaned.

Aaron let himself think about Joanna as he rubbed himself. They would get married in a quiet ceremony, then he'd take her to a secluded hideaway where they could be together. Maybe they'd never leave. He'd make love to her every night, and watch her write every day. They'd be inseparable.

He groaned again and looked at the picture of Joanna, on the verge of release.

Rebecca.

Joanna's face morphed into the woman

who had once loved him. Who had hurt him. Who had made him kill her, the bitch.

"I love you, Rebecca. I know you love me."

"You know it's not like that between us. I don't love you, not like that. Please don't do this to me."

"What do you mean you don't love me? You tell me all the time you love me! Have you been lying to me? Playing with me?"

She stared at him as if he were a stranger. Was that fear in her eyes? Why would she be scared of him? He worshipped her. Her fear made him angry. More than anger, he panicked that she would leave him.

"Aaron, you need to go. Now."

"No!" They were in Rebecca's house. She'd invited him over. He'd been over many times.

(Only twice, and because you made her invite you in.)

Aaron stamped down the dark voice and grabbed Rebecca by the arms. "Did someone make you deny your feelings? That asshole you're working with on the set, Bruce Lawson?"

"Bruce?" She shook her head rapidly back and forth. "I don't know what you're talking about Aaron. You're scaring me. Please, please let me go."

He shook her and her hair came loose. "Don't you understand? We were meant to be

17

together, Rebecca."

"Let me go!"

"Tell me you love me!"

Tears streamed down her face.

"You love me, I know you do, just last week you said, 'I cannot imagine living another day without you.' "

She blinked rapidly, confusion on her face. "What? That was a line from my movie. What are you saying?"

"We've known each other forever, Rebecca."

"We know each other because we're neighbors." She was sobbing, her voice becoming hysterical. "Please stop this!" She opened her mouth and he knew she was going to scream.

A vise gripped his heart, squeezing so hard he couldn't breathe, he couldn't think, blood pumped, louder, hotter, faster, the tightness in his chest blocking out everything.

He didn't know how the knife got into his hand. He didn't even remember bringing it to her house. Suddenly a long red slash cut open Rebecca's cheek and she was screaming, in pain and fear.

Aaron moaned, a pathetically weak sound, as he shook his head, ridding himself of the image of Rebecca's bloodied face. His dick had gone limp without relief. He crumbled Rebecca's picture and threw it against the wall.

Joanna. It wasn't Rebecca in the photograph, it was Joanna!

He rushed across the room and picked up the paper. "I'm sorry, I'm sorry, I'm sorry." He carefully smoothed the picture, trying to rub out the wrinkles, then refolded it, heart racing.

Joanna wasn't Rebecca. She wouldn't lie to him. Aaron had it figured out. Someone had told Rebecca to leave him. That Bruce Lawson. She hadn't wanted to, she'd been manipulated.

(*You killed her Aaron.*)

He didn't want to think about that day. It depressed him because he'd never wanted to hurt Rebecca. He'd loved her. But she lied, and he hated liars.

(*You don't deserve women like Rebecca. Or Joanna.*)

Aaron pushed the dark thoughts from his head, sat in the uneven chair and stared at the cigarette-scarred table until his pulse slowed to normal.

A key in the door made Aaron jump and look around for escape. If it were the cops, they'd burst in, or pound loudly, shouting their presence. Aaron swallowed his apprehension from being on the run for nearly a week.

It was Doug holding two large fast-food

bags in clenched fists. Originally, after the earthquake, it seemed like a good idea to stick close to his cell neighbor Doug Chapman. He had great instincts, could hot-wire a car, and he got them a gun within twenty-four hours. But after living next to the guy in a six-by-nine-foot cell for eighteen months, and being practically tied at the hip this last week, Aaron was antsy. The last thirty minutes while Doug had been out getting food had been the first real peace he'd had in days.

"Fuck, Aaron, we should have gone south for the winter. I should never have listened to you." Doug dropped the food on the table.

"You're free to leave," Aaron said, lips tight. "I'll give you half the money."

"Chill, man. We agreed we were in this together, that two is better than one and all that crap."

"Where's O'Brien?"

"Coming," Doug said. He pulled off his jacket and tore open the bags. "We caught the news while we were waiting. They caught Blackie and his gang over in San Francisco yesterday. I think O'Brien got a little freaked someone would recognize us." Doug nervously ran his hands over his buzz cut, frazzled for the first time since they'd escaped five days ago. "*That guy* got them all."

"Two guys drowned in the bay the night of the quake," Aaron answered. "Your *ghost* didn't get everyone."

"I don't give a fuck about them, *Blackie* was caught. I thought he'd be smart, sure thing."

Aaron shrugged. Doug had a theory about everything, Aaron had learned since Lincoln Barnes died and Doug moved into his cell. Doug's current theory was that someone was tracking all the escapees — a ghost or some avenging angel.

"We gotta get the hell out of here."

"We're already a thousand miles from Quentin," Aaron said. "We got new clothes, some money, we're laying low. I have a place for us. And Blackie was a brute. He was stupid, robbing stores right and left. Aren't you glad I stopped you from joining their gang?"

Doug shrugged, talking with his mouth full. "Guess so. But I swear, I'm gonna go down to fucking Mexico as soon as it's safe. Somewhere where there's no snow. It's twenty degrees out there! *Twenty!*" He slurped his soda.

"Why do we have to go in separate?" Doug continued to complain, shoving fries into his mouth, his face low to the table as if someone would snatch his food at any moment.

"If — and this is a big if — the Feds come up this way, they might be looking for the three of us. So I'll go in alone first, then you and O'Brien come up later. Say you have car trouble. Went off the road or something." Aaron unwrapped his burger and took a bite. *Where was O'Brien?*

"Are you sure?" Doug asked.

"We can feel out the situation when we get to the lodge." His true love Joanna waited for him at the Moosehead Lodge. He didn't want Doug anywhere around Joanna, at least not at first. Aaron needed to assess the situation, make a plan, and decide exactly what they should do. Doug may or may not be part of the bigger picture. Right now, Aaron needed him. But later, when he and Joanna were together? Probably not.

Aaron added, "Maybe there's something else —"

They were interrupted by a knock on the door. Doug pulled out the gun they'd stolen yesterday. Aaron waved him back. "It's probably O'Brien." He opened the door, cautious. He didn't trust the guy. He didn't know him well, he'd transferred into the East Block of San Quentin from the North

Seg only a week before the quake. All they knew about the guy was that he was in for popping his wife and her lover, and was out of appeals. He'd been scheduled to walk the long mile in six months, but the Western Innocence Project had taken an interest.

Innocent. They all had reasons — damn good reasons in Aaron's case — for murder. And it didn't look like the Project had been able to do anything for O'Brien — why would he have gone through the wall if he'd be getting out on some technicality in a few months?

Aaron and Doug still had time and appeals, and neither had a death wish. Would O'Brien take dangerous chances because it didn't matter one way or the other — dead now in a gunfight, or dead this summer by lethal injection? Aaron didn't want to risk it. He had a future — a life with Joanna — and wasn't about to get himself killed.

But O'Brien seemed dead earnest about wanting to make amends with his daughter, who hadn't written or spoken to him since he'd been convicted fifteen years ago.

Aaron asked O'Brien, "Where've you been?"

He held up a ski jacket. "I saw an unlocked car and thought I could use better clothes. I'm freezing." He pulled several pairs of socks from his pockets, tossed a pair at both Aaron and Doug.

"You can say that again," Doug mumbled. "Thanks, man."

"So, are you coming with us to Montana or going back to see your kid?"

O'Brien frowned. "I can't go back yet. The cops are all over the place, I need to lay low, let the heat die down, then go back for my daughter."

"Just so you understand that this is my girl, my rules."

O'Brien nodded. "Absolutely. When do we head out?" He sat down and unwrapped his food.

"Tomorrow morning. Before dawn." Aaron kept his face blank. During his nine years in prison, he'd learned a lot — and something about Tom O'Brien wasn't right. He just couldn't put his finger on it.

"What about the storm they were talking about on the news?" Doug asked.

Aaron waved off his concern. "We'll be ahead of it. Besides, it may be cold, but it's clear."

He listened to O'Brien and Doug bitch about the cold. Something about O'Brien's eyes. They were familiar, and Aaron didn't know why. He'd never met the guy, not until he transferred last week and then not more than two words until the quake.

It was best not to talk to strangers in prison.

But . . . the sense of something predatory lingered. Aaron wasn't going to turn his back on O'Brien.

In less than twenty-four hours, you'll be with Joanna. And finally, at peace.

Two

Present day

Jo had returned to Montana's Centennial Valley four years ago specifically for the silence and the peace, hoping to find a way to go on after Ken and Timmy were murdered.

But sometimes the loneliness of the valley made it all that much more painful. So she jumped at the opportunity to check on the generator, like she jumped at every opportunity to do something to keep her mind and hands fully occupied.

The fierce storm had dumped an inch of snow every hour since noon, the clouds rolling in thick and heavy after one of the most beautiful dawns Jo had witnessed in the valley. Though sunset wasn't technically for another twenty minutes, it was already dark when Jo went to make sure the generator was running efficiently. They had two generators, their primary unit and a backup in case the primary went out. There was no power this far east in the valley. When she'd moved to California after marrying Ken, there were people in the Golden State who hadn't believed she grew up in America without power that wasn't created by a generator. Now she'd come full circle and had returned to the lodge where she had been raised.

The wind whipped the snow around her, pushing and pulling her as Jo shut the doors to the generator shed.

Everything was good to go for the night.

The wind-driven snow had already nearly obliterated her tracks from the main door, but she skirted the railing and started up the stairs. She turned to call for Buckley, her grandfather's two-year-old Saint Bernard. No one lived out here without a big dog for safety. With their keen sense of smell, they could warn of an approaching danger — grizzlies, moose, wolves — before the situation turned life-threatening.

"Woof! Woof! Woof!"

It was an excited bark, a people bark. When Buckley encountered a wild animal, he was trained to come immediately to his

26

master and growl a warning.

"Buckley!" Jo called again, her hand on her can of bear spray attached to her belt. The snow flurries prevented her from seeing either the dog or what excited him.

Peripheral movement caught her attention. She first thought moose, but this was no four-legged predator. It was a man, and he was struggling. She'd never have seen him if the floodlights weren't on. Buckley circled his feet, barked again.

"Hey!" she called out as she approached him.

He was huddled in his ski jacket, a mask over his face, but he was wearing jeans. What an idiot. She bit back her criticism and said, "Come inside." He had to have been near-frozen.

"I-I-I —" he chattered.

"Shh, let's get you warmed up." Jo wrapped an arm around his waist. His entire body was shaking as she helped him the final few feet to the porch stairs. Buckley ran ahead and barked at the door. The stranger grasped the railing, each step a chore. He wore short boots and already the wet snow had fallen inside.

Buckley's noise brought Stan to the door before she could open it. His dark face filled with concern as he helped bring the man into the foyer.

"Karl!" Stan called out, and her grand-father — a tall, lanky white-haired eighty-year-old — rushed in from the den.

"I-I-have a res-res-reservation," the man said.

"John Miller?" Grandpa said.

He nodded. "My tr-truck got stuck."

Grandpa peeled off Miller's wet jacket and helped him to a bench in the entry. Miller had called nearly a week ago and made reservations, but was unsure of his arrival date. The open-ended arrival wasn't a problem because the lodge never sold out during winter.

"We need to get his boots off," Jo said, kneeling in front of him. "Where'd your truck get stuck?" She tugged off one boot. His socks — only one pair — were soggy and icy cold.

Stan said, "I'll get some dry clothes."

"A-About an hour back. It just wouldn't go forward anymore. The wheels kept spin-ning. It got dark fast."

"You've been walking an hour, son?" Grandpa said. "Probably not more than a mile with the wind as it is."

"The storm came in so fast."

"That it did," Grandpa concurred.

Jo had Miller's boots and socks off. Buck-

28

ley tried to get his nose into the activity. "Down, Buckley," Jo said and the dog laid down. If an animal could frown, it was Buckley. He wanted to help. She gave him a quick pat then started in on Miller's gloves.

Trixie, Jo's sister, arrived with a mug of coffee, her mother-hen instincts in full gear. Stan followed with dry clothing.

"Here's some hot coffee," Trixie said.

Jo blew on Miller's left hand as her grandfather worked on his right. They were frigid, but showed no signs of frostbite. Jo had been part of the volunteer search-and-rescue squad since she was fourteen — except for the decade when she'd lived in California. "You need to get in a warm tub."

Stan slipped wool slippers on their guest's feet. "Karl and I will get you settled in your room," he said.

"I'll bring up some hot food," Trixie said.

Miller looked at Jo as if she were the only person in the room. It made her a little uncomfortable, but she pushed that thought aside. The man was half-frozen.

"You were like an angel coming toward me," he said. "I don't know how to thank you. If you hadn't seen me — every step was getting harder. I thought the light was a mirage."

"Thank Buckley." She patted the dog

29

again. Buckley scooted forward until he was the center of attention, resting his warm fur on Miller's feet. "I think we got you inside quick enough. You weren't out long enough for frostbite, and I don't see signs of hypothermia, but it's a good thing you were as close as you were."

Stan nodded. "Couple years back, two college kids got lost on the north end of the valley. Ended up freezing to death in their truck. Fell to sleep and never woke up."

Stan called Buckley off Mr. Miller's feet, then he and Karl helped him stand. He said, "We'll put him in the first room, Jo."

"I'll warm up the stew," Trixie said and went back to the kitchen.

"Do you have your driver's license and credit card?" Jo asked. "I can go ahead and register you, I just need the information."

"Of course."

Mr. Miller reached around to his back pocket. His face blanched. He half turned and Jo saw the large hole in his jeans.

"It must have fallen out. Or it could be in my truck. Probably in the truck. I knew these jeans had a hole, I just didn't think it was that big. I don't want to put you out, I can just rest here a bit and then go back and get it."

"Nonsense," Grandpa said. "We'll take

care of it in the morning. You're in no condition to go back out in this weather tonight."

Jo held back a sigh. Grandpa was from the old school. You always helped those in need. The valley was a throwback. Everyone looked out for one another. When had she lost that sense of community?

Right about the time she'd lost her family.

"Absolutely," Jo said. "We'll take a couple snowmobiles to your truck tomorrow. You'll probably want to get your suitcase as well."

"That's awfully generous of you," he said, smiling at Jo.

"Let's get you settled." Stan and Grandpa walked Mr. Miller upstairs.

Jo collected Mr. Miller's boots, jacket, gloves, and socks. What was he doing coming up here in jeans? The storm *had* come in fast, but she'd hoped her guests were smarter than that, that he would have packed a full snowsuit in his luggage that he might have put on.

She walked through the office to take a look at the guest book. John Miller had called last week to book a room.

Los Angeles.

That explained it. He'd probably never been up this way before. Jo hadn't taken the reservation; it was Trixie's handwriting. She usually asked what kind of previous outdoor winter experience the guest had, so she knew what to expect. In the summer they had additional help, but their winter capacity was usually a fraction of their summer guests. Cross-country skiing and snowmobiling in the Centennial Valley was a wholly different experience than most skiers expected. Only the most experienced should venture out.

John Miller. Funny, that was the name of one of her fictional heroes.

She walked into the kitchen where Trixie was preparing a tray. Buckley passed her and went into the mudroom to his dog bed.

"Ten more minutes and we'd have found his body tomorrow morning — or next spring, considering how much snow this storm is dumping," Jo said.

Trixie frowned and cast a furtive glance at her older sister. "You sound like it's his fault."

"I'm not that callous."

"I didn't mean that."

Jo didn't always know what Trixie meant. She felt there was still tension between them after Lincoln killed Ken, but she'd done everything to dissuade it. It wasn't Trixie's fault that her ex-boyfriend had violated a restraining order and tracked her down.

"That's Montana for you," Jo said. "Bright

blue skies in the morning then *wham*. He *is* from Los Angeles. He probably didn't realize how fast the weather can turn up here."

Trixie squinched up her nose but didn't say anything. Jo was often amazed that she and Trixie, who had both been raised here at the lodge with the same parents, could grow up so different. This had been their home, yet Trixie would rather be anywhere but.

Until four years ago.

Jo shook the past from her mind and said, "I'll take Mr. Miller his tray."

"I can do it." Trixie sounded defensive. Jo watched as her sister limped over to the cupboard where the bowls were stored. Sometimes Trixie's old injuries were barely noticeable, but when the weather chilled, her limp grew more pronounced and Jo knew she was in intense pain.

"I know you can, but —"

"I'm not an invalid, Jo."

Trixie didn't look at her. Anytime the limp or what happened four years ago was brought up, Trixie became combative. Jo knew it was a defense mechanism. Trixie hated not being able to do everything she wanted.

"I know." Jo watched Trixie dish up the stew. She used both hands to balance the

33

tray and left the kitchen, walking slowly.

Jo knew how miserable Trixie felt, but she should be grateful that she was alive. Two people died the day Trixie was shot, and Jo would never forget it. She didn't blame Trixie that the unstable ex-con Lincoln Barnes had tracked her down, but Jo wished that her sister wasn't so bitter about her injuries. She was alive. So was her daughter.

"It could be worse," Jo mumbled. *Much worse.*

A crash jolted her from her reverie. She ran from the kitchen, through the great room, and to the main hall where Trixie had fallen, the tray overturned, the bowl shattered on the stone floor.

Stan ran out of the office while Jo tried to help Trixie up. "It's okay, Trix, it was an —"

Trixie batted her hands away. "Stop, stop!"

She used the wall to pull herself up. Stew had splattered all over her sweater and slacks. Tears glistened in her eyes. She looked at Jo, then turned and walked down the hall where she and her daughter Leah were staying with their grandfather until the storm passed. Jo followed to help, but Stan put his hand over hers, his dark black skin making her skin look even more pale than usual.

"Leave her be," he said.

Jo knew he was right. Trixie was embarrassed and still struggling with the fact that her last surgery had given her no improvement. The doctor told Trixie there was nothing left to do — she was lucky to be able to walk at all. Time and physical therapy would make it a little easier, but she'd always have a bum leg.

But Trixie was an important part of Jo's small family. Jo's husband and son were dead, her parents gone halfway across the world on a mission to teach poor Third World farmers improved agricultural techniques, and her grandfather was getting older and more tired every day. All she had left was Grandpa, Trixie, and Leah, and Jo didn't want to lose them.

You could have built another family.

Could have, would have, should have. It's not like she could just turn off her feelings for Ken and Timmy and love another man, another son.

Where had that thought come from? She hadn't seen or spoken to Tyler in months. And that was for the best.

Why'd you have to push it, Tyler?

"I'll prepare another tray," Jo said, her voice surprisingly rough. She cleared her throat and returned to the kitchen before Stan asked any questions. She'd known him her entire life, he was as much a father to her as her own, but she didn't want to talk to him — or anyone.

She ladled up more stew and sliced a hefty chunk of bread off the fresh-baked loaf. She added a glass of water and cup of coffee, then carried the tray upstairs.

Room Six was the first door on the left. There were six guest rooms upstairs. Her suite was the seventh room, around the corner, and had been where her grandparents had lived for years. Just two rooms, but they had always maintained they didn't need more. When Jo's grandmother died ten years ago, her grandfather had moved downstairs. It was a larger space, where her parents had lived and raised them until joining the agricultural missionary group when Jo was seventeen.

She knocked lightly. "Dinner, Mr. Miller."

The guest opened the door. He stared at her as if he was in shock.

"I hope you've managed to warm yourself."

John Miller was about six feet tall and skinny, though broad-shouldered. He was somewhere between thirty and forty, but Jo would probably peg him on the lower range of the thirties. Short brown hair, quiet blue eyes, and a nondescript face.

Just as Jo was beginning to get nervous with the peculiar silence, he smiled and shook his head as if to clear cobwebs. "I — you caught me off guard. Sorry."

She smiled. "No problem. Do you mind if I put this down?"

"Come in." He closed the door behind her as she crossed to the small table in the corner. The guest rooms were large single rooms with either a queen bed or two doubles, a table with four chairs, sofa, and desk.

She put the tray on the table. "How are you feeling?"

"Better. Lucky."

"Did you drive here all the way from Los Angeles?"

"I —" He paused, as if unsure what to say. Then he blushed. "Yeah, I did. I had a lot to think about, thought the drive would do me good. I left Idaho Falls this morning and it was beautiful. I had the map and didn't think — but the storm came in so fast. Then I almost got trapped in an avalanche."

"Near Lakeview." Jo had spoken earlier to Sam Nash, who owned most of the formerly thriving town of Lakeview. A section of the road between Lakeview and the lodge had been buried, but Nash hadn't yet had a chance to inspect it. They'd heard the avalanche even though it was more than ten miles away — sound traveled far in the valley.

"It seemed to get dark so fast. I have four-wheel drive, but it didn't help. And when I turned on the radio, I got nothing but static. I got stuck, I don't know exactly where. But I thought I was closer to the lodge than I was."

"You're lucky to be alive, Mr. Miller." She was surprised he'd made it this far down the road. In this weather, access was pretty much restricted to snowmobiles.

"John. Please."

She smiled. "Okay, John. The weather is very unpredictable in the winter and you left your truck wearing jeans."

"I wasn't thinking. My aunt used to say I'd forget my head if it wasn't screwed on."

"We'll get you suitable clothing. And when the storm clears, we can go to your truck and get the rest of your things. Why'd you come in through Lakeview? We give our guests directions from Island Park, especially during the winter."

"I left the directions at home," he said. "Thought I'd packed them, but I was preoccupied. So I picked up a map at a gas station in Idaho and that looked like the

38

fastest route."

He continued, "This smells great. I didn't realize how hungry I was."

"Eat. Stay warm. Breakfast is at seven a.m. I didn't mean to give you a hard time, I'm certainly glad you made it here in one piece."

She turned to go.

"Um — are you Joanna Sutton?"

Jo stopped, startled, and looked at him. "Yes."

"I heard you lived here. I just — well, I'm a big fan."

She smiled. "I don't meet many men who read romance novels." Though she had been surprised at the numbers who did, based on her reader mail.

"I read all sorts of stuff. Anyway, it's nice to meet you."

"Likewise. Don't be a stranger. Remember breakfast is at seven sharp, and Stan closes the kitchen at eight."

"You know, I started writing a book."

Jo refrained from rolling her eyes. If she had a dime for everyone who wanted to write a book . . . Instead, she said, "Well, I hope you finish it. Getting to *The End* is sometimes the hardest part of writing."

"I was hoping to have time while here."

"This is a great place for writing. And with

this storm, there's not much else to do. Sorry your vacation was ruined."

Ruined? How could it be, when Aaron was here with Joanna Sutton? Talking to her? He could reach out and touch her. His hand twitched, wanting to feel her skin. Kiss her hands. He wanted to fall to his knees and propose. He resisted, but his pulse raced, his blood ran hot.

"Ruined? I don't think so," he said. "It's perfect." *Just like you. You see it too, don't you? You brought me food, you took off my boots. You kissed my hands, warmed my blood and my soul.*

Aaron stared at Joanna's lips as they curved up. He'd made her smile. He, Aaron Doherty, had made Joanna Sutton smile.

His heart pounded so hard he was certain she could hear it. His blood pumped faster and hotter than the shower her grandfather Karl Weber had started for him, and he broke out in a sweat. Joanna's smile could thaw the soul of any man. But she smiled for him and him alone.

She said in her lyrical voice, "Take advantage of the peace. I know I will. We have plenty of wood for the fireplace and fuel for the generator. Every year it gets like this, and I find not being able to go out forces me to write more. Enjoy."

He walked her to the door, opened it for her. "I will. Maybe . . . I don't know if I'm any good. Would you read something of mine?"

Her smile faltered and he panicked. Had he said something wrong? Then she said, "I don't usually read other people's work . . ."

"I understand." He tried to keep the disappointment from his face. *Don't come on too strong. Don't blow it, Aaron.* "Besides, it's a hobby more than anything. I have another job, I just like to write on the side."

She nodded. She understood exactly what he was saying, he saw it in her eyes, in her half smile. The bond deepened between them, and he relaxed. *This* was a good beginning. This was the way it should be. Comfortable. Friendly. "A lot of people start that way. I wish you a lot of luck, John."

"I don't believe in luck," he said. "Luck is a false belief for people who don't want to work for what they want." He didn't realize until he spoke that he had quoted from one of her books, *Every Little Thing.* His heart skipped a beat and he watched her face closely. He didn't think she noticed, or if she did, she didn't think anything was wrong.

He breathed easier when she said, "Good point. Sleep tight."

And she left.

Aaron leaned against the door, his forehead on the smooth, cool wood, his fingertips reaching for the love of his life.

Joanna.

She was even more beautiful in person. It was all he could do not to gather her up into his arms, embrace her fully, hold her and never let her go.

Joanna.

She'd brought up his food herself, lovingly prepared the stew with her own hands. He turned, saw the rich meal, the hand-sliced bread, the coffee — with cream and sugar on the side. He hadn't had cream and sugar in years. He was lucky to get the watered-down, lukewarm piss they called coffee at Quentin.

Her voice.

Lyrical. Beautiful. Just like her.

Her grandfather had called him *son.* Already thought of him as part of the family.

Aaron could be happy here. He deserved it. He deserved a happily-ever-after, and Joanna would give it to him.

He would never leave.

Why had he ever believed Rebecca was his one and only true love? It was so obvious that Joanna was created for him. Everything that had happened over the last two years had led him directly to her.

If Lincoln Barnes hadn't had the cell next to his, he'd never have known about her.

If the earthquake hadn't happened, if he hadn't been in the right place in the yard at the right time, he wouldn't have been free to find her.

If he'd left Idaho Falls even thirty minutes later, he wouldn't have made it through before the avalanche.

Aaron Doherty was meant to be here, with Joanna, forever.

He'd brought only his backpack from the truck. It held his most prized possessions.

The three books he'd stolen from the library.

Her picture.

And a gun.

He opened *Act Naturally* and started from page one.

Grace Douglass took one look at the man under the hood of her car and thought, if I'm late for work again I'm going to kill someone!

THREE

On days like this, Sheriff Tyler McBride wished he were back home in Texas.

Tyler got off the phone with the Bureau

of Land Management and said, "No surprise, but the Centennial Valley is cut off. Only snowmobile access, and not until the storm passes." Virtually every winter much of the Centennial Valley east of Dillon, Montana, was cut off from vehicular traffic, but the ranchers and others who lived there were more than capable of taking care of themselves.

He was more concerned about his brother's Boy Scout troop who were camping somewhere in the middle of the Red Rock Wildlife Preserve. The storm had come in so much faster than anticipated, and there was no way the kids could get out until it passed.

Tyler's son was out there. Even though he'd never been in the scouts, never gone on more than an overnight camping trip, Jason had wanted to go. And Wyatt had egged him on, dammit. Jason was a city boy, through and through, and not accustomed to this kind of harsh weather.

"Those folks are prepared," Deputy Billy Grossman said.

"Wyatt's troop is up there," dispatcher Bonnie Warren said quietly.

Billy opened, then closed his mouth. "Shit, Tyler, I'm sorry. I wasn't thinking of Wyatt and Jason."

Tyler dipped his head in acknowledgment. "I spoke to Wyatt this morning. He swore to me the storm wasn't going to hit until tomorrow, and they'd be back in Lakeview." He swallowed back his anger. That was Wyatt for you, arrogant, cocky, know-it-all.

"No one expected it so fast," Bonnie, the peacemaker, said.

That didn't appease Tyler. It was his *son* out there in subzero weather with zero visibility. It didn't matter that his brother — his *half* brother — was the scout leader and had been raised most of his life in this terrain.

What Tyler wouldn't give to be back in Texas. A tornado he could handle. It came, it went, you dealt with the aftermath. A foot of snow projected to fall overnight? In Texas, they might get a couple of inches, and it would all be melted within the week.

Montana was not Texas, big sky notwithstanding.

"Get Wyatt on the radio, please," Tyler said to Bonnie. She went to her station to ring up his brother.

Tyler found Grossman brewing more coffee. "When did Nash say he could get the road clear?" Tyler asked.

"They clear it once a week from Monida to Lakeview, provided they have a clear day.

45

Can't do it till this system passes."

Tyler ran a hand through his close-cropped dark hair, his face showing frustration for the first time since the storm had slammed them that afternoon.

"I'm still getting used to the weather up here." As if that could wipe away his anxiety. It could snow for days in a row, then the sky could turn blue and a hot fifty-degree sun would melt the snow into slush.

"The troop met in Lakeview, then skied somewhere near Upper Red Rock Lake to an abandoned homestead," he added. "A three-day winter survival badge test. They were supposed to ski back tomorrow. With this weather, they're stuck for the time being." Tyler was stating the obvious, but the routine of it calmed him. Made him focus. Wyatt knew what he was doing, he would keep the boys safe until the storm passed. They had food and water and emergency shelter.

Jason is in good hands.

It didn't appease Tyler completely.

"The Northside road has been closed for three months," Grossman said. "And there's no way we can use the snowmobiles over the refuge — not just because it's protected land, but it's also too marshy. Even with the freeze, you'll get spots of deeper water that

46

haven't completely frozen. When the storm passes, we can snowmobile around or over the avalanche on the Southside Road."

"The storm's hanging," Tyler said, feeling every one of his forty years. "NWS is saying two more days."

This was mountain country, ski country, fishing and hunting country. Unpaved roads and trails wove throughout the most beautiful land in America. The people in the valley wouldn't be out of touch for long, and they were plenty used to temperamental winters. But inevitably, someone found themselves in trouble. Last year — Tyler's first winter in Big Sky Country — a snowmobiler had been hot-dogging it in the valley and plowed into a fence buried in snow when he mistakenly went off the trail. Got himself cut up and with a broken leg, couldn't move. It took two days to find him, and then the only way they could get him out was on a sled hitched to a snowmobile.

That rescue was memorable for more than just saving the life of Kyle Worthington. That was the day he first met Jo Sutton. But Tyler couldn't think of Jo now. She'd weathered many of these winters, and could take care of herself just fine. He pushed her from his mind and stared at the map, at the spot on the northeast side of Upper Red

Rock Lake where Wyatt had camped out with Jason and the boys.

Wyatt's troop could head west, go around the lake and head back toward Lakeview like they'd come in. Or east toward Elk Lake Road. There were several ranches that way. While most of the valley residents left for the winter, there were still a couple dozen people scattered throughout the area. On the far northeast side of the valley, the Worthingtons owned much of the land bordering the refuge.

Or Wyatt might take the boys south around the lake, toward the Moosehead Lodge where Jo and her family lived.

Any option would be a difficult trip, and they couldn't start until morning. Wyatt was skilled in wilderness survival training. If anyone — other than himself — was capable of saving his son and the other boys, it was Tyler's half brother, Wyatt McBride. But he still had a hard time relinquishing the safety of his son to anyone — especially a brother he barely knew.

While the troop was no doubt prepared for all contingencies, they were still six twelve-year-old boys and one scoutmaster in disastrous conditions, miles away from help.

Billy walked over to the map. "What about

here?" He pointed. "They can cross the creek here and get to the Worthington ranch."

Tyler looked at the map, his eye lingering on the southwest side of Upper Red Rock Lake.

Jo.

As soon as the storm hit, he'd wanted to call her, make sure she and everyone else was all right. But she'd simply tell him she was fine, she'd been born and raised in Montana and a "little storm" wasn't going to faze her.

Not that he would call her anyway. Three months ago she'd made it perfectly clear that their relationship was one-sided. He hadn't believed it then, and he didn't believe it now, but he couldn't force her to see the truth. She was living in another world — a tragic one — and Tyler couldn't compete with a dead man. He refused.

Still, he couldn't get her out of his mind. He missed her, even though he wanted to throttle her.

But if calling her meant saving his son, then he would do it.

Just last week Wyatt had told him to do exactly that. Call her.

"Jo was just caught off guard. Don't give up on her. She deserves to be happy, and as

much as I hate to admit it, you make her happy."

Wyatt was obviously living in la-la land. Tyler had made Jo cry, and he'd felt damn awful about it.

"Bonnie?"

"Still trying for Wyatt, Sheriff."

"When you get a chance," he said, "could you ring the Moosehead Lodge? Wyatt is only a few miles away. It's probably their best destination tomorrow since the storm isn't going to let up."

Bonnie nodded. "Of course, Tyler."

There was plenty of room at the lodge. They'd take care of the boys until Tyler could arrive and bring them all back to their homes.

"How long do you think it'll take?" Tyler asked Grossman. "To get from the homestead to the Moosehead Lodge?"

"They can't do it tonight — they'll need at least four hours, and that's pushing it."

"They all have cross-country skis."

"It's about fifteen miles. A lot depends on the weather. If it lightens up, they'll be fine to get there in a few hours."

"I've got Wyatt up," Bonnie said.

Tyler crossed over to the radio and said, "Wyatt, it's Tyler."

"Checking on me again?"

Tyler let that slide. Wyatt preferred complete control and resented authority. No surprise; their very difficult father had been a Texas sheriff. Now wasn't the time for an argument.

Tyler told Wyatt about road and trail blockages they knew about. "I've been looking at the maps and have a destination for you tomorrow."

"So have I," Wyatt said, his voice sounding far away. "I'm going to the Moosehead."

"That was going to be my suggestion."

"Good, I won't have to defy an order."

In the twenty months they'd lived in the same state and tried to jump-start their relationship, it had been like two bull moose butting heads. Tyler didn't quite know how it had come to this — when they were kids, they'd been friends even though they lived a thousand miles apart and saw each other only a few weeks out of the year. And then — nothing.

"How are the boys?"

"Good spirits. I have them working. I'm going to power down the radio to save on the batteries, but I'll contact you at dawn before I head out. It'll take at least six to seven hours from our position unless —"

"Why that long? It shouldn't take more than four."

Bonnie was on the phone and motioned for Tyler. "Sheriff," she whispered. "I have a male caller who won't give his name and insists on talking to the Sheriff."

Tyler frowned. Probably a nutcase, and right now he didn't need anything to distract him. He held up a finger.

"Wyatt, what's wrong?"

"Ben Ward broke his leg. I've secured it and we've made a makeshift sled for him, but it's going to take too long. I'm going to call Jo and have her come out to the homestead and bring Ben in on a snowmobile."

"What about the Worthington Ranch?" Tyler said.

"Closer as the crow flies, but no way I can get Ben up there. Too steep and rocky." Wyatt cleared his throat. "You have to trust me, Tyler."

Tyler ran his hand over his face. *Trust.* A two-way street, but Tyler didn't say it. "I trust you, Wyatt. I let you take my son." But Jason was more comfortable playing video games than roughing it in the wilderness. It was partly Jason's increasingly solitary lifestyle after his mom died that had prompted their move cross-country in the first place. Tyler wanted Jason to have family, and Wyatt was the only family they had left. But while Tyler and Wyatt came alive in the rugged outdoors, Jason was still a kid raised between San Diego and Dallas, unfamiliar with the demands of rugged terrain.

"I'll call in at oh-seven-hundred hours," Wyatt said.

"I'll be here."

He slammed down the mic. After all these years, why'd he think he could come up here and create a family? Not only was he an outsider in Montana, but he felt like an outsider with his own brother. Why was he surprised? Before the move, the last time they'd seen each other was their father's funeral eight years ago — that, following eight previous years of minimal contact. At the time of the funeral Tyler had been married with a toddler, and Wyatt was doing God knew what. But it was quickly clear that they no longer had the same close relationship they'd had as kids.

"Sheriff? The caller?"

Tyler took the call, more to get his mind off Wyatt and Jason. As soon as the snow let up, he'd be on his way to the Moosehead Lodge to find his son.

"Sheriff McBride."

Nothing. For a moment, Tyler thought the call had been lost. Then, "Sheriff, there are two killers on their way through your town."

"Killers?"

"Escapees from San Quentin."

"Who is this?"

The man coughed deeply. When he spoke, he was out of breath and didn't answer the question. "I don't know exactly where they're going, but I know it's near Dillon and they're looking for a woman."

"Who?"

"I don't know! He never said her name. But she lives near Dillon."

"That doesn't help me much, sir. We're a small town, but not that small."

"Dammit, this is important!" He coughed again.

"Where are you right now?"

"Outside Pocatello. I —" Another long pause. The man sounded distracted. He was lying, Tyler was certain of it. "There was an accident."

"You were in an accident in Idaho? That's outside my jurisdiction. I can get you in touch with —"

"Dammit, Sheriff, would you listen!" The man was breathing heavily. "Two men — escaped convicts from San Quentin named Aaron Doherty and Doug Chapman — are on their way to find this woman. Doherty said she was waiting for him, but he's never actually met her in person. She's pretty, maybe thirty-five or so. He had her picture.

It was cut out of a magazine."

"Can you describe her?"

"Blonde hair, dark eyes, slender, attractive. The photo was taken outdoors on a deck somewhere. Possibly a house. There was a huge mountain range behind her. She was wearing a dark orange sweater and jean skirt. Sheriff, she's in real danger. You've got to stop them. Aaron Doherty's a twisted fuck, a psychopath. He's delusional and he'll kill her, I know it. And Chapman is a loose cannon."

Tyler made note of the names and descriptions. The caller sounded delusional himself, but there was something else — a sense of detail that told Tyler his mysterious caller was telling the truth, even if it wasn't the complete truth.

"Sir, most of the roads are closed except for the Interstate. Even if they are here, they can't get through to anywhere that isn't immediately off the main highway. And without an ID on this woman, I can't warn her. I'll alert —"

"They dumped me at nine. What time is it now?"

Tyler glanced at the clock and frowned, tapping his pen on the desk. "Seven-thirty."

"Seven-thirty p.m.?"

"Sir, do you need medical attention?" Tyler glanced at Bonnie and motioned for her to approach.

"They've had a full day!"

"Sir, have you been unconscious since this morning? I'll get a medical team to you right away. Please give me your exact location." Tyler didn't need it, he could trace the call, but he wanted to keep the man on the line as long as possible. He slid a note to Bonnie. *Locate the call.*

"Sheriff McBride, you have to believe me. This woman is in danger. I was unconscious longer than I thought. Find her. Protect her. Doherty and Chapman are armed and dangerous. They have at least two guns and a knife. Call the state police. They were last driving a Ford truck. Late-model 250. Call the Feds. I'm telling you the truth! Please. Please. I —" The man started coughing again. It sounded like it was coming from far away.

Click.

Tyler looked at the phone and frowned. He described the woman to Bonnie. "Do you recognize her?"

She shook her head. "Can't say. I mean, I can probably list a dozen pretty women under forty who have blonde hair and brown eyes."

Jo had blonde hair and brown eyes. Tyler

56

dismissed the thought, even as his instincts hummed. He said, "What about one who would have been in a magazine?"

There had been a write-up about Jo in a magazine a couple years ago. He'd seen the framed pages in her grandfather's lodge.

Damn, what had she been wearing in that picture?

Tyler couldn't remember. But it had been taken outdoors on the deck of her grandfather's lodge. He asked Bonnie about it.

"I don't remember that. What kind of magazine was it? A ranch magazine? A vacation brochure?"

"Do you think you can peek in the library and see what you can find?" It wasn't Jo. Why would some psycho from Quentin be looking for Jo?

"They're closed, but I'm sure Sally will open it up for me. I might not get in until tomorrow."

"Just as soon as you can, thanks. I can't do anything if I don't know who these killers are after. If they're even here. If they made it before the storm." A lot of *if*s and there were six young boys in jeopardy right now. Still . . .

Jo's on your mind. Do you know how many other women in the area have blonde hair?

But how many blondes were photographed

for a magazine?

"Find out where that call came from, then call the lodge."

He needed more information, but more than that, he wanted to talk to Jo. Make sure she was okay. What if the caller wasn't as delusional as he sounded? What if two escaped convicts were on their way to Jo's lodge right now?

He pushed back the urge to call her himself. After their last conversation . . .

"Do you want to make the call?"

Bonnie was no idiot. She knew he was avoiding Jo. "I'll talk to them, but I need to look something up first. Verify something the caller said."

He left the command center and went to his office. Of course he'd heard about the San Quentin earthquake — who hadn't? — but he was a thousand miles away and would be very surprised if any of those escapees had made it way up here.

But the names had sounded familiar.

He sorted through his memos. Pulled one from the Federal Bureau of Investigation. There had been twelve escaped prisoners all told. All but three had been killed or apprehended.

Douglas Raymond Chapman, 37. Convicted six years ago of three murders. His wife, his girlfriend, and his boss were all killed in the same week. He had a history of violence: barroom fights, six months for his third assault arrest. But he had a college degree and good job. Odd. One day Chapman seemed to have really and truly snapped. A civil engineer from the city of Santa Clara, Chapman hit his boss with a wrench, then disposed of his unconscious body in a sewage treatment plant vat. The man drowned in human waste and toxic chemicals. His corpse virtually disintegrated before it was discovered. Chapman then went home and stabbed his wife to death. Two days later while the police were still investigating, he strangled his mistress.

Aaron Christopher Doherty, 33, was unemployed when convicted seven years ago for the murder of Rebecca Oliver, a well-known actress, and her friend Bruce Lawson. He'd disfigured Rebecca two months prior to killing her outside her home in Glendale, California. Tyler remembered both the attack and the murders — they had been sensational in the press.

There was extensive background information on Chapman and Doherty — known associates, hometowns, details about their crimes. But for the third escaped convict still at large, there was next to nothing.

Thomas James O'Brien, 57. Six feet tall. One hundred eighty pounds. Graying dark hair. Blue eyes. Convicted of two counts of murder in the first degree.

Nothing more. No details of O'Brien's crimes, no background, not even the location of his crime, though Tyler assumed California since he'd been incarcerated at San Quentin.

If the caller was truthful, with the storm how far from Pocatello could the convicts have traveled since early this morning? It would help if he knew where they were headed — something more specific than "near Dillon."

But Tyler's anonymous caller had sounded half-deranged. Injured. Perhaps he had intended to send Tyler on a wild-goose chase. But if he *was* telling the truth, Tyler had more than a Boy Scout troop to find and protect.

Bonnie tapped on his door and entered. "I have the information on that call, Sheriff."

"Shoot."

"You're not going to like it. It was from a disposable cell phone with an Idaho Falls area code, but that's all we have."

Disposable cell. General area.

"Thanks, Bonnie."

60

Tyler glanced back at the FBI memo and picked up the phone. He dialed the FBI contact number. "This is Sheriff Tyler McBride from Beaverhead County, Montana. I need to speak to whoever is in charge about a possible escaped convict sighting."

Blonde hair, brown eyes.

While on hold for the Feds, Tyler pictured Jo Sutton the first day he met her. He'd never forget it.

It was his first official search-and-rescue since becoming Sheriff.

Kyle Worthington had been riding his new Polaris Dragon 700 across the wetlands and hit a fence almost — but not quite — buried in snow. Was thrown from the snowmobile and broke his leg. His ride crashed a hundred yards away and it took him all day to crawl over to it and the radio. By that time he was weak and struggling in and out of consciousness.

While Tyler drove to Lakeview to meet the search-and-rescue team at Sam Nash's ranch, he talked to Kyle over the radio for hours to keep his spirits high. Nash was one of the old-timers, the grandson of one of the town founders. Most of the residents of the once-thriving community had moved on, leaving just a handful of people. Nash had been the only one who really reached out to Tyler when he'd become Sheriff, but even then it seemed perfunctory and forced.

When he arrived, Jo Sutton was already there, standing in Nash's kitchen, giving orders. Her light, golden blonde hair pulled back, curly wisps escaping, softening her face; her eyes as dark as melted chocolate.

"Kyle is somewhere between here and here." Jo put pins on a map that someone had tacked to the wall. "Team A, which I'm leading, will go in from the east. Team B under Wyatt McBride's lead will go from the west, and one of us will find him. I need a medic with each team."

She caught Tyler's eye and cocked her head to the side. "You must be the new Sheriff. I'd recognize you anywhere."

Suddenly all eyes were on him. He had fifteen years as a Texas Ranger, but surprisingly the dozen pairs of eyes stared at him as if he were a rookie. He straightened and removed his hat. "Ma'am."

And still Jo stared. Her dark eyes bored into his own, a half smile on her lips. "McBride," she muttered. "You know how to ride?"

He didn't know what she was talking about, so he said nothing.

"A sled."

Slang for snowmobile. He nodded and said, "I'm also a medic."

She raised an eyebrow. "You can be on my team."

His brother Wyatt was standing on the far side of the kitchen and laughed. Tyler didn't much like being an outsider.

Surprisingly, Jo said, "You got a problem with that Wyatt? Thought you'd relinquished command this year, or do you want it back? I know giving up control is hard for you."

Wyatt cleared his throat. "No, darlin', you're doing fine."

Jo rolled her eyes and said, "Everyone know where they're going and what they're doing?"

Murmurs and nods, a few questions which Jo handled deftly, then Tyler and Jo went outside. She stood off to the side, with four other people on their team getting their sleds ready.

"Jo Sutton." She extended her gloved hand.

Tyler took it. "Tyler McBride."

"I know." He raised an eyebrow and she laughed. "Wyatt told me all about you."

"And you're still talking to me?"

"I ignored some of his adjectives. He might as well have been talking about himself when he called you an arrogant know-it-all."

Tyler laughed, the first good laugh he'd had since moving to Montana eight months before. "You do know my brother."

"We've been friends for a long time. He's a

good guy, under the attitude. When I returned to the valley a couple years ago, he helped me through a really rough time." She turned from him and stared across the vast, silent valley as if surprised she had made the comment.

Tyler wondered what rough time Jo had gone through, and whether she and Wyatt were involved. He thought not — knowing his brother, Wyatt would have already warned Tyler off if Jo was his girlfriend.

He stepped to the side to catch her expression. Melancholy. She was thinking about something upsetting and trying not to. Judging by the tightness in her jaw and throat muscles, she was trying hard not to think about whatever unsettling incident — the rough patch — she'd referred to. Her hands were jammed into the pockets of her ski jacket, more to keep herself contained than from the cold, Tyler suspected. He didn't ask what had saddened her, he figured she'd say something if she wanted to talk.

A moment later she turned to him with a slight smile that didn't reach her eyes.

She said, "Let's go find Kyle. I know a shortcut."

"I thought Team A was supposed to go in from the east."

"Yeah, but I've got a new Polaris I'm testing

for the company. Prototype. Gotta see what it can do, right?"

"What about the rest of us?"

"You'll have to keep up." Her words were light and playful: they didn't match her demeanor. Tyler suspected Jo wanted a few minutes alone.

Something about Jo drew Tyler in like a bee to honey. Her self-confidence coupled with her quiet vulnerability — an alluring combination. He was happy to let her take charge of Kyle Worthington's rescue just to see her at work.

"Sheriff?"

Tyler shook his head and focused on the phone call. He glanced at the clock. He'd been on hold for eight minutes. "This is McBride."

"Special Agent Hans Vigo. Funny that you should call, I'm at a hotel in Idaho Falls, not more than an hour or so from you. My office patched you through to my cell phone."

"Funny," Tyler agreed without humor. "So you know what I'm calling about?"

"Headquarters said you have information about three escaped convicts we tracked from San Quentin."

"Two," Tyler corrected. "Douglas Chapman and Aaron Doherty." He told the FBI agent about the anonymous phone call.

"O'Brien," Vigo muttered.

"Excuse me?"

"I'll explain everything when I get there. We'll be there bright and early, Sheriff."

"As early as possible, because as soon as dawn breaks I'm heading to the valley."

FOUR

It was after eight that evening when Jo finally settled at her desk to write.

The howl of the wind as it whipped the snow around the lodge was the only sound. There would be huge drifts tomorrow morning. Jo hoped their cottage guests were all right. She'd checked on them when the snow first started falling. The cabins were the two closest to the lodge; they didn't have generators but were equipped with propane stoves and wood-burning fireplace insets. They were cozy retreats, perfect for the honeymooning couple as well as the two college kids — Brian Bates and his girlfriend Marie Williams — in the southernmost cabin who had planned to research their joint thesis for an advanced wildlife biology class at Missoula. They'd arrived yesterday and Jo suspected that now the weather had turned, there'd be more romance than

66

working in the field.

She pulled up her current work-in-progress, a story she was calling *Cry, Baby, Cry* to fit her theme of titling all her books after Beatles songs. It had been her editor's idea eight years ago when she called her first novel *Act Naturally*. But this story was much different than her others.

The only time she had missed a deadline was after Ken and Timmy were murdered. Deadline? She'd lost an entire year . . . she didn't think she'd write again.

But then one day not long after she moved back to the lodge, she sat at her computer to order a sweater for her grandfather, and a story idea popped into her head. Her muse had returned, and in the process of writing Jo had found more healing than in the previous year of barely living.

Now that she'd rediscovered her love for writing, she wasn't going to fall into that dark emotional pit again. She could control the pain, control her anguish just fine, thank you.

Her sweeping romances and family sagas had given her a wonderful fan base. She hoped she wouldn't disappoint them with something a little different this time. It was as if *Cry, Baby, Cry* was writing itself, yet Jo was still trying to make it conform to her plan. Jo decided for the first time to let the story take her on the journey, rather than the way she usually wrote with a clear road map.

She was deep into it, on her third page that night, when her eleven-year-old niece ran into her room without knocking.

The sudden movement startled her. "Leah!" Jo admonished.

"Sorry."

"Is everything okay?"

"Mom said to get you. Wyatt McBride is on the radio and asked for you."

Jo saved her document. "Is something wrong?"

"I don't know. Mom didn't say. I think she was mad that he asked for you."

Trixie had always had a crush on Wyatt, who was a year older than Jo and three years older than Trix. But Jo knew Wyatt's heart belonged to one woman, Grace Worthington. And Grace was traveling the world. Living in the Centennial Valley was not in her top ten goals. It hadn't been in Jo's, either, but after Ken and Timmy were killed, this was the only place she had felt safe.

Jo put her arm around Leah's slender shoulders as they went downstairs. She had a special affection for her niece, but was sometimes hesitant to show it. Trixie always acted weird whenever Jo wanted to take Leah out to do something in the valley, like cross-country skiing or snowmobiling over Red Rock Pass. Jo figured Trix was upset that she couldn't do those things with Leah herself, so Jo tried not to push it.

She went into the office where Wyatt and Trixie were chatting on the VHF radio.

"Jo's here," Trixie said.

Jo and Wyatt had a long history. He, Jo, and Grace had been the Three Musketeers growing up, and when they were in high school Wyatt and Grace started dating. When Grace chose a college on the East Coast, Wyatt was devastated. He dropped out of nearby MSU and spent a year in the military. He eventually returned to the valley — told Jo it was in his soul and he didn't feel right anyplace else. He became somewhat of a ski bum while spending the next six years in college, introduced Jo to Ken, and was best man at their wedding.

When Jo returned from California after Ken and Timmy were murdered, she and Wyatt picked up their friendship where it had left off. Wyatt had considered her husband Ken one of his closest friends. He'd even flown to California for the funeral.

"Hey, Wyatt, what's up?"

69

"Gotta little problem. I'm up at the Kimball homestead on the north end of the lake with six Boy Scouts. The storm came in faster than I thought."

He sounded like it was a personal failure that he didn't see it coming. "It surprised us all," she said.

"They often do." Even the weather service was sometimes wrong. "The Ward boy broke his leg. We're shutting down for the night — have shelter, food. We're good. But I need to get him medical attention ASAP."

"I can call in search-and-rescue. Give me your exact location —"

"We're not moving tonight. The storm is getting worse, and we're safe where we are. I set Ben up with a temporary brace and the boys are building a sleigh. But I was hoping we could come to the lodge."

"You're that close? I thought —" She glanced at the map. "Kimball. Right. That's about twelve miles, sticking to the trails."

"Bingo."

"Don't move Ben. I'll meet you there tomorrow morning. Between Trix and Stan they can take care of Ben." Stan had been an Army medic and Trixie had extensive first aid training.

"Are you sure? We can meet you partway —"

"No, if the weather lightens up I can be there in less than an hour. If it's still rough, it might take a little longer. I'll have the sled hooked up, which cuts into speed."

"Perfect. Thanks, Jo. I really appreciate it."

"Don't mention it. Let's talk on the radio tomorrow at seven a.m. so I can give you a better ETA based on the weather."

"Right after I check in with the Sheriff."

"You mean your brother."

Just thinking about Tyler McBride made Jo a bundle of nervous energy. She hadn't seen him in over two months, ever since Thanksgiving dinner at Wyatt's place when she and Tyler had been in the kitchen alone.

She'd been right to put distance between them. It had all happened too fast, too unexpected. She wasn't ready. She didn't know if she'd ever be ready. Why did he have to push it? Dammit, why couldn't he just be happy with the way things were? With Tyler she'd been happier than she'd been in four years. And now . . .

Now Jo missed him.

Wyatt moaned. "Don't remind me. I've never met such a high-and-mighty arrogant know-it-all —"

Jo cut him off and laughed. "Look in a mirror, Wyatt."

"*Touché,* Joanna."

She winced at her full name. No one called her that.

"I'll be waiting for your call. Be careful."

"You, too."

She hung up. Instead of thinking about Wyatt and the boys, Tyler filled her mind. After meeting him on the Kyle Worthington rescue last winter, they'd started seeing each other casually. She knew he was being cautious because his ex-wife had died not long before he moved to Montana. Jo was cautious because — well, she still loved her husband. He was dead, but she couldn't just turn off her feelings like a faucet.

She'd gone with Tyler and Jason to Wyatt's ranch in Ennis. Wyatt had bought a hundred acres and renovated the rundown house himself. He was about halfway done, but what he'd completed was beautiful. Every room had a view — most of wide-open spaces. On a clear day, you could even see Centennial Mountain from the kitchen.

This past Thanksgiving was clear and after dinner the sun had just begun to set in the southwest. The mountains were alive with color, and Jo stopped scraping leftover food into the bucket for Wyatt's animals.

As always, the Centennial Mountains, from any angle, took her breath away.

But that night . . . the vastness of Montana hit her with an intense emptiness, and she descended into the emotional pit she'd been in after Ken and Timmy had died.

Sometimes the past crept up slowly — she knew the sadness would come and she could prepare. But tonight the anguish seized her unexpectedly and all she saw was Timmy's face.

How could she ever replace Timmy? How could she replace Ken? She had loved them so much, her heart twisted at the loss. Her loss. Yes, she was selfish and she knew it, but dammit, they were her family! She had chosen to marry the athletic wildlife biologist who made her laugh like no one else. She had given birth to a beautiful baby boy who should have had a chance to grow up. Nine years wasn't enough.

Hands wrapped around her waist and she almost dropped the plate.

Tyler kissed her on the neck. He was taller, broader, more muscular than her dead husband. And when they made love for the first time, that weekend in September when Wyatt had taken Jason on a scouting excursion, she allowed herself to think that maybe — maybe — she could find love again.

Her heart slammed shut.

She shook her head. How could she explain it to Tyler? He'd been nothing but kind and patient. She touched his cheek, kissed him. "Where's Wyatt?"

"He took Jason out to bring in the horses."

"Jason seems to be adjusting well."

Tyler didn't say anything.

"Don't you think?"

"I think Wyatt's pushing him. Trying to prove something, I don't know what."

"Jason would say something if he didn't like it."

"I don't think so. He's a private kid."

"A little like his dad." She smiled, tried to slide away, feeling suddenly too close, too intimate. Talking with Tyler about his son — his son, not her son. "We should finish clearing —"

Tyler pulled her back, kissed her. His hands found her neck, held her to him, and she let herself relax. The quiet intimacy comforted her. Just her and Tyler, without pressure, without words. Her body heated up, as it always did when Tyler touched her. He was a man of a thousand degrees. She wondered if he'd be comfortable naked in the snow. The vision of them making love in the snow made her grin.

He pulled back an inch, a smile curving his lips up. His green eyes sparkled. Tyler Mc-Bride was one handsome man, a cowboy at heart, and Jo couldn't deny that she was attracted to him.

The first man who had started to weave his way into her heart since Ken.

"I love you, Jo."

She blinked, her body frozen. Love. She pushed it from her mind. He hadn't said it. He couldn't. Too much was at stake when love came into the picture.

"I want to marry you. Will you?"

As if she had already said yes, he kissed her.

Her mouth was open in shock, not response.

He pulled back and in his eyes she saw that he already knew her answer.

"I — I can't."

His muscles tensed and he stared at her. Not talking.

"I'm sorry." She ran from the kitchen. She should have given him an explanation. She should have told him how she felt, about him, about Ken.

About Timmy.

But just thinking about it made the tears come, and she couldn't put her feelings into words. She couldn't explain them to herself, let alone Tyler.

She hadn't seen Tyler since.

The phone rang. "Moosehead Lodge," she

answered, her voice thick. She feigned a cough.

"This is Bonnie Warren from the Sheriff's Department. Who's this?"

"Hi Bonnie, it's Jo."

"Can you hold for the Sheriff?"

Hold for the Sheriff?

"Is something wrong?"

"No. Just a minute, please."

Did Bonnie know about her relationship with Tyler? She didn't think so, but there were only nine thousand people in the entire county of Beaverhead. And they all knew one another. She hadn't advertised it, but they hadn't kept it secret, either.

Why was she worrying about it? It was over. Tyler was calling about Wyatt and the boys, that was it.

"Jo."

His voice was deep and sexy, even though he wasn't trying to be anything but all-cop. Maybe that's why Jo was so attracted to him. He didn't know what he did to her.

"Hi, Tyler."

"Have you spoken to Wyatt?"

"Yes. I'm going out to the Kimball homestead tomorrow morning and bring Ben Ward back. Wyatt will follow with the rest of the boys."

"Thank you."

"There's no need to thank me, Tyler. I've done things like this for years."

Why was she sounding so defensive?

"Jason's out there with them."

"Oh. I'm sure he's fine, he's a good kid, and Wyatt knows what he's doing."

But Jo also knew that while Tyler didn't act over-protective, he kept a discreet, watchful eye over his son. Rightfully, Jo thought. The world was a dangerous place. Balance was hard — when to let them push, when to keep them sheltered.

"I —" What was she going to say? What could she say? "I'll have Jason call you when they get here, okay?"

"I'd appreciate it. Nash called in about the avalanche. That wasn't near you, was it?"

"No. It was about two miles east of Lakeview. We heard it, sounded like it was right in our backyard, but we talked to Nash and he planned to inspect it."

"How is everyone there?"

"We're fine. No problems."

"Any guests?"

"I have one couple who weren't expecting the vast solitude here. I think they're going a little stir-crazy." She was making small talk, and it felt uncomfortable.

"If anyone shows up out of the blue, give

me a call, okay?"

"Why?"

"You never know. You're way out in the middle of nowhere, Jo."

"Everyone here had a reservation, Tyler. Sometimes being in the middle of nowhere is exactly what people need."

"Unless you're going nowhere."

Jo's jaw tightened. "What does that mean? That was uncalled for."

"Was it?" he asked softly.

"Anything else?"

"Do you remember the interview you did for that national magazine a couple years ago? It's hanging up in your lobby."

The sudden change of subject confused her. "Yes," she said cautiously. "Why?"

"What were you wearing in that picture?"

"And this is important why?"

"Just curious."

Jo had no idea what was going on in Tyler's head. "Um, a rust-colored sweater and jeans. No, a jean skirt," she corrected after picturing the article. "Why?"

"Someone was talking about it and I couldn't remember."

"Why do you care what I wore in an old photo?"

"If any strangers arrive at the lodge unexpectedly, call me immediately."

"Now I know something's wrong. What is it, Tyler?"

There was a long silence, which proved to Jo that Tyler was worried about something other than Jason and the scouts. "I don't want to scare you, Jo."

"You're scaring me now."

"I had a strange call this evening from a guy who described that picture of you. He seemed to think that someone might want to hurt you."

"Hurt me?"

Why in the world would anyone want to hurt her? Lincoln Barnes, the vile man who murdered Ken and Tim, had died more than a year ago in a prison fight. Linc was the only person who truly hated her. Jo closed her eyes and took a deep, shaky breath.

"Jo?" Tyler asked softly. "Honey, are you okay?"

"I can't think of any reason why someone would want to hurt me. Linc is dead. I haven't gotten so much as a crank call or nasty e-mail."

"I'm coming to the lodge tomorrow," Tyler said.

"You don't have to —" She stopped herself. Jo would feel safer with Tyler around. More than a sense of security, Jo realized she had missed Tyler. It had been more than two months and he hadn't called after she turned down his marriage proposal. Not that she blamed him. Hell, maybe she didn't want to see him, though the fluttering butterflies in her stomach told her otherwise. "You'll come by to pick up Jason?" she asked.

"And to see you. To make sure everyone is okay."

"Who is this guy with my picture? Do you really think that he's dangerous?"

When Tyler didn't answer, Jo added, "The storm isn't going to lighten up anytime soon. No one is getting to the lodge tonight."

"I'm counting on it. Just be careful."

"What are you not telling me, Tyler?"

Tyler frowned and looked at the information he had about Doherty, Chapman, and O'Brien. How much should he share? He didn't want to scare her needlessly — Jo was right in that no one was going to make it through Lakeview. He'd already spoken to Nash and he was on the lookout for anyone going that way. But the truth was, there was more than one way into the valley.

"I don't want to panic anyone," he said carefully, "but do you remember the earthquake and prison break in California last week?"

"It was all over the news."

"Someone called in a sighting from Pocatello."

"That's on the interstate. They're probably on their way to Canada."

"The witness said that one of the convicts had a picture of a woman. From a magazine. I think it was you."

Silence. Damn, he hadn't wanted to tell her, but what else could he do? She had to be prepared. "Jo? Are you okay?"

"That's why you asked what I had been wearing for the article."

"Yes."

"But you don't *know* that this escapee is coming here."

"No, I don't."

The caller's words came back to him. *McBride, you have to believe me. This woman is in danger.*

He added quietly, "There are three prisoners still at-large. The caller only talked about two of them, but we don't know where the third is, if the three are together, or if they split up."

"Who are they?" Jo's voice was calm and matter-of-fact, but Tyler could imagine her brow furrowed in concentration.

"Aaron Doherty, Douglas Chapman, and Thomas O'Brien. All from California, all escaped from San Quentin during the earthquake. I don't know for a fact that they are coming to the lodge, but you need to be extra careful. I called Nash, filled him in earlier, and he's keeping an eye out in Lakeview. No one is getting through tonight."

"Thanks for telling me. I need to warn the guests —"

"Wait, Jo."

"What do you mean wait?"

"Don't tell anyone."

"I can't keep this information to myself!"

"Can you vouch for every one of your guests? Do you know them, personally? Have they all been there for more than forty-eight hours?"

She paused. "No, but —"

"If you tell one, it will get out. People panic, Jo. You know that. Tell your grandfather and Stan, but no one else. Not until you get the pictures. Is your Internet working?"

"Last I checked, our ISP was down. I'll keep this between us for now. Grandpa and Stan are already settled for the night. I'll tell them first thing in the morning."

"I'll fax you their mugshots as soon as I get them. It won't be long, I already talked to the Feds."

"I'll look for them."

"Lock your door, Jo. And bring a gun upstairs with you."

"Is that really necessary?"

He wished it wasn't. "Just as a precaution."

"Fine."

She hung up, and Tyler stared at the phone.

Why didn't you tell her you love her?

He wanted to talk to Jo, get her to explain herself to him, but not over the phone. What could he say to convince her that loving him wasn't betraying her dead husband?

A phone conversation wasn't going to fix anything. Tomorrow when he saw her, then they'd talk. Maybe he hadn't made it clear to Jo that he wasn't trying to replace Ken Sutton.

At least, he'd explain it to her if he could get through — both through the avalanche, and through Jo Sutton's thick head.

And once he got there and knew Jason and Jo were safe, he wasn't going to leave her side until he knew that the three escaped convicts were nowhere near the lodge.

FIVE

Aaron Doherty listened to Joanna's conversation with a man named Tyler.

On the phone, she spoke softly, and Aaron couldn't make out all the words. But Joanna sounded concerned.

No one knew he was coming here. Doug was in hiding and O'Brien was dead.

Still, something worried her.

Had someone seen them? But even if there had been a witness, no one knew where they were headed. Maybe someone had discovered the missing snowmobile they'd stolen in that pissant little town off South Centennial Road. Doug had wanted to go to the main house and wait until the storm passed. Aaron convinced him it was unwise. Too many unknown variables. They didn't know how many people lived there or if they had weapons.

Had someone in the house seen them and called the cops?

Whatever. There was no way the cops could get here. Aaron had heard the avalanche. It had to have been huge. Maybe there was another way to get to the lodge, but it would have to take longer, right? On his map, the way he'd come had looked the fastest.

Aaron would figure out a way to disable the phone system. He'd assumed that the phones would be knocked out by the storm, but Karl Weber had explained earlier that the lines were all buried. "We don't have electricity out here, we run off a generator, but we have telecommunications," the old man had joked. "Since we've had phone service, over thirty years ago, it's never gone out because of a storm."

Not good. The only phone was in the office, along with a radio and fax machine. Tonight, when everyone was asleep, Aaron would fix the problem. Now he wished Doug was here. He probably knew a way to disable the phones without making anyone suspicious. Doug was a civil engineer, after all — or he had been before he killed three people.

Doug had lived a relatively normal life, as far as Aaron knew. College grad, good job, married. But he'd been violent on and off and then one week for seemingly no reason, he killed three people.

While in prison, the doctors put Doug on psych pills and he became almost docile. At least not so tempermental. But Aaron was a little concerned since Doug had been off his medication for six days now. He didn't seem any different than when they'd been in prison and Doug had been doped up, but Aaron sensed that Doug was getting antsy, like he couldn't stop moving. Aaron didn't want him anywhere around Jo. Right now, Doug was doing exactly what Aaron said, but what if he got it in his head that he should be in charge?

Aaron heard Jo hang up the phone and ducked into another room. It was a small room, maybe a den of sorts. Pitch black, it smelled of pipe tobacco and good cognac. It reminded him of his aunt Dorothy's house in the hills above Glendale. He'd never met his uncle Benny, he'd been dead before Aaron had been born, but the parlor had still smelled like him. Aunt Dorothy would sit there, open up the humidor, the pipe tobacco filling the air. She'd sip cognac and not move for hours.

She'd loved Uncle Benny, turning the parlor into a mausoleum.

It seemed fitting that she died there. Wasn't she better off now, anyway? She'd always said she couldn't wait to die so she could be with Benny again.

And now she was.

Aaron waited in the lodge den, heart thudding, listening.

He'd thought everyone was settled for the night. It was nearly eleven. But when he came out of his room, he'd heard Trixie in the kitchen and Joanna's voice in the office. The fire had been banked for the evening, and Stan Wood and Karl Weber were nowhere to be found.

He'd wanted to familiarize himself with the surroundings. And to learn more about Joanna. That would have to wait.

He listened. Soon, there was no sound but the wind. And still, he patiently waited.

After shooting O'Brien and leaving him in a ditch in the snow outside Pocatello early that morning, he and Doug had continued on to Monida. Aaron didn't answer Doug's questions about why he'd killed O'Brien. Aaron didn't quite understand himself, but when O'Brien made that comment about Joanna being sexy, Aaron snapped. O'Brien had made him nervous from the very beginning. Unlike Doug, O'Brien hadn't been with them the entire time since the earthquake. What had O'Brien been doing? He'd *said* he went to see his daughter, but could Aaron believe him?

Doug stopped asking questions and they drove in silence. The morning was bright and beautiful, but almost as soon as they turned into the Centennial Valley the sky darkened and the weather reports warned of a quick-moving and violent storm.

Still, Aaron insisted that they continue on. Joanna was only *miles* away. He couldn't get this close and not see her.

Doug grumbled, but didn't really complain until they were crawling at fifteen miles an hour in blinding snow. The truck got stuck on the west side of Lakeview, and Doug got really mad.

But Aaron saw the opportunity. There were buildings up ahead, some structures. He convinced Doug to go with him, but then they discovered all the structures had long been abandoned.

Then they saw lights.

Doug was excited. "Let's go pop them and we'll hang out here for a couple weeks. Hell, there's *no one* around. No one will think of looking for us here."

The first building was a garage. Inside there was a truck and several snowmobiles. Aaron had a better idea than killing the occupants of the main house. "Let's take these and go to Joanna."

"No," Doug said subbornly.

Aaron was getting tired of Doug's belligerence. In many ways, Aaron just wanted him gone. But Aaron wasn't sure he could ride one of these things. He sure as hell wouldn't know how to fix it if something happened.

88

And Doug understood all things mechanical.

Aaron tamped down his anger and said, "Joanna has a sister."

"Probably some old hag," Doug muttered.

"*Younger* sister. Very pretty. I think she'd like you."

Aaron was certain Trixie Weber would love Doug. He was a foul, crass brute just like their old friend Lincoln Barnes. Doug liked beating up on women. Trixie liked to be beaten. Otherwise why had she hooked up with a scumbag like Linc?

Aaron wouldn't put a mark on Joanna's flawless skin. That Linc had *hit* her made him want to kill the bastard all over again.

(Who are you kidding? You'll kill her.)

No. Aaron would die first. He'd never harm Joanna. He loved her.

"You'd better not fucking be lying to me," Doug had said. "I hate it here. It's colder than Quentin, and wetter. Shit, I can barely feel my toes."

Aaron had found clothing in a shed. It fit him well, but Doug was bigger and his ski jacket was comically tight. He kept grumbling, but managed to hot-wire the snowmobiles. They sped away from the ranch.

No one followed.

They'd almost died in the avalanche. It

89

had been so *loud.* Deafening. Aaron had never heard anything like it. They felt its tremor behind them and for the first time in his life he thought he would die. But they made it through.

They continued for miles. The first cabin they came to was perfect for Doug. There was food, wood, a stove. And peace. Aaron would love a place like this to share with Joanna. Doug . . . not so much. It was hard to convince Doug to stay in the outlying cabin, but Aaron insisted that he wait it out for a day or two.

"I only have reservations for one," Aaron said. "If we both show up, it'll be suspicious."

"Why the fuck did you do that?" Doug grumbled.

"I made the reservation the day after the earthquake under a false name. I didn't know we'd still be hooked up when we got here." He hadn't thought about it. All he imagined when he called the Moosehead Lodge was that after two years of dreaming, he and Joanna would finally be together. Doug hadn't even entered his mind.

"No one's going to care if you show up with a friend. I don't want to stay here. It's like prison."

"I'll come back tomorrow morning and

we'll work something out."

(Kill him.)

Aaron dismissed the idea. He needed Doug, at least for now.

Maybe he would kill him tomorrow.

Doug complained, but Aaron helped him start a fire in the wood stove and Doug decided that staying warm tonight was the better option.

Aaron had continued to the lodge alone.

Two of them would have seemed threatening. Aaron didn't want Joanna to be suspicious, especially after that phone conversation he'd overheard.

She was even more beautiful in person than in her photograph. When he'd walked into the lodge earlier, he'd seen the article he carried with him everywhere, framed and mounted in the entry.

Montana Romance Writer Simple Country Girl at Heart

There were several photos accompanying the article, including his favorite — Joanna on the wide porch of the lodge, mountains behind her. Her long, golden blonde hair blew in the breeze, her eyes vibrant. Her perfect profile was sharp and aristocratic, but her pure, smooth skin softened her.

Her skin looked even lovelier in person.

Her hair more luxurious.

Her eyes a deeper brown.

Her mouth lush and full.

He was her savior. He had wanted to tell her right when he saw her that he was her hero, but it had to wait. In her books, noble heroes didn't come on scene and tell the beautiful heroine how wonderful they were. Instead, they showed her.

And he would show her. When the time was right, Aaron would tell her that he killed Lincoln Barnes for her.

What man couldn't defend his own woman? Joanna's husband certainly had not been a hero. He'd been stupid and weak, and had been killed because of it. She was better off without such a pathetic man.

When Aaron was certain no one was around, when the watch he'd stolen off the dead O'Brien read 11:38, he left the den.

Silence.

Aaron slid into the office, quietly shut the door and turned on a desk lamp. He knelt on the floor, looking under the desk for a plug. No, he couldn't unplug the radio. That was obvious, and they'd simply plug it back in. Same with the phone lines. He'd have to go outside and find the main box for the phones. But even then, he wasn't sure what to do. Doug would know. He'd have to get Doug to do it in the morning.

The phone rang loudly and Aaron jumped. He whipped around, realized that it was the fax machine, not the phone. The volume button was on the side, and he turned it down, hoping no one had heard it. It rang again, softer.

A fax started to come through.

The first page was a cover sheet with a law enforcement seal, then:

Beaverhead County Sheriff's Department
Tyler M. McBride, Sheriff

Tyler. That's who Joanna had been talking to earlier.

In small, bold block letters the message:

Jo, here are the photographs we talked about earlier. Be careful. I'll be there as soon as I can. Love, Tyler.

Love, Tyler.

Love. Tyler.

What cop signed his memos *love*?

What was Joanna's relationship with the sheriff?

Heat rose in Aaron's face, and he couldn't see anything but the memo in front of him.

I'll be there as soon as I can. Love, Tyler.

Aaron sat on the desk chair, feeling as if his heart had been stabbed with a scalpel. Had Joanna betrayed him with another man? After he had killed for her?

She is too good for you. You know that,

Aaron. She's beautiful. You're average. She's successful, you're nothing. Nothing, Aaron. You'll never be anything. What in the world were you thinking when you came here? She can't love you. No one can love you.

(You'll have to kill her.)

Shut up.

He wasn't like that. Of course he was worthy of Joanna. He was smart, he was handsome, they were meant to be together. They had a future, a grand future. She'd told him over and over that they would live happily together forever. She promised she'd never leave him.

The fax machine beeped and Aaron shook his head, coming out of his thoughts. He saw that three pages had followed the cover page.

Love, Tyler.

The first was Doug Chapman's mug shot. He looked like the brute he was, with a couple days' growth of dark beard, shaggy hair, and small, dark eyes. The shot reminded him of Popeye's nemesis in the old black-and-white cartoons Aaron had watched when he was a kid. But Doug wasn't as fat as Bluto, nor as mean-looking.

Looks were deceiving.

At the bottom of the photo was a physical description. *Douglas Harold Chapman, b.*

*1971, hair: brown, eyes: brown, height: 6'2",
weight: 220 pounds. Distinguishing marks:
Tattoo on upper left arm of rose with the name*
Tanya. *Tattoo on upper right shoulder of eagle
head.*

The next photograph was of Thomas
O'Brien. It was a poor-quality reproduc-
tion. He looked much younger in the picture
than Aaron remembered him. *Thomas Mi-
chael O'Brien, b. 1953, hair: black, eyes: blue,
height: 6'1", weight: 185 pounds. Distinguishing marks: Strawberry birthmark one inch wide
on upper right shoulder blade.*

Then came the last page.

Aaron's mug shot.

He picked all four pages off the fax and
turned for the door. Stopped.

Joanna might be waiting for them. If they
weren't there, she'd call and Sheriff Tyler
McBride would fax them again. Aaron
wasn't sure he could disable the equipment
before then. At least not without being obvious.

He put the cover page, Doug's photo, and
O'Brien's photo back on the fax machine.
He folded his mug shot and tucked it in his
back pocket. Then he clicked off the desk
light and left.

He went upstairs and paced outside Joanna's room. The light was on; he saw it

under her door. What was she doing? What was she thinking? Was she thinking about Tyler?

His fists tightened and he laid them against the paneled wall outside her door, resisting the urge to pound. How could she? How could she do that to him?

He'd have to ask. And she'd tell him. She was honest, he knew that about her. Only a truly honest person would be able to write the books she wrote.

He raised his hand to knock. Dropped it.

Take it slow.

The smart thing would be to wait until breakfast. He realized that as he stared at her door, a wall sconce illuminating the hall. He didn't want to scare her, or even make her feel uncomfortable. Showing up now — near midnight — might do one or the other.

He slowly paced along the hallway, trying to come up with a better reason to knock on her door.

Hunger? No, that was dumb. His room had a small refrigerator with water, cheese, crackers, and grapes. The old man, Joanna's grandfather, had told him if he needed anything else, there was a cabinet in the dining hall marked "snacks" and he could help himself.

What if he said he couldn't sleep and

wanted to talk?

No. That would make him sound like a schoolgirl.

Perhaps he could disable something in his room. Ask her to fix it. But she might think he was weak, incapable of taking care of her.

Aaron grew frustrated. He needed to see Joanna. But he didn't want to blow it. Scare her.

Love, Tyler.

The urge grew and he walked away, down the stairs. Then back up the stairs. To her door. Slowly. Stealthily. He almost knocked.

No.

Down the stairs again.

A noise stopped him. He walked across the lobby, toward the great room, and ran into the girl, Leah Weber, as she bounded across the room with the big Saint Bernard behind her. She wore red flannel pajamas under a red bathrobe, her long blonde hair braided down her back, her pretty face unconcerned at meeting a stranger in the foyer.

"Late for you to be up," he said. Buckley wagged his tail and Aaron scratched the dog on the back. He'd never had a dog of his own. His aunt Dorothy had two poodles — hardly worthy of being called dogs. More like oversize rats. Now Buckley, he was a

97

real dog. A dog Aaron would have been proud to have as a kid.

She grinned. "Shh, don't tell my mom. I just had to get another piece of cake. Stan makes the *best* chocolate cake, and I know Aunt Jo is going to eat it all in the middle of the night."

Aaron agreed. "That was good cake."

Leah asked, "Do you need something?" She licked frosting off her finger.

So young, so innocent. Aaron had always liked kids, and he felt as if he knew Leah Weber well.

Her father Lincoln had talked about her often. Had her picture taped to the cell wall. She'd been younger then, five or six.

Leah had grown into a lovely young woman. What was she now? Eleven, Aaron thought. On the brink of womanhood, but still a child. Still someone to protect.

Aaron had done just that. Leah's father was a crass, violent man who was better off dead. That he'd tried to kidnap the little girl disturbed Aaron on a level he didn't like to think too deeply about. What would Lincoln Barnes have done to such a sweet child? No good, that's for sure. He'd killed another child, Leah's cousin.

"It was an accident, I didn't mean for the boy to die. I wanted what was mine. My

98

woman and my daughter."

Lincoln Barnes's words echoed in Aaron's brain. Remorse from a killer? Aaron wanted blood. Because Barnes had killed a child.

Aaron had avenged the child's death. Someday, Joanna would understand that. Someday, she would get down on her knees and thank him.

"I'm fine," he told Leah. "Just walking around. I couldn't sleep."

"I *know*," she said, rolling her eyes as only a young teen could do. "My mom has me in bed at ten every night, and I tell her why? I'm going to be twelve next month, I shouldn't have a curfew. It's not like I'm going to school tomorrow."

"Enjoy your cake," he said. "I think I'll sit by the fire." The hearth was contained in a huge inset, the flames doing a slow, quiet dance. The room was warm and comfortable.

"See you in the morning." She scurried down the hall to her room, calling for Buckley to follow her.

Meeting Leah was fortuitous. He'd learned something important about Joanna.

He sat on the floor in front of the fire. He would be waiting for his love when her sweet tooth called.

SIX

He'd only been holed up in this godforsaken one-room cabin for eight hours and ten minutes, but Doug Chapman might as well have been back in San Quentin. Why had he listened to Aaron, anyway?

"Stay here, let me go to the lodge alone. It'll be less suspicious that way."

Aaron's excuse was that he'd only made reservations for one person. Who the fuck cared? He could easily have said he was bringing in a friend. But when Aaron started the fire and Doug felt warm for the first time all day, he'd agreed. Fool.

While Aaron was living it up in that big lodge with a sexy woman in his bed, Doug was stuck here with nothing but canned chili from the pantry and the crackers and spray cheese they'd picked up at the rest stop where Aaron had popped O'Brien.

At least he'd also picked up a bottle of Jack Daniel's. Doug needed it, especially after watching Aaron snap. He hadn't thought the skinny kid had it in him.

Doug and O'Brien stayed in the truck while Aaron went into the mini-mart to buy food. The sky was such a striking blue he couldn't believe the news report of a storm coming in later that day.

"I can't believe I'm doing this," Doug muttered.

"Doing what?" O'Brien asked. He sat in the passenger seat of the four-door Ford 250.

"Listening to Dough-head Doherty and coming up to Bumfuck, Montana."

"His girl's up here, right?"

Doug laughed. "Girl. Right. He's never fucking met the bitch. He's obsessed with her picture. I think he cut it out of a magazine or something."

O'Brien asked, "Is she an actress or something?"

"I've never seen her before. But he's in love with her. Or he thinks he is. All I can say is that women are good for nothing but sex, and most won't give it up unless you give them something in return.

"Fucking bitches aren't good for anything but a quick screw. That's my new motto, yessir, a quick screw and then I'm outta there."

"He's never met this woman?"

"Never."

"What's her name?"

Doug glanced at O'Brien. He was too interested, Aaron wouldn't like that. "You saw her picture, right?"

O'Brien nodded.

"Hot babe. Too many clothes, but get them off her and she'd be a fine centerfold. But don't talk about her to Aaron. He's a little crazy when it comes to her."

"And you don't know her name?"

"Just don't talk about her. He gets freaky. Aaron's a whack-job, just remember that. You and me, we do what needs to get done, right? I get you. You popped your wife because she was fucking some asshole."

O'Brien said in a low voice, "Don't talk about my wife. You don't know shit about me."

Doug glanced at him again. "Hey, man, we're all friends here, right? I mean, I don't care what the fuck you did to land in Quentin, all I care about is not going back, know what I mean?"

O'Brien didn't answer, and Doug didn't push it. Aaron slid into the backseat of the truck and said, "I got a new map. It's a lot better."

"The news on the radio is saying that a storm is coming in tonight."

"We'll be there in just a couple hours, long before any storm."

"Where are we going?" O'Brien asked, turning ninety degrees in his seat so he could look at Aaron in the back.

"Montana."

"I figured that, but where?"

"Why do you want to know?"

O'Brien shrugged. "I don't like not knowing where I'm going."

"Dillon area. My girl lives up there."

Doug started the truck and drove along the frontage road that would lead back to the interstate.

"What's your girlfriend's name?" O'Brien asked.

"None of your fucking business."

Aaron placed a bag in the middle seat between Doug and O'Brien. Doug looked in the bag. Food, Jack Daniel's, and a book. "You bought another book? Why?"

"I don't have it," was all Aaron would say. "Go."

"You got some JD. Fan-fucking-tastic."

"Not while you're driving."

"Ass-wipe," Doug muttered.

Doug didn't push it. He pulled back onto the interstate and drove north.

Aaron reached into his backpack and pulled out the picture he looked at all the time. O'Brien craned his neck to get a look.

"Pretty."

Aaron tensed. Doug tried to defuse the situation knowing how Aaron was about the woman. "Hey, look, there's a deer just standing by the side of the road!"

The diversion didn't work.

"Don't even think about her, O'Brien," Aaron said.

"Hey, I'm not, I don't care. I just think she's pretty."

"She's not yours."

"Not saying she is. Does she have a name?"

"You want her, don't you?" Aaron stared unblinking at O'Brien. Doug could see the gun in Aaron's hand. O'Brien couldn't, not from his angle.

"No, I don't want your woman, I have enough women troubles of my own. I was just saying —"

"What? You think she's pretty?"

"Well, sure. She's pretty."

"Think she has nice tits?"

O'Brien paused. Aaron held up the picture. "They're nice."

"What about her ass?"

"I can't really see it from the picture. Do you have others?"

Aaron pressed the trigger. The bullet went into O'Brien's gut. His eyes went wild, in shock. Startled. He didn't know what had happened.

Hell, Doug didn't know what happened, either.

"Pull over," Aaron said.

Doug got off at the next exit, a mile from the stop they'd made.

Aaron carefully put the picture away and stuck the gun in his pants. Doug found a side road. "Stop," Aaron said.

Doug did. He'd never seen such crazy eyes. Even in Quentin, where half the guys were fucking insane, he'd never seen eyes like Aaron Doherty's. Doug feared for his own life. He had a gun as well, but he'd put it under the seat. He didn't want to reach for it now, not knowing what Aaron might do.

He could fucking shoot him, too, and leave him by the side of the road. He'd thought Aaron Doherty was an ass-wipe, but he hadn't realized just how crazy he was.

Doug thought back to Aaron's cryptic comments about the prisoner who had Doug's cell before him. Apparently the guy had been killed in a stealth attack in the dining hall. Aaron had said, "He deserved it."

Doug now wondered if Aaron had killed him. Aaron didn't seem the type. He wasn't wimpy looking, but he wasn't buff or into exercise like some of the guys. Aaron acted more like he was in a daze, like he didn't quite believe he was in prison, but he wasn't going to talk about it. Aaron looked like one of the guys that the fags would like, but Doug knew Aaron had never been made a bitch.

He wondered who Aaron Doherty really was.

And how many people — aside from Thomas O'Brien, who he was now dragging into the ditch — Aaron had killed.

Aaron got back into the truck. "Go."

Doug drove. He didn't say anything about Thomas O'Brien. And he sure as hell didn't say anything about Joanna Sutton, the romance writer.

Doug Chapman didn't want to end up in a ditch.

Aaron Doherty had killed a man for making innocent comments about the woman in the picture. Doug wasn't going to make the same mistake, and that was why he'd agreed to stay in this crappy cabin while Aaron went on to the big house.

Now he was stuck. And dammit, he didn't want to be in prison again, and that's exactly what it felt like in this pathetic cabin.

Sure, he had a bed, and a fireplace, and food, and his Jack Daniel's. But he couldn't *leave*. A prison by any other name . . .

At least he was warm. What the fuck did people think living in the mountains? Shit it was cold. He'd thought Quentin in January was an iceberg, but it was nothing like this. The prison had been dank, an insidious cold that sapped the energy from his bones. But Montana was like the freakin' Arctic.

He should have gone south, maybe to San Diego like Theodore Glenn. Someplace warm.

He'd changed out of his wet clothes, had

106

the fire roaring, but still couldn't rid the awful chill from his bones.

What he wanted was to find a hot woman to screw, get some money, and lay low. He'd liked how Aaron thought things through, even if he was a psycho. All wrapped up in some weird white knight thing that Doug wanted no part of. Killing O'Brien *just like that.* Doug just kept his opinions to himself after that, didn't even mention that this writer woman would probably have nothing to do with Aaron.

Now Doug was stuck in the middle of a freakin' snowstorm in the middle of Bumfuck, *Montana* — without a woman, without money, without a plan. Waiting.

Doug had no intention of going back. Fuck, no, he'd rather die than go back to that hellhole San Quentin. And Doug didn't want to die, either.

He took another long swallow of whiskey. It burned going down, a good burn, a burn that told him he was *free.*

And he'd do whatever it took to stay free.

Doug scooped chili directly from the pot into his mouth with a large spoon.

The chili was good, but what he'd give for a tender steak, a couple beers — yep, that was the way to go. He drank more whiskey and remembered the last time he'd had a nice steak.

The day the cops had arrested him for murder.

Doug threw the pot into the sink, denting the stainless steel. *Murder.* Is that what they called justice nowadays? Like that fucking bitch hadn't deserved to die. *Wife.* She'd been a freakin' ball and chain from the minute they met. Always running on at the mouth, giving him lip. Well, he'd fattened that lip a time or two and what had that gotten him? She'd hit him over the head with a frying pan, right out of the cartoons. And *she* was the one who had a restraining order against him? The cops didn't care what she'd done to *him.*

"Payback's a bitch, Tanya." He laughed out loud. Yeah, he'd gone to prison, but she was dead, rotting in the ground. He'd heard her parents had buried her, and he couldn't stop laughing. She'd always said she never wanted to be buried, only cremated. The idea of worms and bugs eating through her casket freaked her out.

Not that he told her pathetic parents that. He hoped Tanya's worn-out body was being devoured by the bugs she detested. Justice.

Carlos Bagatello had deserved to die, maybe even more than Tanya. But Doug acknowledged that his anger got him in trouble that time. There'd been a witness. Hell, there'd been three witnesses, and that's how the cops nailed him. Not that anyone had actually seen him hit Bagatello over the head with a wrench, or push his body into the sewage treatment tank. More like he'd made a stupid comment about Bagatello as he left. And no one else was on the catwalk above the tank he and Bagatello had been assigned to fix.

And he hadn't really taken care of the knife after slicing Tanya. He'd left it in his kitchen drawer. If he'd known the kid Aaron back then, none of that would have happened. Doug had a college degree and Aaron didn't, but the kid had a sixth sense about these things. He was smart that way.

The only thing Doug regretted was killing Chantelle. What a fine woman. She'd done for him like no other woman had, always ready for him, always wanting him. That was an accident. He'd told the cops that, a total accident. He didn't mean to kill her . . .

"The police came by asking about us today," Chantelle said two days after Tanya had been killed.

"What'd you tell them?"

"We were together that night." She frowned. "Doug, you left at one that morning and didn't come back until after three. Did you kill her?"

"What if I did? We can be together, Chantelle. Just like we want. Tanya was a fucking bitch. She wouldn't give me a divorce."

Tears bubbled into Chantelle's pretty brown eyes. "No, Doug. Not like this. I love you — but you killed your wife! How could you?"

"It wasn't like that —"

"What was it like?"

Doug got on his knees and grabbed her hands. "Chantelle, I love you. We'll get through this. I promise. I have a good job, I make good money, and now I won't have to fork over alimony to that bitch. And we can get that house you want, and —"

She was shaking her head, the tears streaming down her face. "I don't know you anymore, Doug."

She tried to turn away from him, but he was still holding her hands. "No. No!"

"Let me go. Please."

She wasn't scared, not then.

"Chantelle, listen to me!"

"I've listened to you, Doug. You're a coward. You picked the easy way out. A real man would have dealt with his mistakes, not killed them."

"You can't leave me!"

"Let. Go!"

She yanked her hands away and Doug grabbed her ankles and pulled her down. Her head thumped against the hardwood floor. "You don't mean it," he said.

"Yes I do!"

Chantelle always liked it rough in bed, and Doug told himself this was another of her games. He climbed on top of her and she was hitting him. "It's over, Doug. Get off me!"

"You're not walking away. I did it for you. For you, Chantelle!"

"You did it for yourself, asshole!"

He hit her. Her head whipped to the side and she stopped fighting, shock on her face.

He'd never hit her before. Tanya, yeah, but the bitch deserved it. Not Chantelle. Pretty Chantelle. His Chantelle.

"I'm sorry, I didn't —"

She opened her mouth and Doug knew she was going to scream. He clamped his hand over her mouth. He hadn't meant to strangle her. But his hands were on her neck, squeezing, her eyes bulged, no sound came from her mouth . . .

And then she was dead. Too fast, too quick. He hadn't meant to kill her.

He loved her.

But the bitch was going to leave him.

Doug slammed his fist into a painting on the wall. His arm went all the way through and hit solid wood.

"Shit!" he swore and held his hand, shaking out the pain. Nothing broken.

He couldn't stay in this cabin anymore. He was going stir-crazy. But the snow kept falling. It was blowing all around, against the cabin. He'd be buried alive.

He began to sweat. He couldn't be snowed in. Who would find him? What if he ran out of food and water before Aaron came for him? What if Aaron didn't come for him? What if he planned on killing him, just like O'Brien? What if that had been the plan all along? To leave him here to rot?

Screw that. And screw Aaron Doherty. He was going to the lodge and he'd take over. Get that wench for Aaron and kill everyone else. Except for a hostage or two. Keep the women alive. Doug grinned. Yeah, he could use a good lay.

In this weather, they'd have days, maybe even weeks, before anyone came up here. They could stock up, have their fill of women, and be out of the place before anyone found them.

But Doug couldn't do it holed up here in a one-room cabin that was only twice as big as his old prison cell.

He took a long slug of whiskey and felt pretty damn good about his plan. And if Aaron Doherty had a problem with it, he could go to hell. Doug would be happy to send him there himself.

He put on all the clothes he had, even the too-tight jacket. He put the gun in his waistband. He found a sharp knife in the drawer.

Doug preferred knives to guns.

He preferred his hands to knives.

Doug wasn't one to wait. He acted first, knew he was impatient. Which was one of the reasons he'd been caught and convicted in the first place.

But if he was caught now, it would be by a bunch of redneck country bumpkins and he'd kill them.

Murder was easy. Especially when he was an old hand at it.

He couldn't stay here another minute.

He put on the jacket and boots, strapping on snowshoes he'd found in the closet, and left the cabin. Almost immediately, Doug regretted his decision. The snow was falling steadily, blown by the wind, his footprints disappearing behind him almost as fast as he walked. He'd miscalculated where the lodge was. Fortunately, the wind was at his back, pushing him forward. He had to come to something soon, didn't he?

Doug couldn't see anything. It was darker than night, so pitch black that he would have thought he was in hell except that it was too cold. The snow fell so heavy that if he stood for a minute to get his bearings, he'd turn into a snowman. Even with the snowshoes, his feet sank so far into the powder that he feared he wouldn't be able to pull them up.

He would freeze to death.

He considered turning back, but his tracks were gone. He was committed to this course.

He walked straight. As straight as he could. He'd watched which way Aaron had gone; he'd follow. He had a good sense of direction. He'd find the lodge.

And fuck, he'd kill Aaron just for putting him through this.

Doug practically walked into a wall. One minute, he saw nothing. The next, the wall was a foot in front of him and he literally bumped it. A faint light came from around the corner.

Salvation. With one hand on the rough wood, he walked around the cabin until he found the door. The door was buried up to the knob. He tried it.

Locked.

He knocked. If no one answered, he'd just break in. If not the door, a window.

A minute later a man answered. Over his shoulder, the most beautiful woman Doug had ever seen lay in bed, her blonde hair messed up, shoulders bare, breasts covered by a down comforter.

She *had* to be naked.

The man had a lopsided grin on his face. "You're from the lodge, sorry. I didn't know anyone would be coming out tonight."

Doug nodded. "I was checking on the guests, but suddenly the storm got worse and I can't get back."

"Come in, it's too cold to be out." Doug stepped inside and the man shut the door. "How about some coffee?"

"Sounds great."

"Are you Stan Wood? He's the only one we haven't met."

"Stan," Doug said. "Right."

"You're a great cook. Fabulous food," the man said.

"I don't remember your name, I'm sorry. I was just sent out —"

The man laughed as he poured coffee into a heavy ceramic mug. "Greg. And my wife, Vicky."

Vicky waved from the bed.

She must have huge tits, the way the comforter molded to them.

Doug's cock jumped.

He took the mug from Greg, sipped. "Thanks."

Vicky said, "I'll get into something decent."

Doug watched as Vicky pulled a sheet around herself and went into the bathroom.

"My wife's modest," Greg said good-naturedly. "This is her first time here."

"But not yours," Doug guessed.

"I've been to the valley, but not this lodge. I went to MSU and did my thesis on the migratory birds in the refuge. I stayed at the refuge headquarters for a month, on nothing more than a cot. I thought for our honeymoon that a cabin with a real bed was in order."

"Glad you're enjoying yourself."

Greg laughed, sipped his own coffee. "We were planning to go home tomorrow — we live in Seattle now — but with this weather we'll extend the honeymoon a day or three. Can't say I'm sorry about that."

Not sorry at all, Doug thought. He wrapped his hand around the knife in his pocket.

The bathroom door opened and Greg turned his eyes toward his wife. She'd dressed in a white terry robe. Doug imagined she had nothing on underneath.

That was all the opportunity Doug needed. He withdrew the knife from his pocket and shoved it between Greg's shoulder blades.

The man fell to his knees, his mouth open, blood drooling from one corner.

Doug pulled out the knife and Greg crumpled to the floor, his mouth moving soundlessly. He slammed the knife in again, just to make sure he was dead, though Doug was confident the first cut had done the newlywed in.

Vicky screamed. The sound was piercing.

Doug caught her eye. She was fine, but even if she were a pig Doug would have fucked her.

It had been a long, long time since he'd had a real cunt.

Since Chantelle.

Doug smiled. "It's just you and me, now."

Crying, she ran to the main door.

Did she think she'd get far in this weather?

She flung the door open, the blast of cold air filling the room. Doug crossed the room in three large steps and pushed her down, into the snow.

She tried to crawl, shivering, the wind blowing snow all around her.

If Doug had closed the door, she would have frozen to death just feet away from the cabin.

But he had other plans for her.

He grabbed her thick blonde hair and

pulled her back into the cabin, slamming the door shut behind them. He locked it.

"N-n-no," she sobbed, huddled on the floor in water and fear.

"No more games," he growled. He picked her up. Her robe opened, revealing her near naked body. All she wore were panties and a skimpy pink tank top. At first she didn't do anything, she was still catching her breath.

Then she started to fight.

He almost laughed. *This was going to be fun.*

SEVEN

Ever since she'd gotten off the phone with Tyler earlier, Jo had been in a writing rut. Her mind whirled around everything he'd said — and hadn't said — leaving her unable to write or sleep.

She didn't want to think about Tyler, especially when tomorrow was the anniversary of Ken's murder. Four years. The date had been creeping up on her, but this year for the first time she hadn't remembered until today. In the past, she'd feel depressed for weeks leading up to the anniversary of Ken and Timmy's murders, but now — because of Tyler, because of her confusion — she had almost forgotten.

She felt like she was betraying her husband.

Husband? Ken's been dead for four years.

Four years sounded like forever, but it wasn't all that long. And it had been too soon for her and Tyler McBride.

With Tyler, she had tried to put her past aside. And the truth was, she hadn't thought about Ken every night when she couldn't sleep. She had anticipated the future instead of dreading the next day.

Stop. You're just a damn romantic at heart. Love doesn't happen twice in a lifetime. You were lucky with Ken.

But for a while, she had thought it just might. That lightning might strike twice. She felt — what did she feel with Tyler? Safe. Warm. Loved. He was a rock. Solid and patient and smart.

Then he had ruined it by asking her to marry him. She was already married.

Ken is dead.

She *felt* married.

Then why did you sleep with Tyler McBride? Answer that one, Jo.

And she'd felt guilty. Not right after, God no, it had been incredible. Tyler was patient and focused in everything he did, including everything he did in bed. With his entire attention on her, she'd been more than satiated.

It was in the days following when the guilt crept in, along with that tickle of fear that she would forget Ken. And Timmy.

A bath. That would settle her mind, if not her heart. In her bathroom, Jo drew hot water, added lavender scented bubbles, and slid in, sighing. *Yes.* The hot soak would relax her, work out the tension, let her go to sleep and forget about Tyler and the fact that she would be seeing him tomorrow. Let her forget about the ridiculous idea that some escaped convict was fixated on her. Let her forget that her husband and son were both murdered by a psychopath.

She and Ken would never have left the Centennial Valley if it hadn't been for his career, and if they hadn't left he'd probably still be alive. Ken did what he loved to do, and taking the job as a wildlife biologist in the Sierra Nevada outside of Lake Tahoe, California, had been his dream job. As a writer, Jo could work anywhere. She wrote, had Timmy, and they spent every weekend outdoors. Camping. Skiing. Loving.

Though it had been four years since he'd been killed, when Jo really let her emotions go, she realized she didn't grieve for her husband in the same way as she grieved for her son. She'd loved Ken, but Timmy had been their child. She could look at his nine-year-old picture dry-eyed, but when she looked at baby pictures she broke down remembering everything that had been lost. She didn't understand why. Timmy had deserved a future, and it had been cruelly taken from him. From her.

That fateful night rushed back and she couldn't avoid the memories. Maybe it was time she didn't avoid them.

Trixie had gotten a restraining order against her boyfriend, Leah's father. Linc had violated the order numerous times and landed in prison for a year when he attempted to kidnap Leah from school. So Trixie moved from Los Angeles where she'd been living and working as a waitress at a high-end club that catered to celebrities and the movers and shakers of southern California.

While Jo had understood Trixie's need to get out of the valley — it was a hard place to live — Jo had never understood Trixie's wild streak. Trixie wanted to live in the middle of everything. She'd met Lincoln Barnes shortly after moving to L.A. and soon after was pregnant. Grandpa wanted her to move home, but Trixie wouldn't even consider it. She loved Linc, wanted to have her own family even though she was only nineteen. They lived together for a few years, but it hadn't taken long for Linc to show his true colors. He was jealous. Trixie couldn't so much as look at another man or he'd fly off the handle. After Linc hit her, Trixie finally broke it off. Leah was four.

Jo had always suspected Trixie had been abused from the beginning of the relationship, but that she'd kept it a secret. Jo had asked her sister once, but Trix very quickly got defensive. She lied, made excuses, denied — all the signs of a victim of abuse. But at least Trixie had finally found the courage to leave Linc and file a restraining order against him.

It didn't take Linc long to land in prison for violating the court order. When he got out, he went after them again, when Leah was eight. Jo convinced Trixie to leave L.A., offering her and Leah a sanctuary. She and Ken had a big enough house in Placerville, halfway between Lake Tahoe and Sacramento. Trixie and Leah would be safe — Lincoln didn't know where the Suttons lived.

Two months later, when they started to breathe easier, Lincoln Barnes found them.

It was the first Friday in February. Jo had been writing all day while Trixie was out on job interviews. At quarter to three, she left to get the kids from school. Leah was a joy, already a "sister" to Tim. They bickered, but enjoyed doing some things together. Tim thought it was cool that a girl liked video games, and Leah thought it was cool that Tim played guitar.

Jo always wondered now if she'd made different decisions would Ken and Tim still be alive. What if she'd decided to come straight home? What if she'd been suspicious of the pick-up truck in front of the house? What if she hadn't hesitated?

But instead, she'd taken the kids to the grocery store to stock up for the weekend. They returned home an hour later, entering through the back door.

Right into a trap.

"Run!"

It was Trixie's voice from the bedroom. Jo paused, scared but unsure what was going on.

Had those seconds cost Tim his life?

"Go next door," she told Tim and Leah. "Now."

The kids turned to leave, but it was too late.

Lincoln Barnes stepped into the kitchen, a gun to Trixie's head. Leah screamed, and Tim — acting like the man he would never grow up to be — grabbed his cousin's arm and pushed her behind him.

Jo would never forget the look of terror on his face, but also in it a strength older than his years.

"Go!" Jo told the kids again. She had to get them to safety.

With Trixie firmly in hand, Linc took four long strides to the side door as Tim reached for the knob. He hit Tim on the top of the head with his gun and Tim collapsed, unconscious.

"Stop, Daddy, stop!" Leah cried, her eyes darting back and forth from her mother to Tim's prone body.

Jo knelt beside her son, touched him. His head was bleeding. He was still breathing but he needed a doctor. He was breathing — Jo clung to that fact.

Linc said, "Come, Leah. We're leaving."

"N-n-no, Daddy." Tears ran down her face.

"Leave her alone," Trixie shouted. "Take me, leave her alone!"

"Mommy!"

"Shh, Leah, it's okay. Stay with Aunt Jo."

"Fucking bitch sent me to prison! Leah, your mother sent me to prison just because I wanted to see you."

"You hurt Mommy."

"That's a lie."

"You hurt Timmy. Why, Daddy?"

Linc glanced down at Tim and his expression changed. Jo saw the confusion and uncertainty. She pushed aside her fear for her son and said, "Linc, you don't want to hurt anyone. Especially Tim and Leah. Go. We won't call the cops, I promise, I just need to get Tim to the hospital. Please."

"I'm not leaving without my wife and daughter."

Jo stared at Trixie. Wife? She'd never told Jo she'd married him. Was this one of Linc's deranged ideas?

"Just me, Linc. Just me," Trixie said. "Come on, I promise, everything will go back to the way it was before. Please leave Leah out of it, okay?"

"We're a family."

"Don't hurt her!" Trixie cried.

"I would never hurt my daughter. How could you think that?"

Linc pushed Trixie down to the floor and aimed the gun at her.

Leah screamed and Linc flinched. That hesitation saved Trixie's life: the bullet entered her leg, not her chest.

The side door burst open. Ken stood there and took the entire scene in at once. Trixie bleeding on the tile. Leah crying. Jo kneeling next to an unconscious Tim, Tim's blood on her hands.

Ken tackled Linc and the two men hit the

tile. Ken's fist connected with Linc's face, his other hand grabbing the wrist that still held the gun and slamming it against the tile.

Linc was a large, burly man. He hit Ken in the face. "I have no issue with you, Sutton. I want my daughter."

Ken grunted, trying to get the upper hand again.

While the men fought, Jo whispered to Leah. "Run, Leah. Go next door."

"Aunt —"

"Now."

Leah scurried out the open side door. Jo breathed a marginal sigh of relief as she pulled out her cell phone and behind her back felt out the numbers 911, and pressed Send. Then she slid the open phone around the corner of the cabinet.

She positioned herself in front of Tim as best she could. Trixie had crawled over to the opposite side of the kitchen, a trail of blood in her wake.

The grunts from the men brought Jo's attention to her husband and Linc fighting. She looked around for a weapon, saw nothing. Even if she could get to the knives on the far side of the kitchen, they were in a drawer. She couldn't leave Tim unprotected.

Linc's hand was still clenching the gun and a round went off, inches from Ken's head.

Jo didn't want to leave Tim, but Ken was in trouble. Linc was on top of her husband, a large hand pushing down on his throat. Ken grabbed his forearm, trying to pry him loose.

Jo leapt up, pushing a chair in front of Tim in an effort to protect him. She jumped on Linc's back, clawing at his head, hoping to give Ken a breath. To give the police time to arrive.

Linc cried out and threw Jo off him like a wild animal. She landed hard on the tile, stunned for just a moment.

But Ken was free. He took the advantage and slammed Linc's head against the floor.

Linc pushed back, and his gun hand was between the two men. Ken grabbed it, and Jo knew the second before the first gunshot that Ken was dead.

Three bullets rang out in rapid succession. Jo watched Ken's shocked, pained expression.

Linc pushed him off. He looked stunned. "Where. Is. Leah."

Sirens in the distance caught his ear. Jo didn't see Linc run off. She crawled to Ken, sobbing. Cradled his head in her lap.

"Kenny, please, I love you, please hold on."

Blood everywhere. His chest was red and wet, his mouth opened and closed but he couldn't say anything. He had no air. Jo later found out the bullets had pierced her husband's lungs.

Ken stared at Jo and she watched the life disappear from his eyes.

Even after her bath, Jo couldn't sleep. It was after one in the morning when she decided hot tea and chocolate was the only solution to her insomnia.

She pulled on her ratty gray sweats and a long-sleeved T-shirt that had seen better days. It had been Ken's from MSU. She hadn't kept all his clothes, but a few of his favorite shirts comforted her, especially during that first year after his murder. She didn't really think about it now; wearing them had become a habit, and maybe a bit of a good luck charm when writing. To keep the muse flowing.

She couldn't help but wonder if it was these few physical attachments to Ken that stopped her from truly saying good-bye. Was four years long enough? Too long? Too short? She didn't know. She wasn't ready to let Ken go — that's what she told herself. Again and again.

When she was with Tyler, she forgot about Ken — at least on the surface. That scared her sometimes, because she didn't want to forget. At the same time, she knew she had to put Ken's memory to rest if she wanted to have a future with any other man. With Tyler. But if she let her dead husband go, what did that mean for Timmy? She couldn't — she swallowed a sob. It was the anniversary of that awful day, there was no way she'd sleep now.

She walked downstairs, her slippers flapping on the hardwood floors. Grandpa left the wall sconces on low in case any guests left their rooms in the evenings, but to conserve fuel he'd turned every other sconce off, leaving the halls with pockets of shadow and light. She heard nothing, and wondered if the snow had stopped. Peering out the tall grand living room windows, she watched the snow fall steadily, flakes drifting down, keeping the deck, the ground, the valley below all buried. The wind which had whipped something ferocious earlier had stopped, the snow looking deceptively peaceful as it fell to earth.

No wind, no driving gales, just a steady, silent stream of white flakes glowing almost blue in the odd reflected light that Grandpa had on the outside of the lodge.

Coming home had healed her. Had she stayed in California, she would have been alone. She would always miss Ken, she would always grieve for her lost son, but she would survive. And knowing that, knowing she could face tomorrow and whatever it brought, gave her peace.

"I'll always love you, Kenny," she whispered.

A howl of a wolf cut through the quiet storm. Sound traveled in the valley; the animal could have been near or far, she didn't know. The howl was followed by another, then another, as if the first animal had set off a chorus. Odd, she thought, but not unheard of. Perhaps a larger predator was out this night. Most grizzlies were hibernating, but seeing one or two in the winter was not unheard of. Moose were the biggest problem year-round.

Silence again.

She turned toward the kitchen, moving on instinct in the dim light. She opened the cabinet where Stan Wood kept his delectable chocolate cake. Her mouth watered thinking about it.

Only a third of the cake remained. When she'd put it away, there'd been a full half.

"Leah," she said out loud. She couldn't be angry that her niece had her sweet tooth. After all, they'd often found themselves in the kitchen together late at night, and those were some of Jo's best recent memories. Leah had saved her more than any person, just by being Leah.

She pulled down the cake and turned toward the table.

"Hi, Mrs. Sutton."

The cake plate fell from her hands. It hit the wood floor, the crack of breaking glass blocking out her short, startled scream.

Reaching back, she hit the wall and the overhead light came on.

John Miller.

"I'm so sorry." He looked sincerely contrite, knelt, and began to clean up the ruined cake and glass.

"I'll do that," she said, kneeling next to him.

"I didn't mean to startle you. I couldn't sleep."

"It's okay." It was and it wasn't. She rarely encountered guests at night. In the four years since she'd been back, she could count the times on one hand with fingers to spare.

His hand brushed against hers, and for a split second she thought it was on purpose.

Don't be ridiculous. He'd startled her and she was jumpy.

They cleaned up in silence, and she crossed to the refrigerator. "Can I get you something?"

"I don't want to put you out. I'm sorry about your cake."

"It's fine, really. My hips will thank you." She tried to laugh it off, but the way he looked at her made her feel strange, violated. Like he had X-ray vision or something.

You're watching too much television with Leah.

Or, more likely, Tyler's fears had crept into her subconscious. John Miller looked harmless, acted harmless, but there was something slightly off about him. She couldn't put her finger on exactly what bothered her. Maybe it was just her imagination.

John said, "Tea, if you don't mind."

She did mind. She wanted to get back to her room with tea for one. She didn't want company.

Of course she didn't say anything about her feelings as she put the teakettle on to boil. John Miller was a guest, and she'd been raised in a home that prided itself on hospitality. She busied herself getting the cups and saucers. Her grandmother had loved tea, and while Jo preferred coffee day-to-day, tea always comforted.

But she had no intentions of drinking it with John Miller in the kitchen. It had an odd, almost intimate feeling that disturbed her for some indefinable reason. It wasn't like anything was wrong with him — he was nice looking with short brown hair and big blue eyes. He was a little stiff, though at the same time, he seemed to be looking everywhere, not just where his eyes appeared to be focused.

Jo, you are tired. You can't even think straight.

"Milk or sugar?" she asked.

"No, thank you," he said.

"So you're from Los Angeles?" *Boil already!* she mentally told the kettle.

"Born and raised," he said. "I saw your newspaper article in the lobby."

She laughed, feeling a blush rise to her cheeks. She wished her grandfather hadn't done that, but she couldn't very well tell him to take it down. He'd been so proud of her, and she was proud of what she accomplished as well, but still it made her feel like she was on show, or bragging, or something. She shifted, fidgeted with the burner.

"I've read your books," he said.

"So you said earlier."

"I didn't realize when I planned this little trip that you lived here."

"Men don't usually read romance novels." It was a flip comment, and not wholly true. About ten, fifteen percent of her fan mail came from men. Ken used to say if more men read romance novels there'd be fewer divorces.

133

"I particularly liked *All Things Must Pass.* Maybe because your hero shares my name." He laughed.

"John Miller is pretty common," she said. She'd received several e-mails from readers informing her that they, too, knew a John Miller or one of her other characters. Still, she'd never personally met someone with the same name as one of her characters, until now.

The teakettle whistled and she poured the hot water into the teapot and inserted the infuser basket filled with loose tea, just like her grandmother had taught her. The ritual calmed her. Her grandmother always said every problem could be solved over a pot of tea.

"Seriously, I thought the story was poignant. Very relevant to what many couples face. Losing someone."

His voice trailed off and Jo looked at the man in a new light. She brought the teapot to the table, then the cups and saucers and sat down while the tea steeped. Perhaps she'd judged him too harshly. He had startled her, and she didn't like being scared. And maybe Tyler's warning had upset her more than she'd thought.

"You sound like you speak from experience," she said.

He didn't say anything for a long minute, staring into his empty cup. "My wife," he finally said. "Rebecca. Eight years ago."

She reached out for his hand without thinking, squeezed it. "I'm sorry. She must have been very young."

"We were both twenty-five. We'd been married for three years, right out of college. I — I never expected it. It was so sudden."

The tea was ready and she poured. She didn't want to have a conversation about loss, but at the same time the anguish on John's face called to her. He was still hurting, and she couldn't turn her back on people in pain.

"What happened?" she asked quietly, sipped her tea, putting aside her plan to drink alone in her room.

"A car accident. One day she was there — that night she was gone."

A tickle crawled in the back of Jo's mind, but she didn't know why. Something was familiar, but she couldn't place it.

"I read in the article that you lost your husband."

She nodded. She didn't want to talk to John Miller, or anyone, about Ken. He was still hers, to be thought about alone.

"I'm sorry. I shouldn't have said anything."

135

"It's okay. I don't really like to talk about it much." She sipped her tea. "So what made you decide to come to the Centennial Valley in the middle of winter?"

"I have a job offer I'm thinking about. It's a major career change — and I'm just not sure about it."

Another tickle. She'd written a book years ago, *Can't Buy Me Love,* about a man who had done almost the exact same thing — taken a sabbatical from his high-stress computer tech job while contemplating a career change into something more fulfilling, but less lucrative. Her hero, Josh Grant, had gotten lost in Montana, and instead of finding his wealthy friend's vacation house in the Bitterroot Valley, he had ended up at a working ranch in the Centennial Valley, where he'd found both love and hope.

But of course Jo was being ridiculous. There were glaring differences. John Miller had made reservations here a week ago. He'd planned this trip, unlike the fictitious Josh Grant who had gotten lost.

Her best friend, a crime fiction writer in Seattle, had told her that she saw her fictional serial killers in real people all the time. "But you just go with the flow, Jo," Mindy would say. "Because our imaginations are bigger than most people. I know

136

there's not a serial killer on every corner, just like you know happy endings, if real, never last."

She sighed. Mindy was such a pessimist. It was amazing that she successfully wrote any romance into her murder books.

"Did I say something wrong?" John asked.

She shook her head. "Just thinking about a friend of mine. It's nothing."

He frowned and for a moment she thought he was angry. His hand clenched the teacup.

Then it was gone.

"Thank you for the tea, Mrs. Sutton."

"You can call me Jo."

He stood. "I think I can finally get some shut-eye, Joanna. Let me help —" He began to clean up.

"No, I've got it, thanks," she said.

"Are you sure?"

"Of course. You're our guest." She smiled, surprised that she had to force it.

"Very well. Thank you, Joanna, for your hospitality." He winked. "See you on the other side of the night."

She watched him leave, then sank back into her chair.

The other side of the night.

Another one of her heroes used that same phrase. It was cheesy, she'd thought when she'd written it, but her editor had loved it, so she let it stand in the copyedits.

When John Miller said he'd read her books, he'd really *read* them. Remembered them. And while she always liked when fans appreciated her work, this particular fan creeped her out.

Tyler had told her that an escaped convict might be looking for her. Had her picture. John Miller? Her heart raced. Had she just sat down and talked with a killer?

She heard John walk up the stairs, then she went right into the office. There was a fax on the machine. She pulled it off with shaking hands.

The cover page was from Tyler.

Jo, here are the photographs we talked about earlier. Be careful. I'll come as soon as I can. Love, Tyler.

There were two photographs. Jo didn't recognize either man. She sighed. To think that John Miller was an escaped convict from California simply because he'd quoted one of her books. Tyler's comments about someone carrying around her picture had unnerved her.

She was relieved that John Miller was who he said he was. He may be odd, but odd-ness wasn't a crime.

She started upstairs, then turned to check the front door. It was locked. She went around and checked all the other doors, just to be safe. She opened the door to the den and turned on the light. Her grandfather kept his locked gun cabinet in the den. Mostly rifles and shotguns, plus extra cans of bear spray. Tyler had wanted her to have a gun upstairs, but Jo couldn't imagine anyone getting through the storm before Tyler arrived. Still, if Tyler could make it to the valley tomorrow, so could the two men in the fax. She had their photographs and would make copies for all the guests. They were cut off from the world in the middle of this storm, but they could still be smart.

Instead of a gun, she picked up a can of bear spray. It was ultrahot pepper spray, strong enough to repel a grizzly and now part of the mandatory hiking gear. She'd never had to use it, but during one camping trip years ago with her father he'd saved their lives with it.

The bear spray was stronger than pepper spray traditionally used for self-defense. If she saw one of the men in these pictures, she'd take action. They'd be down for at least an hour, enough time to get help, get away, or restrain them until Tyler arrived.

Confident that this was the safest solution, Jo went upstairs. Tomorrow promised to be a full day. She'd take care of her guests, meet up with Wyatt and his troop, bring Ben Ward safely back to the lodge. Plenty to do, and she needed some sleep.

Being cooped up for so long at the lodge had prompted her earlier strange feelings. That was all it was. There was nothing odd about John Miller. She was just restless.

EIGHT

Tyler McBride slept little that night. What was he doing in his warm bed under a down comforter while his twelve-year-old son was in the middle of a snowstorm?

But the stranded Boy Scouts were not his only concern. Two killers were in his jurisdiction, one of which had a fixation on the woman he loved. Back in Texas, Tyler had confronted several stalkers during his tenure as a Ranger; one case ended in murder. The obsession of these psychopaths was not to be taken lightly. If Jo had a stalker from San Quentin, he would most certainly go to her if he could. And when Jo spurned his advances, he could snap.

Jo was in danger, as well as everyone else at the lodge. Still, there were a dozen people at Karl Weber's place and only three escaped convicts. Sam Nash and his grown son, Peter, were keeping watch in Lakeview. If

Doherty, Chapman, or O'Brien showed up, they would call him, alert Jo, and hopefully find a way to detain them.

It comforted Tyler a bit that no one could drive a car to the lodge from Lakeview. Even getting to Lakeview now would be impossible, and Tyler suspected they'd be snowmobiling in tomorrow all the way from Monida. For the first time, the foul weather might be advantageous. Two killers from California wouldn't have been prepared with snowmobiles, or expect anything like this storm.

To pass the time while he worried about his son and the escaped convicts, he read one of Jo's books. When Wyatt had introduced them during the Worthington search-and-rescue last winter, he'd mentioned Jo was a published author. That had intrigued Tyler enough that he looked up her books on Amazon one night and ordered a couple. He never planned on reading them after he realized they were romance novels, but one night when he couldn't sleep he'd picked one up.

He'd read almost all of her books since. They intrigued him, different than the military and political thrillers he generally preferred. They weren't what he expected. Jo's novels were as much about family and forgiveness as they were about romance. And she infused them with a hint of humor that he didn't see in her sad brown eyes.

In Jo's novels, there were insights into human behavior, love, and honor. Tyler couldn't help but admire them.

Reading Jo's books always gave him pleasure, but at the same time made him acutely aware of the loneliness of his own life. Of how he was raising his son, how he hadn't pushed Jo after Thanksgiving. How could he compete with Saint Ken?

That's not fair.

Maybe not, but he knew Jo still felt married to another man. Tyler had hoped he'd given her enough time and patience to accept him in her life, but after she turned down his proposal, he couldn't help but wonder if and how Jo compared him to Ken. It was impossible to compete with a ghost. He wouldn't even try.

But isn't that what he'd done by proposing in the first place? Trying to force her into making a choice? Tyler loved her, and dammit, he knew she loved him — even though she hadn't said it in so many words. She had gone out of her way to visit him. When he'd mentioned Jason's trip with Wyatt over Labor Day, she had shown up on his porch with an overnight bag in hand.

Making love had knocked down barriers neither of them had even known were there. During the year since they'd met, from the Kyle Worthington rescue until his ill-fated proposal, Tyler and Jo had found every opportunity to be together. She may not have *told* him she loved him, but he saw it in her actions, in how she touched him, in how she smiled. He understood the loss of her family was a tragic obstacle, but he thought she had accepted him — wanted him — in her life. Tyler certainly wanted Jo as his wife, his best friend, his lover, Jason's mother.

But he'd been wrong to propose then. Tyler had seen panic in her eyes. The way she looked at him. As if she was betraying her husband.

Tyler wouldn't do that to Jason or to himself. So he didn't call her, didn't talk to her. When she was ready, Jo would come to him in the flesh, just like she came to him in his dreams.

Tonight was no different.

He slept a couple hours, a rough, uncomfortable sleep mixed with worry for his son and fear for Jo. He woke up unrested, leaving for the station at dawn after a quick shower and shave.

The storm had temporarily halted. The snow had stopped falling, but the air was thick with mist, the sky dark and foreboding. The NWS said the worst of the storm had passed and there would be occasional flurries, but right now visibility was nil and Tyler didn't see it getting better anytime soon. On a typical day he'd walk the few blocks to work. Today, even in his four-wheel drive, it took him ten minutes. The snowplow would be coming through later to clear the main streets, but Tyler suspected most people would remain indoors for the bulk of the day.

When he'd moved up here with Jason, Wyatt wanted them to live on his ranch outside Ennis, but Tyler wasn't comfortable enough with his relationship with his brother to move in with him. They'd never found common ground with their father; Wyatt hated him and Tyler didn't. Though dead, Richard McBride still stood between his sons.

They didn't have a traditional childhood.

Tyler didn't even remember his mother, who'd been his father's mistress. She'd been killed in a car accident when he was two. If he closed his eyes and concentrated long enough, quietly enough, he could sometimes smell her perfume, something flowery and very faint. It was probably his imagination, but he liked to think it was a real memory.

After she died, Richard McBride brought Tyler, his bastard son, to live at his house with his wife — informing Gabrielle for the first time that he had fathered a child with his mistress.

Controlling and vindictive, Tyler's father only got worse when Gabrielle took Wyatt and moved to Montana when Wyatt was nine and Tyler was eight. Tyler couldn't blame her.

After she left, Gabrielle allowed Wyatt to visit them in Texas for one month every summer and a week during Christmas and Easter. The only thing Tyler didn't know was why their father hadn't fought for custody. Richard McBride was not a man who gave up what was his. Tyler had always wanted to ask, but never had.

Tyler had always looked forward to Wyatt's visits, and when the boys were young they were best friends. And then, like a switch, when Wyatt was eighteen he stopped coming. Tyler knew he hated their father. He was hurt that his half brother hated him as well.

Or so he felt at the time. Hindsight and maturity told Tyler that Wyatt's abrupt silence had everything to do with their father, not him, but it was still a surprise when Wyatt contacted him about the open

Sheriff's position after the sitting Sheriff suffered a severe heart attack and needed to retire.

With Sharon gone and a son to raise on his own, Tyler took the position. Besides his son Jason, Wyatt was the last of Tyler's family, and he'd wanted to reclaim the brother of his childhood. But after twenty months, they hadn't made a lot of headway. The McBride men weren't talkative, and to solve problems you had to talk about them.

Tyler found a house in town, though in hindsight maybe he should have made more of an effort to live closer to his brother. He'd planned on looking for some acreage outside of Dillon, a place where he could raise some horses like he'd done as a kid, but being near the station had its benefits.

Like today.

He dumped out the lukewarm pot of coffee the graveyard shift had brewed, and made a fresh pot, then asked the two deputies manning the station overnight for a report. It had been surprisingly quiet. The biggest averted disaster was two kids who had been playing in the snow yesterday and disappeared. They'd been found late that night in a neighbor's tree house, too scared to come down when the ladder fell, and no one had been able to hear their shouts over

146

the wind.

Now they were safe. At home, in warm beds.

Where Jason should be.

You're all I have, Jason. Just hang in there.

He poured himself coffee and took it to his desk.

Born and raised in Texas, he'd joined the Army at eighteen as much to get away from his father as to see the world. But after six years, he took his free college education from the government at the University of Texas in Dallas. Met the beautiful Sharon. They dated, she got pregnant, they got married.

It didn't last. Sharon moved to California with their son and Tyler only saw Jason a couple times a year. Hardly the opportunity to be a good father. But when Sharon came down with a particularly insidious cancer, she and Jason moved back to Texas.

You were always a good father, Tyler. I should never have moved so far away. I thought I was living my dream, but it was a nightmare. Forgive me.

Of course he'd forgiven her. What else could he do? She died two months later, painfully, and he was left with a son he barely knew, who resented him if he gave it a thought.

The main door opened, letting in a draft of cold air.

"Another day in paradise," Tyler said.

"Paradise?"

Two men walked into the Sheriff's main office. The one who spoke was about five foot ten, fit but a tad on the heavy side, about forty-five, wearing a suit without a tie and a ski jacket. The taller, younger man had close-cropped dark hair and dark eyes, wore a tie and jacket, but with jeans. That almost threw Tyler, but no doubt about it: These two men were the Feds he'd been expecting.

The younger man's eyes assessed the room immediately, then focused on Tyler.

"Sheriff McBride?"

Tyler stood. "That's me. You must be from the Bureau."

The younger Fed flashed his badge. "Mitch Bianchi, Fugitive Apprehension, FBI. We checked the trace on the call from Pocatello. Disposable phone. We couldn't get a trace, and the phone hasn't been used again. Has he called back?"

"No." Tyler glanced at the other man, who extended his hand.

"Hans Vigo, Quantico." His smile reached his pale blue eyes. "Saturday I was in sunny San Diego tracking a fugitive down there.

148

Can honestly say I miss it."

"You said yesterday on the phone that you were tracking three of the convicts north," Tyler said, motioning for the Feds to help themselves to coffee.

Vigo did, putting cream and sugar in his and handing Bianchi a Styrofoam cup of black coffee. "Mitch called me on Saturday and said that one of our convicts had been spotted in Salt Lake City. I met up with him there. We missed them, tracked them to Pocatello, but couldn't get a good location. Had one witness at a fast-food restaurant who thought she saw one of them." He pulled the picture of Doug Chapman from his file. "No car in the lot that she could see, so we canvassed the motel across the highway. The manager was less than helpful, but believes he saw Doherty." He put Aaron Doherty's picture in front of Tyler.

"I got those last night from your headquarters," Tyler said.

"Good. Get them out to everyone. These are the last three convicts still at large and we want to get them before they hurt anyone."

"The caller told me that Doherty had a picture of a woman. I think I know who it might be."

"Joanna Sutton," Mitch Bianchi interjected.

Tyler stared at him, a vein throbbing in his neck. Though his fears were confirmed, the knowledge didn't stop the panic in his heart. He turned to Vigo. "If you knew Jo was in danger, why didn't you tell me last night?"

"I didn't know until a few hours ago," Vigo said. "I contacted my office and they have been going through the prisoner's personal effects. Doherty had an extensive library. Most of the books were written by Joanna Sutton. He'd underlined certain passages. They'd obviously been read multiple times."

"I spoke to Jo last night and told her to be on the look out for the convicts," Tyler said. "I faxed her the mug shots. She's going to be careful. But there was an avalanche on the South Centennial Road, and I alerted the Sheriffs in both Madison County and in Eastern Idaho. But with this weather, they can't get there, and Jo said no one had come in who didn't have a reservation."

Vigo breathed an audible sigh of relief. "That's good. And actually, we can use this to our advantage."

"How so?" Tyler asked Vigo.

"We know that Aaron Doherty is trying to

150

find Joanna Sutton," said Vigo. "He knows where she lives, or at least the general area. If we can get to the lodge first, we can set up a trap."

"I'm not using Jo as bait."

"She's not bait. She's already there, she's already in his sights. We get there first, we can protect her and catch a killer at the same time."

Tyler saw the merits of the plan. "We're not going to stop looking for him before he reaches his destination. Jo has had enough tragedy in her life, she doesn't need to be subjected to some psycho stalker."

"Do you know her well?"

"Well enough."

"So you know that her husband and son were murdered four years ago," Bianchi said bluntly.

Tyler nodded. "Your point?"

Vigo said, "The man who killed the Suttons was in the prison cell next to Aaron Doherty."

"I don't understand." Tyler said. "Did this Doherty have something to do with the Sutton murders?" Jo rarely spoke of that time, but Tyler thought only one man was responsible for killing Ken and Tim Sutton.

Vigo said, "No. But we think that Doherty killed Lincoln Barnes, the man convicted of the murders. He was stabbed with a home-made shiv in the San Quentin dining hall. No one saw anything, at least they weren't talking. The warden believed Doherty had something to do with it, but no one said a word that would have incriminated Doherty."

Tyler assessed the information. "What did Doherty have against Lincoln Barnes, and what does it have to do with Jo?"

Bianchi said, "We think that Doherty found out why Barnes was on death row and in some sort of twisted obsession, killed him as vengeance for the Sutton woman."

"You're not implying that Jo had —"

Vigo put his hand up. "Mrs. Sutton is not a suspect in anything, Sheriff. What we're concerned about is Doherty's M.O. He has obsessed on women in the past, probably more than the two times we know about. In high school, when he was a minor, he disfigured his girlfriend — received proba-tion." Vigo shook his head in resigned disgust. "The second was Rebecca Oliver."

"The actress," Tyler stated.

Vigo nodded. "Doherty disfigured her when she spurned his advances. In her report to the police, she said he had built up this entire fantasy about her when he confronted her in her home. He sliced her face then ran off, went into hiding. The police were looking for him, but he kept a low profile. Two months later he killed her and a male friend in her house while she was recuperating from plastic surgery."

"I heard about the case. And you think this freak is fixated on Jo?" Tyler thought back to what the caller had said about Jo's picture. That Doherty looked at it all the time.

"Yes. And the call you received proves it. We need to get into Centennial Valley."

"You'll get no argument from me. But why Jo? Does this Doherty know her?"

Vigo shook his head. "I've been reading his psych profiles. No one nailed his psychosis, but I'm willing to stake my reputation on a diagnosis. He's an erotomaniac."

Tyler said, "In layman's terms."

"The best-known erotomaniac is John Hinckley, Jr., who fixated on Jodie Foster and fully believed that she loved him and they had a relationship. Of course, there was no relationship and Ms. Foster had no knowledge of Hinckley's plans to assassinate President Reagan. But in his mind, Hinckley believed that he and Ms. Foster were romantically involved."

"And you're saying that Doherty believes that he and Jo are 'romantically involved?'"

"Yes," Vigo said. "Doherty doesn't have the same background as Hinckley, but erotomania is rare. Men who exhibit these tendencies start at a young age — postpuberty. While they do not have normal relationships with their mothers, they are not physically abused. There is usually an emotional or physical detachment from their mother. Erotomaniacs have delusions of grandeur — specifically, that individuals in public positions have feelings for them. Doherty fixated on Rebecca Oliver, an actress who he believed was acting just for him. When Doherty's house was searched after the first attack on Ms. Oliver, every movie she'd made was in his possession, including a pirated version of her unreleased film. And now we have found Ms. Sutton's books left behind in his cell."

Tyler let the information sink in, his fear growing. "He killed Rebecca Oliver."

Vigo nodded. "But not immediately. I'm not saying that we have the luxury of time, but we do have the element of surprise. I have an agent tracking down one of his relatives, to see if we can learn anything that could help us.

"On every level, Aaron Doherty functions like a normal, intelligent man," Vigo continued. "The difference is his delusion: In his

154

mind, he fully believes that Jo Sutton returns his feelings. He may have even convinced himself that she pursued him — by writing books — and he is simply responding to her. He has reasoned everything out. The problem with a true erotomaniac is that they have manic qualities; they will first fully believe that they are completely worthy of the love of the public figure, to the extent that they will do everything they can to ensure that the object of their delusion can only be with them. But they can plunge quickly into despair and doubt themselves. They become suicidal. If he was on an upswing, Jo would be safe. He would convince himself that everything she said and did confirmed their love. But when the delusion is exposed or denied, that's when he gets dangerous. Not only to himself, but to others."

"The best thing we can do is get to the lodge and be waiting for him," Tyler said. "If he shows up."

Vigo nodded, then Bianchi said, "Doherty is most definitely dangerous, but not in the same league as his pal Douglas Chapman."

"Chapman killed his girlfriend," Tyler said, glancing at his notes, "his wife, his boss."

"He has a short fuse. Not as bright as

Doherty, not as methodical, but violent and unpredictable."

"Unpredictable in the sense that he has a temper and he's not taking court-ordered medication since the breakout," Vigo said. "But we can assume two things. First, that Doherty is in charge."

"How so?" Tyler asked. "It looks like Chapman had a record even before murder."

"Yes, but Chapman is a disorganized killer. He attacks on the spur of the moment, without premeditation or forethought. The guy used a knife from his own kitchen to kill his wife — rinsed it off thinking that would take care of the fingerprints and blood as well. He killed his boss for getting on him for being late to work — that was the morning after he killed his wife — and then went to visit his girlfriend and killed her the following day. He doesn't plan ahead. There was plenty of evidence to convict him."

"So he'll kill first, ask questions later. I think I'd rather take my chances reasoning with Doherty."

"Doherty is smart and unpredictable. Chapman will slip up."

"Let's hope so, before anyone gets hurt," Tyler said. "My deputies are checking on all the roads to find the best way into the valley. We have something else at stake here."

"Which is?"

"There's a Boy Scout troop going to the Moosehead Lodge. They were caught in the storm and one of the boys is injured. My brother is the troop leader, and he's bringing them to the lodge because it's the closest and easiest access from where they are now." Tyler looked at the map. "But Jo is already on alert, and since the fugitives haven't shown up yet, the chances that they'll get through before us are slim. What about the third convict? O'Brien?"

"We believe the caller," Vigo said. "That Doherty is with Chapman only. Which means your anonymous caller is O'Brien."

Bianchi spoke. "I've been tracking Thomas O'Brien since the escape." For the first time, Bianchi sounded like more than a reactionary Fed. "This is completely confidential, Sheriff."

Tyler nodded.

"We believe that O'Brien has tracked down several of the escaped convicts and detained them for police. Three were beaten and restrained, then an anonymous call came into authorities. But —" He stopped and glanced at Vigo who nodded.

Bianchi continued. "Raymond 'Blackie'

157

Goethe and his band of merry men were causing widespread panic in the San Francisco area. The local cops couldn't get the drop on them. Goethe killed two cops when he was cornered, then disappeared without a scratch. Three days ago, O'Brien contacted me and told me where they were. We staked it out, caught them immediately when they returned after a robbery. O'Brien was there, took out Goethe himself." Bianchi was on the verge of saying something more, but stopped himself. Tyler's interest was piqued, but he didn't say anything. "O'Brien slipped away. I had him, and he disappeared."

"Why would one convict help you capture the others?"

"O'Brien was once a cop," Vigo said quietly.

"Why was he in Quentin?"

"For killing his wife and her lover — who happened to be a prosecutor," Bianchi said.

"From your recollection, the caller sounded like he'd been injured, correct?" Vigo asked.

Tyler nodded. "He indicated that he'd been unconscious for an extended period of time. He said there had been an accident."

"If there was, all traces of it are gone or buried in snow," Bianchi said. "And so is O'Brien. If it was O'Brien who called."

"It's the logical explanation," Vigo said, "but we can't assume anything." He glanced at his phone and frowned. "I need to take this."

Tyler pointed down the hall. "There's a small conference room at the end of the hall. Feel free."

"Thanks." He flipped open the phone. "Agent Vigo." He turned around the corner.

Bianchi said, "We're here to help. Any resources you need. You told the people at the Moosehead Lodge about the convicts?"

"Yes, and faxed the mug shots. At least they'll be on alert. I'm concerned about the kids going to the lodge if there is danger."

Billy Grossman came in. "I have a way in," he said. He spread a map across Tyler's desk. "I spoke to the Sheriff out of Island Park, and the problem there is that the roads across the mountains and Red Rock Pass are impassable right now. At least, they are not advising it. We can't go in the back way. Because of avalanche warnings the BLM isn't letting anyone through. But I just talked to Nash and he said the avalanche is passable."

"Passable?" Bianchi said. "What, we drive right over it?"

Tyler grinned and Billy laughed. "In a manner of speaking. There are no paved roads in the Centennial Valley. Half the acreage is a wildlife preserve. The rest is owned by a dozen or so families. Ranches, mostly. Some vacation homes. The Moosehead Lodge, and another great place over by Elk Lake. Cross-country skiing and snowmobiling are the two big winter activities, but in the summer you have fishing, hiking, mountain biking, wildlife activities — a lot more. The only way to get around the valley once the snow is laid down is on skis or snowmobiles."

"Does Nash have some for us?" Tyler asked.

"Yes, he's going to get them gassed and ready. If we leave in the next thirty minutes, we'll make it to Lakeview before the snow starts falling again."

Tyler glanced at his watch. It was ten to seven in the morning. "All right. Seven-thirty we head out. Call in Al Duncan to join us, and have Keith Lofton fill in for me while I'm out. He can handle any other emergencies that come up, but make sure that he knows everything we do about the convicts. I'm going to radio my brother and fill him in on the potential danger. Maybe there's someplace else we can send the troop."

"Is that safe, Tyler?" Billy asked. "The

160

storm isn't over. And with the Ward kid having a broken leg . . ."

Billy didn't need to finish the thought. Tyler had been thinking the same thing. "What's safer, Billy? Keeping the boys out at the Kimball homestead for another two or three days, or getting them to safety where there *might* be a problem, but where none exists now?" He pinched the bridge of his nose. It was a lose-lose situation. But no matter what, he needed to tell Wyatt of the potential threat. Chances were that his brother would make it to the lodge before Tyler, and Tyler would have to trust him to protect not only his son, but the woman he loved.

"Bonnie, can you get Wyatt on the radio?"

NINE

Mitch had known Hans for fifteen years, since they'd met on the transport to Kosovo as part of a special Evidence Response Team to uncover mass graves and help identify victims. They'd become friends, good friends. They'd worked together on a half dozen cases since. Hans had been the best man at his wedding.

So when Hans stepped back into the room, Mitch immediately detected a ripple

161

of anger beneath Hans's calm expression. Hans motioned to Mitch. "I need you for a minute."

On alert, Mitch followed him down the hall. Before the door had clicked closed, Hans said, "You lied to me."

Hans spoke with quiet rage, as only a man with complete control over his emotions and a steadfast equilibrium could do.

"It was important."

"You used me."

"Hans, you don't understand —"

He raised an eyebrow. Mitch swallowed and paced. There were few people in this world that he respected more than Hans Vigo. Largely because Hans hadn't given up the field. He still went where he was needed. He'd pushed to be assigned the Theodore Glenn case. He pushed for a lot of things and always got them.

"You've used up your tokens, Mitch. You'd better talk fast. And I'm still sending you on the next flight back to Sacramento."

He should have factored in Hans's friendship with Meg, but Mitch had needed Hans's diplomacy and clout to get this far.

He'd been *this* close to Thomas O'Brien. So close he could taste it. When a predator smelled his prey, when he visualized the capture, knew he was about to spring the trap . . . and then the entire plan went to hell.

"The man saved my life."

"O'Brien?"

Mitch dipped his head. "I was loaned out to the San Francisco regional office. With so many convicts on the loose and the locals focused on public safety and emergencies after the quake, they needed additional help. I was assigned O'Brien, but almost immediately was pulled off. I called Meg, she hadn't done it. It came from higher up, and not in the FBI. She told me to pull back — since when does Meg pull back?"

"Megan plays by the rules."

Mitch bit back a stinging comment. He and Meg had a complex history, and at first he'd thought that's where all the crap was coming from. Now, he wasn't as certain. "I was following a fugitive."

"Protocol demands that you inform the local field office of any leads. Your supervisor expressly told you not to go to Salt Lake City."

Mitch had no response.

"Then you ask me to meet you. I trusted you, Mitch. I came without so much as a question. And then Meg calls me and says you disobeyed a direct order and haven't returned her calls."

163

"Look how close we are!"

"You have to return to Sacramento."

"No. Dammit, Hans! You need me." Hans raised an eyebrow. "You know what I mean," Mitch clarified. "I'm one of the best. I'll find them."

Hans didn't say anything, just stared at Mitch.

"You can talk to Meg, explain it to her," Mitch said.

Hans asked, "Explain *what* exactly? All I see is an arrogant FBI agent who thinks he doesn't have to answer to anyone. You go off half-cocked, don't tell your boss, don't tell *anyone* and think that you'll be forgiven? Meg went out on a limb for you —"

"Don't go there." His ex-wife was the last person he wanted to be indebted to.

"You want me to talk to Meg, you tell me what I'm supposed to say. Because right now I'm ready to send you up the river. I will not be lied to, I will not be used, and I will not let even *you,* a man I call a friend, tell me to manipulate someone I like and respect."

When Mitch didn't say anything, Hans said, "I was best man at your wedding, and I was there when the marriage fell apart."

"You knew it would."

"Call me psychic."

Hans *was* pissed. In all the years Mitch knew him, he'd rarely heard sarcasm.

Mitch told Hans everything that happened during the Goethe shoot-out. "I lost track of O'Brien in San Francisco. Then he calls me a day later. I have no idea how he got my phone number, how he even knew to find me. I think he was following *me* while I was trying to pick up his trail again. He tells me where Goethe's gang is hiding out. That they're about to take down another store, but will be back. And to wait for his signal.

"We stake it out and he's right. They come back. He's with them. Armed. I'm thinking, what the fuck? He's going to get himself killed. Or he set a trap for us. But something he said made me wait. SWAT wanted to go in as soon as they had a shot, but I — O'Brien told me he'd been the one to catch three of those guys. The man has balls, I give him that. And I didn't want him dead. I wanted to talk to him. Hell, I don't know. Being pulled off the case, then having O'Brien call me? My gut just said wait, so I held everyone back. I'm waiting, waiting — and he looks right at me. He sees my hiding place.

"Then you know what the guy does? He shouts, 'Drop your weapons! This is the police!' "

165

Mitch shook his head, remembering the scene vividly. "O'Brien has cover, SWAT drops in, takes everyone out immediately. Two of Goethe's gang fall. I walk into the scene, gun drawn, and out of nowhere a woman screams and jumps on me with a knife. Blackie's girlfriend." He rolled up his sleeve, showed Hans the fresh scar to add to a dozen others. "She sliced my arm. O'Brien was right there, took her out, and then Blackie went after him. O'Brien didn't hesitate. He fired, then disappeared." Mitch shook his head. He didn't know whether to admire O'Brien or lament the fact that a dozen cops had missed him. "I still don't know how he did it."

Hans said nothing for a long moment. "You feel like you owe your life to this man. You know he's a killer."

Mitch nodded.

"Why did you lie to me? To Meg? To everyone you work with?"

"I don't want him to get himself killed. I can talk him into turning himself in."

"He eluded SWAT in a secure building. He's not going to turn himself in."

"I think he's looking for something."

"Are you telling me everything?"

Not quite. "All I know, Hans."

"Meg is furious."

"I know." Mitch had been avoiding her calls for two days. "I'm sorry to drag you into the middle of this."

Hans sat on the edge of the table. "If I didn't like you and Meg so much, I wouldn't be here right now. But that doesn't change the fact that you breached protocol and can be suspended or fired over this." He held up his hand before Mitch could say anything. "I'll talk to Meg, but only if you return to Sacramento."

"But —"

"But nothing. O'Brien isn't with Chapman and Doherty. You know it, and I know it. From what the caller said, it must be O'Brien. Chapman and Doherty must have figured out who he was or were suspicious. Tried to get rid of him. The man has nine lives, I'll say that much."

"I'm not leaving you here on your own."

"The Helena field office is perfectly capable of providing backup, and Sheriff McBride is solid. I did some background work on him last night and he can more than hold his own."

"There's no way Helena can get here in twenty minutes before you leave for the lodge."

"But they'll be here soon enough. I promised Meg you would be on the next flight to

Sacramento."

"In this weather?"

Hans shrugged. "So, next flight might not be for a couple of days. You might as well put yourself to good use and help us track a couple fugitives." He paused, then added softly, "I know how a case can get under your skin so bad you'll do anything to work it."

"Thanks, Hans." Relieved, Mitch started to open the door.

Hans pushed it shut, stared at him, and spoke with a firm voice. "Don't thank me yet, Mitch. You violated my trust, and I won't forget it anytime soon."

Aaron had come downstairs early, while everyone but Stan Wood slept. The old black man worried Aaron yesterday — something about the way he'd looked at Aaron in the foyer that set off his warning bells.

After ten minutes, Aaron learned Stan was like that with everyone. Suspicious. But when Aaron offered to help with breakfast — "I need something to do with my hands" — Stan handed him a butcher knife and told him to dice up a pile of potatoes.

"You're a long way from L.A., John," Stan said.

"Yes, sir."

"What brings you up here?"

Aaron paused for effect, though he had his story down. "A major decision."

"Life-changing?"

"Yes, sir."

"This is a good place for thinking. Sometimes people come up here to think and never leave."

"How long have you lived here?"

Stan sipped black coffee. "Going on thirty years."

"It's so — quiet." That had been the first thing Aaron noticed when he woke up early that morning. Dead silence. The storm had kept the wind whipping half the night, but now it was calm. Some might call it peaceful.

It made Aaron nervous.

"That it is," Stan agreed.

"And you've been thinking for thirty years."

Stan laughed, a deep, guttural sound that made Aaron think the man didn't laugh much. "When we stop thinking, we die, young man. But I did my heavy thinking years ago. Now, I contemplate lesser evils than my past. Like how long it's going to take you to dice up those potatoes."

Aaron busied himself at the task, a little disturbed at being criticized by Stan, but with an urge to please him that he didn't understand.

Aaron barely remembered his father. Aaron and his mama moved around so much that Aaron didn't see his dad for months at a time. Even when he stayed with his paternal grandparents, his dad rarely visited.

Joe Dawson hadn't wanted him. That's what Ginger Doherty said.

There were few male figures in Aaron's life, and none that lasted more than a couple months. His paternal grandfather had been a foreboding man, not one Aaron could confide in or ask for advice. And the last time he'd seen his dad? He'd been six or seven.

"Don't bring him here again." Grandfather glared at Aaron's mother. "I won't have you putting Lottie through this again. She cries for weeks after you take the boy."

"He's your grandson. Your flesh and blood," his mama said. No one knew Aaron was eavesdropping. He was good at hiding.

Even when he didn't hide, people often didn't notice him.

"I told you we would take him in if you'd stop coming by."

"I'm not giving you my son!"

170

"But you'd sell him fast enough, wouldn't you?"

Grandma Lottie came into the room, tears in her eyes. "Ginger, I love Aaron. Please let him stay here. With us. We'll provide for him. Give him a good, stable home."

"And what about me? He's my son!"

"You haven't acted like a mother since the day you gave birth!" Grandma Lottie said. "You complained that you were fat and then had a tummy tuck!"

"How can I provide for my son without a husband? Oh, wait, you didn't teach your own son to take care of what is his."

"Leave Joe out of this."

"What, he has a couple minutes of fun and gets out of his responsibility, but I have to pay for it the rest of my life?"

"We'll take care of Aaron. Give up your parental rights, and we'll give him a real home."

Aaron sat around the corner just out of sight, arms hugging his legs, back flat against the wall, breath caught in his chest. He didn't know what he wanted. When he was here, he missed his mama something awful. He loved the way she smelled, the way she held him, the way she told him that he was her little man. But Grandfather was smart and Grandma Lottie let him lick the spoon when she made sugar cookies. And she told him he was the best angel in the school choir . . .

Mama hadn't even come to the play.

He wanted to be with his mama, but he didn't want to leave Grandfather and Grandma, either.

What were parental rights? Sometimes his grandparents would talk when they thought he was sleeping. They said bad things about his mama. Especially Grandfather. Why did they hate his mama? Why couldn't they all live together and be happy? Why did his mama make him move all the time and live with strangers?

"How much?" Mama asked.

Grandma Lottie sobbed. "We don't have a lot of money, Ginger! We'll buy Aaron's food and clothes and we can start up a college fund —"

Mama laughed. "College? I never got sent to college. I love Aaron and he's mine. He's the only thing that is all mine, and you're not getting him. Not unless you have a good reason for me to give up parental rights."

"Aaron is not a possession!" Grandma cried.

Silence. It lasted nearly forever to Aaron as he huddled alone.

"Get out." Grandfather had spoken. His voice was barely audible, but Aaron started shaking.

No, Grandfather, I don't want to go. Don't make me leave.

Grandma Lottie started crying. She ran around the corner, saw Aaron. Her eyes widened and she gathered him into her arms.

"I love you, Aaron. I'll always love you." Her tears soaked into his cheek and shirt. He wanted to tell her he loved her, too, but he couldn't talk.

"Aaron!" his mother called.

Grandma Lottie ran into the living room with Aaron around her neck. "We can sue for custody. We can fight for him."

Mama laughed. "No judge is going to give grandparents custody over a baby's own mother."

"He's not a baby anymore, Ginger," Grandma Lottie said. "He's a little boy and you're going to ruin him."

Anger flashed in his mother's eyes. "Ruin him? No more than you ruined your own son. Give me my boy."

"Joseph!" Grandma Lottie shouted at his grandfather. Aaron's ears were ringing. "Joseph, do something!"

"Give him to her."

"No!"

"Lottie, please." Grandfather sounded like he was going to cry. Mama said real men didn't cry. "Think of Aaron, this isn't helping him."

Grandma Lottie sobbed. Mama pulled him from her arms.

They left without another word.

"Is this good?" Aaron said to Stan, his voice thick for reasons he didn't understand.

Stan put a hand on his shoulder. "Very good, son."

Joanna came into the kitchen. She looked at him, gave him a half smile. "You're up early, Mr. Miller."

"John."

"John. Right. Sorry." She poured herself some coffee, added cream and sugar. "I was going to take the Trotskys and the MSU kids breakfast and lunch and make sure they don't need anything else. The NWS anticipates more snowfall this afternoon, and I want to meet up with Wyatt and the boys as soon as possible."

"I can check on the guests," Stan said.

"No, no problem, seriously. It'll only take me a few minutes."

"Why don't you take John here?" Stan suggested.

"It'll only take me a minute —"

"I'm a little concerned about the Sheriff's fax, Jo," Stan said.

Aaron looked at Joanna. "What fax?"

174

She waved her hand as if it were nothing. "A couple convicts who escaped from prison. Tyler — Sheriff McBride — thinks they're in the area, but as you know from this weather no one is getting through."

"Do you have a description?"

Stan pulled copies of the mug shots from a drawer. "Here you go."

Aaron looked at the pictures, frowning.

"Recognize them?" Stan asked.

Aaron shook his head. "I'm glad to say no, I haven't seen them."

Stan put the pictures away. "Jo, just to be on the safe side." He nodded at Aaron.

"I have my bear spray," she said.

Does she not want to be with me? Aaron watched her eyes, tried to read her mind. Why didn't she like him? What was she hiding? Did she have something going on with this Sheriff Tyler McBride?

He stared at the knife next to the diced potatoes.

Blood dripped from the tip. He had it in his hand. Below him was Rebecca Oliver, her arms and chest sliced up, blood seeping into her sheets, her big blue eyes staring at him.

Why Aaron why Aaron why . . .

He closed his eyes, swallowed, carefully said, "I'm happy to help."

175

Stan smiled. "Good. Let me get you a snowsuit. I think you'll fit comfortably into one of my old outfits, before I put on this extra twenty pounds." He patted a stomach that didn't look all that large. "Jo?"

She nodded. "Great."

The tension fell from Aaron's body. The blood was gone from the knife.

She did want him, after all.

After Tyler told Wyatt about the escaped convicts, he called the lodge. The phone rang repeatedly, before a breathless Trixie answered.

"Moosehead."

"Trixie, it's Tyler McBride."

"Hi, Tyler."

"Is Jo around?"

"She's taking breakfast to our cabin guests."

Tyler's chest tightened. "Alone?"

"Alone?" she asked as if he'd asked if she were naked. "What do you mean?"

"Did Jo tell you about our conversation yesterday?"

"About the convicts? She showed Grandpa, Stan, and me the pictures you faxed. They're not here."

Tyler felt marginally better, but fear still tickled his gut, and he always trusted his instincts. "Just to be on the safe side, stay close to the lodge, okay?"

"We will. You know Jo is going out to meet Wyatt later, right?"

"Yes. I'm on my way, Trixie, but it may take all day to get there."

"I'll make sure there's enough dinner for you."

"And a couple deputies."

Her voice lost its flirtatious humor. "Why so many?"

"We need to get the boys home, that's our number one responsibility. And until we know exactly where the escaped prisoners are, I'm not leaving."

"Why? Are they coming here?"

Jo hadn't told her family everything, Tyler realized. Maybe it was for the best that they didn't know how personal the visit was for one of the killers.

"We're not sure," he said. "We're going off an anonymous call. I should know more when I get there." He wasn't going to tell Trixie about her ex-boyfriend's run-in with Doherty, not over the phone. She knew Lincoln Barnes was dead, and good riddance, but there was still Leah to think about. And if the Feds were right and Aaron Doherty had killed him, Tyler wanted to tell Trixie in person.

"Trixie," Tyler added, "please be careful."

He hung up and Bonnie came in. "Sam Nash is on line two."

Tyler picked up the phone. "Nash, Billy told me you're loaning us your best sleds. I appreciate it."

"Someone broke in to my shed and stole two snowmobiles."

Tyler stiffened. "Two?"

"I thought I heard something yesterday, but I was helping Old Bud Landry bring in feed for his cattle — there was a delay in the delivery, and the truck couldn't get past Monida, so Pete and I brought it in on Landry's sleds. I thought the snowmobiles were those damn Worthington teens again, being stupid. Turns out they were my own sleds I heard."

"Could they hold more than one person?"

"They're single-rider sleds, but two could fit."

Great. That didn't tell him if all three convicts were at large in the valley, or if his caller was correct that there were only two.

"I'm leaving in ten minutes. If you need me, Bonnie will tap you through to my radio."

He hung up, dialed the lodge again.

The phone rang. And rang.

Twenty rings later Tyler slammed the

phone down. "Billy! We're leaving now."

TEN

Jo hadn't wanted to take John Miller with her to deliver breakfast and check on the guests at the two cabins. But Stan had put her on the spot and she didn't want to be rude.

"Okay," she said, bounding into the kitchen at quarter to eight. "Where's my little helper?"

Stan gave her a look and handed Trixie two plates. "Got it?" he asked.

"I'm not going to drop them," Trixie snapped and left.

"He's already outside." Stan watched Trixie leave to serve Cleve and Kristy Johnston who were sitting in the formal dining room on the far side of the foyer. "On the deck. He has some thinking to do."

"Don't we all?" Jo said, not meaning to sound callous. "I talked to Wyatt earlier this morning and I'm going to head out to the Kimball homestead by nine — as soon as I'm done with this. I want to get Ben Ward back before the snow starts again, and NWS predicts it'll be falling heavy by two at the latest."

"You should bring someone with you. At

179

least until we know more about where those convicts were headed. I don't like the idea of you out alone when there could be escaped prisoners in the area."

"Nobody knows where they are. They might be anywhere in Montana or Idaho — or Wyoming for that matter. Heck, they could have made it up to Canada, which would have been the smart thing. And you have their pictures, so we know who we're looking for."

"Yes, we do." Stan turned and Jo saw the gun in his waistband in the small of his back.

"Stan —"

Stan hated guns. He'd served two tours of duty in Vietnam and had been a strung out drug addict and alcoholic when he panhandled Karl Weber in Bozeman thirty years ago. Karl had been guest lecturing at the university for a week, and when he returned he brought Stan with him.

Jo had been seven or so at the time, and all she remembered about Stan was that he'd been big, black, and very sad.

Now he was part of their family. She couldn't imagine him not being in her life. She didn't know everything about his history before he moved to the valley to be Karl Weber's right-hand man, but she knew he detested firearms and never carried when he went out. Bear spray was his weapon of choice.

She touched his arm. "Everything is going to be okay, Stan."

"I'd feel a lot better if you had someone with you. I'll go if you don't want a stranger."

She shook her head. Stan had been having heart trouble for the last few years. He was on medication, and she didn't want him overdoing it.

"I'll take John, okay?"

"Thank you. I'll feel better when the Sheriff gets here."

Me, too.

Ten minutes later, Jo had on her snowsuit and favorite boots. She wasn't keen on taking John Miller with her, but she didn't want Stan to worry. She met John on the deck. He looked into the distance, toward where you could see Upper Red Rock Lake — if the visibility were better. Now, all that was in front of them was a quiet pale gray mist.

"Ready?" she asked, feigning cheerfulness.

She led John outside to the snowmobile shed. The temperature was still in the low twenties, but so far this morning the snow was holding off and visibility wasn't half bad. "Have you ridden one of these before?"

181

"It's been a long time," he said. She appreciated his honesty.

"It's like riding a bike," she said. She gave him a quick rundown on the controls.

"It's coming back to me," he said. "Are you going to all the cabins?" he asked as they started out.

"No, just the two we have occupied. We offered to move them to the lodge yesterday morning, but they wanted the privacy. Each cabin is fully self-sufficient. It can be peaceful."

The honeymooners were about two hundred yards directly west of the lodge. It was the best cabin on the property, with a fantastic view of the valley and a small private deck. The college couple was about three hundred feet south of the honeymooners, as you start up the mountain — easy to get to on a well-worn trail, but more difficult in this weather.

"Why don't we split up?" Jo suggested. The snow had started trickling down, and it could worsen quickly. She'd hoped it would hold off until that afternoon, and now all she wanted was to leave as soon as possible to bring the scouts back before the weather made it impossible.

"I'll take that cabin," she said, pointing to where the MSU kids were, "you head for the Trotskys. Greg and Vicky. Just hand them the basket, ask if they need anything, make sure they have enough wood."

John seemed undecided, so Jo said, "Or we can do it together. It's just the weather is turning and I want to get back quickly."

"Where are you going?"

"Do you see that cabin?" She pointed to the barely visible cabin among the trees. "Two college kids from MSU are up there. I'm going to walk up, but you can take your snowmobile all the way down to the Trotskys' cabin. Just follow that tree line — it's marked — and you'll be fine."

"Okay. Thanks, Joanna."

Aaron watched Joanna put on snowshoes, then turned his snowmobile toward the cabin downslope. Greg and Vicky Trotsky. He glanced over his shoulder and saw Joanna walking up the snow-covered mountain trail, visible only because of her bright red jacket.

Aaron wasn't exactly sure which cabin Doug was in, but it definitely hadn't been occupied, and it seemed to have been much farther out. In reading the Moosehead Lodge brochure in his room, he'd learned that there were seven cabins on the property.

But what if he was wrong? Aaron couldn't chance it. He listened carefully as Joanna went up the slope to the college kids' cabin. He was certain Doug wasn't there — it was too wooded, too steep. They'd been able to drive the snowmobiles up to the door of the cabin yesterday.

If Chapman hurt her, Aaron would kill him. He didn't want to kill anyone. He only resorted to violence when he had no choice. It was never his fault when he had to kill.

Worse than killing Doug, though, was that Joanna would learn his true identity if there was a confrontation. Aaron couldn't have that. Last night they'd bonded over tea and conversation. He'd relished every moment of their time together. Every word they shared. Her large brown eyes watching his, her delicate hand playing with her hair, twirling the ends round and round her finger. She was truly interested in what he had to say, touching his hand in sympathy when he'd told her about losing Rebecca.

"I love you, Joanna," he murmured into the quiet, cold morning.

Doug could ruin everything. It had been smart of Aaron to let Joanna and the others see Doug's mug shot. That meant Aaron could force him to stay away. He might have to get out of going with Joanna to meet the Boy Scouts, as much as he hated the idea. He'd miss the opportunity to bond with her as they'd done last night. But he had to tell Doug that Joanna knew what he looked like. Doug had to stay away. Far away.

He knocked on the door of the honeymooners' cabin. He heard, "Who is it?"

He recognized that voice.

"Doug?"

The door opened. Doug stood in the entry half-naked. His face was flushed, a fresh set of scratches on his chest. A bruise covered one cheek and he had another on his side.

Behind Doug was a man, facedown, dried blood on the back of his T-shirt. He wore sweatpants. On the bed a woman quietly sobbed, a scarf tied around her mouth. Her hands were tied to the bedposts with fishing line. Her wrists bore red welts and cuts that continued to bleed. She was naked and the bed was bare. Dark bruises marked the inside of her thighs, blood was smeared on the mattress.

"What have you done?" Aaron shut the door firmly behind him. There was a simple bolt lock. He slid it closed.

"Is that food? Great. I'm famished." Doug took the box from Aaron's hands and sauntered over to the table, oblivious to the dead body he had to step over to get there.

"Dammit, Doug! I told you to stay put."

"Shit, I was going stir-crazy. Flat-out insane."

"It hasn't even been twenty-four hours."

"I felt like I was back at Quentin. I had to get out." Doug opened the box. "Hot coffee." He poured from the thermos into a cup and breathed in the rich scent. "Good stuff."

"Do you realize they're going to find out what happened here?"

"We'll be long gone." He gulped the coffee.

"The owners come to the cottages every day to bring food and supplies. And when the snow lets up —"

"Anyone comes, I'll pop them."

"You can't kill everyone! Let me think."

"You think, I'll eat."

Aaron looked at the woman on the bed. She wasn't blindfolded. Not only could she identify Doug, she could now identify Aaron. She'd have to be killed. Aaron didn't relish the thought, but he'd make Doug do it.

Then tomorrow, he'd make a point of going out with Joanna again. He could delay the discovery of the bodies until he took Joanna away. He had wanted more time — at least a week — to win her heart, but now he realized he'd have to work faster. Especially if the Sheriff was on his way to the lodge.

It would work out, he convinced himself. After all, she'd been very attentive to him last night. And today, asking him to join her while delivering meals to the guests, and then to help the Boy Scouts. Wouldn't it be pleasant to run this place with Joanna? Together. Working as a team. Lovers, friends.

In her book *Every Little Thing* the heroine had lived in a large, run-down home in San Francisco. The hero, an architect, had bought the building to renovate and turn into a high-class spa. Instead, they'd worked together to create a quaint bed-and-breakfast, fell in love, and married.

He could see himself in that role. Working with Joanna to keep the Moosehead Lodge afloat. Her grandfather was old — probably eighty — and she couldn't do it all herself. She needed a man. She needed him. Aaron.

John Miller.

"Yo, Aaron?"

"You'll have to kill her."

"She's my distraction, buddy. You want some? I'm worn out." Doug laughed.

How had Aaron ended up with this vile human being as his partner? Aaron wasn't about to have sex with any woman except

187

Joanna. And he wouldn't take her against her will. She would offer her body to him freely, out of love and passion, not fear.

"Joanna is going to be here any minute."

"Want me to help you restrain her?"

Aaron's hands clenched and unclenched. He slammed a fist on the table, knocking over the thermos of coffee. He didn't notice the hot liquid spill across the wood, onto the floor.

"Fuck, man —"

Aaron whispered, "You touch her and I will kill you."

Doug blinked, stepped back. Started cleaning up spilt coffee.

"Just saying, man."

"Kill the woman and go back to where I left you yesterday. Do not leave. The Sheriff faxed over our mug shots."

Doug stopped cleaning and glared at him. "What about you?"

"The machine jammed. I helped clear it, erased the memory," Aaron lied easily. "But your page already had come through. Everyone there knows what you look like."

"I can't believe this! You said we'd have that place to ourselves. It's in the middle of nowhere, no one would think of finding us, but the cops know we're here? How the fuck do they know we're here? Who told them?

Who saw us?"

Aaron had been thinking the same thing. He shook his head. "Maybe the clerk at the gas station where I bought the map."

"That's stupid," Doug said. "Why would she remember you? You know how many people go into gas stations and buy maps?"

She'd commented on the romance novel Aaron had bought. "You like Joanna Sutton?"

"Yes," he'd replied.

"Me, too. I read them as soon as they come out."

Doug said, "Maybe you didn't take care of O'Brien."

"He was dead."

But he hadn't been dead when Aaron had left him in the ditch. He was bleeding from the gut. No one could survive without medical attention. O'Brien had been left in the middle of nowhere. Only a few hours later it was snowing so hard, he'd certainly have frozen to death if he hadn't bled to death first.

Aaron didn't need to tell Doug that.

"It's the only way this will work. Do it."

A sound. A snowmobile. He jumped up, parted the curtains a fraction. Joanna had just started her snowmobile. She was looking at the cabin. *Stay away. Stay back.*

"I have to go. Do what I say, Doug."

189

"Or what? You going to kill me like you killed O'Brien?" Doug had his hand on his gun.

Aaron glanced at Vicky Trotsky. Almost felt bad for her. She didn't ask for this, not like other women. "Kill her before you leave. She can identify you, and me."

Vicky tried to scream and fought the ties. Aaron turned from her, unbolted the door. "If you fuck this up, Chapman, you're dead."

"Ooo, big threat." But he didn't sound so tough — he knew Aaron was dead serious. "Fine. But I have all day, right?"

"No one will be out here tonight, I'll make sure of it. Be out before seven tomorrow morning."

"That'll give me plenty of time for some more fun."

Vicky whimpered and strained, the fishing wire cutting deep into her wrists.

"Keep that up," Aaron told her, "and you'll kill yourself." He turned to Doug. "Don't make her suffer."

Eleven

Jo left Brian and Marie with a full breakfast, sandwiches for lunch, fresh water, and extra coffee. She had told them about the convicts, but didn't make it more dire than it was: Three convicts *might* be in the valley and they *might* find their way to the lodge. It was a lot of maybes and not a lot of facts.

"Just be careful. You have a can of bear spray, it'll stop a human predator as easily as a four-legged one."

She left them, trudged down the slope and didn't see John. She couldn't see the Trotskys' cabin in the mist. If it were a clear morning, it would have been great snow for cross-country skiing. She loved going out after a storm, crossing the valley over to the Worthingtons' just to say hello to their closest — at fifteen miles — neighbor.

She was back at the main trail and still no John. She started her snowmobile and was almost to the Trotskys' cabin when John Miller stepped out, closing the door behind him.

"Is everything okay?" she called over her idling snowmobile.

"Fine," he said and mounted his snowmobile. "Ready?"

"I should say hello." She reached to turn off the ignition.

"No, I sort of caught them in, um, sleeping." John blushed and glanced down.

She laughed, embarrassed for John. "Honeymooners. I'll check in on them later."

191

Something niggled at the back of her mind, but she didn't know what bugged her. She shook her head, and led the way back to the lodge.

They put away the equipment and entered through the mudroom. Jo felt great. Just being outdoors for a half hour had invigorated her.

"Hungry?" her grandpa asked.

"Famished," she said. "But we need to eat and run. I want to head out to meet Wyatt as soon as possible."

John said, "You have a fantastic place here, Mr. Weber."

"Thanks, son. My Joanna and I built it from next to nothing."

John glanced at Jo. "My grandmother," she explained. "I'm named for her. My sister Trixie is named after my paternal grandmother."

"I never knew my grandparents," John said. "It must be awful nice to have them in your life."

"It is." Jo kissed her grandpa on his cheek. "I'll take care of feeding Mr. Miller," she said. "What about the other guests?"

"Everyone has already come down."

"Where's Stan?"

"Checking on the generator. We ran the

gasoline pretty low last night, he's topping it off."

"How are we doing on fuel?"

"We have four more tanks. Each will last three days. If we conserve more, we'll get another day out of each."

"Next week I'll refill them in Lakeview."

"We might have to go into Dillon for it. Nash is the only one still selling gasoline, and he doesn't have much storage anymore."

Jo told John to sit down, then she went about making fresh scrambled eggs and toast. She retrieved sausage and potatoes from the warming oven and prepared two plates.

"You didn't have to go to all this trouble," John said.

"Nonsense. You helped me, I'm happy to cook up a little breakfast." Jo used to love to cook because Ken had a fantastic appetite, especially after working outdoors all day. But it had become a lost art since moving home.

John leaned over his plate and ate as if he hadn't eaten in a week, not looking at her, focusing solely on his food.

"Our morning trek made you that hungry?" she asked lightly, though that funny feeling came back that something was off about John Miller.

He looked up, startled. "Yeah, I guess I didn't realize quite how hungry I was. Excuse my poor manners."

She waved her hand in dismissal. "I like a man with a healthy appetite."

It was a flip comment with absolutely no sexual connotation, but immediately Jo wished she could take it back. Something behind John's eyes changed. It was as if she had just declared her everlasting love and he was about to say the same thing in return . . .

She stood, picking up her plate, and walked briskly to the sink, feeling hot and uneasy. Obviously she was reading far more into an innocent comment, and an innocent look, than had been intended by either of them.

"Can I get you anything else?" she asked without looking at John Miller.

"More coffee would be great."

She forced a smile on her face as she refilled John's cup. "If you're doing okay, I need to check on a few things before we head out to the Kimball homestead, so if you'll excuse me?"

His face fell, but he nodded.

"I'll meet you here in thirty minutes?" she asked.

"I'll be here."

Why had that exchange bothered her? There was something . . . strange. John seemed as if he were reading a script, every sentence calculated. She shouldn't be so judgmental. Some of the people who stayed at the lodge were downright weird. Like Yancy Izziary and Glenda Marsden who came up every spring for two weeks. Even with their ritualistic meditations, naked walks through the woods, and habit of eating dirt, they might be considered normal — after all, they owned a software company in the Silicon Valley. But their habits were nonetheless strange and Jo had never bonded with them.

She reminded herself that she was in the hospitality business. She didn't have to like everyone, but she did have to treat each guest politely and professionally.

She ran into Stan coming in the main door. "Everything good?"

"No problems," he said.

"Did you hear anything from the Sheriff? Wyatt?"

"I think Trixie talked to Tyler earlier on the phone. She's in the root cellar if you need her."

"I'll talk to her, then get Wyatt on the radio and tell him I'm on my way."

"I'm going to shower. Be careful out there, Jo. You're taking John, right?"

"Yes, Stan. I promised." She kissed his cheek. "Don't worry about me."

"Can't help it." He squeezed her shoulders. "John seems a bit like a lost soul. I think getting out will do him good."

Stan walked down the hall to his room on the other side of the den.

Jo set the radio for Wyatt's frequency and tried to bring him up. Silence. But he may have his radio off to save the battery. Still, she should have something, even static.

She flipped through all the major frequencies, trying to reach anyone.

Silence.

Something was wrong.

She looked over the radio. All appeared to be in working condition, but the equipment was old.

The door opened and she jumped.

"Didn't mean to scare you, honey."

She grinned foolishly. "Sorry, Grandpa. I can't get Wyatt on the radio. I tried other frequencies, but I can't reach anyone."

"Let me look at it. Why do you need to talk to Wyatt?"

"I wanted to let him know that I'm leaving for the Kimball homestead in about ten minutes."

"I'll see what's wrong, then tell him you're on your way. Can you help Trixie down in the root cellar first?"

Jo left her grandfather with the radio and went down to the root cellar.

It was icy cold. The insulation kept it from getting as cold as outside, but there was no heat. Fortunately, the lighting was good and she saw Trix filling a box with supplies.

"Why didn't you get me?" Jo asked, taking the box from her sister. "I'm happy to help."

"I can bring a box of food up," Trix snapped. "Why do you insist on treating me like an invalid?"

"You can do anything, Trix, but why should you work in pain if you don't have to? The stairs down here are dangerous." She sighed. "Okay, I didn't come down to pick a fight." Jo looked over her shoulder. No one had followed her down. "I wanted to talk to you about the fax from Tyler. I'm going out to Wyatt and the troop, and I want you to —"

"If you're going to tell me what to do, just forget it."

"Stop being so defensive."

"I can't help it!"

Tears coated Trixie's eyes.

"Trix, what's going on?"

"It's everything. You, and Grandpa, and even Leah treat me like I'm a fragile doll waiting to break."

"I don't."

"Yes, you do. But — it's been four years, Jo. I thought when Linc was killed in prison I'd finally get over it, but I can't. It was all my fault. I saw you looking out the window this morning. Your face. You were thinking about Ken and Timmy. And it's my fault they're dead."

Jo grabbed her by the arms, shook her once. "It is not your fault, Trixie! Dammit, how many times do I have to tell you I don't blame you for what happened? Lincoln Barnes killed Ken. He killed Timmy. He nearly killed you and took Leah. He alone is responsible. Don't ever forget that!"

Tears streamed down Trixie's face. "How can you forgive me when I can't forgive myself?"

She limped to the stairs. Jo called her to come back, but Trixie kept going.

Dammit.

Jo leaned against the shelf and took several deep breaths. Had she brought this on? Had her own anguish over Ken and Tim subconsciously told Trixie that she blamed her? *Did* she blame her sister?

Maybe on some level. Trixie had always

198

done what she wanted without regard to consequences. Running off to Los Angeles. Hooking up with Lincoln Barnes in the first place. But Trixie had a good heart, and Jo knew she'd never hurt anyone on purpose. What had happened to Ken and Tim was a tragedy, one Jo would never forget.

She'd never talked about losing her family, not with anyone. She didn't want to put her pain into words, as if that might make it hurt more. And maybe it was because she feared she would cast blame on her sister.

But would it have been better if her sister had died, too? Because had she made another choice, had she left Trixie back then to Lincoln Barnes and his gun, Trixie would be dead.

And Ken and Tim would be alive.

Damn, damn, damn!

She gathered the supplies and brought them upstairs.

And walked right into John Miller.

"You didn't come back and I was worried," he said.

It hadn't been that long, Jo thought, but didn't say anything. "I was helping my sister. Can you bring this into the kitchen for me? I need to get some bear spray and then we'll be off."

"Bear spray?"

"In case a grizzly is out. Rare this time of year, but known to happen. If I was on foot, I'd bring Buckley with me, but since we're taking the sleds I can't take him."

"Bear spray." He grinned and Jo relaxed. Maybe her earlier concerns about John Miller were unfounded. She was just edgy and uptight.

Then he said, "Sounds great. Just you, me, and miles of winter wonderland."

He winked and walked away with the supplies, whistling.

Jo shuddered.

Ken had said the exact same thing to her when they first met. How could John Miller know that? A coincidence? It wasn't a highly original statement, but . . .

Till There Was You. It was one of her older books, about two young lovers whose families despised each other because of a long-ago land dispute in the Centennial Valley. She'd based the story not only on history of the area, but some on her and Ken's courtship. She and Ken used to take daylong trips on new powder, and it was on one of those fictional trips that her hero and heroine realized they loved each other and it was up to them to bring their families together.

Just you, me, and miles of winter wonderland.

Ken had said those words. So had her fictional hero Jim Hedstrom.

She deeply regretted asking John Miller to join her on the twelve-mile snowmobile ride to the Kimball homestead.

Then she had an idea. A damn good idea. She knocked on Craig Mann's door. His eighteen-year-old son, Sean, answered. "Hi, Ms. Sutton."

"Is your dad here?"

"Right here." Craig was forty-something and physically fit. He and Sean had come to the lodge every winter for the last five years for skiing and father-son time.

"How would you two like to help escort a group of Boy Scouts stuck in the valley?"

"Sounds better than sitting around the lodge all day," Craig said. "We'll get ready and meet you downstairs in five minutes."

"Thanks."

The way Jo figured it, the four of them — Craig, Sean, John, and herself — could take the two-seater snowmobiles out to the Kimball homestead. Ben would be on a sled; Wyatt could ride with one of the men, and she could double up the five remaining boys.

Safety in numbers, she thought.

TWELVE

It took Tyler nearly thirty minutes to drive down the interstate to Monida, and it would be at least two hours before he, his two deputies, and the Feds hit Lakeview. If the snow didn't fall heavier than the few wisps that started as they left Monida.

He was about to radio Bonnie to patch him into the lodge. The ringing phone had to have been a glitch, or no one could hear it. Phone lines simply didn't go out in the valley. They were buried, and he'd never heard of a problem.

Bonnie came on almost immediately. "I have Wyatt on the radio."

"Patch him through."

A minute later, Wyatt said, "Tyler."

"Everything okay?"

"Karl Weber radioed me. Jo is on her way now."

"When did you talk to Karl? I talked to Trixie earlier this morning, but haven't been able to reach anyone by phone since."

"About ten, fifteen minutes ago. He was having radio trouble earlier, but it's fixed."

Tyler didn't like the coincidence of radio trouble coupled with not being able to reach the lodge by phone, but at least Wyatt had spoken to Karl.

"Karl didn't sound worried or distressed?"

"Not really — he asked if I knew about the escaped prisoners, and I told him that we had talked."

Tyler said to Wyatt, "Don't tell me that Jo left the lodge alone."

"No. She brought several men with her. Karl said the weather was too unpredictable for the scouts to hike to the lodge, so we're going to double up on snowmobiles and probably arrive before you get there."

"Who did she leave with?"

"Karl didn't say. Must be guests from the lodge. Any word on the prisoners?"

"No," Tyler said. "But Nash said two of his snowmobiles are missing."

"Stolen?"

"Appears so. I wanted to give Jo another warning. She's a smart woman, but she's also stubborn."

Wyatt agreed. "Yes, she is."

"Is there anywhere other than the lodge where you can take the boys? What about that place near Elk Lake? Or the Worthingtons'?"

"Both places are too difficult to reach with an injured boy," Wyatt said. "The valley is nearly four hundred thousand acres. The chances that two killers will stumble over us, slim to none. And I'll hear a snowmobile from miles away. Sound carries extremely well out here. I'll be cautious."

"Tell Jo about the theft when you see her."

"Anything else you want me to pass on?"

"Nothing I won't tell her myself when I see her. We're about four miles from Lakeview. We should meet up around the same time at the lodge."

"Do you really think these guys are a threat?" Wyatt asked.

Tyler glanced at Hans Vigo in the seat next to him. Why would the Feds have come all the way out here unless they thought there was a real threat? There was something to their concerns, and his own fear.

"Just keep your eyes and ears open, Wyatt."

"Yes, Sheriff." Wyatt hung up and Tyler winced. He hadn't meant to sound so bossy. It came with the territory. Was that why he and Wyatt couldn't regain the brotherhood they'd shared as kids? Because they had both grown up into strong-willed, stubborn men who didn't like to explain themselves?

Tyler was about to radio Bonnie again to patch him into the lodge — he'd like to talk to Karl Weber himself, tell him about the *personal* threat to Jo — when Mitch Bianchi shouted from the backseat, "Stop!"

Tyler slowly braked. Slamming on the

204

brakes could have put them into a skid or spin. Before they fully stopped, he saw the same thing Mitch Bianchi had.

A car roof.

Tyler motioned for everyone to remain silent as they exited the police 4X4 truck, guns drawn. If there was someone in the car, it was doubtful they were alive. But if somehow a killer had survived, he was trapped, and trapped animals attacked first.

They approached slowly by necessity, the snow soft under their boots. The car was off the road, but barely. Most likely it had gotten stuck. Tyler remembered that, according to the anonymous caller, the killers were driving a Ford 250 truck.

The vehicle looked like a truck, the bed full of snow, the cab almost completely covered as the wind had blown drifts of snow around it. Tyler motioned for his deputy to get into the bed, and Bianchi took the front. Tyler approached the side and kicked the snow off the window.

Empty.

"It's the same type of truck that Chapman and Doherty were last seen in," Bianchi said. "What are the odds?"

"It's theirs." Tyler took a shovel from his vehicle and scooped snow away from the door so he could open it.

"How can you tell?"

"Look." He pointed to a map on the floor. It wasn't just that it was a map of eastern Idaho and southwest Montana. There was blood spatter on it.

Bianchi came around and held the door open against the pressure of the snow while Tyler picked up the map. There was more blood on the dashboard, much of it smeared as if someone had tried to clean up. As if to prove the point, Bianchi gestured to the rear bench seat. Bloodstained napkins from a fast-food chain had been tossed into the back.

"I think this confirms that our anonymous caller was Tom O'Brien," Bianchi said.

"How so?"

"Let's say the 'accident' Tom O'Brien talked about was that his two buddies were onto him," Bianchi said.

"Onto him? I don't get it," Tyler said.

"We told you earlier that we have reason to believe that Tom O'Brien has been tracking the fugitives on his own, detaining them until authorities arrive. I'm thinking that somehow O'Brien slipped up, maybe said something he shouldn't. Chapman has a hair-trigger temper. We suspected he'd stolen a gun. So O'Brien slips up and Chapman shoots him. Tosses him from the truck outside Pocatello."

"O'Brien is one lucky son of a bitch," Grossman said. "To survive with a bullet hole for hours in this weather."

"Could be he ran, passed out somewhere — a public restroom? Maybe he stole another car? We don't know," Bianchi said. "But it makes sense, including his waiting half a day to call it in."

"O'Brien said he was in an accident," Tyler said, considering what Bianchi was saying and trying to reconcile that to the facts as he knew them.

"Accident my ass," Bianchi said. "Accident in that he slipped up *accidentally*. But he didn't say *car* accident, did he? No, they shot and dumped him, thinking he was dead or dying." He slammed his fist on the roof of the truck. "If I was only in Pocatello, I could find him!"

"Mitch," Vigo said quietly. The other Fed took a step away, hands fisted, but didn't say anything. "We need to get to the lodge as soon as possible."

"Let's go," Tyler said. The abandoned truck was only a mile from where the snowmobiles were stolen. The killers had more than enough time to make it to the Moosehead Lodge. Unless they had been injured or lost. With luck, they were dead in

207

the snow.

Vigo didn't move.

"What are you thinking?" Tyler asked, eager to get moving.

"His body would be here," Vigo mumbled. He stared at the interior of the truck, deep in thought.

"Hans?" Bianchi asked after a long minute.

"Chapman was driving. O'Brien was in the passenger seat. Doherty was in the back. Doherty shot O'Brien."

Tyler stared at the cab, trying to see what Hans Vigo saw. As the senior Fed explained what he believed happened, Tyler could picture it unfolding right before them.

"Chapman was driving because he's the grunt man. He can't sit still. He would *have* to drive. And Doherty would be fine with that because he wanted to think, to fantasize about Joanna Sutton. To build up the relationship in his mind, so that when they saw each other he would believe she felt exactly the same as he did.

"O'Brien was looking for a chance to take control of the situation. He couldn't take them together. That's why he called Bianchi when he had Blackie Goethe's gang cornered. He knew he couldn't take them all, so he tipped his hand, put his own freedom

208

on the line. With Chapman and Doherty, he'd probably thought he could separate them, take one of them down first, then the other."

"What happened? How did he trip up?"

Hans climbed into the cab, then into the backseat. He stared at the seat belts, then settled in the middle. "Doherty sat here. That way he could see both Chapman and O'Brien. He didn't trust Chapman because he's a hothead. He didn't trust O'Brien because he's smart. And — and because he disappeared for a couple days. He left to trap Blackie Goethe's gang. He had a good excuse, something that sounded right on the surface, but Doherty is suspicious by nature. He wouldn't trust him. He'd want to watch him. But he didn't shoot him because he thought O'Brien was going to turn him in."

"He shot him because of Jo," Tyler said, suddenly putting the facts in perspective. "O'Brien was in the passenger seat with the map."

"Exactly. He was trying to figure out where they were going, who they planned on seeing. Probably joking around a bit. Trying to get them to trust him. But he said the wrong thing about Jo Sutton."

"Guy talk," Bianchi interjected. "Something seemingly innocuous, like how hot she was."

"He knew what she looked like, but not her name," Tyler remembered. "Doherty had a picture. O'Brien wanted to warn her, but didn't know who she was. He started asking Doherty questions about her."

"He asked the *wrong* questions," Vigo said. "They didn't know O'Brien was trying to send them back to prison. Doherty thought that O'Brien was trying to steal his girl."

"Jo Sutton is not his girl," Tyler said.

Vigo shook his head as if to clear it. "Sorry. I sometimes get overinvolved in my profiles."

Tyler nodded, feeling a touch self-conscious by his reaction. Jo was *his* girl. If only she would realize it.

Her words that night came to him loud and clear.

"I feel like I'm still married."

Jo Sutton belonged to a dead man. And until she made peace with that, she wouldn't be able to open up to him.

But damn if he was going to let some psychopathic obsessive killer near her.

"I may be wrong," Vigo admitted as he clambered out of the truck. "It's just an educated guess."

Bianchi said, "Your educated guesses are

usually right on the money. And it fits what we know about Doherty's personality and O'Brien's phone call."

"Let's move," Tyler said.

"And put these bastards back in prison," Vigo added.

"Sounds like a plan to me," Tyler said, relieved to be moving again.

Aaron rode directly behind Joanna, who led the twelve-mile trek to where the Boy Scouts were waiting. They were going at a steady 10- to 15-mile-per-hour pace, primarily because visibility was poor. But it wasn't snowing, the few flakes falling almost as an afterthought.

Aaron didn't feel the cold, he barely felt the motor of the snowmobile beneath him. His jaw was locked tight and he stared at Joanna's bright red ski jacket.

Why had she asked two other men to join them?

The excuse that they could bring the boys back together rang hollow. Why hadn't she thought of that at first? Why all this deception? Why didn't she want to be alone with him? Hadn't they planned this lover's interlude, time to really get to know each other as they rode to save the Boy Scouts?

An anguished cry caught in his throat. She

didn't love him like he loved her. How could he believe he was worthy of such a beautiful, smart woman?

(You're pathetic, kill her now.)

He was a convicted murderer, a man who couldn't provide for Joanna. How could he keep her happy? How could he care for her and make sure she had everything she wanted? When they were on the run, constantly looking over their shoulders. How could he expect her to live like that?

She'd do it if she really loved you. And if she doesn't love you, kill her.

(Kill her now.)

No, no, no! He didn't want to kill her. That was something Doug Chapman would do, kill a woman because she made him mad. He'd killed his wife to get rid of her so he could be with his girlfriend, then he killed his girlfriend when she wanted to leave him because he killed his wife.

The irony made Aaron laugh out loud. No one heard his cackle over the loud hum of the snowmobiles. Did Doug even see the ludicrous life he led?

What about Aaron? He was a nobody, and Joanna must see that. His nothingness was plastered over his face, in his words, an average man in an average body with an average mind.

You're smart, Aaron. Very smart. If she doesn't see that, she needs to die.

No! Dammit, he didn't want to kill her. His chest heaved and he couldn't catch his breath. How could he take away something so beautiful and precious?

Tell her the truth.

That he killed Lincoln Barnes? Then she would know he was one of the escaped convicts.

She'll forgive you.

Or better yet . . . he could apprehend a killer. He could risk his life to save hers. Put a bullet in Doug Chapman's gut, just like he did to that letch Tom O'Brien who was staring at Joanna's breasts in the picture.

He would save her life and she would fall in love with him.

Aaron needed to figure out exactly how to set it up. And fast. Before the damn Sheriff Tyler McBride — *Love, Tyler* — arrived.

Joanna looked back over her shoulder and pointed her finger to the northeast. They were curving around. He had no idea where they were, but Joanna had a marvelous sense of direction. Such a smart girl.

His chest swelled with pride. She belonged to him.

THIRTEEN

Annie Erickson poured coffee for the well-dressed FBI agent who was sitting at her small oak kitchen table.

"Thank you for agreeing to talk to me," he said.

She glanced at his card. QUINCY PETERSON, ASSISTANT SPECIAL AGENT IN CHARGE, FBI SEATTLE REGIONAL FIELD OFFICE

"You wanted to talk about Aaron?"

"Yes, ma'am."

"Have you found him?"

"We're closing in on him, but we need some additional information to help us pinpoint his exact location and his mind-set."

She glanced down. Though the federal agent looked like a nice, handsome man not much older than Aaron, his job was to put poor Aaron back behind bars.

"Ms. Erickson? You testified at Aaron's trial. You asked for leniency because of childhood abuse."

"The judge didn't listen to me. But he wasn't there — he didn't watch that woman destroy that little boy."

"But you were there."

"From the day Aaron was born, Ginger

214

left him with friends and family until she had no one left who would take him. I wanted to adopt him, to raise him as my own — she knew I loved him, and she took him away from me. I loved him more than she ever could!" Annie looked down at her own coffee cup, remembering the last time she'd seen Aaron as a boy. He'd been thirteen. When Ginger left with him, Annie knew she'd never bring him back.

"How did you know Ginger and Aaron?"

"Ginger's mother and mine had been friends when we were kids."

"You and Ginger weren't friends?"

Annie shrugged. "Not close. We grew up in Los Angeles, went to the same school, lived nearby. Since our moms were friends, we saw each other often."

"Did you know Aaron's father?"

She'd never met Joe Dawson, but he was as much to blame for what had happened to Aaron as Ginger. If he had a backbone, he would have fought for custody of his son. His parents were good people and would have taken care of Aaron. But Joe was as selfish as Ginger.

"Joe Dawson didn't want to be a father. Aaron wasn't the only child he fathered out of wedlock. Last I heard he has four kids out of four different women. His parents stepped in and he married the mother of the last child, but I don't know if they are still together."

"You know a lot about the family."

"I did. Until my mom died two years ago she kept in contact with Ginger's mother."

"Do you know if Ginger's mother is still alive? Do you have an address?"

"I don't think so. The Christmas card I sent last year was returned. She was the same age as my mom, eighty-three. Maybe she went to a home. My mom thought she had Alzheimer's, but Ginger's mom hated going to the doctor."

"Do you know where Ginger Doherty is now?"

Annie shook her head. "I heard from friends that when Aaron was a sophomore in high school — frankly, it was amazing he didn't flunk out of school what with Ginger moving him every couple of months — she left him with her great-aunt in Los Angeles. Glendale, I believe. She was supposed to come back for him in two months — she told everyone she had a job on a cruise ship — but she never returned. Not surprising. She never showed up when she promised she would his entire life."

"You never knew what happened to her?"

Annie shook her head slowly. "I thought

she'd either just forgot about him completely, or hooked up with some other guy who didn't want kids. I had Aaron for eight months while she shacked up with a sugar daddy in Florida. The bastard didn't like kids, so she never told him about Aaron. Aaron was seven then, and that was the only stable year of his entire life. Then you know what she did? She showed up one morning *two weeks* before the end of the school year and just took him. The relationship didn't work out and she wanted to spend time with Aaron. Then I heard from my mom that she left him with her mother not a week later." Annie's voice cracked. Every time she thought about Aaron or Ginger she became upset.

"So you can see why the judge was wrong to give that poor boy the death penalty. I never doubted he did what they said he did — there was evidence, I know — but I wish the system could see that he was just a wounded little boy."

Agent Peterson was taking notes, his face solemn and nonjudgmental. Annie liked him.

"And you never heard from Aaron after his mother took him when he was thirteen?"

"Well, I visited him in prison after his arrest for killing poor Rebecca Oliver." She sighed. "I ache over that. If only I'd had the money to fight Ginger for custody. But — it wasn't just money, I suppose. What claim did I have to him? Why didn't the schools do something? His grandparents? His father?"

"Do you know Joanna Sutton?"

"The romance writer?" Annie glanced down again. "He asked me if I would bring him her books. He'd read one in the prison library and wanted more. They were wonderful family romances. I thought he could learn what love was really about, that his mother wasn't typical and, in fact, was abnormal."

"Did you know that Aaron was writing her letters?"

"I —" She swallowed uneasily.

"Did you send letters for him? Receive letters?"

"Am I in trouble?"

"No, ma'am."

Annie bit her bottom lip and played with her coffee cup. "I know I broke the rules — but just that one time. When he asked me to send a second letter, I read it first and never mailed it. I realized what he was doing."

"And what was that?"

"He was turning her into another Rebecca

Oliver. He had this idea that the actress was in love with him. He wrote me letters, at least twice a month, telling me about their dates, what she said to him, how much he loved her. I had no idea it was all in his head. And then he started writing that he and Joanna Sutton were pen pals, that she was helping him write a book, and the prison gave them special permission to be together.

"I didn't believe it, not after reading the second letter he asked me to send, but I didn't want to hurt him so I played along with his fantasy. I mean, he was in prison. Who could he hurt? Why are you asking me about her? He didn't — oh my God, he didn't hurt her since the escape?" Annie felt ill.

"Not yet, Ms. Erickson, but whatever information you have about Aaron's feelings toward Ms. Sutton would help us determine what his next move might be."

Annie swallowed a sob. She pictured young Aaron, big blue eyes looking out the window for a mother who never arrived on time. Young Aaron making sure he was clean, his clothes pressed, his hair combed all the time, just in case his mother showed up that day. Ginger didn't like dirty little boys . . .

"It's my fault."

"What?"

"Mrs. Sutton responded to his first letter. I didn't send it from the prison, but instead put my return address on the envelope. I was going to bring it to him, but after reading the second letter, I decided against it."

"When was this?"

"Two years ago."

"Do you remember anything about the letters?"

"I still have them."

Stan went upstairs to change the towels in the guest rooms. He found it odd that in John Miller's room he saw several of Jo's books on the desk. He crossed over and immediately noticed that three had a library's Dewey decimal code and the letter S for "Sutton" taped to each spine. Did he buy them at a library fund-raiser? Maybe. They all looked well read.

He opened one of them and saw underlined passages. Who on earth marked text in romance novels?

What did they really know about John Miller? He hailed from L.A. and had made his reservation a week ago, out of the blue. He hadn't been referred by anyone. He said he needed time to think, which wasn't surprising to Stan. But he didn't seem the type to cotton to thinking time. And he had attached himself to Jo readily enough.

You sent this fellow with Jo.

Had Stan made a mistake?

He went through John's room. There was nothing personal in it except for the clothes he'd worn yesterday. He'd worn Stan's clothes today, including a snowsuit. The only thing he'd brought with him from his truck were romance novels? *Jo's* romance novels?

Stan noticed a piece of paper folded and tucked into one of the books. He picked up the book, extracted the paper and carefully unfolded it. If his fears were unfounded, Stan wanted to be able to put the paper back as it was.

He stared at a photograph of John Miller. A mug shot, complete with the height marker behind him. It was a fax — and the header read *Beaverhead County Sheriff's Department, Dillon, Montana.*

Sheriff McBride had faxed over the mug shots of *three* convicts, not two.

John Miller, aka Aaron Doherty, had stolen his own.

Stan had to warn Jo.

She was in the middle of nowhere with a killer.

■ ■ ■ ■

Jo was pleased with their progress: They made it to the Kimball homestead in just over an hour. They'd been moving at fifteen miles an hour most of the time except for two delays. On their return, they wouldn't be able to go that fast hauling Ben Ward safely, or with the scouts sitting double on the snowmobiles. She was a little concerned about fuel — the added weight would drain their gasoline much faster, but as long as they rode steady and stayed on the main trail they'd make it. She had a two-gallon backup tank that she could tap into and siphon off if necessary.

Wyatt stood outside the cabin as Jo approached. "Heard you coming way back."

"Snowmobiles aren't built for stealth."

Wyatt glanced at the three men disembarking from the other sleds. Jo explained, "I don't like the weather right now. I'm thinking we should get you all back to the lodge quickly, rather than letting anyone ski in."

Wyatt held up his hand to stop Jo's explanation. "I spoke with Karl an hour ago. He told me you were coming with help. I should have thought of it myself."

Jo said, "I don't think we're going to be able to take your equipment. We're already doubling up some of the kids. Why don't you figure out how best to distribute everyone? It'll be slow going, but we'll all be back safe in less than two hours."

"Sounds like a good plan. I can come back for our stuff tomorrow or the next day."

She pulled out an insulated box from the straps on the back of her sled. "Stan sent some sustenance."

"Great."

Jo introduced Wyatt to the three men. "John Miller, from Los Angeles, and Craig and Sean Mann from Seattle. The Manns have been to the lodge before."

Wyatt shook their gloved hands, motioned them inside.

The Kimball homestead was simply an abandoned log cabin that had withstood harsh winters for more than fifty years, largely due to the craggy cliff to the north which protected it from the worst of the wind. Holes had been repaired, the roof replaced a couple summers back by Wyatt's former scout troop, and the land had been used for winter survival scout events for as long as Jo could remember.

The roof and the walls did little to stop the cold, and the inside was not much warmer than the ten degrees it was out-doors, though a fire burned in the river rock fireplace.

Jo started unpacking the sandwiches and hot chocolate for the boys, coffee for her and the men. She saw Jason sitting next to the injured Ben, who was up against the wall, close enough to the fire so the warmth did him good.

Jason looked so much like his father that for a moment, her heart skipped a beat.

She approached and squatted next to the boys, handing them cups of hot chocolate. "Hi, Jason."

"Hi, Jo." He didn't look at her; just stared at his cup. She didn't know what exactly he knew about her relationship with his father. She hadn't talked to him since she'd turned down Tyler's marriage proposal.

The last person she wanted to hurt was a boy still grieving over the death of his mother. She had no right to have insinuated herself into the McBride family. Why hadn't she thought about Jason more when she first started seeing Tyler?

Because she hadn't wanted to think about Jason. Thinking about Jason inevitably made her remember Timmy.

Timmy would have been thirteen, a year older than Jason.

She realized how callous she'd been toward Tyler's son, as if he weren't an important part of who Tyler was. Or maybe — maybe subconsciously Jason was more important to her, and more important in her rejection of Tyler, than she'd realized.

She squeezed his arm and made him look at her. "Keeping watch over our patient?"

He shrugged, sipped the hot chocolate. "It's my fault."

Ben shook his head. "It's not."

"It was." He said it so emphatically that she knew nothing Ben — or Jo — could say would change his mind.

Ben piped up. "We were climbing the rocks over at that trail that leads to Red Rock Pass. My foot went in between two boulders and just snapped."

"It was an accident," Jo said.

"He was my partner," Jason mumbled. "And it was my idea to climb the rocks."

"It wasn't your fault."

"I was supposed to be looking out for him."

"You are supposed to look out for each other. It was an accident. If he hadn't stepped in the wrong hole in the wrong way, it wouldn't have happened." Jo wanted to hug Jason, but suspected he'd be embarrassed. And the thought of holding a boy . . .

any boy . . . made her throat constrict.

The last boy she'd held was her dying son before he went in for surgery.

"The pressure on his brain is so strong that he'll die in less than twenty-four hours if we don't relieve it." The doctor, a squarish man with wire-rimmed glasses, had looked at her as if somehow this was all her fault.

Or maybe that was her, looking in a mirror.

"Then do it!" she demanded.

"I don't think he'll survive the surgery."

What?

She hadn't spoken the question, but it vibrated in her head. What did he mean, Timmy wouldn't survive the surgery?

The doctor stared at her, and when she didn't speak, he said, "Timmy will die without surgery. The extent of the internal bleeding is so great that without surgery to stop it, he can't survive. But because of where the bleeding is, and the extensive contusion inside his skull, I don't think we can stop it and repair the damage in time."

"What are his chances?" she asked in a voice so low she might as well not have spoken at all.

"Most optimistically, twenty percent."

"Twenty percent? That he'll die?"

"That he'll live."

Because time was crucial, Jo held Timmy

while the nurses prepared him for surgery. He looked like he was asleep, his face calm, but his skin was too pale, his cheeks too hollow.

"It's time."

Time. She'd only had minutes. Nine years, one month, ten days, and minutes . . .

In the cabin, Jo turned to Ben, gave him a smile, blinking away the threatening tears. "You holding up okay?"

Ben sighed dramatically. "Mr. McBride won't let me do anything. I've just had to sit here and do nothing."

"How does your leg feel?"

He shrugged. "It hurts if I move, but it's kind of numb now. And Mr. McBride put on a splint."

"I see that. He did a great job. You know you get a free ride back to my place."

"I'd rather drive the snowmobile myself."

Jo laughed. "I'll bet. It won't be long. Next season."

"That doesn't help."

Jo handed them both sandwiches. "Eat up, we have about a two-hour trek ahead of us and we need to get going pretty quick. I'm going to talk to Wyatt and start moving things along."

Jason shrugged, bit into his sandwich.

Jo didn't push it, relieved when she walked away to talk to Wyatt. He wasn't in the cabin. "Where'd Wyatt go?" she asked Craig Mann.

"He's using the radio."

He could have done it inside — unless he didn't want the boys to overhear.

She went outside. The wind had started to whip up, sending small flurries of snow to and fro like a vigorously shaken snow globe. Damn, it had come on suddenly. She saw Wyatt next to the snowmobiles and walked over.

He was on the radio. He stared at Jo and frowned.

"What's wrong?" she asked.

"The weather is getting nasty. We have to get going now."

"I agree. Who are you talking to?"

"Tyler. Here, you give him the ETA and I'll get the boys ready. You're going to pull Ben on your sled, Craig Mann and his son can take Kevin, he's the smallest, and Miller and I will each take take two boys."

She nodded and took the radio from Wyatt. "Tyler?"

"Jo. You made it safely."

"Did you doubt me?"

She tried to make light of it, but Tyler's voice was grave.

"The prisoners stole two of Nash's snow-mobiles. We're nearly to Lakeview right now and Nash will lead us around the avalanche. Fallen trees and boulders are blocking the road, so we need to make about a quarter-mile detour around, but we'll make it."

"The wind is picking up, throwing the powder around."

"The NWS is predicting another ten inches overnight, starting by five."

"We'll be back long before then."

"Be careful, Jo. With snowmobiles, the killers could be at the lodge already. Did you know your phone is out?"

"Our phone?"

"Yes. I talked to your grandfather over the radio."

"Must be something with the box outside the house. I can check it when I get back." She didn't want to be scared just because a wire got knocked loose in the storm — it happened on occasion — but she couldn't help but wonder if it really was an accident.

"There are seven cabins on your property, right?"

"Yes. And there are a couple vacation homes between Lakeview and the lodge as well, but they're not on the road. I don't think they'd be easily found, unless you knew they were there."

"We'll check those later. I want to get everyone into the lodge. It'll be much easier to keep people safe under one roof."

Jo almost hit herself. "We have two cabins occupied. I didn't think there was an immediate danger, not one that would warrant moving them."

"Who are they?"

"Greg and Vicky Trotsky are newlyweds. Greg worked at the refuge one summer. And two college kids working on a big project in the second cabin."

"I'm going to radio your grandfather and ask him to move them to the lodge before the weather gets worse. I can't protect people if they're spread all over."

Wyatt came out with John and Craig, giving instructions.

"We need to get going," she said glancing at her watch. Ten-thirty a.m. "We should be back by one. I'll see you soon."

"I love you, Jo."

Click.

He'd hung up. She stared at the radio, in shock more than anything else. Her throat thickened. He still loved her? After she turned down his proposal? After she told him that she still felt married?

You slept with him, but you can't marry him? What's with you, Jo!

She glanced at the cabin and immediately thought about Jason, and knew then that it wasn't Tyler she was scared to commit to.

"Joanna!" John waved to her, trying to get her attention. She put up her finger in a "just-a-minute" gesture and went back into the cabin to help organize the boys. They had stored the equipment they couldn't take in the corner. Wyatt had all the food in his pack — they couldn't leave that for grizzlies or wolves to hunt down. She made sure the boys were dressed properly and sent them out one at a time.

Jason and Ben were the last. "Is he really going to be okay?" Jason asked, eyes cast down.

"Yes," Jo said. "Your uncle knows what he's doing. The splint is solid and you've kept him off his leg. We'll get him to the lodge and Stan — he was a medic in the army — he'll give him a once-over. Nash will come in from Lakeview and patch him up."

Jason's eyes shot up in surprise. "Dr. Nash is a veterinarian!"

Jo laughed, rested her hand on Jason's arm. "He's been known to work on people. He delivered my son . . ." Her voice trailed off and her face froze. She rarely thought about the day Timmy was born. She expected the pain to hit her, physically, in the heart. Instead, a dull throb spread throughout her body, a quiet angst, but not debilitating. She didn't cry.

Jason whispered, "Are you okay?"

She nodded. And meant it.

Wyatt came in and said, "The boys are ready. Help me bring Ben out?"

"Jason, want to grab Ben's stuff and follow?" Jo asked.

Jason followed as she and Wyatt carried the injured boy outside and strapped him into the sleigh. "It's cold now," Jo told him, "but there's a built-in heater. You'll be toasty in no time."

"This is totally cool," Ben said, grinning at Jason, who secured Ben's pack with bungee cords on the bottom of the sleigh.

Jo wrapped a waterproof blanket tight around Ben's body. "Just don't move around, okay? It'll be a couple hours. Maybe a nap is in order."

"Do you have music?"

"Sorry, pal, heat only."

Wyatt pulled an iPod out of his pocket, put the buds in Ben's ears, the device in his hand. "Enjoy."

"Thanks, Mr. McBride!"

"Don't thank him," Jason teased, "he only likes country music, like my dad."

"I like country," Ben said.

Her snowmobile radio beeped. She said

to Wyatt, "Make sure that you have every-thing you need and that the boys didn't leave any of their food out. Wouldn't want you to be mauled by a hungry bear when you return tomorrow."

"You're all heart." Wyatt squeezed Jason's shoulder, then went inside the cabin.

Jo picked up the radio. "Hello, Jo Sutton here."

"Jo, it's Stan."

"We made it just fine, we're already about to move on out. We'll be in time for a late lunch."

"Are you alone?"

She glanced around. Jason was leaning over the sleigh talking to Ben. Thirty feet away were the other three snowmobiles, the boys standing around, checking out the gauges and talking to the Manns. Where was John? There, talking to one of the boys. Wyatt hadn't come out of the cabin yet.

"Sort of. Why?"

His voice was low. "Jo."

"You're going to have to talk louder."

"Put the receiver to your ear and listen."

She did what he said.

"John Miller's real name is Aaron Doherty. He's one of the escaped convicts."

She couldn't have heard right. Her blood ran cold.

Jo looked over at where John Miller was standing with one of the scouts, showing him the features of the snowmobile. He glanced over as Jo stared, and she quickly looked away.

"Are you sure?"

Stan had to be wrong. How could an escaped prisoner from San Francisco make it all the way up here to the Centennial Valley? Why would he?

Tyler said one of the convicts had her picture.

That didn't make any sense. None of this made any sense! Why her? Her chest tightened and she was thrown back in time, to another day when a violent criminal threatened those she loved.

She'd been alone with him. He'd seemed odd, but could he be a killer? Had she led a killer to six innocent boys?

She swallowed bile as she listened to Stan's confirmation.

"Yes. He stole his mug shot off the fax machine. I found it in his bedroom. There is no doubt, Jo. Are you okay?"

No, she wasn't okay. But she'd have to find a way to pretend. To protect the boys, she had to make believe nothing was wrong.

"I'll talk to Wyatt," she whispered.

"Be careful."

Careful. She'd been talking to a convicted murderer for the last twenty-four hours. Had breakfast with him. Brought him out here even after getting that funny feeling about him when he quoted one of her books this morning.

Why'd he come here in the first place? Why was he so interested in her books? In *her?*

She glanced at Jason and Ben. She had to tell Wyatt, but she didn't want to leave the boys unprotected. Wyatt would have a gun. Why hadn't she listened to Tyler and kept a gun with her? But even if they confronted John — Aaron Doherty — he might still hurt someone.

Lincoln Barnes had never meant to kill Timmy. Her son was simply in the way of Linc getting what he wanted.

If Tyler was right — if one of the convicts wanted her for some insane reason — she had to get away from the boys. Right now they were occupied. She'd get to Wyatt, tell him, and they'd figure out what to do.

Just pretend everything is normal.

Normal. Right. Should she leave Jason and Ben alone to warn Wyatt?

She was doubting herself, doubting her instincts because of what happened to Tim.

John Miller — *Aaron Doherty* — was star-

235

ing at her from thirty feet away. She was wearing her ski mask — a saving grace if she couldn't keep the fear out of her expression.

She turned to Jason and said as casually and quietly as she could, "Hey, I need you to go to Wyatt right now and tell him I have a, um —" She didn't want to alarm Jason. What would Wyatt understand? Of course, the Highway Patrol codes they also used in search-and-rescue. "I have a 10–106." *Suspicious person.*

Wyatt was smart. He'd understand and come out prepared.

"A 10–106? What's that?"

"An inside joke," she said, forcing a false lightness in her voice.

"O . . . K . . ." Jason said as if he thought adults had strange jokes.

She didn't want Aaron Doherty anywhere near the injured Ben Ward. She watched Jason trudge toward the cabin. It was slow going because the boys had to leave their snowshoes and skis behind. She started toward where Craig and Sean Mann were handing out helmets to the boys. Maybe she could alert them to Doherty.

Doherty approached her faster than she could get to the Manns. She met him halfway, wanting to keep him as far from the boys as possible. She felt trapped. She didn't know if she was doing the right thing, but she didn't know what else to do. What if Doherty had a gun? Tyler had said the convicts were armed. What if Doherty took one of the kids hostage? Jo couldn't bear the thought of another mother losing her son.

She put on her best game face. "Hi, John. Ready to head back?"

"Who were you talking to?"

"Talking to?" Her voice cracked and she coughed to cover up her nerves.

"On the radio."

Did Doherty sound suspicious, or was that her fear?

"Stan," she replied. "He wanted to make sure we arrived safely." *She was talking too fast. She needed to smile. Smile, Jo!*

She tried. She gave him a half smile.

"But didn't you already talk to someone on that guy's radio?" He motioned toward the cabin.

Jo glanced over to where Jason had stopped to watch her talking to Doherty. *Go, Jason! Get inside!* She willed him to keep moving toward the cabin. After what seemed like eternity, he did.

She breathed a brief sigh of relief.

"Joanna," Doherty said, "what's going on?"

"Oh, that call? That was, um, Sam Nash over in Lakeview. He's a veterinarian and I wanted to make sure that he could get through the avalanche today to take a look at Ben's leg. We don't have a doctor here in the valley, you know, but Nash is great, handles a wide variety of medical situations." She was rambling. She needed to give Wyatt time to act.

Please understand the code. Please, Wyatt, know what I mean.

She forced a smile on her lips, but he was watching her eyes through the ski mask. She swallowed, shaking. She was going to blow it. She was going to get the boys killed.

No.

Out of the corner of her eye she saw Jason enter the cabin and relaxed a fraction. No one was going to die. Everything was going to be fine.

"You seem — different," Doherty said. "Did the veterinarian have news about the escaped prisoners?"

"Oh, no, nothing like that," she said quickly.

She didn't realize she'd averted her eyes when she spoke until after the words left her mouth.

238

Doherty did.

"You're lying."

She wanted to laugh and deny it, but what would she do if someone who wasn't an escaped convict accused her of lying? She'd be indignant.

"Why on earth would you say that?" She stared directly into his eyes to show him she wasn't afraid, when inside she was terrified.

His eyes scared her with their intensity.

Unconsciously, she stepped toward the cabin. "Mr. Miller, I think you're being presumptuous —"

The door of the cabin opened. She and Doherty looked at the same time.

Wyatt didn't have a ski mask on, and his face was hard. "Get away from her," Wyatt said.

Wyatt had a gun in his hand. He'd reacted too fast, now Doherty knew for sure they were on to him.

Doherty grabbed Jo from behind, held her to him. "Come with me, Joanna."

"Let her go," Wyatt demanded.

"Shit!" Doherty exclaimed. Cold metal pressed into Jo's neck. "Who told you, Joanna? Who told you?"

"Don't hurt anyone. Please don't hurt the boys."

"I'm not going to hurt a kid! I don't kill

kids like that bastard Lincoln Barnes."

Linc? What did Doherty know about Linc? What did he know about Timmy? Oh, God, this was a nightmare.

"Just back away, John, back away from Jo and we'll talk, okay?" Wyatt said.

"Stop it!" Doherty yelled.

Now all eyes were on them. Doherty was backing away from the cabin, toward the closest snowmobile. He pulled Jo with him, then turned his gun toward the Manns. "Get away."

Craig and his son herded the boys like cattle away from both the cabin and Doherty's gun.

"Okay," Doherty said, "we're going to do this my way. You're coming with me, okay? Then no one will get hurt. Just you and me, Joanna. That's the way it's supposed to be."

Jo stared at Wyatt. He was slowly shaking his head. "John, I don't know what you want, but you don't want to do this."

"Stop talking!" Doherty shouted at Wyatt. Quieter, to Jo, he said, "Please, Joanna."

She hesitated.

Doherty turned the gun toward where Ben Ward lay strapped — trapped — in the sleigh thirty feet away.

"I'll come with you!" she exclaimed. "Don't hurt him."

Doherty turned the gun back on her. "Good. Good!" He sounded happy. "Let's go."

"Jo's not going anywhere with you," Wyatt said. He stepped out of the cabin.

Before she knew what he was doing, Aaron aimed the gun at Wyatt and fired.

Oh, God, Wyatt, no!

Wyatt dropped to the ground.

Aaron pulled her shocked body the remaining feet to the snowmobile. She started to fight.

"Stop, or I'll kill every one of them. I don't want to, I really don't want to."

He touched her cheek with his gloved hand. "You know me, Joanna. You know I wouldn't hurt anyone. I love you. I wouldn't hurt anyone unless you made me." His eyes hardened. "Get on."

Shaking, Jo slid her leg over the snowmobile. Aaron Doherty was not sane and she didn't know what he would do. She didn't know him, she'd just met him yesterday. He thought he loved her? Unreal. He was unstable. She had to go with him, get him away from the boys. She couldn't risk their lives. What if Wyatt had been one of the scouts? Jason?

She dry heaved. *Wyatt, please be okay. Please live.*

Aaron jumped into the seat behind her, his gun pressed against her side. He turned the ignition.

"Drive."

Craig Mann crossed over to Wyatt. Jason stared at Wyatt's body in front of the door. Wyatt was struggling to get up, blood spreading across his shoulder and dripping into the white snow.

Aaron took charge of the snowmobile and they started off too fast, almost tipping them end-over-end. He regained control and within a minute, Jo couldn't see Wyatt, Jason, or the cabin.

FOURTEEN

Doug tired of Vicky Trotsky quickly that morning and slit her throat in one clean slice.

Aaron had said he didn't want her to suffer.

Aaron wanted him to go back to the first cabin. Aaron probably wanted him to sit and heel and sit at the back of the bus. Asshole.

Doug was tired of taking orders from Aaron. He'd heard the snowmobiles leave well over an hour ago, didn't know what was going on, but that meant there were fewer people at the lodge. Easier to gain control.

But he'd been stupid. He'd left his gun at the cabin. No fucking way he could take anyone hostage with a knife. Might be able to slice one or two, but what good would killing someone be if he still got caught?

Guns kept people under control. He'd sneak in, find someone by themselves, and then he'd have a hostage. Get everyone in one room, have them tie each other up, and he'd be in charge. Warm, in the big house, eating well. As soon as this shitty weather passed, he'd grab a truck and get the hell out of here. Take a hostage to drive, he had no idea where he was or how to get out of here.

But maybe Aaron was right. Maybe he should lay low, go back to that cabin they'd found. They'd left the snowmobiles they'd stolen behind the cabin, shielded from casual observers. They were probably buried in snow by now, but Doug knew where they were.

He could just leave fucking Aaron Doherty. The kid didn't seem to want him around, anyway. And after all he'd done for him! If it weren't for Doug, they wouldn't have even had the guns. And he was the one who hot-wired all the cars they stole, he was the one who'd gotten the snowmobiles running. Damn, Aaron treated him like a sewer rat rather than the smart guy he was. He might not have acted as smart as Aaron, but who was the one with the college degree? That's right, good old Doug Chapman had a degree in civil engineering.

His head ached, and he blamed it on the Jack Daniel's he'd consumed the night before.

He stared at the dead woman on the bed, the blood drying on the mattress. He remembered killing her. The anger that had been building up inside all week. The rage that had gotten him in trouble all those years ago when he'd been drinking. But he had it under control, cut out drinking too much which made his anger harder to ignore. Then Tanya had to start fucking with him and he let the bitch have it.

You didn't want to kill Chantelle.

God, he missed her.

He turned his eyes away from Vicky Trotsky. She was just a nobody, Doug couldn't bring up any real emotion or regret.

No emotion except the bubbling anger he'd never understood.

He looked out the window, saw nothing and no one. Nothing at all. The damn wind was kicking up snow all over the place and it was loud. How could the wind make so much noise? He'd always thought snow was silent, but there was nothing quiet about this blizzard.

In the daylight, he had seen there were marked paths leading to the lodge through some sparse trees. He'd watched which way Aaron and the hot writer had gone. Other trees were marked as well. That would lead him back to his cabin — and his gun.

"Thanks for a great party, baby," he said to the dead woman and left.

He'd give Aaron another chance, Doug thought as he hiked back to the cabin where he'd left his gun. But if Aaron fucked with him, Doug Chapman would invade the lodge and take over. He hated doing nothing.

And if anyone tried to stop him, he'd kill again to feed the angry monster inside.

Tyler and his men arrived at Nash's house off South Centennial Road ten minutes after Tyler spoke to Jo. Agent Vigo immediately got on his cell phone. The Centennial Valley had virtually no cell phone service, however there were certain pockets that the locals called "phone booths," several of which were in Lakeview.

245

Tyler talked to Nash, who drew him a map on how to get around the avalanche. The detour would add only fifteen minutes to their timetable.

As soon as Tyler and his deputies packed their supplies into the snowmobiles which Nash had already fueled, he motioned for Vigo to wrap up the conversation — they needed to get on the road. The wind had really whipped up the fresh powder and while there was no new snowfall, visibility was poor.

Vigo approached and said, "That was my contact in Seattle, Quinn Peterson. He spoke with Annie Erickson, one of Aaron Doherty's temporary guardians.

"She confirmed everything in his file — Doherty was raised by friends and family his entire life, being uprooted by his mother when she felt like it. She also said that Ginger Doherty disappeared when the kid was sixteen. Left him with a great-aunt and went to work on a cruise ship. Never returned. Peterson is running down that lead."

"You think bringing the mother here is going to help us catch him?" Tyler asked. "We don't have the time."

"Actually, I suspect she's dead," Hans said.

"Why?"

"Peterson ran her social and nothing popped since the year she disappeared. She received paychecks from King Cruises for three months after leaving Doherty with his eighty-two-year-old great-aunt Dorothy Miles. She died three years later, left everything to the kid. A house, some money.

"So I'm thinking if what Ms. Erickson says is true," Vigo continued, "that Ginger Doherty hooked up with men right and left — that maybe one of them killed her."

"Nothing in the files on her? No death certificate?"

"Nothing we can find, but Peterson already put out an alert to the locals. Maybe there's a Jane Doe out there that matches her description."

"How is this going to help us catch him?" Tyler asked, anxious to leave.

"We need all the information we can get," Vigo said. "The more we know about Doherty's background, the greater chance we can predict what he'll do next."

"I *know* what he's going to do next," said a frustrated Tyler. "He's going to track down Jo if we don't get to her first."

Vigo glanced at Bianchi, then said, "Peterson has letters that Doherty attempted to send to Jo Sutton through Ms. Erickson. The first letter was mailed to her — Erickson didn't see anything harmful, it was a simple fan letter. Jo wrote back, a generic response — something like *Thank you for writing, I'm glad you enjoyed my book.* Erickson intended to give it to Doherty, but after reading his second letter, she decided to keep it from him and send no other letters to Jo."

"What did it say?"

"It implied that they had a relationship, that he knew she wrote for him because that was the only way they could share intimacy."

Tyler hit the side of the garage. The mere thought that some psychotic bastard would butcher Jo's innocent and beautiful stories angered him.

"Erickson never mailed them — and Doherty was distraught when Jo didn't write back. The prison authority just informed us that they uncovered dozens of letters Doherty had written to a 'Joanna.' They were hidden in plain sight — he'd highlighted words and letters in her books that, when read together, were messages for her."

"It's sick." It was more than sick — now Aaron Doherty was trying to make his fantasy real. Jo was in danger and Tyler hated that he wasn't with her to protect her.

"It's in line with what I surmised earlier," Vigo said. "He has delusions — but not the wild-eyed delusions you expect from drug addicts on the street or the mentally ill."

Nash approached them. "You're all ready to go."

Deputy Grossman called from Tyler's truck, "Sheriff! Stan Wood from the Moosehead is on the radio. Says it's urgent."

Tyler strode over, picked up the radio. "Stan, it's Tyler. What's wrong?" His heart raced. The two people he loved most — his son and Jo Sutton — were in danger.

"I found Aaron Doherty's mug shot," Stan said.

"I faxed it last night along with Doug Chapman's and Thomas O'Brien's."

"We only saw O'Brien's and Chapman's. I found Doherty's in John Miller's room, folded in one of Jo's books. Doherty and Miller are one and the same."

Stan's words sunk in immediately. Tyler almost didn't want to say it. "John Miller was one of the men who went out with Jo to bring back Wyatt's troop."

"Yes."

"Does Jo know?"

"I called and told her."

Shit. It would have been safer to have let Doherty think he was in the clear. To return to the lodge with Wyatt and the boys where Stan would have the upper hand.

"I'll contact them. Get everyone into the lodge and keep them there, including your guests staying in cabins."

He hung up and dialed into Wyatt's frequency. Nothing. He tried again. And again. And again.

Someone finally picked up the radio. "Hello?"

"This is Sheriff McBride. Who's this?"

"Kevin Sampson, sir. Are you coming to save us?"

Kevin sounded scared. "Son, put Wyatt on."

"He's hurt."

"Ms. Sutton?"

"She's not here. Mr. Miller took her." Kevin spoke fast. "He had a gun and they left on a snowmobile."

"Mr. Miller?" Tyler repeated. His blood ran cold.

"He shot Mr. McBride and took her. You're going to get them, right? Jason says you're the best cop."

Doherty had shot Wyatt and taken Jo. Tyler's world was collapsing around him. He felt helpless this far from everyone he cared about.

"Is Wyatt okay?" He feared the worst.

"I think so. I don't know. Mr. Mann is doing something."

Tyler rubbed his temple. "Put Jason on."

"I can't."

Tyler's frustration and fear grew. "Just put him on, son."

"He's gone, too."

"What do you mean gone?"

"He left right after Ms. Sutton and Mr. Miller. Following them, I think."

His son — his twelve-year-old son — was tracking a killer in the middle of an impending blizzard. He'd throttle him. What *had* Jason been thinking? *Dear Lord, I just want my son back. My son and my girl.*

The killer has Jo.

"Put Mr. Mann on. Now."

"Yes, sir."

Why hadn't one of the men gone after him? Why did Jason feel compelled to be so reckless? A moment later, a voice said, "This is Sean Mann. My father is trying to stop Mr. McBride's bleeding."

"What happened?"

"Not quite sure, except that Ms. Sutton got a call on the radio and then Miller just flipped out. He had a gun and said she was coming with him. When Mr. McBride tried to stop him, Miller shot him."

"How is Wyatt?"

"He was hit in the right shoulder. My dad says he'll probably be okay if we can get

251

him to a doctor."

Tyler surveyed the valley. There was no way Life Flight could get in here, the ceiling was too low. But Nash was a veterinarian. Not ideal, but the best they had under the circumstances.

"Get Wyatt back to the lodge ASAP."

"We only have two snowmobiles and there are eight of us. Even with the kid on the sleigh, we can't all go."

Shit. Tyler had to both get to the lodge and find Jo and Jason. And he had to get those boys safely from the homestead to the lodge. All right now.

"This is what I want you to do. Either you or your father take Wyatt and Ben Ward to the lodge. I'll have a doctor meet you there. The other needs to stay with the other four boys until someone can get there, okay?"

"Yes, sir."

"Can you do that?"

Another voice came on the radio. "Sheriff, this is Craig Mann. I heard your request. I'll take Wyatt and the boy in. I think the others are safer here — there is plenty of food and water and the shelter is sound — until we know where the convicts are."

"John Miller is Aaron Doherty, one of the convicts. Which way did he take Jo?"

"West."

The lodge was southeast from the homestead. Where was Miller taking her? He hadn't had time to scout out the area. He might have a map, but it wouldn't show residences. All the vacation homes were either north or south, accessible from the North or South Centennial Road. Nothing west that Tyler could think of.

It was only twenty degrees. When night came, it was supposed to drop to minus twenty. They had no provisions to survive the night exposed. Most snowmobile tanks held nine gallons. They got — maybe — ten miles a gallon.

Tyler had to find them. And the only way was to follow their trail.

"Mann, you bring Wyatt and Ben in like you said. Sean will stay with the boys. I'll go directly to the homestead and track Miller from there. I'll send my deputy to the lodge with the doctor." It would have been better to send Mann here to Lakeview, but the lodge was closer.

"What if one of the other convicts is there?"

"There's only one more other than Doherty. Doug Chapman. He should be considered armed and dangerous, got it?"

"Yes, Sheriff."

"How's Wyatt?"

"I stopped the bleeding, but he lost quite a bit. He's conscious. The bullet is still in there. I know first aid, but this is out of my league."

"I'll be there as soon as possible."

Everyone was looking at him when he hung up the radio. He didn't need to repeat what had happened. "Nash, can you go to the lodge?"

"Absolutely. And if you need to bring the scouts here instead of the lodge, do it. Peter can go with you." Peter was Nash's son, a military veteran of thirty who didn't say much and had been standing quietly next to his father the entire time.

"Agreed. When we arrive at the homestead, we'll contact the lodge and ascertain whether it's safe to bring the boys there. Otherwise, they'll come here."

He continued, "Bianchi, Billy, come with me and Peter to the homestead. Peter can lead. He knows the valley better."

"We'll take the lodge," Vigo said.

"Be careful. We don't know if Chapman is dead or alive."

Gun within easy reach, Stan walked up the slope to where the college kids were staying. He knocked briskly on the door, then stepped back.

"Who is it?"

"Stan Wood from the lodge."

"How do I know?"

"Look through the window."

Stan stepped to the right. The shutters opened and Brian Bates looked out.

The door opened a moment later. "Sorry. Jo said there might be some trouble coming this way and not to let anyone in."

"The Sheriff would like you and Marie to come to the lodge. He's on his way with reinforcements."

"Is that necessary? Is there really a problem? I thought it was just a precaution."

The pretty, petite Marie wrapped her arms around Brian from behind. "Are we in danger?" she asked, her big blue eyes looking from her boyfriend to Stan.

Stan said, "One of the convicts was a guest at the lodge under a false identity. The Sheriff is on his way to apprehend him now — he went out with Jo on a rescue. We don't know about the second. It would be safer if everyone was under one roof."

"Okay, give us a couple minutes. We'll pack up our stuff."

Stan nodded. "I'll go down and talk to the Trotskys. Meet me down there in ten minutes."

Brian closed the door and Stan walked

down the steep slope, his snowshoes giving him purchase. The trees on the slope shielded him from the worst of the wind, but he could barely make out the cabin beyond. He'd lived through twenty-nine winters here, didn't particularly like them, but for him the splendor of summer made up for the brutality of winter. Nowhere on earth came close to the peaceful radiance of the Centennial Valley in June and July, when the birds came and stayed for a time.

Knowing what came in only a few months sustained Stan during the worst of winter. He approached the Trotskys' cabin and listened.

The howl of the wind. Snow falling from the trees. The scurry of rodents across branches. He heard snowmobiles in the distance — they were miles away. He couldn't tell if they were coming from the northeast, where Jo was picking up the scout troop, or from the west where the Sheriff was coming in. Sound carried far in the valley.

He knocked on the door. There was no sound from inside, but they might be napping. Stan had never married, but he'd been young and in love once. Before the war.

He knocked louder. Again, silence. He withdrew his gun. The blinds on the two windows were closed. He couldn't see in. He slowly turned the doorknob.

Unlocked.

He pushed open the door, standing to the side. Phantom gunfire rattled around his head and he broke out in a sweat. He clenched the gun and glanced through the opening.

Vicky Trotsky was naked, tied to the bare mattress, her neck a red river of blood. Bruises and welts covered her body. Her empty eyes stared at the heavens, as if pleading for mercy.

Did her husband do this to her?

Stan hated the thought, guilt washing over him when he saw Greg Trotsky dead on the floor.

No one else was in the cabin. He slammed the door shut on the violence, unable to see anything but red behind his closed eyes. Had Stan done this by sending Aaron Doherty down here with Jo to deliver breakfast?

But there hadn't been enough time for him to rape and kill Vicky. Had he done it the night before? Was that why he was so eager to go with Jo?

Stan had assumed, when Doherty left the other two killers' mug shots on the fax while taking his own, that it was a sign that the

257

other convicts were out of the picture, either dead or elsewhere.

Stan didn't want to go back in the cabin, but he had to. He had to know what happened there.

He opened the door and crossed first to Greg Trotsky. His body was tight and hard, a sign of rigor mortis. Stan crossed to Vicky's body. He picked a sheet up off the floor and covered her nakedness, wanting to give her some semblance of dignity in death. Her body was still warm to the touch.

Stan had seen enough death in Vietnam to know that Greg had been killed hours before his wife.

In Stan's mind, there was no way that Aaron Doherty could have killed the Trotskys. He'd been visible around the lodge in the evening and in the early morning, and he wasn't gone long enough this morning to come down here to rape and brutalize this poor woman.

Even if Doherty hadn't murdered the couple, he had to know the truth. He'd been inside the cabin this morning. He must have seen Greg dead, and Vicky beaten and restrained. And he did nothing. Nothing, because the killer was Doherty's partner.

There was another killer at large. And no one knew his whereabouts.

FIFTEEN

Doherty was driving the snowmobile far too fast on the trail, especially with the fresh powder and swirling wind. Visibility was so poor Jo wasn't sure exactly where they were headed, but the compass on the control panel of the sled indicated they were traveling almost directly west.

What trail went west from the Kimball homestead? Jo didn't know this quadrant of the valley well enough to know for sure, but she made a logical guess that Doherty was heading to the refuge center. It was vacant in winter, but its location would be on the maps her grandfather had provided every guest in their room.

She prayed Wyatt would be all right. Maybe it was a flesh wound.

There was so much blood.

Jo couldn't let herself think about that now. She had to focus on where they were going and how she could get out of this situation. Doherty had control over the snowmobile, but she was sitting in the front. Wasn't there something she could do?

Doherty's face was buried in her neck and when he licked her skin it was all Jo could do to prevent herself from forcing a crash on the snowmobile and being done with it.

She didn't know what his plans were, why he had obsessed on her, where he was taking her. Visibility was poor, but at least they weren't driving blind.

She didn't want to die. Making Doherty crash the snowmobile into one of the drifts wouldn't be a smart move, not at the speed they were going. They were going too fast for the weather. Maybe she wouldn't have to do anything on purpose and Doherty would get them both killed.

At least the boys were safe. That was all that mattered, really. Six young boys who had their entire lives ahead of them. If Jo died saving them, it wouldn't be for nothing.

She would see Timmy again.

And you'll never see Tyler. You'll never be able to tell him you love him, too.

She had to make a stand. She had to choose to live her life again after four years of living only in her fiction. Or she had to choose death. Because while she had gone through all the motions of life, it wasn't until she laid eyes on Sheriff Tyler McBride that day at Nash's that she truly felt alive for the first time since her husband and son had been killed.

She had to live to tell Tyler. To apologize for running out on him at Thanksgiving. To explain her fear that she would be replacing Timmy with another son.

She owed it to Tyler, and to herself, to face that fear.

She had to gain control of her situation. But how?

"I love you, Joanna. I've always loved you." Doherty spoke in her ear. Her stomach turned. If she was going to see Tyler and Jason again, she'd have to stay alive. And that meant finding out what Doherty had planned. Maybe she could buy time. She had one huge advantage — winter survival skills.

"We're going too fast," she said. The windshield helped with sound control, but it was still difficult to talk over the roar of the sled.

"I know what I'm doing."

"You've never lived here. The drifts can come up suddenly." The wind had calmed a bit, but swirls of powder intermittently obscured their view.

"We're on a trail."

"That doesn't always help."

"I know where I'm going."

"Where? The refuge?"

"None of your business."

"Aaron, please — you don't want to hurt me."

He sounded shocked. "I would never hurt you, Joanna. I love you. I'm your hero."

"If you are my hero, you need to let me go."

She wanted to tell him she had another hero, the Sheriff, and he was coming for her, but her instincts told her that wouldn't be a wise move. She didn't know why Doherty had been in prison, but she understood now that he'd been the one with her picture, that he had been the one obsessed with her. He thought he loved her.

Her friend Mindy had once talked to her about research she did on one of her serial killer books. Jo had blocked out most of the conversation — Mindy could be a little too creepy about stuff like murder and mayhem. But something she'd said had stuck with Jo.

"Stalkers who kill think that if they can't have you, they won't let anyone else have you. It's similar to abused spouses — the husbands beat their wives out of control and anger, and if they threaten to leave the husband can't handle it. No woman, no wife, can just walk out. They have to die first. It might not even be that well thought-out, just a deep down psychotic break."

While Mindy wasn't a psychiatrist, her explanation described Trixie's relationship with Lincoln Barnes. Lincoln couldn't tolerate Trixie leaving him. Jo didn't think Lincoln wanted to kill Trixie so much as to beat her into submission to come back to him.

The idea of playing along with Aaron Doherty's warped fantasies made Jo ill, but if it would get her out of this dire situation, she'd do it.

Though Jo wasn't positive she knew Doherty's ultimate destination, they were definitely following a trail that led to the refuge.

Doherty must have studied the map closely as well as the trails, but his knowledge was still limited. If they found themselves off the trail it would be difficult to find it again. They could be lost for days in the valley in this weather, even with the compass. Too many natural barriers to blockade them. Those same barriers also prevented help from easily finding them.

"Are you cold?" he asked.

"Yes," she responded truthfully.

"Isn't there a heater on this?"

"Yes, but it'll use up the fuel faster and we're already a half-tank down."

"We're almost there." He flipped on the heater. Hot air blew in her face and warmed her gloved hands.

He must have memorized the distances of the trails because even Jo wasn't certain how far it was from the Kimball homestead to the refuge center. At least ten miles, as the crow flies.

A snowflake fell and hit the windshield. Then another. The weather was turning again, and it would be as nasty as the night before.

She had to find a way to escape.

She was about to speak to Doherty, try to get him to talk about his plans, when she heard something. She'd been hearing it on and off for a while now. It was a snowmobile, and at first she thought it was the echo of the Polaris. But there was a distinctly different pitch. It sounded like an Arctic Cat. In fact, the Arctic Cat that Sean Mann had driven out to the homestead.

Had Sean been following them the whole time? He could have easily followed their wakes in the snow.

It gave her hope, more hope than she had a minute ago. Because she knew about trails not on the map, ways to get back to the lodge by using her compass and knowledge of the valley.

But she didn't know how far behind Sean was. He could simply be following them — had he taken the radio? Maybe he was tracking them and letting Tyler know where they were. But how could he know? Everything looked the same in the middle of the valley — lots of white and gray and drifts all over. Fluorescent trail markers stood out to keep them on course.

Then again, maybe he was following them to their destination and when they stopped, he would call Tyler. Except he wouldn't know when they stopped until he came upon them. And by that time it would be too late — as soon as Doherty turned off the Polaris, he'd be able to hear the Arctic Cat nearby.

Shit.

Sean Mann was in danger because of his noble and heroic act of following them. She'd have to figure out some way to distract Doherty — except how could she distract him? Especially since the Arctic Cat was gaining on them.

Aaron Doherty didn't act like he was stupid. Irrational, obsessive, but he wasn't a wild-eyed psychopath. When Lincoln Barnes had broken into their house in Placerville to kidnap Trixie and Leah, he'd been half-deranged, his eyes darting back and forth, trapped. His anger was directed at Trixie, but he took it out on anyone in his way.

Doherty didn't have that rage, at least not at this moment. He seemed almost calm. As if they were on a fun ride through the valley.

At least Jason is safe. If Tyler lost his son . . . Stop it, Jo. She had to stop thinking about it. Every time she did, she thought about Timmy. It was getting harder and harder to keep her emotions in check, and now was not the time to break down.

Doherty breathed heavily into her neck as he banked right and sped up. "You smell good."

She shivered, feeling dirty and contaminated with Doherty's arms tight around her as he drove the Polaris, his breath on her neck. Thank God she had her ski mask on. She wouldn't have been able to hide her distaste otherwise.

She contemplated jumping. They were going about twenty-five miles an hour — in this weather they should have slowed down to fifteen to twenty. But she could easily fall wrong and break her neck. And she might be stunned, giving him more than enough time to turn around and find her.

She had worn a bright red snowsuit for safety. Now it might get her killed.

Could she find a way to throw him from the sled and keep going? He held her so tightly she could barely breathe let alone jump. And he had the gun. If he shot her out here, without help, she'd die.

They skidded and Jo contemplated bumping him off the back of the sled, but with him holding her she didn't think she could get him off without falling with him. "You're going too fast," she repeated.

"Don't tell me what to do," he said, but slowed down a little. She felt the tension in his body. Did he have a plan? Or had he just taken her because she now knew who he was?

They skidded again.

"You have to slow down," she demanded. "You're going to get us both killed."

"If I'm going to die, I would rather die with you."

Oh, God, he had a death wish. He wanted to kill them both.

"Please, Aaron, don't do this. You don't know this area, I don't want to die."

"Why?"

He stopped the snowmobile, but didn't turn it off. The Arctic Cat was getting closer. She glanced at the gauges. Fuel was half gone.

"Tell me, Joanna, why do you want to live?" He turned her face toward him. In the ethereal gray of the blowing snow, his dark blue eyes probed her. He looked so normal, and his eyes were calm. Too calm.

He was in complete control of whatever emotions he had.

He squeezed her jaw when she didn't answer right away.

"Because I love it here. This is the most peaceful place on earth. It's my home."

"You want to live because of a *place*?"

"And my grandfather. My sister. My niece. My friends." *Tyler*. But she didn't say that. Remembering Mindy's words, she suspected if Doherty knew about Tyler he'd kill her now.

"But you don't have anyone," he said.

"What are you saying?"

"Your husband is dead. Your son is dead."

"Don't talk about my son." She would not allow this man to use Timmy's memory in any way.

"What made you go on? Why did you want to live after Lincoln Barnes killed your family?"

She'd often asked herself that exact question in the weeks after the murders. There were nights she fell into such deep despair that it was only by the grace of God that she hadn't killed herself.

But she'd never seriously considered it, had she? No. Ken wouldn't have wanted her to. Both her husband and son loved life so much that to end her own was unthinkable.

Fear crawled up her spine. How did he know about Lincoln Barnes?

"Did you know Linc?" she asked.

"Very well," he said.

The Arctic Cat was getting closer. So close that Jo feared Doherty could hear it.

He said, "I killed Lincoln Barnes. I killed him for you, Joanna. Because he stole your family. I love you, Joanna. I found justice for you."

Nothing he could have said would have surprised her more. She didn't know what to think, but she feared Aaron Doherty knew far more about her than she could even imagine. The realization chilled her deeper than the icy wind.

"You killed Linc? Why?"

"He had the cell next to mine. He's the one who told me about you. He blamed you for keeping Trixie from him. Then I found your books in the prison library. I read them. I knew then that you were the only person in the world who understood me. Remember in *Tomorrow Never Knows*? John Miller was your hero. His mother had left him with his grandparents so she could live a wild life. My mother was just like her. John couldn't find love because he didn't know how. You taught me what love is all about."

"Love is about trust. You shot Wyatt. How

can I trust you?"

"You'll learn."

He tilted his head up. The Arctic Cat was close, very close. "Someone followed us. You stopped because you knew!" He hit her.

"You stopped the —" But he didn't let her finish. She swallowed blood from her cut lip.

He turned off the Polaris and pocketed the key. "Don't move," he said.

He jumped off and walked toward the sound, gun in hand. His boots sank deep in the snow. He figured it out quickly and started walking on the path left by the Polaris which was partly packed and easier to traverse.

Jo couldn't let anyone else be hurt or killed because of her. She got off the sled and, praying the sound of the approaching sled masked her movements, she opened the seat and pulled out a can of bear spray. Doherty didn't know they kept extra cans in each snowmobile.

Silently, she retraced Doherty's steps. He was so focused that he didn't notice her. Only fifteen feet away.

The Arctic Cat was around the bend. *Bend* was figurative. It was really the way the drifts had piled up from the wind. They blocked the sled from view, but she saw snow being tossed up and out.

"Aaron, don't!" she shouted to distract him from the Arctic Cat.

He whirled around, surprise in his eyes. "I told you to stay put!" He took a step toward her and she lifted her arm and deployed the highly concentrated pepper spray that could stop a grizzly attack in seconds.

Jo had never seen the impact of bear spray on a human being. Doherty fell to his knees with a scream of such pain and agony that for a split second, Jo felt guilty.

The Arctic Cat rounded the drift. She waved frantically, hoping the driver would stop.

Doherty buried his face in the snow, lifted his head. His eyes were red and swollen shut behind his mask. He didn't have the gun in his hand. He screamed, *"Joanna!"*

Doherty collapsed again in the snow. Was he dead? No, he couldn't be — bear spray was pepper spray. It was debilitating, but not lethal. Jo watched as Doherty turned his face in the snow. His eyes were closed, his mouth opened and closed as if gasping for breath.

He tried to move but couldn't. Was he groaning or was that the wind? Jo didn't wait to find out. She took the opportunity to get away.

The wind was blowing from the north, so the pepper spray was dissipating to the south. She walked clumsily over a snowdrift, sinking deep, thankful she had on her waterproof mukluk boots that prevented the snow from seeping into her shoes. Still, the cold air was tinged with the spray and she coughed repeatedly as she made her way around where Aaron had collapsed.

The Arctic Cat stopped and the driver sat there. He looked small for Sean Mann. The driver wore a bright blue snowsuit with a fluorescent green strip across the front and back.

Jason.

"Jason? Jason, what are you doing?"

He took off his helmet and ski mask. He looked exactly like a younger version of his father, dark hair a little longer and mussed. He was a handsome boy, and would grow into a fine young man.

"He shot my uncle. I didn't want him to hurt you too."

He'd saved her life, she was certain.

"You are a brave young man. I am so proud of you." She kissed him on the cheek. "Put your helmet back on, we have to go. I don't know how long he'll be incapacitated."

At least twenty minutes. Probably longer. But she couldn't let him catch up with her and Jason. The snow was coming down faster.

She assessed where they were. They could retrace their path and go back to the homestead, about an hour away. Or they could go south and skirt the edge of Upper Red Rock Lake. The problem with that was there were no snowmobile trails on that side of the lake. There were fences and rocks and other obstacles now hidden in the snowdrifts, and with the snowfall getting worse, she couldn't risk being stuck in the middle of nowhere without a radio.

What would Tyler do? Craig Mann would have called him on the radio, told him Wyatt had been shot. And when Tyler learned Jason had gone after her and Doherty, he would follow. That meant he would go first to the homestead and track them from there.

She slid behind Jason and considered driving past Doherty to disable the Polaris. Then she heard Doherty cry out followed by a gunshot. He'd found his gun. There was no way she'd bring Jason any closer to that psychopath.

She retraced their path, moving too fast for her comfort, but she had to get out of Doherty's target range as quickly as possible. They rounded the snowdrift and she slowed to twenty miles an hour.

"Thank you, Jason," she whispered, blinking back freezing tears as she hugged him tightly.

Sixteen

Aaron couldn't breathe. His lungs were on fire. The oxygen that kept him alive was barely enough. His eyes burned. His skin felt like a thousand ants crawled just beneath the surface. The icy snow helped, but he still couldn't move.

He would find her. Find her and wrap his hands around her neck. Shake her. *Why, Joanna?*

She wanted him to die. After all he'd done for her. He'd killed for her. He'd taken vengeance in his hands and done something right for once in his life. Killing Lincoln Barnes made him the hero he knew he could be, the hero he wanted to prove to Joanna he was.

And she had hurt him.

He rose to his knees and crawled two feet before collapsing in a fit of violent coughing.

He would freeze out here, twenty feet from freedom. He couldn't think, he couldn't feel anything but intense pain throughout his body and the piercing wound to his heart.

Joanna had left him.

While he was dying in the snow, she'd driven away with someone. A man. A man like that evil Bruce Lawson who had lied to sweet Rebecca about Aaron, filling her head with vicious untruths.

He didn't know how long he lay in the snow. His right hand gripped his gun, but it was so cold he didn't know if he could move his fingers. For the first time since Joanna had betrayed him, the powerful cold of the snow was more painful than the burn of the pepper spray.

He looked up, the snowmobile seemed so far away. The wind slapped him in the back, the swirling snow taunting him. *Joanna didn't appreciate your sacrifices. Look what you did for her! And she betrayed you.*

Love, Tyler.

The Sheriff of Beaverhead County, Montana.

She wasn't worthy of Aaron's love and affection. She wasn't worthy of anything. She had betrayed him for a cop.

You killed her friend, Wyatt.

He'd interfered. Why couldn't he have just let them go? Why did he have to get involved? Aaron didn't want to kill. All he

275

wanted was Joanna. Was that too much to ask?

Maybe he should just lie down here and wait for night. He would die in the snow, freeze to death. He was nobody, a speck of dust in the universe. Who would miss him?

(You pathetic animal. Get up and find the traitor.)

He crawled two more feet.

She'd used him. Flirted with him. Teased him. Then she turned to a cop for affection.

He didn't deserve that kind of treatment. She should be *thanking* him for all he had done for her. What had the cops ever done? They could have killed Lincoln Barnes for her, but they had a so-called code of ethics. They'd arrested Linc, but he didn't suffer for what he'd done to the Suttons. He'd been in prison before, gotten out, and killed.

Aaron blinked. His eyes still burned, but he could see a little better. He slowly rose, stumbled, and knelt to catch his breath. He coughed, his nose burned, but he breathed easier.

Slowly, he crawled in the icy snow, over the tracks the snowmobile had made. He saw Joanna's footprints on the path, deep impressions in the snow, and he cried out. She'd stood here and wounded him. She might as well have shot him through the stomach with a shotgun.

Still he continued forward, the coughing subsiding, his chest feeling like he'd been run over by a truck but he finally could take a deep breath. He didn't know how long he'd laid prone in the snow, but it took him twenty minutes to reach the Polaris once he started moving. He collapsed onto the seat, found the key in his pocket, and turned the ignition. The air wasn't hot, but it was warmer than the cold surrounding him.

He hoped Joanna knew it was her fault he had to shoot that guy. He hadn't wanted to kill him, but she'd left him with no choice.

Aaron refrained from screaming out loud, but his head pounded with a bright pain. The pain of betrayal, of loving the wrong woman. Should he resign himself to a life of misery?

In the pain, he saw his past. The past he had thought Joanna knew and understood. She'd written about his life. She had loved him at one time. Just like his mother.

He was nine and his mama said she'd be back for his birthday.

He sat in the living room of his mama's friend. Annie. Annie was nice, one of the nicer people his mama left him with. He knew Annie wanted to keep him all the time, but his mama said no. So he moved around. Last time he was with Annie for three whole months, and then his mama picked him up and said he had a new place to live. He was going to his grandparents'. Annie cried when he left, and he wanted to cry too, but he didn't dare.

His mama would call him a crybaby, and then she might never come back for him.

"Don't you look nice, Aaron?" Annie said brightly. But Aaron saw that she was sad.

He wanted to ask the only question he wanted the answer to — when was his mother going to be here? — but he didn't. Because even he didn't want the truth.

Annie would have answered, "Soon."

But that was a lie; both he and Annie knew it. He didn't want Annie to lie so he didn't ask the question.

Soon, to Ginger Doherty, could be a few minutes or a few weeks.

He sat with his hands folded in his lap, as his mama liked. His pants were pressed, his shirt clean, his hair gelled back. He was presentable. He'd even spit-shined his shoes like his grandfather had taught him.

His mama would keep him this time.

Minutes turned into hours. Hours into all night. Annie tried to get him to come to the dinner table and eat. She'd made his favorite — meat loaf, mashed potatoes and gravy —

but Aaron didn't want to spill on his clean shirt or pressed pants. What if mama walked in? She wouldn't hug him, just tell him to change.

She'd done it before. Aaron learned that he had to be perfect for her affection.

But that was okay. He was good at acting perfect.

He sat up all night. He didn't sleep. Annie cried in her bedroom. He'd heard her on the phone leaving messages.

"Ginger, where are you? You promised to be here today! Aaron is waiting."

"Ginger, dammit, pick up the phone!"

"This is the last time, Ginger. I won't watch his heart break again. You are hurting your own child and you're too selfish to see it!"

Aaron ignored Annie after a time. Annie didn't understand Mama. Annie didn't understand that his mama had a perfect life and she needed a perfect kid all the time. That's why she couldn't keep him with her. Little boys made messes.

It was three days later when Ginger Doherty breezed in. "Happy Birthday!" she said.

She gave him a hug, his face in her breasts, smelling of rose and soap and cleanness. "You are Mama's beautiful boy. Nine years old today!"

Annie stood in the doorway, her face tight. "His birthday was on Monday."

Mama gave a dramatic sigh and glared at Annie. "His birthday is today. I should know, I gave birth to him. I have someone I want you to meet. We're going out to dinner to a really fancy restaurant. Go get changed into your best clothes, Aaron. I know you'll be a good boy."

Aaron ran off to change, but he heard Mama say, "Annie, I knew I should never have brought him back to you. We'll leave tonight."

"Please, Ginger, let me keep him. I love him."

"He's not your son. He's mine, and you can't have him."

Mama came down the hall as Aaron was changing. "Pack your things. We're going to visit friends after dinner."

Annie pleaded. "Don't take him, Ginger. You'll only leave him with someone else, someone who doesn't care about him like I do."

"He's not yours to care about," Mama said.

No one cared about him, not then and not now.

"You shouldn't have lied to me, Joanna," Aaron whispered in the wind, his voice raspy and throat sore from the pepper spray. "You promised we would be forever. You promised you'd never leave me."

The heater was warming up, but to get it hotter he'd need to get moving. Aaron wanted to follow Joanna. He could track the snowmobile. Who had found them? Aaron hadn't gotten a good enough look. Must have been one of the other two men, Craig or Sean Mann, who'd come for her.

He'd kill them both. How would Joanna feel about that? How would she like to know she was responsible for everyone dying?

But what if the Sheriff had already reached the homestead? What if he was at the lodge? What if they'd found Doug or where he and Doug had hidden the snowmobiles?

Too many ifs.

He had to find a place to regroup and plan. He looked at the mileage on the Polaris. He'd kept track of how far they came and he was about two miles shy of the refuge center. He had planned to stop there, make sure no one had tracked them, then go into Lakeview, near where the truck had stalled. That way, he could go down South Centennial Road west to the Lima Reservoir and, hopefully, find a car to steal. Take Joanna far from the valley, far from anyone who could influence her.

Aaron would convince Joanna that only he was her hero, her White Knight. And if she tried to leave . . .

She wouldn't. Aaron would not allow it.

Before any of that could happen, he had

to find her again. And if she didn't come willingly? He'd start killing.

Don't make me kill, Joanna. Please don't make me kill anyone.

(You like to kill, Aaron. Admit it.)

He continued on the trail to the refuge, but he didn't stop. Instead, he turned south. He would skirt Upper Red Rock Lake and should be back at the lodge before dark.

Chapman better be waiting for him.

It was one in the afternoon when Tyler arrived at the Kimball homestead, an hour after he and his team had set out from Lakeview, but with the way the wind tossed up the snow and the gray fog hung low over the valley, it could have been dawn or dusk. All sense of time and place seemed to be lost.

Tyler assessed the situation and assured himself that Sean Mann and the four scouts in his charge were safe, then he radioed the lodge. Karl Weber answered immediately.

"Did Craig Mann arrive with Wyatt and Ben?" Tyler asked.

"Yes, about twenty minutes ago," the old man said. "Nash is with Wyatt."

"How is he?" Tyler asked.

"Alive."

"You don't sound encouraged."

"He needs a doctor. Nash is good, but he's no surgeon."

"But he'll be okay until we can take him over the mountain." Tyler spoke as if his words were the truth.

"It needs to be sooner rather than later. Problem is, there's no way to get over Red Rock Pass in this weather. And it's going to get worse tonight. The NWS said by tomorrow morning it will clear some and we should be able to get him out, but there are no guarantees."

Tyler pushed back his concerns for his brother, though it bothered him that he and Wyatt had spent the better part of two years circling around each other rather than reclaiming their family. He vowed to put all that behind him. He prayed he got a chance to talk to Wyatt and apologize for being so stubborn.

"I want to get the kids out of the lodge as soon as possible. Until I know that both escapees are in custody, no one is safe. Did Stan get your cabin guests into the lodge?"

"Tyler, it's Hans Vigo. We've had a situation. The Trotskys are dead."

"Trotskys?"

"The newlyweds. Stan found them. Duncan and I are heading down there now, but Stan gave us a report. The male victim has

283

been dead at least twelve hours. Probably between eleven and one last night. The female victim has been dead for less than three hours. She had been repeatedly raped and beaten, tied to the bedpost with fishing wire which cut her down to the bone. Then she had her throat slit."

"Was it Doherty?"

"Chapman, more likely," Vigo said. "Doherty didn't have the time to rape Mrs. Trotsky. According to Stan, he arrived about five p.m. last night. He had a reservation in the name of John Miller, and claimed his truck got stuck and he walked in. He was convincing. He was seen last night in the late evening, around midnight, and he helped Stan with breakfast in the morning. He then went with Jo to the Trotsky cabin. He was inside, but not for long. He had to know what was happening. My guess is that Chapman was there and Doherty covered for him. He may have even known from the beginning and that's why he went with Jo to deliver breakfast."

Tyler's gut tightened. That psycho had been under Jo's roof since yesterday. Watching her. Following her. Insinuating himself into her routine. Why? Why had he played such a sick game, then waited until now to grab her?

"Why now, Hans? Why did Doherty wait to kidnap Jo when he could have done it last night or this morning without fanfare?"

"He wanted to court her. Win her over. When that didn't work and she learned his real identity, he was forced to take her."

"Any sign of Chapman?"

"No. There were some tracks leading away from the cabin, Stan said, but the wind has messed with them. Duncan and I are going to follow them after we check the Trotsky cabin for any clues to Chapman's whereabouts or plans."

"Is the lodge secure?"

"Peter Nash, Craig Mann, Stan, and Duncan are on the entrances now. Everyone is armed. Karl Weber is manning the radio. We fixed the phone — someone had pulled the wires directly from the box outside of the house. It only took ten minutes to re-hook everything. I've been in contact with the FBI Field Office in Helena and they are on alert, waiting for the ceiling to lift so they can bring in a helicopter full of reinforcements."

"When?" asked Tyler.

"That's the million-dollar question. Not before tomorrow."

Tomorrow didn't help Tyler track or find Jo and Jason.

"Mitch and I are going to track them now. There are clear tracks, but we don't have a lot of time. I'm sending Sean Mann and the boys back with Deputy Grossman. Be on the lookout for them."

"Will do. Be careful."

Tyler hung up. *Be careful.* He'd said the same thing to Jason when he left for the scouting trip three days ago. Not *I love you,* not *Have fun,* but *Be careful.* He'd been worried that Jason would get lost or hurt himself or freeze overnight. He'd never imagined he would take it upon himself to chase a killer in the middle of ten-degree weather with a pending storm.

Tyler stepped out of the cabin. Make that beginning storm. The snow was falling heavier.

"Billy, stay with the boys at all costs. Get them safely to the lodge and stay inside." Out of earshot, he told his deputy about the Trotsky murders. "Be alert."

To Mitch Bianchi, he said, "Ready?"

"Let's go." They got on the snowmobiles and started out.

The wind was beginning to obscure the path Jason had taken, but it was deep enough to follow. Jason must have been following directly in Doherty's path, making it wider and deeper. Whether on purpose or necessity, it was smart.

Ten minutes out, Tyler held up his hand. Mitch pulled alongside him. Tyler pointed to his ear. *Listen.*

Over the idling of their sleds, they heard another snowmobile, this one moving fast. It was hard to tell exactly where the sound was coming from, but it was coming closer.

"Move to the side of the trail," Tyler told Mitch. They pulled over about ten feet, turned off the sleds to get a better sense of location.

"It's coming —" Tyler couldn't even finish his thought. The Arctic Cat snowmobile came quickly into view at the edge of visibility. "Cover me," he said to Mitch. He stepped into the path of the sled and waved his arms.

The sled slowed, then stopped. The rider in the back jumped off, said something to the other. Tyler tensed, fearing a hostage situation.

The second rider disembarked and pulled off his helmet and mask.

Jason.

His son stood there and waved to him. Tyler had never been so happy, so relieved, to see anyone. Jason was grinning ear to ear and said something to the other rider loud enough for Tyler to hear.

"I knew my dad would find us, Jo!"

As Tyler watched, Jason hugged Jo tightly. She took off her mask and kissed him on the cheek, then said, "Go see your dad. He was worried about you."

Tyler met his son halfway. He hugged Jason tightly, eyes burning with unshed tears. He wanted to throttle Jason for doing something so dangerous as going after a killer, and at the same time he was so damn proud of him.

"Don't ever do anything to scare me like that again," Tyler said. "I'm so glad you're safe. I love you, Jason."

"I love you too, Dad." Jason's voice was as rough with emotion as his father's.

"I'm also proud of you," Tyler said. "I was scared to death. That man is a killer."

Jo came up behind them, put her hand on Jason's shoulder and said softly, "He saved my life, Tyler."

Tyler looked at her over Jason's head. There were bruises on her face and dried blood on her lip. Tyler tensed in barely contained anger and asked, "Did Doherty hurt you?"

She shook her head. "I'm okay. I don't know what he had planned. I think he was heading for the refuge center. There's a three-room research facility there, closed for the winter."

Tyler wanted to take Jason and Jo back himself, but now that they were safe, capturing Aaron Doherty became his new number one priority.

"Can you take Jason back to the lodge?"

"Yes, but —"

Tyler interrupted Jo. "I have to go after him."

"The storm's coming in, Tyler. It's at least two hours to the refuge center. What if I'm wrong? What if he has other plans?"

Mitch joined them on the path. The snow had blanketed his shoulders during the short time he'd stood still. "She's right, Tyler. We can't fight the elements." Mitch introduced himself to Jason and Jo.

Tyler wanted Doherty for putting the woman he loved in danger. For shooting his brother. For jeopardizing his son's life.

"How did you get away?" he asked.

Jo hesitated.

"Tell me the truth."

"I'd heard the Arctic Cat — it has a distinct sound. And I thought it was Sean Mann since he'd driven it from the lodge. Then Doherty heard it and stopped. He had a gun and I was terrified he would shoot the rider. I didn't really have a plan. I got the bear spray out of the seat and sprayed him while he was distracted. I didn't know the other rider was Jason until Doherty was down. We didn't wait to find out what condition he was in. We took off instead."

"Good," Tyler said, his voice rough and thick. He hugged Jason again, then reached out for Jo. "You're right, we need to get back to the lodge." He didn't want to say anything about the Trotskys around Jason.

As if in agreement, the wind whipped up powder around them, the falling snow swirling, making it impossible to see more than a few feet ahead.

"How's Wyatt?" Jo asked.

"He's okay, but he needs a doctor. Sam Nash came in with us and is tending to him, but he needs surgery."

"Uncle Wyatt is going to be fine, though, right?" Jason asked.

"Of course," Tyler said with more confidence than he felt. "Jason, want to ride with me?"

"Do you mind, Jo?" Jason asked.

"You go with your dad."

Tyler leaned over and kissed Jo lightly on the lips, then whispered in her ear, "Thank you for saving my son."

Doug Chapman smiled as his hands busied themselves in the fading light.

He hated the snow. He hated the cold. He hated Montana. He couldn't believe he'd let that obsessive brat convince him to come up to *meet his girl*.

What a crock of shit.

He'd watched from the tree line as a couple cops — by the way they moved and acted he figured they were cops — raided the cabin where the dead people were. They had no idea how close he was. Doug hated the snow, but it had its advantages, especially when it was swirling around in the wind like camouflage.

As soon as they'd gone back to the lodge, Doug returned to the cabin he and Aaron had found when they first arrived in this frigid wasteland. He'd spent half the day mapping out the area using the map Aaron had brought him before he left to go with his bitch to get the damn Boy Scouts.

"See how we can get out of here," Aaron had said. "As soon as I get Joanna, we'll leave. Meet me back at the cabin where we hid the snowmobiles." That cabin was circled on the map.

Doug could give a flying fuck about the bitch, unless Aaron shared her. She had a fine ass, one he'd be willing to share but he sensed Aaron wouldn't be so generous. He had it bad for the bitch, so bad he was risking his neck for her, and what did that say about him? That he was led around by his prick, no doubt.

Doug would have none of that. He'd follow the plan because it was actually kind of smart, he could see that, but he'd kill the bitch if she interfered. No woman was going to hold him back. He was going to get out of this trap Aaron had walked him into.

The cops would be all over these cabins first thing in the morning. But wouldn't they get a surprise?

He smiled again as he drained the last of the Jack Daniel's. Doherty's plan was smart, and it would work. But no way was Chapman going to put his neck on the line again. This was Aaron's game, and he'd go along to get the fuck out of Dodge, but if Aaron wasn't back by morning, he was shit out of luck. Doug wasn't about to wait for him.

SEVENTEEN

Tyler made sure all the people at the lodge were safe — there were eighteen adults and seven kids. The kids were in the safest part of the house — Karl Weber's rooms on the downstairs floor. There was no outside entrance except for a double door leading to the deck, which Deputy Al Duncan guarded. Tyler had put most everyone not connected to law enforcement in those rooms. The Johnstons had a room on the second floor and the college kids took another upstairs room.

And Jo. She had gone upstairs to shower and change. He'd wanted to follow her up. But first he had things to do.

The storm tossed snow all around the lodge. Looking out the tall windows from the great room, Tyler couldn't see anything beyond the edge of the deck, and even that was fuzzy. The storm both protected them from predators — Chapman and Doherty would have a hard time getting to the lodge even if they were holed up in one of the outlying cabins — and made them blind to a threat.

Tyler made sure every entrance was covered, then went into the den where Wyatt was on a pullout bed. Nash sat in a chair in the corner. "Good," Nash said. "You keep him from getting up while I get some more coffee."

Nash left and Tyler pulled the chair closer to where his brother lay. Wyatt's chest was bare and Nash had bandaged the wound. Blood had seeped through, but it wasn't spreading. The room was warm: A space heater was in the corner, set on high.

Wyatt tried to sit up. "Don't," Tyler said, "or I'll have to find a way to restrain you."

"I'll be fine."

"You have a bullet in you."

"Nash said Jo and Jason are safe."

"Yes." Thank God. Tyler didn't know what he would do if he lost those he loved the most. He finally had a small sense of what Jo had suffered these four years since her loved ones were killed. He began to understand her fear of opening her heart again. Now that he did, he could help her accept and return his love.

"Stupid kid," Wyatt said with affection. "What was he thinking?"

"He wasn't. He acted first. He's a Mc-Bride." Tyler grinned and told Wyatt how Jason had found Jo and how Jo incapacitated Doherty. He feared for her all over again and took a deep breath. She was safe.

"Where is he?"

"We don't know. Jo thought he was heading to the refuge center, but we couldn't get out there before the storm hit hard. We barely made it back as it was."

"Maybe he'll freeze to death."

"I sure hope so," Tyler said, "but we can't assume anything. We made a faulty assumption that because Doherty only took his own mug shot that Chapman wasn't a threat.

Not true. We have two killers. They'll be more dangerous together. I'm hoping that they had a falling-out, but we can't count on it."

"Thank God Jo and Jason are safe."

"You can say that again," Tyler concurred. "I haven't been really fair to you, Wyatt."

"Don't get all emotional on me."

Tyler ignored the comment. He had come to Wyatt to say his piece, and he was going to say it. "I didn't know what to expect when I moved here. I wanted my big brother back. But we've both changed. I said a lot of things in the past that I regret."

"Don't. You were right, most of the time."

"I was stubborn and let a feud I didn't understand come between us."

"Between me and Dad."

Tyler nodded. "I never understood it, and at the funeral all I wanted was to make peace, to have my brother back, but you —" He stopped. Tyler had promised not to cast judgment on Wyatt's past actions. Isn't that why he was here? To hold out the olive branch?

"I made a scene," Wyatt said. "I'm sorry about that. I wasn't at a really good place in my life eight years ago. Hell, I was practically living in the Cattle Stop." The Cattle Stop was the larger of two Dillon bars.

"Before Dad died, I tried to leave Montana. I went to New York City."

"That's a big change." Tyler couldn't picture himself or his brother in New York City.

"My old girlfriend had moved there and I was still hung up on her. She thought I was a simple country boy, and she wanted more. I tried to want more, too. But it didn't work and I came back feeling like a failure. Then Dad died and reminded me that he'd always told me I'd never do anything with my life, that I was a disgrace to the McBride name. Why? Because I hated the military and got out as soon as possible? I didn't want to be a cop and follow in his footsteps? And — he hurt my mom. I couldn't forgive him for that. And I guess I started to blame you."

"Why did you tell me about the job opening here?"

Wyatt paused, then said, "I missed having a brother. And I knew you weren't to blame for Richard McBride's warped version of fatherhood. It's amazing that you turned into such a great dad when you had a pathetic role model."

"You've been a terrific uncle to Jason," Tyler said. He felt everything inside shift and settle, and the old hurts and misunderstandings washed away.

"Getting him stranded in the middle of the worst storm this winter? Yeah, sure."

"I'm serious, Wyatt. What he's learned from you since we moved here — last year he didn't even know how to ride a snowmobile, and now he can track one? He relied on his instincts, and I have you to thank for that."

"Well, okay, I'll take some of the credit." Wyatt grinned, though Tyler saw the pain in his eyes.

"Do you want me to get Nash?"

"No, no, I'm fine. I'm going to get one more thing off my chest since we're having this man-to-man chatfest. I'm not sorry for what I said about Sharon."

"Why even bring it up?"

"Because I think you're still beating yourself up over a failed marriage that wasn't your fault."

Tyler didn't want to talk to his brother, or anyone, about his failed marriage. It was a black spot on his heart, and he was embarrassed that he'd been manipulated for so long.

"I don't —"

Wyatt interrupted. "Tyler, you're one of the good guys. You've done everything right by Jason, even after his mother took him from you."

"I let her," Tyler said. And he'd regretted it every day.

"Because you didn't want to put a little kid through a major custody battle. Sharon's family had money. They would have taken everything you had."

"It was never about the money," Tyler said.

"Sharon betrayed you and took your son. You did the right thing, and you've been beating yourself up ever since. I don't regret telling you that the only decent thing Sharon ever did was come back and make it easier on Jason when she was dying."

Tyler tried to tamp down the anger. Why had Wyatt brought this all up again? So he told him exactly why he'd been furious that day after Sharon's funeral.

"Jason overheard you, Wyatt. I agree with you. Sharon was selfish. But she loved Jason, and she did end up doing the right thing, and I don't want Jason's memory of his mother tainted."

Wyatt paled. "Shit, Tyler, I didn't know. I'm sorry."

Tyler released a pent-up breath and rubbed his face with his hands. He was exhausted. "It's water under the bridge, Wyatt. From today on, we're brothers again in every sense of the word."

"Then I have one more confession."

"I don't know if I can handle anything else today, bro."

"I'll make it short and sweet. You've always been a rock, Tyler. You always had a plan, a vision for your life that I never had for mine. I was envious for a long time. Dad loved you more — no, don't deny it, it was true. I blame him, but I no longer blame you, and that's why I called you when Sheriff Talbot had the heart attack. When Talbot called me — he knew I had a brother who was a cop — and told me he was retiring, I thought of you."

"I'm glad you did. I'm glad I moved up here. And I'm particularly pleased that Jason has such a great role model in his uncle."

Wyatt reached up and Tyler grabbed his hand, held it. "We're going to get you to a surgeon in Island Park tomorrow first thing."

"I know Nash is worried about the bullet, but I'm going to be just fine."

Tyler was worried, too. "Well, do what he says and don't move, okay?"

"Is that an order?"

"Damn straight. You know what an authoritarian I am."

"I have an order for you, brother."

Tyler grinned. "I don't think you're in

much of a position to order me around."

"Hey, you give me a couple weeks to get my strength back and we'll go one-on-one on the basketball court."

"You're on. Your request?"

"Give Jo another chance."

"I'd always thought you disapproved of our relationship." Tyler put his elbows on his knees, his hands dangling in front of him. "You were friends with her husband."

"Ken Sutton was a great guy. He treated Jo really well, loved her more than anything. They were good together. And if he hadn't been murdered in cold blood, they'd have lived until a ripe old age, celebrated their Golden Anniversary and all that. But that wasn't in the cards, and Jo still deserves to be happy."

"I wonder if she knows that," Tyler said.

"It's true I didn't like the idea of you dating Jo at the beginning."

"I could tell. I thought you had a thing for her."

Wyatt laughed briefly, then winced as his shoulder shook. "I love her like a sister. But Jo had so much tragedy in such a short time, I didn't want her to get hurt."

"I'm not a love 'em and leave 'em kind of guy."

"I realized that soon enough, and I also

noticed how much happier Jo was after you came 'round. So I changed my mind. All I'm saying is, just because she got scared and ran out, don't let her keep running."

Tyler grinned. "I'm way ahead of you, Wyatt."

"Then why the hell did you let me talk like some chick?"

Tyler laughed and Nash came back into the room. "How's our patient?"

"Same," Tyler said, "but it hurts when he laughs."

Dressed in jeans and a sweater, her hair still damp from her hot shower, Jo sat at her desk and took a picture out of a drawer she rarely opened. Ken and Timmy. It had been taken only a few weeks before they were murdered, at Lake Tahoe. They'd gone skiing, bringing Leah with them. Trixie hadn't wanted to come, which had been fine with Jo — her sister needed time to figure out what she wanted to do with herself. As far as Jo was concerned, Trix and Leah could live with them indefinitely.

Jo stared at Ken, his sun-bleached blond hair partly hanging across his tan face. She touched his hair, as if brushing it off his face. "Kenny, I love you. I'll always love you. But I'm happy with Tyler. I think you'd like him." They were different in so many ways. Ken was talkative, outgoing, and full of nervous energy. Tyler was quiet, steadfast, and solid, his energy fully contained, rippling just beneath the surface. But in the ways that mattered — loyalty, strength, honesty — they were similar. They had the same values that Jo shared, about home and the importance of family.

She touched Timmy's picture and choked back a sob. The tears didn't come. "I miss you Tim. I miss you so much."

She'd feared that somehow, if she loved Tyler and married him, that Jason would replace Tim. But no one would ever replace Tim. No child could. He had been her son, she loved him, and she would always remember the nine years they had together. Holding him as an infant. Watching him take his first step, ride his first two-wheel bike, glide down the ski slopes behind his father.

No one could take those memories from her, and for the first time in years she let them wash over her, remembering the joy and not the tragedy.

Today she realized that loving another child — another boy — wouldn't diminish the memories of her son.

A knock on the door startled her. She

glanced at the clock. It was after seven. She could hardly believe that a mere twelve hours ago she'd thought John Miller was just a quirky guest as they were getting ready to meet Wyatt and the scouts. She'd had enough shocks for one day, but it wouldn't be over until Doherty and Chapman were behind bars.

She opened the door. Tyler stood there, his face drawn, his eyes weary. It had been a longer couple days for him, with Jason trapped in the blizzard and knowing the killers were in the area.

"Come in," she said, closing the door behind him.

"How are you doing?"

"Okay. The shower helped."

"Good."

Tyler grabbed her by the arms and kissed her, one arm wrapping around her waist, the other finding her hair and twisting it in his fist.

No tentative kiss. This was a kiss of possession, of desperate need.

Jo opened her mouth and Tyler pulled her body even closer to him. She had no place for her hands except around his neck, and he almost pulled her off the floor to bring her closer.

The kiss slowed down, moved to her neck,

her ear, her head, back to her lips. Slower, almost sweet.

"I would have killed him if he had hurt you," he whispered, pulling her face into his shoulder and holding her. "I couldn't think straight when I found out Doherty had taken off with you. And then Jason followed. What on earth was he thinking?"

"He'd just watched his uncle get shot. I don't think the poor kid was thinking much."

Jo touched Tyler's cheek, made him look at her. She saw love and so much more. She saw a future she could have. If she could believe that true love could happen twice in a lifetime.

"Talk to him, Tyler. He needs to know you're proud of him."

"He's eating dinner with the boys. I'll talk to him tonight." Tyler looked deep into her eyes. "Jo, I need to know that you're not going to run away again."

She turned from him, but he didn't let her go. How could she explain the complexity of her feelings, the intensity of her emotions, when she barely understood them herself?

"Look at me, Jo."

She turned back to him and their eyes locked. His powerful look said, *I won't let you run away, I love you.*

She drew in her breath as he kissed her. A light, feather of a kiss.

"I love you, Jo. I loved you from that first day at Nash's when I watched you organize the search-and-rescue team. I loved you when you both nurtured and lectured Kyle Worthington. I loved you when you came to me Labor Day and gave me your beautiful body. I felt like I'd won a lottery I didn't know I'd entered. And I loved you even after you ran away from my proposal."

He offered a wan smile. "Nothing has changed the way I feel. I can't turn off my love. I will wait for you as long as it takes for you to make peace with Ken. Just as long as I know you're not going to keep running from me. That you'll let me stay in your life, that you'll let me help in any way, no matter how small or how large."

"I —" She couldn't say it. She couldn't say anything. Here was a man who was giving her a second chance at love. She glanced at the picture of Ken and Tim on the desk. "I — want to try, Tyler. I'm scared."

Every muscle in his body relaxed. Had he been as nervous as she?

"I don't want to forget them," she whispered.

"Look at me." She did. "I can't compete

305

with your dead husband, Jo."

"It's not a competition."

"You've made it into one. I can see it in your eyes, a constant comparison. You know you do it. Sometimes I think you force yourself to think of him whenever we get close."

"It's not like that," she whispered. But Tyler was right. She did try to remember Ken more after she'd spent time with Tyler. That wasn't fair to Tyler, or to Ken's memory.

"It isn't?" He stepped toward her.

"You don't understand."

"Try me."

What could she say? She didn't even understand it herself. Ken had been gone for four years. "You're the first man who has made me want to forget I ever loved someone else."

Tyler touched her face, his voice softening. "I don't want you to forget Ken. I want you to stop putting him up as a shield whenever I get close. I'm done with that, Jo. I've never had an affair with a married woman, and I'm not going to start now."

He kissed her again, taking her breath away, then he let her go, his mouth inches from hers as he said, "You seem to think that true love only happens once in a lifetime. Unless you get over that idea, we haven't got a chance. You have to accept the fact that you're a single woman and not run away like a cheating spouse."

She nodded, chin quivering. "I'll try."

"That's all I ask. As long as I know you are trying to make us work, I will wait for you as long as it takes."

"I don't deserve you." She wrapped her arms around him, rested her face against his chest. She felt safe, warm, *loved* here in Tyler's arms. She belonged here. With Tyler.

"Nonsense." He stroked her hair, kissed her head, and held her. "Why don't you come downstairs and be where I can keep an eye on you?"

"I'll be down in a bit."

He stepped back and tilted her chin up. "Don't be long." He kissed her. "Will you be okay alone if I go down and talk to Jason?"

She needed the time to think. "I'm fine. Promise."

He kissed her again and left.

Jo sat back at her desk and looked at the picture of Tim and Ken. "I love him," she told the photograph. "I hope you understand."

Now if only she could gather enough courage to admit it to Tyler. Because once she did, there was no going back.

Aaron sat very close to the fire in the cabin. He didn't think he'd feel warm again.

Doug was pacing, nervous and angry.

"I can't believe it! You fucking fool. You got me to come with you, only to get trapped in the middle of a blizzard with cops all over the place."

"They're all at the lodge. No one is out tonight. If we stick to the plan, everything will be fine."

"Plan? You fucking idiot. Why'd I let you talk me into staying? I could have gotten out of here this afternoon before the snow started shitting on me out there. I had time, but no, you said you had a plan and I thought, okay, we'll do it your way, but you fucked up!"

"It wasn't my fault."

"Right. The bitch had bear spray on her." Doug barked out a laugh.

"Don't call her a bitch," Aaron said, his voice low. He didn't like Doug's reaction to the change in plans.

"She was supposed to be our hostage, our ticket out of this dead end. Instead, we're trapped and the cops are going to be all over this place at the crack of dawn."

"I have a plan for that."

"No. Not another stupid plan!"

"Listen to me."

"I'm done listening!"

Aaron clenched his jaw. He guzzled the water bottle he'd found in the pantry. He hadn't realized how dehydrated he'd gotten out there in the snow. It had taken him hours longer than he'd thought to get from the refuge center back to the cabin. He'd almost backtracked a couple times, and his fuel got dangerously low. Still, he kept going, following the lake and then the compass. And he'd made it.

After what he'd endured today, he didn't need Doug Chapman's bullshit. He had more important things to worry about, namely how to convince Joanna that he loved her, that he'd killed Lincoln Barnes because he loved her. If only they'd had more time so he could have explained. Then she'd realize the depth of his feelings.

She had loved him once. All those books she wrote for him. The way she looked at him when they'd first met. She'd wrapped her arms around him, took him in, gave him food and shelter. They'd bonded over tea. She loved him, she'd just been surprised when she found out who he was, that was all. She would love him again when he had a chance to talk to her.

"Doug," he said quietly.

"What?" Doug snapped.

"Have you ever made a bomb?"

"Bomb?" His eyes lit up. "No, but I can."

"How?"

Doug looked around the cabin, diverted from his rant. "There's not a lot I can use here, but there's propane for the stove. I think I can fix something, but I don't know how stable it'll be and how the cold will affect it."

"I don't need to move the bomb. I want to blow up this cabin."

"Why?"

"A diversion."

It was obvious from his expression that Doug didn't understand. "I guess, but where will we go? There's a fucking blizzard out there. We'll freeze our asses off before we get to the lodge."

"It's for tomorrow. What I need is something that has a time delay."

Doug frowned, his brows furrowed, thinking. "So we're not going to be stuck here?"

Aaron shook his head. "It depends on the weather in the morning, but if the visibility is good enough for the cops to come here, then it's good enough for us to get to the lodge."

"Where there are more cops."

310

"We don't know how many there are. They can only come in on snowmobiles. I think most of them will be out looking for us."

"And if we do something stupid, they'll find us."

Aaron wanted to shoot Doug and be done with him. Instead, he took a deep breath, drank more water, and said, "I'd like to find a way to blow up this cabin by setting a bomb of sorts that will explode when the door opens. That'll serve two purposes. It'll let us know when the cops arrive here — the farthest spot from the lodge — without us being anywhere nearby. Instead, we'll be hiding in that spot you found today."

"Near the lodge."

"Exactly. Then we go in, knowing there'll be minimal coverage. We grab Joanna and leave."

"And go where?"

"There's a fire tower in Lakeview."

"Fire tower?"

"Yeah. It's one of those tall forest ranger buildings, where they watch for fires. The one in Lakeview is closed, hasn't been used in years, but it's still maintained by the Forest Service. We'll break in and be able to see anyone approach for miles off."

"If the snow stops."

"Then we'll radio the Sheriff and tell him we want a helicopter to take us out of the valley."

"That'll never work. The cops don't just let you fly off in one of their choppers."

"They will if it saves Joanna's life."

Aaron had no intention of killing Joanna, of course. She would be coming with them. But the police didn't know that.

"It won't work."

"It might."

"What about the truck? It's still in Lakeview."

"Buried in snow. Battery probably frozen."

"We could jump-start it off one of the snowmobiles."

"You think?"

"Oh, yeah. I'm good with cars. I can get that truck running again. We just need to get there."

"That might work even better. You get the truck running, I radio the Sheriff and tell him he has three hours to get us a chopper. But we don't wait that long, we just get the hell out of here."

"He thinks he has time, but he has none."

"Exactly."

"I want a hostage, too."

"You can have her sister. Trixie Weber is your type."

"Hell, any woman with a decent pair of tits is my type."

Aaron bit back a retort. He hated Doug's vulgarity, but now wasn't the time to piss him off. "So, do you have an idea about a bomb?"

"Well, there's nothing here to create an explosion when the door opens, but I might have an idea that'll work if we can time it just right. All we need is a couple candles." Doug opened a drawer and pulled out two thick white candles. "Just like these."

Doug seemed pleased with his plan, and Aaron trusted him on things like this.

Aaron leaned back and closed his eyes, letting the warmth of the fire lull him into a half sleep.

Joanna.

Joanna Sutton had screwed with the wrong man, and if she thought she could get away with it, she had another thing coming.

It's not her fault. It's that man. That Love, Tyler.

Tyler McBride, Sheriff of Beaverhead County. The man who had faxed the mug shots in the first place. Joanna had spoken to him on the phone the other night, quietly, intimately.

313

She doesn't love Tyler. She loves you, Aaron.

No she doesn't. She hurt him. She hit him with bear spray, left him to die in subzero temperatures.

How could she do that to him? She tried to kill him.

No she didn't. She could have taken your gun while you were laying in the snow. She could have shot you. But she left you alone, with the gun and the snowmobile. She didn't want anyone to know that she loves you.

As if it had really happened, he vividly remembered the way Joanna looked at him, the way she touched him, her quiet words of support and encouragement throughout the day. The knowing smiles, the flirtatious glances.

Their kiss the night before. After tea. She kissed him, he could picture the scene clearly, feel her lips on his. She wouldn't have kissed him if she didn't love him.

What he couldn't remember, he made up. He vividly smelled her clean, fresh, all-female scent. *Soft.* Her smooth skin. The taste of herbal tea on her lips. The way her delicate hand caressed his face, his chest, his cock.

"I love you, Aaron. We'll be together soon."

We'll be together soon.

I'm coming for you, Joanna. We'll leave this place and make our own family together. I'll get rid of Doug as soon as I can.

The first book he'd read of hers was *All You Need Is Love* and he knew that Joanna Sutton could read his heart.

The hero had been raised by relatives who didn't want him. First his grandmother, who died; then his aunt who despised him; then his older half brother, a drunk who blamed the hero for everything bad that had ever happened to him.

By the end of the book, the hero had found someone who loved him for who he was, and he learned that his mother had left him to protect him from a father who wanted him dead.

Which explained a lot about Ginger Doherty, Aaron surmised.

He'd put himself in that role. And his mother was a noble woman. She had done what she had to do to protect the son she loved more than anything.

(*She didn't love you.*)

Aaron shook his head, squeezing the voice from his mind.

(*That's why you had to kill her.*)

No. He hadn't. He loved his mother. She made sacrifices for him, huge sacrifices. She loved him.

And he loved Joanna. He wanted to give her a second chance. But he realized he couldn't do it with all those people around. She wouldn't understand. She was scared because someone had scared her. Someone had told lies about him. Who did she think he was? What he needed was time with her. To show her how he could care for her, how much he needed her.

And she loved him for who he was, nothing more, nothing less. She would thank him for avenging her husband's murder, her son's death. She would hold him, pull him to her breast, tell him she loved him, that she would never let him go. That he meant more to her than anything or anyone. That he was the center of her universe.

They would run away, far from all these people who thought that he was something he wasn't.

It's all just a misunderstanding.

Joanna loved him. She did.

EIGHTEEN

Jason wanted to check on Wyatt that evening, so Tyler brought him to the den for a visit. Wyatt was sound asleep.

"Is he going to be okay?" Jason asked, his face full of concern. Too much worry for a twelve-year-old.

Tyler closed the door and took Jason down the wide foyer to a bench in the corner. They sat side by side. Tyler said, "Sam Nash and Peter are going to take Wyatt to Island Park tomorrow by snowmobile."

"It *is* serious."

"I'm not going to lie to you, Jason. Wyatt is stable, but he needs medical attention. He may be fine, but we don't know and right now Nash is concerned about his blood pressure and the fact that the bullet is still in his body. Bullets can do funny things, depending on where they are lodged. He needs X-rays to make sure the bullet didn't do additional damage. And there're other things to worry about, so moving him is the smartest thing to do."

Jason nodded.

"I'm going to do everything I can to make sure Wyatt lives. He's my brother. I love him."

"You never talked about him before."

"Before what?"

"Before we moved here."

"We didn't talk much ourselves. You know we had different mothers. Wyatt's mother didn't like Grandpa anymore, and well, let's just say Wyatt and I grew up and grew apart.

But he's my brother and I love him, and I'm glad we came here to Montana so you could get to know him." Tyler took a deep breath. He remembered with clarity his fear when he heard Jason had gone after Aaron Doherty. "You've really grown up since we came here. I know you didn't want to move in the first place."

"I didn't know what to expect." Jason looked down at his clasped hands.

Tyler put his son's hands in his own. "Jason, I am so proud of you."

"You're not mad?" Jason looked at him.

"I was scared to death that something would happen to you, but I can't be angry with you. Not when you acted on instinct. If it weren't for you, Jo could have been seriously hurt by Aaron Doherty. The man is extremely dangerous." Tyler took a deep breath. "I'd prefer if you didn't put yourself in harm's way again, but I know that'll be wishful thinking. You're a lot like your uncle."

"I'm like Uncle Wyatt?" Jason sounded pleased.

Tyler smiled. "I'm the one with the dangerous job but Wyatt was always the risk taker. Skateboarding, mountain climbing, river rafting. He'd be the first to take a dare, and he'd usually win, even if he broke a bone or two in the process. I admire that about him. I've always been more cautious."

"Uncle Wyatt said he likes that you think things through, says you're a smart guy."

"He said that? When?"

"We just talk sometimes. Is Jo going to marry you?"

"How — I mean, I didn't —"

"Uncle Wyatt told me you proposed to her."

Wyatt had a big mouth.

"I should have talked to you first, I suppose."

"I like her."

"So do I."

"You didn't love Mom."

"That's not true."

Jason didn't say anything and Tyler wondered what he was thinking. When the silence went on too long, Tyler said, "Would it be okay with you if I married Jo?"

Jason nodded. "When?"

"I don't know. She hasn't agreed."

"Why?"

"Because she misses her husband and son."

"I miss Mom sometimes."

"I know you do. And that's okay."

They sat there for a long time, but this time the silence was comfortable. Tyler put an arm around his son, eyes hot with pride.

Jason was growing into a fine young man.

Jo couldn't write or sleep and she realized she hadn't eaten dinner. It was nearly midnight when she slipped on her sheepskin house boots and went downstairs. Deputy Billy Grossman and her grandfather were sitting in the entry, Buckley at Grandpa's feet. All three lifted their heads to watch her come down the stairs.

"Is everything okay?" Grandpa asked.

"Yes. I thought I'd make some tea. Can I get you anything?"

"We're good."

She scratched Buckley on the head and looked out the window. The floodlights were on, but only a swirling sheet of white could be seen. This blizzard was worse than last night's. But she felt surprisingly safe — there was no way Aaron Doherty could get to her or anyone else tonight.

She felt a pang of guilt wishing him dead. Freezing to death was an awful way to go. But he had shot Wyatt and held a gun on a young boy.

He had killed Lincoln Barnes.

For her. She shivered, not from cold.

He'd also known that Doug Chapman had killed the Trotskys. Doherty had let him.

He didn't do anything to save Vicky. Tyler had explained the time line to her, that Doherty couldn't have killed them, but he had to have known. He'd gone into their cabin. Brought breakfast. Told Jo everything was fine.

She kissed her grandfather on the cheek and tried to put the disturbing thoughts aside. "How are you?"

"I should ask you the same thing."

"I'm so sorry about this."

"Sorry? It's not your fault."

It wasn't, she knew that, but it was because of her that Aaron Doherty had come here in the first place. Irrational to blame herself, but there it was.

"I know, but . . ." She sighed and put her head on his shoulder. "I love you, Grandpa."

"I love you, kiddo."

"Do you know where Tyler is?"

"I think he's in the kitchen with the FBI agents."

She kissed her grandfather on his thin cheek, leathery from spending so much of his life in the rugged outdoors. "Are you sure I can't get you anything? Some more coffee? Maybe some food?" she asked both her grandfather and Billy.

"We have a thermos, but thanks," Grandpa said.

"Just let me know if you need anything. Or if you want to get up and stretch, I can stand watch."

"You need to sleep."

"I don't know if I can," she admitted.

She walked through the darkened great room. If they had lit it up, the windows would have turned the room into a fishbowl. A fire roared in the enclosed fireplace, casting shadows on the walls. Any other night the fire would be comforting and romantic; tonight the flames reminded her of the flames of Hell. Sean and Craig Mann sat in the far corner watching the back doors. Everyone was on alert. The tension was palpable.

The kitchen was empty when she got there, but she heard Tyler's voice, low, in the office. Not wanting to interrupt his conversation Jo made tea. She put a kettle on to boil, then looked at the file folders and papers on the table.

Some were notes that one of the FBI agents wrote on a yellow legal pad.

Doherty exhibits signs of obsessive-compulsive dissociative disorder. See criminal history. Erotomania with severe mood swings. Ginger Doherty was a single mother, Doherty never knew his father (Joe Dawson — Peterson checking on him and grandparents.)

Mother left him with friends and relatives most of his life. (Annie Erickson, testimony — review.) Ms. Doherty worked military communications for ten years. She took assignments that would take her out of state or country. Never owned property or rented in her own name. Lived off others. See court transcripts, spec. testimony of Annie Erickson during penalty phase of State of California v. Aaron Christopher Doherty.

Mother's last known whereabouts King Cruise Lines, San Diego, CA. Disappeared 1986.

Did Aaron Doherty kill his mother? Did he kill his great-aunt? (Peterson getting records — Dorothy Miles, Glendale, California.)

Jo flipped through papers looking for the testimony and instead found something far more disturbing.

Joanna.

The fax was of a letter in small, perfect handwriting, crammed tight on the page. She read on, hands shaking.

I discovered your books last month and have read almost all of them. I am searching for the rest, and in the meantime will reread each and every one. You have a gift, and insight, that amazes me. It's like you know me, know what I'm thinking and feeling. You understand me like no one else has ever tried to. For that alone, I am eternally grateful.

Like the hero in *All You Need is Love,* I was raised by a single mother who protected me by sending me to live with relatives all over the country. It wasn't until I read your book that I understood that she did it for love, not for selfish reasons. I loved her, but didn't understand, not until now.

You must have an eye on the souls of all us tortured heroes, those of us who have persevered through trauma and heartbreak.

My wife was murdered in cold blood. I miss her so much. When I read your book *Don't Pass Me By* I realized that we share so much of the same pain. We were meant to be together, Joanna. You don't know me personally, but you know my heart, you know how much I love you, how I will forever protect you . . .

There was nearly a ream of paper, pages copied from a book and, judging by the header, faxed to the lodge that evening from the Federal Bureau of Investigation in San Francisco.

The pages looked very familiar. She picked up the top sheet and realized this was *her* book that had been copied. In the margins of every page were words so tiny she had to squint to read them. It was a letter of sorts, written to her, in the margins of her own book.

Dearest Joanna:

I know who killed your husband and son. I will avenge you. I am your hero and someday we will meet and you will know the truth. . . .

A moan escaped her throat. Seeing the words in his tight handwriting was worse than hearing him tell her. He'd been obsessed with her for years, but she'd never known. She might have quietly lived her life here in the Centennial Valley never knowing that some psychotic killer had *avenged* her. She hadn't asked for it, dammit! What had she done to attract the attention of this lunatic?

"I think your water is done."

Jo jumped up, knocking papers onto the floor. Agent Hans Vigo walked over to the stove and turned off the teakettle. She hadn't noticed the loud shrill whistle until he'd removed it.

"I'm sorry," she mumbled. "I —"

"You shouldn't be reading this. Some of it is disturbing."

She picked up the copies from her book off the floor. "How long has he been obsessed with me?" she asked.

"Two years."

"Why?" Her voice was a whisper.

Hans poured the hot water into a teapot and put in a couple bags that Jo had taken out when she started the water. He brought the pot to the table with two mugs, put them down, and took the papers from her clenched fists. "It has nothing to do with you."

"My books . . ."

"He would have obsessed on someone else if not you. You understand that, right? If not you, it would have been another woman. Aaron Doherty has what we shrinks call 'obsessive-compulsive dissociative disorder.' I'd even go so far as to diagnose him as schizophrenic or an erotomaniac, but some would argue against that."

"So he's crazy?"

"Crazy is such a misused and misunderstood term. Any human behavior we don't understand we label as 'crazy.' Some people say it's crazy to play the lottery because the odds are stacked dramatically against you. Some people say it's crazy to want to have kids in this violent world. Others say it's crazy *not* to want them. Crazy is used to define any human behavior we disagree with.

"But clinically, 'crazy' means 'insane,' and I know I'm in the minority on this, but I don't think most serial predators are insane."

"So if Doherty's sane, what then?"

"I don't think we can know exactly, at least I can't without talking to him, but from this" — he waved his hands at the stacks of papers — "I can predict his behavior. At least in such a way to hopefully stop him before he hurts anyone else."

Jo didn't want to ask, but she couldn't help herself. "So what is he going to do?"

"He's going to try to convince you that he's a good person."

"Me?" She poured tea for both herself and Agent Vigo.

"You're the object of his fantasy. He wants you to understand and approve of his actions, particularly his killing Lincoln Barnes. In his mind, he killed for you. That bonded you to him — you 'owe him one,' for lack of a better phrase. And because he risked his life, because he killed, he expects you to love him. It's circular reasoning — his fantasy is that you are already in love with him, but at the same time he killed Barnes to make you love him. He wants your understanding, approval, and affection."

She shook her head. "Maybe he did, but he must hate me now. I shot him with pepper spray, then ran away."

Hans sipped his tea. "At that particular moment, yes, he did hate you. I suspect he rendezvoused with Doug Chapman somewhere. Most likely at the refuge you thought he was going to, but he could have planned to meet him at one of the cabins, or perhaps a vacant summer vacation home."

"It would have taken him two hours to get back here, and then to find the cabin in the blizzard — by that time even Tyler and I were having a hard time staying on the trail and I know the valley better than most."

"He may not have made it, you're right. But we have to assume that he did and he is planning something. Delusional people can convince themselves of anything. He probably wanted to kill you after you left him. He then would want to kill himself, feeling that he was unworthy of you. But over time, he'll generate another fantasy in his head. Maybe that he surprised you with the revelation that he killed your husband's murderer. He's justifying your reactions in his mind, giving you a second chance, if you will. He did the same thing with Rebecca Oliver."

"Who?"

Hans paused. "I thought Tyler told you."

Tyler walked into the kitchen from the office. "I didn't have a chance. After the

Trotskys — I didn't want to lay everything on you at once."

"Tell me now," she said.

"Rebecca Oliver was an actress and Doherty was her neighbor. He broke into her house and killed her and her friend."

"Oh, God."

Hans said, "I think it's important to understand his cycle. He didn't kill her right away. A month before the murders, he defaced her. In that attack, he was essentially giving her a warning. He was angry — like he was with you today — but then he stood back and assessed the situation. Convinced himself that Rebecca didn't understand exactly what he wanted or who he was. He wanted to convince her. He sent her letters, which the police promptly confiscated. She never saw them. But at the same time, he was shrewd. The police were looking for him, so he disappeared. But he still found a way to watch her — he broke into another house across the street during the days when the owner was at work. He saw the police watching his house and hers. He believed she had betrayed him — in his mind, for the second time. He disappeared, went underground, before re-emerging later to kill her. The day after a tabloid newspaper reported that she'd been released from the hospital after plastic surgery."

"And he eluded the police all that time?" Jo asked, incredulous.

"Doherty is resourceful and smart. If you know what you're doing — keep a low profile, act like you belong — you'd be amazed at what people see and don't see."

"Are you okay, Jo?" Tyler asked.

She shrugged. "I'm not sure."

Tyler tucked a lock of hair behind her ear. "You should get some sleep."

"Not now." She poured herself and Hans more tea. "Want some?"

"No thank you. I've had enough coffee to keep a small army awake all night."

Jo rubbed his knee under the table. "What about food?"

"Stan had venison stew for everyone when we returned. I should be asking you the same thing."

"That was hours ago. Let me heat some. There's nothing better than stew at midnight." She squeezed Tyler's knee and caught his eye, then went to the refrigerator to take out the leftovers.

"Hans, do you think Doherty found shelter?" Tyler asked.

Hans sipped his tea. "Yes. I looked at the map that's in the guest rooms. There were trails marked, emergency shelters noted, times and mileage. I think he had a destination in mind when he took Jo this morning. But I also think he had a backup plan. He could be at the refuge, or hiding out in a cabin waiting for the storm to break."

"We'll check every cabin the minute the blizzard breaks," Tyler said. "Don't give them time to leave."

"I agree."

"You said earlier that in understanding Doherty we can predict what he'll do next."

Hans nodded. "That's always our goal. We've had a crew at Quantico reading Jo's books, and they've hit upon a common theme. Love, forgiveness, and redemption. That's exactly what Aaron wants. He wants Jo's love and forgiveness because in that, he'll be redeemed."

"What am I supposed to forgive him for?" Jo asked, stirring the stew. She walked over to the breadbox and took out half a loaf of homemade bread, put it in the oven to warm.

"Things you don't even know about. He thinks you understand him and, in that understanding, you will de facto forgive anything he does. You will support him in anything and everything. In his fantasy, you were created for him. You live to be with him."

"Which means," Tyler said, "that — in his mind — if she refuses to go with him, she needs to die."

Hans nodded. "Yes."

Jo picked up her tea with surprisingly steady hands. Sipped. The men watched her. She put the mug back down. "How do we catch him?"

Agent Mitch Bianchi walked into the kitchen with a yawn. "Mr. Nash is back sitting with Wyatt. He's running a low-grade fever which may be nothing, or may be an infection. We'll need to watch him. I went in and checked on the boy with the broken leg. Stan did a good job with him, though we should get him to a doctor as soon as possible." He looked at the cups on the table. "Tea," he said flatly.

Jo stood. "I can make some coffee."

"Don't trouble yourself."

"No trouble," she said.

"Actually, I'm done with caffeine for the night, though a tall glass of milk sounds good about now."

Jo took out a couple glasses and a carton of milk. She found some cookies in the pantry and put them out as well. All three men reached for them. She went to check on the stew, stirred it, then dished up four bowls and put them on the table with the warmed bread. "To soak up all that caffeine," she said.

"So you want to know how to catch these guys," Mitch said, taking a hefty bite of stew.

"You're the expert in fugitive apprehension," Hans said. "What do you suggest?"

"If they're not frozen by now?" He swallowed. "Okay, we have to think like them. Chapman, he wants to get out of here as soon as possible. Killing the Trotskys was killing time, as far as he was concerned. He's bored and scared — he doesn't want to go back to prison. Which means he'll be stupid and dangerous."

"I called in for reinforcements," Tyler said, "but it'll take time for them to get here. And we're going to be losing Nash and Peter — they're taking Wyatt and Ben to Island Park as soon as the blizzard breaks."

"What about calling on the Worthingtons to help?" Jo asked. "Their ranch is northeast of here. The parents live there and a couple of their kids and grandkids. It's one of the last working ranches in the valley."

"How close?"

"The main house is fifteen miles up the road to the east, closer to Elk Lake."

"Could Chapman have made it there?" Mitch asked, concerned.

"We talked to Nash in Lakeview when we

first had the confirmed sighting," Tyler said. "Nash is a volunteer deputy and he has a phone tree of sorts. He contacted everyone in the area to be on the lookout for them."

"But Chapman's armed," Mitch said.

"So are the Worthingtons," Jo said. "They raise cattle and sheep and their boys are mostly grown men. They're trustworthy people, but if they see a stranger who doesn't look right, they aren't going to turn their back on him."

"Any other residences nearby?" Mitch asked.

"There's only about a dozen families who live here year-round," Jo said. "Us, the Worthingtons, Nash — a couple others around Lakeview, a few near Elk Lake. Most people who come here on vacation do so in the summer, though there have been people who'll come in if the weather is predicted to be good enough for skiing, usually closer to the spring," Jo said.

"We'll contact the Worthingtons in the morning and see if they can spare anyone. I'd like to get the kids out of here as soon as possible, but I don't want to spare a deputy. We need people here to search for Doherty and Chapman, and others to guard against them."

Peter Nash entered the kitchen. "Only

Kyle Worthington and his brother Lance are at the ranch," the veterinarian's son said.

"Where is everyone?" Jo asked.

"Elizabeth had her baby a couple days ago and they left before the first storm hit."

"I didn't know," Jo said. Elizabeth Worthington Stuart lived in Missoula. "We can't use Kyle or Lance. They're kids themselves." Kyle was seventeen and Lance two years older.

"But would their ranch be a good place to take the kids?" Tyler asked.

Jo nodded. "It'll be a trek. Only if the weather clears some. They could double up on the snowmobiles and get over there in an hour, maybe a little more. It's a pretty straight shot on South Centennial Road, provided there're no major impediments."

"Billy Grossman can take them," Tyler said.

"What?" Jo asked.

"I need to get the boys and Leah to safety, but I don't want to lose one of my deputies."

"What about Craig and Sean Mann?" Mitch said. "They proved themselves today."

Tyler nodded. "Good idea."

"I think you should send our female guests, Kristy Johnston and Marie Williams, with them," Jo said. "Kristy hasn't handled this crisis well, and Marie is so young. We have plenty of snowmobiles. Enough if their men want to go with them. After what happened to Greg and Vicky . . ." The knowledge still made her ill. She'd known Greg. She'd liked him, and his new wife. Shared dinner with them their first night here.

"I'll talk to them tonight," Mitch said. "I'd like to have as many men here who are versed in self-defense, but I don't think either Brian Bates or Cleve Johnston are ready for this."

"I have FBI SWAT out of Helena on standby," Hans said. "They'll be here in less than three hours after they get weather clearance. But what are we going to do about Doherty and Chapman in the meantime?"

"I've been thinking about that," Mitch said, "and I think the best course of action is to sit tight. Get the kids out as early as possible, but then complete lockdown."

"Make them come to us," Tyler said, understanding Mitch's methodology. "You said Chapman was restless."

"Bingo. He won't be able to sit still another day. He's been in hiding for two days, he's going to be half-crazy. I hate doing nothing," Mitch added, "but sometimes

336

the key to fugitive apprehension is to wait them out."

"Sounds like a plan. I think we've done all we can tonight," Tyler said. "I'll talk to the Manns about escorting the kids tomorrow."

"I'll talk to Trixie about Leah," Jo said. "I'm sure she'll agree."

"And I'll take the two couples," Mitch said.

"That leaves me to clean the kitchen," Hans interjected.

"You don't have to do that," Jo said. "I can take care of it."

"No, I'd like to. It'll relax me, give me time to think."

They split up and Jo found Trixie in their grandfather's suite. The scouts were asleep in sleeping bags on the floor of the living room. The door to the right was her grandfather's bedroom; the door to the left was where Trixie and Leah were staying. Deputy Al Duncan was sitting up at the single door leading to the deck.

"Ms. Sutton." He tipped his head.

"Deputy." Her heart lurched as she stared at the sleeping boys. Timmy could have — should have — been one of them.

But today, she had helped ensure that six families — including Tyler — had their sons brought in safe. They'd be going home tomorrow.

"Is something wrong?" Trixie asked.

Jo hadn't seen her sister sitting on the far side of the room at the kitchenette table where their grandmother used to play solitaire in the wee hours of the morning when she couldn't sleep. Trixie was doing the same thing. Jo hadn't noticed the faint sound of cards sliding against cards until it stopped.

"No." Jo carefully wove her way among the sleeping bodies, noticing Leah lying on the side closest to Trixie. It was just like her niece to not want to be left out. She bent down to pull the blanket up. Love swelled. Whatever awful things had happened that day four years ago, Leah had come out of it quite a wonderful girl.

Jo sat down across from Trixie. "I was talking with Tyler and the federal agents. They're going to move the kids to the Worthington ranch first thing in the morning, if the blizzard passes. I think Leah should go with them."

In the faint light, Trixie shook her head. "She'll be a sitting duck! Look at what happened to you when you went to the Kimball homestead. You were nearly killed. Wyatt was shot."

"It's not Leah they want."

338

"How can you be so sure?"

"The FBI agents think —"

"They don't know anything. They haven't been able to catch these guys for nine days! They came all the way from California to Montana. It's ridiculous to think that they can stop them now."

Jo shook her head. "You're being fatalistic."

"Me? That's a switch."

"Shh."

"Don't shh me!" But Trixie glanced at Leah and lowered her voice. "I'm scared."

"Me, too."

"How can they protect all those kids?"

"Tyler is going to ask Sean and Craig Mann to escort them."

"No deputy?"

"I think the Manns proved themselves today, Trix. If we take them to the Worthingtons, it's a clear shot up the road. They can get there without trouble on the snowmobiles, ninety minutes max."

Jo softened her voice, touched Trixie's hand. Her sister was trembling. "You can go, too."

"What about you?"

"I'm staying here."

"But it's you he's after."

"That's why I don't want to be anywhere

near the kids. It's safer for them. If anybody's watching, they'll know I'm not with them. They won't follow."

"How do you know?"

"I just know." Everything Agent Vigo had said to her made sense. She didn't understand Doug Chapman's motivation, but Aaron Doherty wasn't going to go after a bunch of preteens. He wanted her.

"You think Leah will be safe?"

"It will be safer than staying here."

Trixie bit her lower lip. "O-Okay," she whispered.

"What about you?"

Trixie shook her head. "I'm not going."

"There's something you need to know." Jo glanced over to where Leah slept on the floor. Made sure her breathing was even, calm, that she was really asleep. Then she turned to Trixie. She had debated whether to share this information with her sister, but if the roles were reversed Jo would want to know the truth. It would come out in the media sooner or later. Jo leaned forward and whispered, "Aaron Doherty killed Linc in prison."

Trixie's eyes widened. "No."

"He did. He told me, and the FBI confirmed. He killed Linc in some sort of vengeance revenge thing because Doherty was obsessed with me, or my books. I'm really not sure how it started, but it's true."

"When the prison authority told me Linc was dead, I thought — I don't know. But not this."

Jo squeezed her hands. "I know it's hard. We'll get through this. Trust Tyler. He knows what he's doing. And there are four other cops here. They'll find the two creeps and we'll finally feel safe again."

Trixie shook her head. "Safe? I haven't felt safe in years."

NINETEEN

Jason told Deputy Duncan that he couldn't sleep and was going to get something to eat.

He'd heard every word Jo and her sister said.

He left the suite of rooms and walked to the main lodge kitchen. He'd hated Montana when they first moved here. There was nothing to do. His Internet connection kept getting kicked off, television was on satellites that half the time didn't work because of the mountains, and there was no movie theater in Dillon. They had to drive an hour just to see a stupid movie. In Dallas, even though they were in the suburbs, there was a ten-screened theater ten minutes in one direction, fifteen in the other.

But there was something about this place that he had grown to like. Like he was home.

Stupid thought, he knew. He'd never been here before, and when his dad told him they were moving to Montana he pitched a fit. He hadn't wanted to come. He didn't want to do *anything,* really, because life had gotten so complicated after his mother divorced his dad and moved him to San Diego.

Then she got sick and brought him back. Died while Jason sat there holding her hand. She'd been so beautiful once, but the cancer ate her from the inside out and she was nothing but a hollow shell of the mother he knew. She hadn't been perfect, but she'd loved him. And Jason would always remember that.

Moving to Montana seemed like running away from memories of his mom, and he didn't want to do it. But he didn't like Dallas and had no one to turn to, no one but a dad he barely knew. He liked the beaches in San Diego, but he didn't like the kids who teased him about his Texas twang so cruelly that he'd worked hard to lose it.

He'd hated his dad for a long time. Why hadn't he visited more often? Why hadn't he let Jason come home?

He knew the truth now, though his dad

didn't think he knew anything. His dad thought Jason didn't pay attention, that when he was into his video games his ears suddenly stopped working.

Not ever.

He wanted to make his father happy, and he didn't know how. But he knew he couldn't make him worry, not like he did after his mom died and his dad thought he was depressed.

"You, um, want to talk to someone?" Dad had asked one night after Jason got up at three a.m. Apparently neither of them had slept well in the months after Sharon Mc-Bride died.

"No," he said.

"Well, let me know. You can talk to me, or," he said quickly, "anyone you want."

Jason hadn't wanted to talk to anyone but his mom, to find out answers to questions only she knew, but she was dead.

Jason opened the refrigerator, looked around. He really wasn't that hungry. He closed it and jumped at a voice.

"Hi, Jason."

There was a small light next to the stove. Jo Sutton walked into the kitchen and asked, "Can I get you anything?"

"Naw. I just couldn't sleep." He felt sheepish.

"I saw you sneak out of Grandpa's wing."

"I wasn't sneaking."

"Okay, not sneaking."

"Where were you? I didn't see you."

"Sitting in the great room next to the fireplace. I couldn't sleep, either."

"Where's Dad?"

"In the den with Wyatt. He fell asleep in the chair. He needs a couple hours shut-eye. We have a busy day tomorrow."

"I heard."

Jo walked over to the refrigerator and took out a gallon of milk. "Milk helps me sleep." She poured two tall glasses and handed one to Jason. "Sit."

He did, looking at the milk. He sipped, then guzzled half of the glass. "Nothing better than cold milk," he said.

"I agree." She sat across from him. "You doing okay?"

He shrugged.

"You acted bravely today, Jason. You are definitely your father's son."

"You think so?"

"I think so."

"I want to be a detective someday. Maybe."

"That's a good goal."

They didn't say anything for a long time.

Then Jo said, "You have something on your mind."

"Something Dad said earlier."

She didn't push him, and Jason was glad about that. He wanted to talk to her. She just might be the only person who really understood his feelings.

"Dad said you won't marry him right now because you still miss your husband and son."

She didn't say anything and Jason feared he'd said something wrong.

"I'm sorry, I shouldn't have said anything."

"No, it's okay. He's right."

"I miss my mom, too," he said quietly.

Jo reached out and touched his hand. "I know you do. It'll never go away completely. But it gets easier."

"Are you sure?"

She nodded. "It's okay to miss her."

"My mom made mistakes."

"We all make mistakes."

"But I feel guilty when I think about them. Because she's dead. And I want to make it up to her, but I can't."

"Try really hard to only remember the good things. No one is perfect, but your mother loved you."

Jason's voice caught as he said, "But she

took me away from Dad. He didn't fight for me."

Jo's heart went out to Jason. He had been holding so much back for so long. Tyler had told her early in their relationship about his ex-wife Sharon. She'd cheated on him and Tyler gave her a second chance. Then she cheated on him again, and filed for divorce.

Tyler might have won custody, but he didn't want to put the then-six-year-old Jason in the middle of an ugly legal battle. Sharon had threatened to fight him tooth and nail.

But when she was dying of cancer, she came back and Tyler had taken her into his home, getting to know a son he'd only seen a couple times a year, before his ex-wife died. It had been hard on Tyler, but it was equally hard on Jason. Harder in many ways.

"You know why he didn't fight for custody."

Jason shook his head. "He never told me."

"You should ask him."

"Do you know?"

She nodded.

"Tell me."

Jo didn't want to get in the middle of it, but Jason was a boy and she did understand how sometimes boys couldn't talk to their fathers about feelings. It made them think

they were less manly. But with women —
with mothers — it was easier.

"He didn't want a big, nasty fight with
your mom. And she didn't want to share
you. The love a mother has for a child is
powerful."

"She used me to hurt Dad."

"No. She loved you."

"I know. She loved me a lot, but —" Jason
didn't continue.

Jo squeezed his hand. "Remember the
good times. Remember how it felt when
your mom hugged you. Remember her
laugh. What was her favorite flower?"

"Red roses, I think."

"When you get home, plant a red rose-
bush."

"I don't think they'll survive in the snow."

"There's some miniature roses you can
grow indoors."

"Really?"

She nodded. "Then when you look at the
roses, you'll remember only the good stuff.
And that's all that's worth remembering, Jason. All the other stuff — the mistakes —
we can't think about."

"Does it work for you?"

Jo looked down. It hadn't, not for a long
time. She'd forgotten every mistake, every
flaw to the extent that she had idealized her

marriage, put her husband on a pedestal that no man could topple. No one could compete with her memories of Ken because he had become flawless in her mind. A saint.

"Yes. But for a long time, I missed my husband and son so much that I was living in the past. I didn't want to forget them."

"I don't want to forget Mom."

"You never will. And I'll never forget Ken and Timmy."

"Does that mean you won't marry Dad?"

"No. It means that I have to put everyone in their place and then I'll be ready. Do you understand?"

Jason nodded. She wasn't sure he did, or if he was just humoring her. She wasn't even sure she understood.

"You okay to go back to bed? It's going to be a long day tomorrow."

Jason nodded. He stood, walked around the table and spontaneously hugged her.

"Good night, Jo."

Jo sat there for a long, long time.

I love that boy.

And for the first time she battled the guilt and won.

The silence woke Aaron.

For nine years he'd lived in a six-foot-by-nine-foot prison. He might as well have

348

been in an open coffin. With all the solitude he had in prison, there had never been total silence.

Silence.

The wind had stopped. There was nothing but a quiet blanket over the valley. He glanced at his watch, one he'd stolen off the dead O'Brien. Three-ten. Still time before they put their plan in motion.

Doug couldn't make a bomb to detonate as Aaron wanted, so they came up with another idea with the same premise.

Aaron could quote the entire article written about Joanna that he carried with him everywhere, so he didn't need to pull it out of his pocket to remember a passage that rang ironically true now.

Jo says she plans out all her novels in detail. "I like a clear road map of where I'm going," she said.

When asked if she'd ever gone on a detour, she laughed. "Many, many times. But I've always discovered when I reached the end of the story that I had laid the foundation of the detour, even in my notes, often without realizing it."

That's exactly what Aaron and Doug were doing tomorrow. A detour that Aaron had unknowingly created yesterday morning.

When Joanna had left him at the top of

the cellar stairs, Aaron decided to see what was down there. Not with a specific reason in mind, just a curiosity since he had thirty minutes before he had to meet his love.

He'd put the box Joanna handed him down, flicked on the light, and went down the narrow stairs. The cellar was dank, musty, and cold. Shelf after shelf of canned food lined the walls. Peaches, apples, prunes, sauces, jams, more than Aaron could count. He wondered if Stan Wood did all this, or maybe Joanna. She lovingly prepared all this food for them to share through the years, marking and dating each jar with her perfect script.

There were six windows in the basement, three on one wall, three on another. What did they need with windows down here? He crossed over to one. They were all locked from the inside, three feet wide and two feet tall.

Big enough for someone to slip in.

He unlocked one window on each side and pushed them open just a fraction against the snow.

Just enough to get fingers underneath from the outside and pull all the way open without too much sound.

At the time, he didn't think about why he would need to break *in* to the lodge considering that he was a guest.

But now? Now, it was the only way he could get inside.

I'm coming, Joanna. Wait for me. Dream of me.

Forgive me.

(She'll never forgive you.)

Aaron shook the errant voice from his mind. Of course she would forgive him. She loved him.

Last night they had made love. She'd come to his room wearing a pale blue gown. She wore nothing beneath and he saw her nipples hard, pushing against the filmy fabric.

"Joanna."

"I've been waiting for you, Aaron."

"You know who I am?"

"I knew the minute I saw you." She took his hand. "I've dreamed of you forever."

He touched her face with the back of his hand. "I love you."

"I'll never leave you, Aaron. I'll be with you forever."

And she took him to bed . . .

Aaron bolted upright. The light had changed. He'd fallen asleep.

"Must have had a nice fucking dream." Doug laughed. He was standing in the kitchenette drinking coffee.

Aaron looked down and saw the wet stain spread across the blanket that had covered his naked body.

"We don't have a lot of time, so clean your dick off and get dressed," Doug said, eating food he'd stolen from the dead Trotskys' cabin.

Aaron went to the bathroom, red with embarrassment. If he didn't need Doug for this part of the plan, he should kill him now.

He looked in the mirror, his face still red and puffy from the bear spray Joanna had hit him with yesterday.

(Kill her.)

He shook his head violently back and forth, trying to rid himself of the tempting voice.

He didn't want to kill Joanna. He loved her. He loved her dammit!

His fist slammed into the mirror. It shattered around him. Blood dripped onto the porcelain sink.

Aaron's breath quickened as he watched the blood ooze in rivlets down the side of the sink.

Pounding on the door. "Stop jerking off, Doherty, and get your ass out here. We have to go or it'll be too late."

Aaron rinsed the blood off his hand and

the dry sperm off his cock. He dressed and stepped through the doorway.

"I'm ready. Let's go."

TWENTY

The silence woke Jo.

She slid out of bed. Dawn hadn't yet broke, the sky was still overcast, but the blizzard had passed. No snow fell; no wind wrapped fresh powder around the lodge like a cloak. Taking Wyatt and the kids to safety had become a whole lot easier.

Jo dressed quickly. If Chapman and Doherty were out there waiting for daybreak to attack, their job in the lodge was to get the kids off immediately.

Jo entered the lobby as Tyler spoke in low tones to his deputies, the FBI agents, the Manns, and Sam Nash.

"Everyone is going to the Worthingtons'. When you get there, if possible a Life Flight helicopter will come for Wyatt. If not, then Nash will take him over the pass into Idaho.

"Craig, you and Sean are to stay with the kids at all times. I have no reason to believe that Doherty or Chapman have gone east toward the Worthington ranch, but be careful and fully alert. I spoke with Lance Worthington just a few minutes ago and he said everything was clear. He and Kyle have plenty of provisions.

"The Johnstons are going with you along with Marie Williams. Brian Bates is going to help us keep watch. Any questions?"

"Are we taking the kids down to the shed?" Nash asked.

"No. We'll bring the snowmobiles here to the front door. I want to do it before the sun rises. We don't have a lot of time. The storm has lifted and Agent Bianchi and I feel if Doherty and Chapman attack, it'll be not long after daybreak."

"Then we'd better get going," Nash said. "We need to fuel up and —"

"Stan and Brian already left to fuel the snowmobiles."

Jo said, "You're going to need all the snowmobiles to get that many people to the Worthington ranch."

"All but one," Tyler said. "In case of an emergency. I'm hoping we're not going to need it."

Hans spoke up. "I talked to the Helena office this morning. They can't fly yet — the storm moved north into their flight path — but they predict liftoff within two hours."

"Three hours to get here," Tyler said. "That means we only need to hold down the fort for five hours. Then we'll have a

SWAT team holding it down for us, with enough people to start a manhunt. If these bastards haven't shown themselves by then, we'll go out and find them."

"Let's get moving," Mitch Bianchi said.

The bite of the predawn morning chilled Jo as soon as she stepped out, but she relished that the air was clear. Already she could tell the sky was lightening. They might see blue today.

The weather could turn so quickly here, from brilliant blue to a blizzard in hours. Sometimes the blue sky would last for weeks; other times, it would disappear between dawn and noon.

But she'd take every blue-sky minute she could find.

Tyler stopped her from going down the steps. "Go back inside. Get the kids lined up. They're to bring nothing except the essentials Stan packed for them."

"But —"

"Don't argue with me, Jo. We don't know where these two are. They could be watching us now."

"You're right."

He touched her cheek with the back of his hand. "It's going to be over soon. Then we can focus on us."

He didn't wait for her response, but with

rifle in hand he stood sentry on the deck as Nash and the others went to the garage to retrieve the snowmobiles.

Jo had been raised with guns, but she'd never seen so many out at once. She pictured a scene from the Wild West, with the menfolk protecting the ranch from bandits. She looked out the front window, then turned to make sure the kids were ready.

"Trixie, where's Stan with the emergency provisions?"

"He went down to the root cellar about twenty minutes ago."

"I'll go help," Jo said

She opened the root cellar door and flipped on the light, thinking it strange that Stan hadn't turned it on. Maybe he'd already come up and Trixie hadn't seen him.

Stan was sprawled at the bottom of the stairs. "Oh my God, Stan!" The stairs were very narrow. She'd always been afraid that her grandfather was going to fall and break his hip. Now Stan —

It wasn't until Jo reached the bottom of the stairs that she realized they weren't alone.

Aaron Doherty stepped from behind a high stack of boxes. The pepper spray had made his face swell, his eyes were still red. He held a gun on Stan.

"Don't scream or I'll kill him. I promise you, he's not dead. Yet. He was kind to me, I didn't want to hurt him. But if you betray me again, I will shoot and it will be your fault. Do you understand?"

She nodded.

He took three steps toward her. She unconsciously took a step back. He grabbed her arm and pulled her to him. With his gun hand aimed at Stan, he patted her down. "Making sure you have no gun or bear spray." He backhanded her and she stumbled, tripping on the bottom step and sitting down hard. "That was for attacking me yesterday. But I forgive you. You didn't understand. By the end of today, you will understand I will never leave you and we'll be fine."

She found herself nodding as her terror increased. How was she going to get out of this without anyone getting hurt? One look at Aaron's face told Jo that he expected to kill someone today.

And that person may well be her.

Aaron pulled her up. "Let's go."

As the sky lightened, Tyler felt uneasy. Nothing specific, but something wasn't right.

He got on his walkie-talkie. "McBride to

Bianchi."

"Here."

"You at the garage?"

"We're about to come up, just a minor problem here. Mechanical."

"Hold on a minute."

"Something wrong?"

"I don't know."

Tyler listened to the random plops of snow from the trees. He walked across the deck to where Deputy Billy Grossman was on the far side. "I'm going to walk the perimeter."

"I'll cover you."

Tyler went down the steps, slowly circled the lodge. He was only a quarter way around the building when he saw it.

Footprints outside the root cellar window. The snow had been shoveled away and the window pried open.

Running too slow in the fresh powder, he got on his walkie-talkie. "Mitch! They're in the lodge. Get up here ASAP."

"McBride — all the snowmobiles have been sabotaged. None of them will start. We're on our way on foot."

Tyler took the stairs two at a time, slipped, caught himself on the railing. He flung the rifle over his back and had his service pistol in hand. He tried the door.

Locked.

He pounded on the door. "Jo!"

Gunfire popped inside the lodge. *Bang-bang-bang.* Tyler hit the deck, crawled out to the snow, found a relatively safe place crouching in the wet snow.

"Report!" Bianchi called over the radio.

"One of them is inside." Tyler looked for Billy. Saw he had overturned a heavy wood table and was behind it, gun aimed on the door.

Shit shit shit! They'd had the damn house secured, then they left. Thought the women and children were safer inside. Doherty and Chapman had to have been watching and saw who left the house. Still, they didn't know how many men they had.

Then he realized Chapman could have been watching the lodge yesterday while Doherty was out with Jo and the scouts. If he counted heads, he'd have a damn good estimate. When had they gotten into the cellar? Sometime during the night? Right before dawn? Were both of them inside or just one?

Tyler needed to get inside, but he was too broad to crawl through the cellar window.

Which meant so was Chapman. He couldn't have gone that way. Doherty had to be the only one inside.

How could Tyler use that to his advantage?

He heard a snowmobile in the distance.

The gunshots must have been a cue for Chapman to bring the sled. Aaron had a hostage.

The front door opened and Tyler trained his gun on the opening.

It was Jo. Just above her lip was a smear of blood. Doherty had hit her. Tyler's jaw tensed.

"Jo —"

She shook her head. Right behind her Aaron Doherty had a gun at Trixie's head.

Jo watched Tyler's face from his position at the bottom of the steps. He barely moved, but his face turned grave.

"What happened?" he asked.

"He was in the root cellar. Stan is unconscious at the bottom of the stairs. Someone needs to help him."

The snowmobile was approaching. There was no way they could fit four people on one snowmobile.

"Doherty!" Tyler called. "Let them go. If you end this now, no one will get hurt. I'll tell the prison authorities you cooperated."

Doherty laughed. "I'm already a dead man, cooperation or not. I'm not going back to Quentin. You're just jealous about Joanna and me. Don't think I didn't read that love note you sent her. *Love, Tyler.* You bastard."

Using Trixie as a shield, Aaron fired his gun at Tyler. It came close, damn close. Doherty was a good shot.

"Hold your fire!" Tyler called.

"Fuck you, Sheriff McBride." Doherty fired again, but this one was far off. Tyler had moved from Aaron's best angle.

"Don't, Aaron. Please," Jo begged.

"Do you love him?" Aaron demanded.

"No, Aaron. I only love you. You know that. Haven't you read my books?"

Doherty's face softened almost imperceptibly. Then his expression grew stern again as he looked at Tyler. "I need you to move away, or my friend won't come closer. He's waiting for my signal."

"FBI SWAT is on their way," Tyler said. "You can't get out of the valley."

"That's what you think. Sit by the radio, Sheriff. I'll be in contact."

"I'm not letting you take them."

"You don't have a choice. There's a bomb ticking in the lodge. And all those kids are going to die."

Tyler's eyes widened. He glanced at Jo.

"He's telling the truth," she said, her voice catching. "He has both gas stoves open and on, blew out the pilot light. A lit candle on a shelf. It's only a matter of time — ten, fifteen minutes — before the gas rises and the candle ignites it."

Aaron laughed. "Everyone is locked in the root cellar right beneath the kitchen. I doubt they'll survive the explosion."

From Jo's petrified expression, it looked like Aaron was telling the truth. "Please, Tyler," she said. "I'll be okay. Save the kids. Please."

All his training, every instinct, told Tyler not to let Aaron Doherty leave with two hostages.

But there were seven kids, two old men, two women, and his injured brother inside that house. If there were an explosion, some or all of them would die.

"Time is running out," Doherty said. "It's going to take Doug at least five minutes to get here after I give the signal."

Tyler listened. The snowmobile was idling somewhere, but where he couldn't see. It could be a mile away or behind a tree, the way sound carried out here.

Mitch Bianchi rounded the corner, gun in hand, aimed at Doherty's head. He was steady as a trained sharpshooter.

"Sheriff!" Bianchi called.

"There's a bomb inside," Tyler responded.

"And I'd be careful about opening that back door," Doherty said. "A draft could stir the gas around and *boom!*"

Jo looked so lost standing in the middle of the deck. Trixie was white as a ghost, her entire body tense, a whimper coming out of her throat. But she was light, easy to carry, and not putting up a fight.

Seven kids are going to die if you hesitate another minute.

"It's okay, Tyler. Please let us go."

Shit. He didn't want to, he knew it was wrong, but Tyler was trapped. Even if he could take Doherty out, Jo and Trixie were in the line of fire. And the makeshift bomb inside . . .

"Go." It was the hardest thing Tyler had ever done.

Aaron whistled. Within two minutes, Chapman drove up, towing another snowmobile behind. He stopped when he saw Tyler.

"You need to stand down, Sheriff. Move to the corner of the house."

Tyler did as he was told, though he didn't let go of his gun — hoping, wishing for an opportunity to kill Aaron Doherty.

Chapman brought the snowmobiles up to the porch stairs. He released the tow. Doherty said, "Go, Joanna."

Jo walked down the stairs. Chapman grabbed her, held a knife at her throat.

"Don't touch her," Doherty warned. They traded Trixie and Jo. Now Doherty had a gun on Jo, and Chapman had a knife on Trixie. This time Trixie screamed, but it was short-lived. Chapman nicked her neck and said, "Next time I'll slice your throat. Just like I did that babe in the cabin."

They got on the snowmobiles and took off down the road. Tyler could have shot either man in the back, but there was no guarantee the bullet wouldn't go through their body and into Jo or Trixie.

"Shit!" Mitch shouted. "Fuck!" He started toward the door.

"Careful!" Tyler exclaimed. "Jo confirmed the bomb."

The two men slowly entered the lodge. Mitch said, "You get the kids, I'll take care of the bomb."

"Gas buildup in the kitchen. Watch it."

Tyler turned to the root cellar door. He unlocked it and shouted. "Everyone up the stairs, single file, don't push."

Leah was first. "Stan's down there, hurt. He's moaning. I don't know what's wrong. Help him!"

"Go outside and follow Deputy Grossman." Over his shoulder, he told Billy, "Get them as far away as you can."

The kids, then the female guests. Karl was

helping Stan Wood stand. "He has a head injury," Karl said.

"I'll get him upstairs. You go."

Karl started up the stairs. Mitch called down, "All clear."

Tyler helped a dazed Stan up the stairs, sitting him on a bench by the front door. The smell of gas filled the air.

"Mitch! We have to get out — the gas!"

"It'll take a few minutes for the gas to dissipate, but I got the trigger — two lit candles — taken care of. The place would have blown in less than five minutes," Mitch said, his voice calm as if he encountered bombs daily. "Good call on your part. I don't know what the damage would have been, but with all the wood in this place, it would have been one helluva fire."

"What do we do now?" Tyler said.

"We track those bastards."

"Doherty said he would call. Maybe he wants to make a trade."

Hans Vigo entered the lodge. "What the fuck happened?"

Tyler quickly filled him in.

"Yes, he'll call, but he's not going to make a trade. He'll want to buy time to get out of the valley."

"We need to track them," Mitch said.

"Agreed," Tyler said. "But when they stop

the sleds, they'll hear us. Snowmobiles are loud and the sound echoes."

"Forget the snowmobiles. They were sabotaged."

"All of them?"

"Damn straight. Nash and his son are still there trying to repair them, but hell if I know how long it's going to take."

"We need at least two — one to take Wyatt to the hospital and one to track them."

"I'll go to the garage." Stan's voice was thick with pain.

"You need to rest," Karl said. His eyes were watery and he stared at Tyler as if begging him to save his granddaughters.

"What about when he calls?" Tyler asked. "If I'm not here, he might do something rash."

Hans said, "I'll stay and patch him through to you."

"Will that work?"

"It'll have to. These two have proven to be very resourceful. We can't let them get too far or they just might disappear altogether."

TWENTY-ONE

Aaron had Joanna in front of him on the snowmobile as they sped on the fresh powder along South Centennial Road. That it was even called a road amused him; no cars could drive on the snow that had accumulated.

Joanna shivered and Aaron turned the Polaris's heater on high. She wasn't dressed for the weather — having left the lodge in jeans, a sweater, and short boots — and he didn't want her to be cold. He wrapped his body around his love to protect her.

(The bitch tried to kill you!)

Aaron frowned. The pain from the bear spray attack was becoming a distant memory, but he still remembered not being able to breathe. The thought that he was going to die.

Even now, his throat burned.

He shook his head, pushing frightening thoughts of killing Joanna from his mind. He didn't want to kill her. He loved her. She had come with him. She was sorry. He *knew* she was sorry. Why would she have come with him today if she didn't feel bad about what had happened between them yesterday?

With the clear weather, it wouldn't be long until they reached the fire tower in Lakeview. It was thirty-five miles away, and they were pushing forty on the snowmobile. The sled could go up to a hundred miles an hour, but that would be dangerous, and he wasn't going to risk Joanna's life.

The fire tower offered them a hiding place. It would also prevent anyone from sneaking up on them, and buy them time. He'd considered breaking into an unoccupied house, but with only him and Doug to cover entrances, it would be hard to know how many had followed, or see their approach. The fire tower would give them a clear view of the valley.

That they were able to walk out of the lodge with Joanna and her sister, in front of all those cops, put Aaron on cloud nine.

It had gone so much easier than Aaron had thought it would, even after the rocky beginning.

He'd easily gotten into the root cellar while Doug went down to sabotage the snowmobiles. He'd heard voices inside, but no one was out yet, and it was still dark, dawn barely coming through.

The plan was that after Doug sabotaged the snowmobiles, he'd go back to where they hid the sleds they'd stolen from Lakeview and fill them with gasoline he'd taken from the lodge. He'd then wait for three gunshots which meant that he should start for the lodge.

The gunshots meant that Aaron had everything set up.

Stan Wood had surprised Aaron in the root cellar and Aaron hit him over the head. The old black man went down and for a moment Aaron felt bad about that. He didn't want to hurt Stan; he'd been kind to him. But he checked his pulse and it was strong. Just unconscious, not dead. That was okay. Aaron flicked off the light from below so that anyone who came in wouldn't immediately see poor Stan.

The surprise of Stan's presence in the cellar threw Aaron off for a moment. He'd originally planned to sneak into the lodge and find a hostage. He would set the makeshift bomb — Doug was brilliant in figuring out the candle and gas trick — and demand that Joanna go with him.

But after hitting Stan, Aaron had to rethink his plan. There were a lot of kids running around — six or seven. If he could get one of them, Joanna would do anything he wanted.

As he was about to go upstairs and implement his plan, Joanna turned on the cellar light. He had to think fast. Put the gun on Stan and demand that Joanna be his hostage.

It worked. She would do anything to make sure no one was hurt. That helped.

It was Joanna who told the kids to go

down into the cellar for safety. Trixie was the last to go down, and Aaron said, "Not you."

"Aaron, please, just me," Joanna said.

"I want her to come with us."

"Why?" Joanna looked scared, then she said, "She'll just get in our way. Be a third wheel."

"For Doug."

Joanna paled, and Aaron added, "I won't let him kill her, okay?"

When Trixie hesitated, Aaron aimed his gun down the cellar stairs. "Don't know who I might hit."

His finger was on the trigger. He would have pulled it, but Trixie shut and locked the cellar door as he instructed.

He smiled. "Good girl. The kitchen."

He set up the bomb. It didn't take long. Doug said he wouldn't have a lot of time, the gas could explode in ten minutes or thirty.

So he fired the gun three times into the couch — he really didn't want to hurt anyone — and Joanna screamed. "Please, Aaron, please leave Trixie. Don't do this."

He glared at her as he changed hostages, taking Trixie in hand and holding the gun to her neck. "Go out the front door and don't do anything funny or I'll kill her. And

370

your friends won't have time to stop the explosion. Are you willing to risk it?"

Joanna shook her head and started for the door.

"Let him kill me, Jo!" Trixie shouted. "Run!"

But Joanna didn't run. She listened.

Why she gave a rat's ass about her sister baffled Aaron. She must not know the truth.

Aaron had tried to tell Bridget, his first true love, the truth, but she wouldn't listen.

Bridget Hart. What a beautiful name. Bridget. Hart. Aaron had dated her in high school. They were "a couple." An "item." They'd gone out for over a year. He had loved her. He would have given her the world. And she had said she loved him. She gave her body to him, told him how after graduation she wanted to get married and have kids together.

She lied. She lied over and over again. One terrible day she left him.

How could you walk out on someone you said you loved? How could you *leave* and then claim you loved them no more?

Bridget told Aaron he was too controlling. She needed "space," and all those other clichés that really just meant *I've been lying to you for the past fourteen months, nothing I said was true.*

A month later — *twenty-seven* days after she broke up with him — she started dating a football player. Trevor Keene was smart *and* an athlete and Aaron knew he could never compete.

He had to remind her that she loved *him,* Aaron Doherty. He was worthy of her love, dammit, worthy of her! Didn't she see that? Had Bridget been playing a game to make him come after her? Did she want him to fight for her? He could do that. He'd be glad to.

He'd followed her. He had to convince her that he was her one and only true love. Instead, Aaron learned he was nobody.

Trevor did everything for Bridget: opened doors, held her hand, helped her with homework. What did Aaron, who had been told by every teacher that he didn't live up to his potential, have on star athlete and valedictorian Trevor Keene?

Nothing.

The despair — the deep, bone-piercing pain of failure — hit Aaron hard. Of course Bridget left him for a better man.

His own mother had left him over and over again for better men.

He'd almost killed himself then. He'd wanted to, he had one of his uncle's old guns, a simple revolver. He could shoot himself in the head and that would be the end of it.

His mother wasn't around to care. He couldn't do it in the house. Aunt Dorothy might find him, and he didn't want to upset her. She'd been kind to him, as kind as Annie Erickson when his mother left him with her all those years ago.

Fleetingly, he wondered what his life would have been like if Annie had been his mother. Or Aunt Dorothy. If he'd never had Ginger Doherty in his life. If he'd never loved her so hard that it broke apart his insides.

In the end, he didn't kill himself, didn't even come close to it — hadn't even loaded the gun. But an idea formed in his dreams that night.

Bridget was beautiful. Would Trevor love her if she wasn't beautiful? Aaron would. He'd love Bridget no matter what, even if she was scarred and ugly.

Aaron decided to prove it. And when Bridget got herself cut up, Trevor dumped her. Oh, not right away, that would have been tacky, but he did, nonetheless. He left her and went to college and didn't take her with him.

Aaron would have taken her back even though she'd given her body to that asshole who didn't love her. He would have taken her back because true love demanded it. It demanded that he still love Bridget with her cut face, her betrayal, her black and twisted core that let her walk out on him in the first place.

She turned him in. She told the police he'd cut her face. He was still a minor, and he went before a judge. She took pity on him and gave him probation and counseling. He said he didn't mean it. And he hadn't truly wanted to hurt Bridget. He'd only wanted her to love him like before.

Aaron shook his head, remembering where he was. Joanna was here with him because she wanted to be. She wasn't running, he hadn't even had to put a gun to her head to get her to cooperate. There was still hope. They would make it work.

It had to work. She was his last hope.

He glanced at Doug up ahead, riding with Trixie Weber, the wife of that murderous bastard Lincoln Barnes. Just proves that women don't know what's good for them. If she were a good sister, Trixie would be helping him win Joanna's heart. Hadn't he proved himself to both of them? Lincoln Barnes had shot Trixie, almost killing her. He would have taken Leah away from her. He was a certified scumbag, and Aaron had taken care of him — not only for Joanna, but for Trixie too, and her daughter. To protect them. Barnes would never hurt them again, thanks to him. He was dead. Dead, dead, dead . . .

Aaron pulled off his glove with his teeth. He needed to touch Joanna. Like Bridget, like Rebecca, Joanna was beautiful. Her skin was soft. As they drove, his finger went down to her chin, ran along the tender curve of her neck. She didn't flinch, didn't move. His breathing quickened. He pulled her hair to the side and kissed the back of her neck.

His plan was working. They'd radio Sheriff Tyler McBride and tell him to get a helicopter for their escape. They'd ask for some money just for good measure.

Aaron had no plans to be anywhere near where the helicopter landed. By the time the cops figured out they'd been tricked, he and Joanna would be out of the valley and starting their new life together.

He sped up, passed Doug and motioned for him to stop. "Turn it off."

Doug did as he said.

Aaron listened. No one was in pursuit. Brilliant idea disabling the snowmobiles, even if it had been Doug's.

"Okay, let's go." Aaron started the Polaris.

This time he led the way.

Karl Weber came into the lodge's office. Tyler was listening to a conversation between Hans and the Helena field office. They were predicting departure in less than an hour. The SWAT team was suiting up.

But it would take nearly three hours to get here. Where had Doherty taken Jo?

"Tyler, I have news," Karl said.

Tyler escorted Karl from the office. "Are the snowmobiles working?"

"No, but Jo's Polaris is missing. It must be one that the convicts are using."

"Doherty took a Polaris yesterday at the Kimball homestead."

"That's Jo's personal sled. It has GPS tracking."

Tyler allowed himself a sliver of hope. "We need to turn it on."

"I'll make the call."

Tyler motioned for Hans to wrap up the conversation. The lodge had just the one landline.

"George Worthington and I decided to put GPS on all our sleds after his son Kyle was lost last year. I didn't know I'd need it to track Jo's kidnapper."

Karl Weber had aged a decade overnight. Tyler put a hand on his shoulder. The man had once been large and physically fit. And while he was in decent shape for an eighty-year-old man, he had developed a hollow appearance that hadn't been there the last time Tyler had visited the lodge.

"We're going to find her and Trixie. I promise."

Karl nodded. Tyler refused to give this worried grandfather anything but good news.

Hans hung up, and Karl called the service that provided GPS tracking. "There's one problem," Karl said while he was on hold. "The GPS service is sporadic here in the valley. We may only get a glimpse of where they are, then it'll be gone. Because our Internet service is down, we need to rely on the tracking company to let us know where they are."

"I'll take whatever we can get. If we can send a SWAT team to their location rather than wasting time here, I'll take it."

Tyler was antsy. He wanted to go out, wanted to follow them, but there was no way to do it without a vehicle. "Is there any hope for the sleds?"

"They pulled out wiring. Simple and effective," Karl said. "It's a matter of getting everything hooked up in the right way. Agent Bianchi is down there with Porter,

Nash, and the Manns. They're working as fast as they can."

Tyler willed them to go faster. Out of the corner of his eye, he saw Jason in the office doorway.

"Son, I need you to stay with your friends." Tyler had put the kids in Karl Weber's suite. He didn't want to worry about them.

"I want to help," Jason said.

Tyler clapped a hand on his son's back. "I know, but there's nothing you can do right now."

"I don't want to sit around and do nothing!"

"I know. But —" He stopped and imagined himself as a twelve-year-old boy. Wanting to be a man, but not there yet. Wanting to help, but not having the experience or skills to do so.

"How's Leah holding up?"

"Okay. She was crying earlier."

"Go get Leah and take her to talk to Wyatt. Uncle Wyatt is going stir-crazy and I don't want him doing anything dumb like trying to get up. Leah could use a distraction so she doesn't worry about her mom."

Jason looked skeptical. Tyler said, "It's important that Wyatt stays still."

"Okay, Dad, I'll do it."

He left and Tyler watched him walk down the hall to find Leah. *He's a good kid.*

Karl was still on the phone. When Tyler turned back to him, Karl said, "They've turned it on. No signal yet. They're going to watch. I'll stay on the phone if you like. There's call waiting in case one of the FBI folks tries to get through."

"Thanks, Karl. I'm going down to the garage and see if I can help on the snowmobiles."

The sky had whispers of blue when Tyler went out. It was up to thirty degrees, and the forecast was for a high of forty-one. Amazing, when yesterday didn't top twenty, with a low of minus twenty-two. In Dallas, there were cold spells, but nothing like this. Nothing like these frigid winters. It was enough to make him want to go back to Texas.

But his family was here. Wyatt. Jason was growing into a fine young man. They'd bonded here when they'd barely spoken in the years before Sharon died. Montana was now home.

And Jo. There had been a change in her yesterday, and while she didn't say it in so many words, Tyler suspected that she was finally making peace with her past and would be able to commit to him.

First, he had to get her away from a killer.

"Any progress?" he asked when he walked into the garage.

"We're working on it," Mitch said.

"No pressure. Except that the lives of two women are at stake."

Tyler bit his tongue when Mitch glared at him. He shouldn't have been sarcastic. They knew very well what the stakes were.

"Can I help?" he said.

"Are you a mechanic?" Mitch said.

"No."

"Then let us do it. Nash has magic hands."

As if on cue, Nash turned the ignition of one of the sleds and it came to life.

"Let's get another," Mitch said, optimistic.

Tyler's walkie-talkie beeped. "Vigo to Mc-Bride."

"Go ahead," Tyler said.

"We have a location on the sleds. They're moving west on South Centennial Road. They're halfway between here and Lakeview right now."

"Where do you think they're going?" Tyler asked almost to himself. "Back to their truck?"

"Possibly, or maybe they think they can steal a truck in Lakeview. They'll need to refuel there. Otherwise, they won't make it out of the valley. There's nothing between

Lakeview and the Lima Reservoir, according to Karl, unless you know where you're going, and I don't think they do."

"No, they're retracing their steps. They want out, and they don't know the fastest way would have been for them to go east. They're going the way they came."

"They said they would be in touch. Probably want to negotiate safe passage."

"Don't know that I would believe them, but we need to be prepared for anything."

"Karl just said GPS has lost them, but they were still heading toward Lakeview when the signal cut out."

"Thanks." He said to Nash, "Is there a faster way to Lakeview than South Centennial Road?"

"Nope."

"Then let's get another ride fixed and get the hell out of here. I've got a bad feeling."

TWENTY-TWO

"Absolutely not." The group stood beside the snowmobiles as Doug Chapman shook his head slowly back and forth. He stared at the fire tower a mile off South Centennial Road.

Jo watched the exchange between the men with fearful interest. She didn't know what

Doherty had planned, but it was obvious they hadn't agreed previously on this part of the plan.

"Once we're up there, we'll be able to see for miles," said Doherty. "We'll know when they're coming. There's no way they can get to us."

"And we'll be trapped," Chapman said. "They'll surround the place and we won't be able to get out."

"We have Joanna and her sister," Doherty said.

Trixie whimpered. Jo wrapped her arm around Trix and whispered, "It's okay."

"No, it's not!" Trixie said.

Chapman glared at her. "Shut up."

Doherty said, "We'll radio the Sheriff and make our demands. We're going to tell him we're at the refuge center. I made the trail yesterday, and refreshed part of it this morning. There's no reason to think that we're not there."

"Then why trap ourselves up there?" Chapman looked up.

The fire tower was no longer in use. Routine flybys by the Forest Service took care of the fire watch. But not too long ago, keeping watch had been part of Sam Nash's job. As Jo recalled, he'd move into the fire tower at the beginning of the fire season and keep watch over the valley. Times changed. For better, and for worse.

"What about that town we passed on the road?" Chapman asked.

"Town?" Doherty frowned. "There was no one there."

"There were new buildings. We could keep our ears open, but we won't be a hundred feet in the air."

Jo realized Chapman was afraid of heights.

Both Chapman and Doherty were right — if they went up the tower, they'd be trapped. But there was no way anyone could approach without being seen — unless another blizzard hit. Jo looked up at the sky. As the clouds moved northeast, it was becoming bluer.

Still — there was a steady wind, and the temperature hadn't risen much even with the sun. Jo suspected that by nightfall another storm would move in.

This particular fire tower was sparsely furnished. When Nash had done his fire duty, he'd bring up a portable generator, a radio, and an ice chest. There was a cot and desk — whether they were still there or not, Jo didn't know. It was a solitary job, and one of his sons would relieve him every Saturday afternoon until Monday morning. It was a life Sam Nash preferred.

Jo had been falling into the same quiet, functional despair of the Nash family, she realized. Twenty-two years ago, Emily Nash had tragically died in a skiing accident. Sam and his three sons had never fully recovered. The two oldest sons had moved from the area. Peter, who had watched his mother die, had stayed in the valley, except for his three-year stint in the military.

Is this the life Jo wanted? Living day in and day out with nothing but memories to keep her warm?

Did she really think that Jason was somehow a threat to her son's memory?

She needed to talk to Tyler, to explain, to make things right. She needed to get out of this mess so that she could truly put the past behind her.

Jo remembered what Hans Vigo had said last night about Aaron Doherty's personality. He was delusional; he believed she loved him. She had to play off that. Then maybe she and Trixie could get out of this alive.

She whispered in Trixie's ear, "Trust me."

Before her sister could respond, Jo stepped forward. Chapman and Doherty both turned to her. There was a gun in Chapman's hand.

She put her hands up. "Aaron, can we talk? In private?"

"What —"

Chapman interrupted. "Don't trust her."

Doherty glared at him, then turned with suspicious eyes on Jo. "What's wrong?"

"The town isn't a real town, not yet. There's a developer of sorts trying to resurrect the past glory of Lakeview, when it was a mining town nearly a hundred years ago. He's building a western-style town and eventually will have a small motel, shops, a restaurant. He thinks." Jo rolled her eyes. While in concept the idea was wonderful, people didn't travel this far out for shopping and good food. They came here for peace and recreation.

"Don't listen to her," Chapman said.

Jo looked at Aaron. "There's nothing inside the buildings. No heat, no food, no water. Most are incomplete. And the fire tower — I hate to agree with your friend, but he's right — we're no better up there. You can see for miles, but there're not even windows up there. It's going to be ten degrees colder and with the wind —" She glanced at Trixie. Her sister was freezing, but was doing her best not to show how cold she was.

She lowered her voice and stepped next to Aaron. Touched his arm. Looked into his eyes.

"Trix is hurting. In the cold, her leg is awfully painful. Please — we need to get her someplace warm."

"Where?"

Jo tilted her head, watched as Doherty looked over at Trixie with concern apparent in his face. He cared. He didn't want Trixie to suffer.

She could use that.

"Sam Nash's house."

Chapman interrupted. "What the fuck? You're going to listen to this bitch? We should have taped her fucking mouth shut."

Jo stepped partly behind Doherty, as if she were intimidated by Chapman. Okay, she *was* intimidated. Chapman was a wild card. She couldn't predict how he would act, but she needed Aaron on her side.

"Who lives there?" Doherty asked her.

"Sam Nash and his son Peter, but they are both at the lodge right now. Their house is only two miles from here. There's heat and food. The best thing is, it's on a knoll. You'll be able to see anyone who comes up the drive. I swear, Aaron. And if you get there and don't believe me, come back here. It's not that far."

"No," Chapman said. "I like the town."

"Fine," Jo said, glaring at Chapman. "Go to the town. It's five miles in the opposite direction, but we'll do it. And then you'll see that I'm right."

"A house would be nice," Doherty said to Chapman.

"You can't trust her!" Chapman exclaimed.

"We'll know soon enough if she's lying." Doherty looked down at her, touched her chin. Jo used every ounce of control to not flinch.

"Aw, fuck. There better be some Jack Daniel's or I'm going to kill someone." He stared right at Jo.

Doherty stepped in front of her, blocking Jo from Chapman's murderous glare.

"Let's go," he said.

He turned to Jo. "Are you cold?"

"I'm okay."

He put his hands on her arms and rubbed them up and down. The friction warmed her, reminding her that she was in fact very cold. Her feet felt like ice cubes. If she was out too much longer, she would start to fade.

"I'll get you warm," he said.

She shivered as he wrapped his arm around her and led her back to the snowmobile. As they climbed on the Polaris, he nuzzled her neck. "I'm so sorry we didn't have time for you to pack some clothes."

"I'm okay," she said.

"I'll buy you anything you need as soon as we get away."

"That sounds nice."

His words chilled her more than the cold air.

Her plan better work.

TWENTY-THREE

Tyler sat in the entry scratching the Saint Bernard Buckley between the ears. Thinking. They had one snowmobile working and he had wanted to take it to pursue Jo.

Instead he'd let Nash take Wyatt to the other side of Red Rock Pass, where a Life Flight helicopter would meet them to take Tyler's brother to the nearest hospital.

It was one of the most difficult decisions he'd made in his life, but if they didn't get Wyatt to a doctor as soon as possible, he would die. He had developed a high fever and was going in and out of consciousness.

Hans stepped out of the office. "Doherty is on the radio. He wants to talk to you."

Tyler jumped up, startling the dog. He strode over to the office.

Tyler took a deep breath and picked up the radio.

"This is Sheriff McBride."

"I want transportation — a helicopter — to take us out of the valley."

"You know I can't do that."

Hans Vigo had his ear close to the receiver to listen to the conversation.

"You don't have a choice. I have two hostages, and until Doug and I are free and clear you're not going to see them again."

"Let me talk to Jo."

"Jo. Why do you call her that? Why not Ms. Sutton?"

"I don't know what you mean."

"Keep your hands off her, Sheriff. She's not yours."

"She's not anyone's," Tyler said. "She's not property."

"She's mine. And she knows it. She wrote books for me. Just for me. And she wants to be with me now, especially now that she understands everything that I've done for her. All for her."

Hans motioned to keep Doherty talking in that vein.

Tyler said, "You killed Lincoln Barnes for her."

"That vicious Neanderthal blamed Joanna for taking Trixie away from him, but I saw the truth. A woman needs a man who can take care of her. Romance her. Give her what she wants and needs. Linc was a vile, violent man. He's better off dead. He would have died eventually. I just sped up the process."

"I understand," Tyler said.

"I doubt that."

"Truly, I understand. I would have wanted to kill Lincoln Barnes for what he did. You're not like him, Aaron. You're better than that. I'll tell that to the prison authorities."

"That's a laugh. You'll still send me back there. I'll still be on death row. I'll still be dead in a couple years."

Hans had scrawled on a piece of paper: *Offer a deal.*

"What if I can get you into another prison? A federal penitentiary. Someplace nicer than Quentin."

"I don't want to go back to *any* prison. I want to live my life in peace with Joanna."

Tyler's hand tightened on the receiver, but he kept his voice even. "I need to speak with her to make sure she is alive before I can negotiate."

"No. I don't trust you. You can talk to her sister."

A moment later, the high-pitched voice of a very nervous Trixie came over the radio. "T-tyler?"

"Are you okay? And Jo?"

"We're okay."

She sounded terrified. Damn, he wanted to hear Jo's voice and know for himself that she was okay.

"Have they touched you? Hurt you?"

"No —"

Doherty came back on the radio.

"Enough. You know they're alive and well and I wouldn't hurt Joanna. Despite what she did, I forgave her. That's what you do when you love someone. You forgive them."

Tyler's heart turned cold. *That's what you do when you love someone.*

"What do you want?" Tyler said quietly.

"I want a helicopter in two hours. At the Red Rock Refuge Center."

"And you'll let Jo and Trixie go?"

"Not until we're out of the valley."

Tyler knew Doherty had no intention of letting Jo go.

"I have a proposition."

"You're not in a position to negotiate, Sheriff."

"I'll be your hostage. Let Jo and her sister go, and take me instead."

"I'm not an idiot, Sheriff. You have two hours. If the chopper isn't here, Trixie Weber is dead."

"Aaron, listen —"

Doherty turned off his radio.

Tyler slammed his fist on the table. "I can't let Jo and Trixie on any helicopter with those killers!" He ran a finger along the map on the wall, found the refuge center. That had been Doherty's destination yesterday. They'd been gone for less than two hours, but since the weather was now clear they could have moved. It would have been easy for them to make it to the refuge center.

Hans said, "They're not there."

"Why do you say that?"

Karl Weber answered. "The Polaris is in Lakeview. The GPS picked them up a few minutes ago and now they're stationary on Nash's property."

"They're at Nash's house?" Mitch said.

"Makes sense," Tyler commented. "It's shelter, food, water, provisions. They can refuel and go anywhere — even out of the valley. While we fumble around sending everyone to the refuge, they have more time to get away."

"Unless they're planning on going to the refuge when they know the chopper is there or on the way."

Tyler shook his head. "Doherty doesn't want anyone else around. He doesn't trust anyone — a pilot or me, or even Jo. He wants to get them out of the valley where he'll be in control. Jo isn't going to risk

392

Trixie's life or that of an innocent bystander. She's playing along."

Hans said, "Maybe she's the one who convinced him to go to Nash's house, knowing about the GPS. As long as she continues to play along, she's okay. But if Doherty suspects that she's fooling him —"

He didn't need to finish. Tyler knew that if Doherty went into a rage, Jo would be the first to die.

"Mitch, how close can we get to Lakeview on a snowmobile?"

"I wouldn't go closer than two miles. Then if they hear anything, they'll think we're going to the refuge. But if we get too close, they'll know we're onto them."

Tyler issued orders. "Karl, stay on line with the GPS. If Jo's sled moves, I want to know. Mitch, you and I will go on the first available snowmobile. Do you ski?"

"It's been awhile."

"Get out a pair and practice. We'll go in on skis from five miles out. Grossman and Duncan can take the second sled, if we can get another working. Hans, can you stay here and be the command center?"

"Absolutely. Helena just gave word that they're moving out. Their E.T.A. is two hours and twenty minutes."

"Good. Keep in contact with me and I'll

let them know where to land. Craig and Sean Mann can stay with the kids. I want them in Karl's suite, no exceptions."

Tyler turned to Mitch. "Let's see how Stan is doing on those snowmobiles."

They were standing in Nash's big country kitchen, waiting.

Doherty and Chapman argued about everything. They argued about whether to tie Jo and her sister up. (Doherty said no, Chapman said yes.) Chapman wanted to keep them locked in the cellar, Doherty refused. ("I need to see Joanna," he said.) Doherty wanted to leave immediately, and Chapman said they had to have a firm plan before they ventured outside again. ("It's fucking thirty-one degrees out there," Chapman said after looking at a thermometer.)

Doherty agreed to tie Jo and Trixie back-to-back in chairs in the kitchen, but he wanted to leave as soon as Doug got a truck running.

"We need to refuel and we need a better plan," Chapman said.

"You refuel the snowmobiles and I'll study the maps," Doherty said. "By the time you get back, I'll have a plan and we can go."

"Shit, Aaron, I don't want to go outside again."

"You're going to have to eventually. We have thirty-five miles to reach Monida, which is like a ghost town. But we should be able to nab a car there."

"See, that's a plan I can live with."

Doherty was on a roll. "We'll get a car and head south."

"I like it. South. Warm. And what are we going to do about money, dude?"

"I'll toss the place. There has to be something around here that's valuable. Maybe some cash, jewelry."

"And guns," Chapman said.

"So do we have a deal? You fuel up, I'll find money, and we'll go."

Chapman reluctantly put on his ski jacket again. "Just as long as I never have to see, feel, or breathe snow again after this."

On his way out, Chapman ran his hand across Trixie's chest. "Nice tits, babe," he said with a wink.

"Asshole," Doherty muttered under his breath when Chapman was out of earshot.

Jo watched the entire exchange seemingly without interest. She was trying to find a way to play the two men off each other. Doherty didn't like Doug Chapman. Did he dislike his foul mouth? Or was it his drive toward violence, the way he manhandled Trixie? How could she use that to her advantage? They couldn't leave, not yet. It would take at least forty minutes practically flying on snowmobiles for anyone else to make it to Nash's place. She had to delay. She had to give Tyler time to get here. So far, her plan was working. As long as they turned on the GPS, Tyler would know their location.

"Aaron?" she said.

He stopped studying the map and crossed over to her, squatted next to her. He touched the side of her face gently, as if caressing a lover. His expression was like a puppy who wanted to please her. Jo swallowed and forced herself not to flinch.

Instead, she smiled. "I don't like Doug."

"He can be helpful in certain situations."

"He's crude. He touched Trixie inappropriately. I don't like the way he looks at her. I think he's going to hurt her."

Trixie gasped. Though Jo knew she wasn't acting — she was shaking uncontrollably — the timing was good.

"I won't let him," said Aaron. "But why do you even care about her?"

"She's my sister."

"You're more forgiving than I am."

Jo wanted to ask what in the world he knew about family, but instead she said, glancing demurely down, "I don't like the way he looks at me."

Doherty tensed. He grabbed Jo's leg and squeezed. But by the look on his face he didn't know he was hurting her. She swallowed her pain.

"He looked at you?" Doherty asked slowly.

"Yes," Jo said.

"I'll kill him before he touches you. You know that, right?"

She shrugged. "I want to believe you, but —"

Doherty frowned. "I've told you the truth from the beginning."

"You told me your name was John Miller."

"Because I wanted you to get to know the real me first."

Jo wasn't sure where she'd gone wrong, but Doherty suddenly sounded less friendly. What had she said to piss him off? What could she say to bring him back to nice, overprotective boyfriend?

"I trust you," she said. "I just wanted you to know."

He nodded, stared in her eyes. He leaned forward, his lips about to touch hers. She instinctively turned her head. It wasn't something she planned, she couldn't stop herself. If she'd had a warning, maybe she could have kissed him. But it had been a surprise.

He grabbed her head, turned her to face him. With his hands hard against each side of her head, he said, "You will not deny me what's mine. I thought you understood that this is for the best. You have too many ties here. We need to get away to be truly together."

He kissed her. Jo blanked her mind, fearful that he would do something worse. Her wrists pulled against the binds. Her fingers tried to untie the knots, but they were too tight.

"I'm not going to hurt you," he whispered in her ear, "unless you betray me again. I've forgiven you for yesterday. I won't forgive you for today. There will be no third chance."

He stood and left the kitchen.

"Trix," Jo whispered as she heard Doherty on the stairs, "can you work on the knots?"

"What are you doing?" Trixie asked. "You're playing games with him. Don't do that. Don't play games. They're going to kill us. First they're going to rape us and then they're going to kill us!" She verged on hysteria.

There was no doubt in Jo's mind that Doug Chapman would rape one or both of them. But she also believed that Aaron

Doherty didn't want to attack them. He wanted Jo to be his girlfriend, his wife, *his.* Jo hoped that as long as she played along with his sick fantasy, she'd buy enough time for Tyler to find them.

But she wasn't sure she understood all the rules to the game, or even if he might change them without warning. The only thing she knew for sure was that Tyler would find them if they stayed at Nash's. If they left, their chances of survival diminished.

"Trix, listen to me," Jo said, her voice low. One ear listened for movement on the stairs, or the sound of the door opening. "Tyler will find us here, but we have to stall."

"He thinks we're at the refuge!"

"Shh. The Polaris has GPS tracking. Remember, we installed it last year?"

Trixie was silent. "You really think they'll find us?"

"Yes, but we have to play along. Just for a while. Can you work on the knots? Help me. We have to get out of the ties. If we can get out, I know where Nash keeps his guns."

"I'll try."

"If we can't, just play along and stall."

"I don't know if I can. That man Chapman is so gross. But John Miller — I mean, Aaron — he scares me. He sounds normal, but his eyes — they are wild now."

Jo knew what Trixie meant. In some ways, Aaron Doherty resembled the boy next door. His tone was calm, but his words and the intense way he looked . . . Jo hoped she could pull this off. She mentally reviewed what she'd learned the night before from Agent Vigo. How Aaron had been abandoned repeatedly by his mother, left with relatives and friends all over the country.

What mother would do that to her son? What mother could be so cold as to abandon a little boy for weeks, months at a time?

She'd have never left her son like that. Jo tried to imagine what it was like for Aaron to grow up without a father, and with a mother who came in and out of his life on a whim. Who missed birthdays, school events, recitals. Timmy had loved soccer, and Jo and Ken had gone to his every game. She'd watched most of his practices as well. Sure, when she was close to a deadline she'd bring her laptop to the field and write while the boys kicked the ball around or scrimmaged, but she'd loved watching her son be, well, be a little boy.

She tried to feel sympathy for Aaron, but it was hard. He'd shot Wyatt, left him in the middle of nowhere. He'd kidnapped her and Trixie, not just to get away, but because he was obsessed with Jo. He'd killed Lincoln

Barnes in a misguided quest for vengeance. Vengeance for *her*.

Jo was glad Linc was dead. When he had been given the death penalty, she'd had mixed feelings because of Leah. The poor child was the innocent in the whole mess.

So Jo never brought it up. She didn't talk about Ken or Tim with Leah, not more than a few words. That wouldn't have been fair to her niece. Leah had cared about Ken, had adored her cousin Tim. She had good memories, as well as the bad.

Jo needed to share more good memories with her niece. So that she didn't remember Tim as the boy her father killed, but as the cousin she played soccer and video games with.

Just like Jo needed to remember the good times and not that last day.

"I'm sorry," she said to Trixie.

"Sorry about what? You've been a pillar of strength. I — I don't know how you're doing it."

"I'm sorry about how I've made you feel responsible for Ken and Tim's murders. It's not your fault, it never was, but I think maybe in the back of my mind I put some of the blame on you. That's not fair. You didn't ask for Lincoln Barnes to be a violent killer, you didn't ask him to come to the house. You were running for your life and he found you. It's my fault."

"No, Jo, it's not. Please —"

"Listen, Trixie. I'm serious. Linc was obsessed with you. I guess I never realized it until now, watching Aaron. It's not normal, it's psychotic. Linc would have chased you anywhere. If you came back to the valley, he would have come here. I should have taken the kids away, or been more careful. Something . . ." Jo drew in a shaky breath. "You're my sister, Trix. I love you."

"Oh, God, Jo, I don't deserve your forgiveness —"

"Shh." Jo thought she'd heard the door open. It slammed shut a moment later and both she and Trixie jumped.

"Aaron!" Chapman called.

"I'm upstairs," came a muffled reply. "I found some guns."

"Good."

Chapman stepped into the kitchen. "Well, well, well, I find two pretty sisters all alone."

He straddled Jo on the kitchen chair, his foul breath on her face, his cold hands on her neck. "You're a fine woman, Jo. A *fine* woman. Nice ass, nice tits, nice face to look at. Aaron doesn't want to share you, but hell, maybe he won't be around *all* the time, you know? We could have a little fun, just you and me."

He ground his pelvis into her and kissed her hard on the lips. She turned her face and he laughed in her ear. "I don't like kissing all that much, anyway. But I sure do like my women tied and helpless."

He reached under her sweater and pinched her nipples. Jo refused to show a reaction, but she couldn't stop the tears of pain springing spontaneously to her eyes. She felt dirty, disgusted, and petrified.

Chapman heard the footsteps on the staircase at the same time Jo did. He got off her, then did the same thing to Trixie. He was kissing Trixie when Doherty walked in.

Jo watched the look of distaste cross Doherty's face. "Get off her, Doug. Wait until we get in the clear. Are the snowmobiles ready?"

"They're fueled and right where we left them," Chapman slid off a sobbing Trixie.

"It's okay," Jo whispered, though she didn't fully believe it.

Stall, dammit! Think of something!

Chapman said, "I'm fucking tired and cold. Let's eat first, get up our strength if we have to be on those rides for hours."

Jo said, "Aaron, I hate to agree with him, but he's right. There's nothing in Monida. We probably won't be able to get food or anything until dark."

When Doherty didn't look like he would cave, she added, "I haven't eaten at all today, Aaron. But I finally have my appetite back."

He touched her lightly on the face and she smiled. She hoped it looked warm and friendly. All she wanted to do was spit in his face.

"For you, my love. Twenty minutes. That's it. Then we have to go."

TWENTY-FOUR

Tyler and Mitch rode double on one snowmobile; deputies Grossman and Duncan were on the second. They followed the fresh impressions in the snow left by the two killers who had Jo and Trixie. FBI SWAT was on their way, but they were still two hours away. Tyler couldn't wait that long.

Hans would radio only if Jo's Polaris changed location. Right now, it was stationary: on Sam Nash's property. They were unlikely to take any of Nash's other vehicles. Even Nash's four-wheel-drive truck probably couldn't get out of the garage with this much snow on the ground. Nash had a snowplow, but it moved slowly. Even with Chapman's mechanical skills, if he could figure out how to operate it, would they chance taking the slow-moving truck? Tyler didn't think so.

Either Doherty had planned on meeting at the refuge after he knew the helicopter was on its way, or he never had any intention of meeting them and was buying time. Time to escape.

Doherty and Chapman already had weapons, but at Nash's they could have acquired an arsenal. Nash had several shotguns and rifles. Tyler had his sidearm and a shotgun Stan gave him, and Mitch and his deputies were armed, but in a standoff, Doherty and Chapman would have the upper hand.

There was more blue than gray in the sky, and even though Upper Red Rock Lake was miles from the road, Tyler could see the sun reflecting off the still water. The lake was too deep to completely freeze, but it was cold enough to turn the top inch to ice.

Though the weather seemed perfect, with a projected high of fifty, Karl Weber said he suspected another storm front would move in quickly. The NWS predicted twenty-four hours, but Tyler trusted Weber's judgment — he'd lived through more surprise storms than most.

Two miles from Nash's property, Tyler stopped the snowmobile and they disembarked. They'd made excellent time because visibility was good and they had the trail Chapman and Doherty left.

The four men put on cross-country skis. They each had a walkie-talkie, and Tyler had the portable radio to keep in contact with the lodge. They couldn't move as fast as the snowmobiles, but they skied steadily about seven miles an hour. Tyler was grateful that he'd made a point of refreshing all his winter sports skills when he'd moved to Montana. Otherwise, he'd be lagging behind.

In twenty minutes, they'd be within sight of Nash's property. They'd assess the situation and form a plan of attack. A plan that didn't put Jo and Trixie in more danger than they already were.

Bong.

Jo jumped when the grandfather clock in Nash's living room announced the time, the deep, guttural chime vibrating in her head. She'd been here many times, had often heard the forlorn sound, but today it seemed particularly ominous.

"Time to go," Doherty said as he untied Jo and Trixie.

Did Tyler have enough time to track the GPS in the snowmobile and make it out here? She thought she'd heard the roar of snowmobiles far in the distance, but then they'd stopped, or perhaps they'd turned in another direction.

Bong.

"Please, please leave us alone," Trixie said. "You can just leave, we can't go anywhere or tell anyone. Leave us here and go."

"We'll only slow you down," Jo said.

Doug Chapman laughed. "You're hostages, babe. We're not letting you go anytime soon."

Aaron stared at Jo, an odd look on his face. Had she tipped her hand?

Bong.

"Everything is going to be fine," he told her.

"No!" Trixie cried when Chapman grabbed her.

Doherty stared at Trixie with disgust. "You, we don't need." He pointed his gun at her.

Jo screamed, trying to put herself between Doherty and the gun, but he held on to her upper arm so tight her arm burned. "What are you doing?" she asked.

"You really don't know what she did, do you?" Aaron said.

Bong.

"Aaron." Jo's eyes darted back and forth

between Doherty and Trixie.

"Trixie? Are you going to tell her or am I?"

"Stop this right now, Aaron." Jo's voice was stronger than her frayed emotions.

Chapman leaned over and backhanded Jo. She would have fallen down if Doherty hadn't caught her.

"Don't touch her again." Doherty turned his gun on Chapman.

"You're letting the bitch make demands of you?" Chapman said, furious the gun was aimed at him. "Get that fucking gun away from me or I'll kill you." It sounded like an idle threat considering Doherty had the upper hand. Jo pictured them firing simultaneously and killing each other. She would have laughed at the absurd vision if she weren't so fearful for her life.

Bong.

"Do not call her a bitch," Doherty said. "You will treat Joanna with respect."

"She's playing you, Aaron. She's been playing you all day."

Aaron blinked rapidly. "Everything is going to be fine once we get out of here."

"So what are you waiting for?" Chapman mocked.

"I want Trixie to tell the truth," Doherty said, "for once in her life."

Bong.

Trixie shook her head. "You don't know me. You don't know anything about me! Leave me alone!"

"I was in the cell next to Lincoln Barnes. I know a lot about you, Trixie. More than you ever told your sister."

"Shut up!" She lunged for him, and Chapman grabbed her and held her back.

"What are you doing, Aaron? Let's get out of here."

"Not until Trixie tells Joanna the truth."

Jo looked from Doherty to her sister. There was something on Trixie's face. Jo's gut turned and bile rose to her throat. She didn't want to believe anything Aaron Doherty had to say. The man was a killer. He had kidnapped her. But . . .

"Leave her alone," Jo said quietly. "Please, Aaron."

Bong.

Doherty turned to Jo, touched her face with the muzzle of his gun. His expression soft and almost loving, but his eyes were hard and distrustful. "No secrets, Joanna. Okay? No secrets between us."

"Stop, Aaron. Let's just go."

A little voice scratched and clawed at the back of Jo's mind. She wanted to know whatever secret Aaron Doherty knew about her sister. All the doubts, all the fears, came rushing back.

No, Jo, don't go there. She's your sister. She's Leah's mother. You can't go back. You can't have what was stolen. Just forget . . .

But the doubts she'd had for four years grew. She looked at Trixie, didn't say a word.

Tears streamed down Trixie's face. "Jo, I'm sorry."

Bong.

"Tell her!" Doherty screamed and Jo jumped. "Tell her you married Lincoln Barnes!"

Jo stared at Trixie, but relief flooded through her body. She'd wondered for a long time whether Trixie had married him when they were in L.A., but Trixie had denied it. There were a few hints here and there, but Jo didn't push it because it had become unimportant. When Linc called Trix his wife the day he killed Ken and Tim, Jo had thought he was delusional. Now she knew he wasn't: Linc had told the truth.

"It's okay, Trixie," Jo said. "That's water under the bridge. Linc hurt a lot of people. I don't care that you married him. You were a different person then, and you got away from him. You protected Leah, and that's the most important thing."

Instead of Trixie looking relieved, she

410

became more irate. "Why do you forgive me so easily? Why, Jo? After everything . . ."

"Tell her!" Doherty screamed.

Bong.

"I — I —"

Sobbing uncontrollably, Trixie sagged, and Chapman let her fall to the ground.

"Aaron, just fucking get it out," Chapman demanded. "I want to go. Everything's ready. We're wasting time because you're playing a fucking game."

Bang! Bang! Bang!

Jo stared wide-eyed as Doug Chapman staggered backward from Doherty's shots. His gun went off once, into the ceiling. Plaster fell to the floor like snow. There was no blood at first, which made it more surreal to Jo — Chapman wore a thick ski jacket. As she watched, blood seeped from the bottom and dripped to the floor.

His mouth moved, but no sound came out. Chapman fell with a thud and didn't move. Doherty didn't show any reaction. He simply frowned and shook his head.

Bong.

"Tell her, Trixie." Doherty's voice was so low Jo almost didn't hear him. Trixie shook her head back and forth.

"No, no, no!" She sobbed.

"It's okay, Trix." Jo's heart raced as her

eyes moved from Chapman's dead body to her sister's terrified, tear-drenched face. Jo didn't know how to stop this insanity.

"Tell her, Trixie!"

"I forgive you," Jo said, wishing she could go to her sister, but Doherty held her too tight. "The past doesn't matter."

"Tell her!" Doherty screamed.

"It's my fault," Trixie sobbed. "It's my fault Ken and Timmy died."

Doherty asked Jo, "Didn't you ever wonder how Linc found you? Didn't you wonder how he knew where you lived?"

She had, but after Timmy died it hadn't seemed important. It was almost ethereal, like she should ask the question but she was in a daze. And then the trial . . . it never came out. She didn't think the question had ever been asked. And deep down, she hadn't cared. Her husband and son were dead, that was all that mattered.

Jo looked at Trixie. Everything made sense now. Her sister's self-blame. That she came back to the valley even though she hated it here. Why she resented Jo spending time with Leah, while at the same time almost forcing Leah on Jo.

Guilt.

Bong.

"It doesn't matter," Jo whispered, though

412

it did matter. And now that the question had been raised, how could she forget? But that was something to deal with when she and Trixie got out of this.

Doherty just shot his partner in cold blood. He's going to kill you. You have to get out of here, get Trixie out of here. Nothing else matters.

Trixie sobbed, looked up at Jo, her face a mask of agony and pain. "I — I called him. I told him to meet me at a restaurant on the highway. I — I wanted to go with him. I knew I couldn't take Leah, but I had to b-b-be with Linc. He didn't show up, and I was so mad, but he followed me. He wanted Leah more than me. He followed me to your house. I'm so sorry, Jo. I didn't know he was going to hurt anyone."

Hurt? He'd killed a man and a little boy because Trixie had led him to their house.

"I'm sorry, Jo. I wish I'd died that day."

Bang.

Jo screamed. Trixie's mouth opened and blood flowed from the corner. *"NO!!"*

Doherty let her go to her sister, hold her. "I'm glad," Trixie whispered. "I'm glad I'm dead. Take care of Leah for me. You were always a better mother."

"Hold on, hold on," Jo cried, cradling her sister in her arms. The bullet had gone into

413

Trixie's chest, almost dead center. Jo's head and heart hurt, she couldn't think about what Trixie had done in the past. She loved her sister. "Please don't die." *Oh, God, please not again. Don't take anyone else from me. Don't let Trixie die!*

"She's better off dead," Doherty said. "Now you've been avenged. We're going now, just you and me."

Bong.

It was noon. Jo's life would never be the same.

TWENTY-FIVE

Tyler glanced at Mitch. Neither man had to say a word. They'd both heard the gunfire.

Heart racing and fear spurring him forward, he and Mitch took on a burst of speed. Nash's house was off the road, his drive covered by snow, but a marker showed Tyler they were at the right place to turn. They had to slow for the turn, and their momentum only brought them halfway up the knoll.

"Shit," Tyler muttered. Nash's simple, two-story farmhouse was only a hundred yards away.

"We'll go parallel to the house," Mitch

said, cutting across and parallel to the road below.

Tyler followed, but time was crucial. Who had been hurt?

Another gunshot pierced the air, then a scream.

Jo.

Mitch whipped around, stared at Tyler. He said, "Keep your cool, Sheriff. We don't know what's happened."

Mitch was right, but the woman he loved wasn't at the mercy of a psychopath.

Mitch motioned toward the garage. The door was open. He put a finger to his lip. They skied to the door, peered in.

Empty.

"Shit," Mitch said. The sleds were probably closer to the house, which meant the killers could get away and Tyler and Mitch wouldn't be able to pursue them.

Another scream cut through the silence, and Tyler and Mitch moved as quick as possible to the main house.

Aaron Doherty stared at Jo. "You're coming with me. I got rid of them. It's just you and me."

"Please," Jo begged, "we have to get Trixie help."

"Why do you still care about her after she

betrayed you?"

"She didn't do any of it on purpose." Trixie wasn't breathing. Jo felt for her pulse. Faint and fading. She was dying.

"We have to go. Right now."

"No. No!" Jo was panicking. All thought of playing along with Doherty vanished. She eased Trixie down on the floor, opened nearby drawers looking for dish towels, found them under the sink. She tried to stop the blood. Too much blood. It was Ken all over again.

"No, Trixie, please," Jo sobbed. "Leah needs you."

Doherty pulled Jo up. "She's dead. Come now or I'll have to hurt you. Don't make me hurt you, Joanna."

Jo glimpsed movement outside the kitchen window, far down the slope heading to the garage. Skiers? She saw a glint of metal near her foot. Chapman's gun. She kicked it next to Trixie, then stumbled and collapsed next to Trixie's body. "I love you, Sis. No matter what." She hid the gun under her sweater and prayed Doherty didn't notice.

"She doesn't deserve your love." He jerked her up and pulled her in front of him. His expression was clouded, but he looked sad. "No more games, Joanna. We're leaving now."

She pushed aside the anguish that filled her and only thought one thing: *Get away from Aaron Doherty.*

She went with Doherty as far as the porch, then collapsed into a ball at his feet. "No, I won't go with you! I don't care anymore."

"What do you mean?"

"You killed my sister!"

"She was a whore! She brought Lincoln Barnes into your house. She's the reason your husband and son are dead! I avenged you. I take care of those who hurt you."

Jo pushed aside her conflicting emotions and anguish that Trixie was dead inside the house. No matter what she might think of what her sister had done, Trix didn't deserve to die.

Had Jo done the wrong thing? Had the decision she made to play along with Aaron's psychosis resulted in her sister's murder?

Jo pushed the disturbing thoughts from her head. She had to deal with this crisis, find a way to delay or distract Doherty.

"Trixie might not be dead. Please, Aaron, you're not a killer. Not like Doug Chapman. If she dies, Leah won't have a mother." Jo knew Trixie was gone, but she hoped to appeal to whatever humanity might be left in Doherty.

"I'm sorry about that," he said. And Jo believed him. "We can send for Leah when we're settled."

Her stomach roiled. She couldn't go with him. He might act contrite, but he was an unpredictable killer.

"Are you crazy?"

Jo tried to take back the words, but they were already out there and Doherty's face twisted in anger.

The gun was in his belt, but he reached for a knife instead. The knife was as terrifying as the gun.

"You've been lying to me all along," he said.

"No —"

"Doug was right. You don't care about me. You've been playing me!" Doherty held the knife up as if he would stab her. Jo screamed, her hands instinctively moving to her face.

A sound startled him. He looked right, left, confused. His arm came down and Jo gasped at the sharp pain across her lower cheek and arm.

She cried out, started to crawl away, trying to gain traction on the icy porch to get up and run.

He said, "See if anyone but me loves you with a scar across your face."

He raised his arm again. Jo reached under her sweater and pulled out Chapman's gun. She aimed it at Doherty.

He reacted faster than she thought anyone could. He kicked her hand and her finger pressed the trigger, trying to keep the aim at his body. The gunshot echoed as it went wild, the gun falling from her hand. Jo scrambled for it, but Doherty kicked her down. She tried to get up, and over her shoulder saw a knife coming down . . .

She rolled, blood coating her arm. She couldn't think about the blood or the pain. *Get away. Run.*

Jo got up on all fours and moved as fast as she could. She slipped, but so did Doherty behind her. She thought she heard a shout downslope and glanced over her shoulder. Doherty was ten feet away, but he'd stopped, listening. She ran, tripping down the stairs, then glanced back.

He was gone.

A snowmobile roared to life and sped away. She stood, tried to run in the snow, but her boots sunk down too far, making it impossible to run. She fell into the powder, the icy cold soothing her hot, throbbing cheek and arm.

If he's behind you, he'll stab you in the back.

She heard another snowmobile and her

mind played tricks on her. Had Doug Chapman survived the attack? No. She'd seen his eyes. They were dead.

She crawled, tried to roll over to shield herself from a pending attack.

A man loomed above her. She opened her mouth to scream, then said, "Tyler!" She sobbed in relief and anguish as he gathered her up and carried her back to the house.

"Jo, where are you hurt?"

She hugged him, the panic and fear still making her heart race. "He killed Trixie. He killed her."

"Shh. I need to look at you."

"No, no, please, Trix — Oh God, Tyler, she's dead." Jo clung to him as if she were drowning.

"Where's Chapman?" he whispered.

"Dead," she said. "Aaron shot him."

"You're bleeding. I need to stop the blood." He eased her onto the couch.

"I need to see Trixie. Please. If she's alive —"

She stumbled into the kitchen and Tyler caught her by the arm to keep her from falling.

Trixie lay exactly where Jo had left her. Jo sat heavily next to her, checked for a pulse. Nothing. Listened for breathing. Nothing.

Then the tears came. "Why, Trixie? Why?"

Tyler inspected Chapman's body. He didn't say anything, but the way he turned his back to the killer Jo knew he was also dead.

Tyler squatted next to her, checked Trixie's vital signs. "There's nothing you can do, Jo."

"What if I hadn't tried to manipulate Aaron? I don't know why he shot her." But she did. A twisted sense of revenge. The knife wound across her left cheek stung when salty tears slid down her face.

"Jo, I need to check your injuries."

No matter what Trixie did four years ago, she didn't deserve to die. Not gunned down.

She brought Lincoln Barnes into your house. And she was dead.

"Leah can never know," she whispered.

"Jo, honey." Tyler picked her up and carried her from the bloody kitchen into the living room and placed her on the couch. He put an afghan over her shaking body, rolled up her sleeve to look at her arm. "We'll tell Leah together."

Jo closed her eyes. "She can't know the truth."

"The truth? That her mother was murdered? Shh, you're not thinking straight."

She heard cloth tearing and opened her eyes. Tyler was tying a band of material around her bleeding arm. She couldn't feel her fingers.

Tyler didn't need to know about Trixie's failings, either. She'd keep her sister's secret.

With her uninjured arm, she reached for Tyler. He clasped her hand.

"You found us."

"I'm so sorry we weren't here sooner. We didn't want to make noise so we skied in."

"I thought I saw skiers." She winced as Tyler tightened the makeshift bandage around her arm. "We?"

"There were two snowmobiles parked outside the door. Doherty took one, and Mitch Bianchi followed on the other."

"They were getting ready to take us, and I was so scared you'd lose the GPS signal. I was stalling. But if I didn't stall, Trixie would still be alive. If I'd just done what they wanted —"

"Stop." Tyler kissed her to shut her mouth. "Stop that. No second guessing. You did the right thing. If you were on the sled, there would be no way we could follow on skis. We were banking on the fact that the sleds were stationary."

"Can you track Doherty? On the GPS?"

"We'll try. Are you okay?" Tyler's voice cracked. He touched her face with shaking hands. "I thought — when I heard the gunshots — I can't lose you, Jo."

"I'm okay." She rested her head on his shoulder, her heart finally slowing. For one too-brief moment she let everything just wash away and breathed in Tyler.

Noise from the porch made her jump. Tyler jumped up, gun in hand. "McBride!" A voice called from outside.

"In here!"

Grossman and Duncan walked into the living room on full alert, guns drawn.

Tyler said, "Chapman's dead. Doherty killed him and Trixie Weber. Mitch went after him on his own. Billy, go get my radio for me — I left it in the garage with the skis. I need to call Vigo and tell him where to send the SWAT team."

The asshole was gaining on him.

Aaron pushed the Polaris as fast as it would go. He was practically flying over the snow. The first drift he jumped scared the hell out of him, but he managed to stay on the sled, feeling at one with the machine.

She betrayed you. She was going to kill you.

No.

Yes. She had Doug's gun. She shot you with bear spray yesterday, and today she was going to shoot you with a gun.

"I killed her sister," he said out loud.

423

The bitch deserved it. Of all people, Trixie had wanted Linc Barnes. He hit her and she liked it so much she was going to run away with him.

Linc had told Aaron everything while they were in prison. How he called Trixie on her cell phone every day, begging her to come back. He'd finally convinced her to meet with him, but in public. "She didn't want me to see my daughter. She was willing to let another man raise my daughter, but not Leah's own father!"

Linc followed Trixie to Joanna's house, but Leah wasn't there. That's when he lost it.

"I didn't mean to kill anyone. I just wanted what was mine. My daughter and my wife. Mine."

Aaron didn't regret killing the bastard, or Trixie Weber. The bitch deserved it.

So does Joanna.

He tensed on the sled, urged the machine faster. Faster.

Joanna had betrayed him. She would have killed him. She had lied to him, over and over.

Just like Rebecca. Just like Bridget.

Like his fucking mother.

Ginger loved you.

He shook his head rapidly back and forth,

424

trying to force the thoughts from his head. His mother had never loved him. He was property. A possession. She used him as a pawn with his father — who he didn't even remember — with his grandparents, and all the strangers she left him with.

When Annie wanted him — she loved him, wanted him to live with her — Ginger came and took him away.

Why didn't you fight for me Annie? Was that all a lie, too?

Who could he believe?

Clink-clank.

The bastard was shooting at him!

Aaron glanced to the left: too steep. To the right: deep drifts, looking like white sand dunes.

He didn't know where he was, but he had to get away from whoever was shooting at him.

Up ahead he saw a fallen tree. It was huge, and Aaron had no time to think.

He veered sharply to the right, barely slowing down. The edge of the road was steeper than he thought and he was flying over a drift, thirty or forty feet above the ground.

The thrill was terrifying and exciting.

He landed and would have crashed except he veered left, then right, around a high drift. It was a maze and he could get lost.

So could the cop chasing him.

Like something out of the movies, Aaron saw a snowmobile fly over him. No one was on it.

The cop had been thrown off. Probably broke his neck.

Aaron wasn't waiting around to find out. He felt in his pocket to make sure he still had the map. Good. He aimed his sled northwest and kept going.

Twenty-Six

FBI SWAT landed at Nash's house thirty minutes later. Tyler left Jo in the house with Duncan and Grossman while he went to talk to the Feds.

Mitch wasn't back, and he wasn't answering his walkie-talkie.

Ten armed SWAT officers exited the helicopter. The commander approached Tyler, took off his helmet. "Agent Hunter Blackstone. You must be Sheriff McBride."

Tyler took his hand, they shook.

"Agent Vigo said one target is dead, one civilian is dead, and one target is at large."

"Yes. Aaron Doherty escaped on a snowmobile. One of your men followed him."

"My men?"

"A Fed. Agent Mitch Bianchi."

"Bianchi's here?"

"Hans didn't tell you?"

"Not in so many words."

"Is there a problem?"

"Problem? No problem. Bianchi is one of the best. I just thought he was heading back to Sacramento."

"If he is, he's doing it on a snowmobile." Tyler frowned. "I haven't heard from him in over thirty minutes."

"Roger that. I'll send my pilot and half my men to do reconnaissance and see if we can spot the pursuit. Which way did they go?"

"West," Tyler said. "You should be able to track the wake of the sleds. They kick up a lot of snow."

"Good to know." Blackstone walked quickly back to the chopper. Tyler couldn't hear what he said, but six men reboarded and the bird lifted off. Blackstone returned. "My pilot is concerned about the weather."

Tyler glanced at the cloud-spotted blue sky. "How soon is it going to turn?"

"There's a nasty storm front heading in from the southeast. It's going to come in hard and fast. We'll lose visibility in three, four hours max."

Tyler would never get used to the weather

in Montana. "Then we'd better find Mitch and Doherty before you're grounded."

"Have you taken care of the bodies?"

Tyler shook his head. "They're still in the kitchen. One of the victims is the sister of the survivor."

"Sorry," Blackstone muttered. "My men will take care of them." He looked around. "Where can we put them?"

"The garage." Tyler pointed downslope. "Do you have body bags?"

Blackstone nodded. "Can we use this house as a command center?"

"Yes. The owner is transporting my brother to a doctor on the other side of the mountain."

"Your brother?"

"He was the scoutmaster shot yesterday."

"Right. We'll secure this place. No one will be able to get in without our sanction. You take a breather. You've been on duty 24/7 for three days, Agent Vigo said."

The way Blackstone said "Agent Vigo" showed that Hans's colleagues gave him a huge amount of respect.

"I won't be able to relax until I hear from Mitch," Tyler said.

"We'll find him. We have some state-of-the-art sensors on the bird."

"Good. After you find him, find Doherty.

I have a bad feeling that he'll come back again for Jo."

"We'll be ready for him."

Aaron followed his map to a house near the Lima Reservoir.

He'd heard the helicopter searching for him. Or for the cop, who was probably dead. It didn't matter, the farther he rode west, the farther away the chopper sounded.

When he'd first arrived at the lodge, he'd used information he found in the office to identify all residences in the area. He carefully plotted them on his map. At the time he wasn't sure if he would need them, but he also knew he had to get Joanna away from her family in order to convince her of his nobility.

Now he was alone.

It was getting dark, and it wasn't even four in the afternoon. He'd been riding for nearly four hours, had recently switched to the backup tank. He'd burned a lot of fuel running from the cop, so he kept the sled steady at twenty miles per hour once he knew the helicopter hadn't spotted him.

The blue sky turned dark gray. Clouds rolled in like something out of a horror movie. Thunder rumbled in the distance, sounding far more foreboding in the valley than it ever did in the middle of a city like Los Angeles.

Aaron stopped as the first snowflake fell. He took out his map. He wasn't sure where he was, and though he knew he'd traveled over seventy-five miles, he'd been zigzagging. He *thought* he was only a few miles from the Lima Reservoir, but what if he was wrong?

The snow fell deceptively soft around him as he stared at the map. Shit, he didn't know where the fuck he was.

That wasn't true. He'd gone mostly northwest. He'd kept a good eye on the compass. Which would put him about . . .

He looked at the map, then at his surroundings. What if he was wrong?

He couldn't afford to try to find this one house only to find he was miles from where he thought. If he ran out of gas in the middle of nowhere . . .

It's Joanna's fault.

He slammed his fist on the Polaris's instrument panel. Damn, damn, damn. He should have taken her with him.

She didn't want to come with you. She doesn't love you. She lied to you. All these years, it was a joke. One big joke on you.

Eight years ago when he went back to Rebecca to explain, to beg for forgiveness, he'd realized what a joke she thought he was.

He'd quietly snuck into her house. She had an alarm system, but he knew the code. It surprised him she hadn't changed it, but maybe she hadn't known he knew. Or maybe she wanted him to come to her.

A man was with her. The same actor who had been bad-mouthing Aaron to Rebecca all these months. It was his fault, not hers. Aaron believed that up until he overheard . . .

"Rebecca dear, are you feeling all right?" Bruce Lawson's voice was prissy. Condescending.

Why had she let him in the house? Into her bedroom?

"I'm fine."

Such a beautiful voice. Aaron closed his eyes and imagined Rebecca speaking to him so kindly, so lovingly.

The sound of movement, then Lawson said, "Better?"

"Much."

The smooch of a kiss.

Aaron tensed. Lawson had kissed Rebecca. Touched her with his lips. Not okay. Not okay at all.

"You've been a godsend, Bruce." Rebecca sighed. "I wouldn't have made it all these weeks without you."

"You're still worried."

"Of course I am. They haven't found him."

"The police are looking for him. He wouldn't be so stupid as to show up anywhere near here."

"I don't know. He — there's something not right with him."

"Of course not! He hurt you. The guy's a lunatic."

"He thought there was something going on between you and me."

"Who cares what he thought?"

"There wasn't. Not then."

"What are you saying?"

"You've been a rock, Bruce. I never thought — I guess, with your reputation . . ."

"Don't believe everything you hear, darling."

Smooch. Silence.

Rebecca said softly, "Thank you for staying with me."

"I'll stay with you as long as you want me to."

Aaron didn't remember killing them. He witnessed the scene disembodied, as if looking at himself from afar, in freeze-frames. Coming into Rebecca's room. Bruce Lawson charging him, Aaron slicing him with three strokes.

Slit, slit, slit.

Rebecca screaming.

Stabbing her. The police said he'd stabbed

her thirty-two times. He only remembered the first one. Then pulling his knife out and looking at her face. The shock.

I loved you I loved you I loved you I loved you.

He groaned, his hand aching as if he'd today stabbed Rebecca thirty-two times. He stared at the Montana map. He had to be right.

He would find the Jorgensen farm. He would refuel. Then he would hunt down Joanna and cut her heart out.

Like she'd cut out his.

If anyone tried to stop him, they'd die, too.

TWENTY-SEVEN

The storm teased the valley, rolling in fast but bringing with it just an occasional flurry of flakes. Weather didn't ground the helicopter; nighttime did.

Tyler went back to the lodge with Jo on the last run of the chopper. They'd found Mitch almost immediately — he'd been thrown from the sled while in pursuit and had hit his head hard. Snow wasn't as soft as it appeared. Agent Bianchi was damn lucky he didn't break anything, including his back.

In case Doherty returned, Mitch stayed with half the SWAT team at Nash's house. At dawn, weather permitting, they'd start the search again.

The rest of the team was at the Moosehead Lodge. Grossman and Duncan had escorted the Boy Scouts and remaining lodge guests to the Worthingtons' house before nightfall. Tomorrow morning, a charter helicopter would take them over the pass to reunite with their families. Except Jason. Jason hadn't wanted to go, and Tyler didn't force him to. The lodge was safe — cops outnumbered civilians. Jason was in the den with Buckley. Tyler thought that maybe it was time Jason had his own dog. Tyler had a dog most of his childhood, until Kip was hit by a car and had to be put to sleep. He hadn't been able to have another pet, but Jason was a boy, and boys needed dogs.

Tyler stared at the closed door leading to Karl's suite, knowing Jo was in there with her family, telling them about Trixie. He wanted to go to her, to take care of her, but Jo needed this private time with Karl, Stan, and Leah.

After triple-checking that Jason was safe in the den, Tyler went into the kitchen where Vigo was talking with Agent Hunter

Blackstone. Tyler poured himself coffee and sat down across from the senior agent.

"You couldn't have done anything to save her," Hans said.

Tyler didn't respond. What could he say? He'd been running through the day from beginning to end and thought of a million different things he could have said or done, but every scenario ended up with someone dead.

"How's Mitch?" Hans asked.

Blackstone answered, "In a foul mood with a bear of a headache."

"He's lucky he's alive, hotdogging it after Doherty on his own," Hans reprimanded. "Probably thinks if he gets injured in the line of duty he'll have a pass when he gets back to Sacramento."

"Excuse me?" Tyler asked.

"It's nothing," Hans said.

"Like hell it is," Blackstone said. "Mitch defied orders tracking Thomas O'Brien up this far. He wasn't supposed to leave the Sacramento region. Then he was ordered back and he never went. I sure as hell wouldn't want to get on Meg Elliott's shit list."

"She doesn't bite," Hans said.

"I have my doubts."

"Mitch will be okay, as long as he doesn't

mouth off," Hans said.

"I don't understand." Tyler didn't understand how the FBI worked, but he'd assumed Mitch Bianchi was assigned to this case.

Hans explained. "Mitch is a damn good cop. More than dedicated. But he sometimes has a problem following orders, and the FBI is not the place to regularly defy authority — right or wrong. Mitch was supposed to stay in Sacramento; instead, when Thomas O'Brien was sighted, he followed rather than calling the appropriate regional office."

"I'm glad he did," Tyler said. "He's solid."

"That he is, and loyal."

"If you need anything from me," Tyler said, "I'll gladly testify that Mitch has been a great agent to work with. Smart and sharp."

"If you want to write a letter, that'd be good for his file," Hans said. "By the way, Nash called right before you arrived. Wyatt's safe and in the hospital. He's going into surgery tonight, but the prognosis is good."

"Glad to hear that." More than glad. Tyler had been worried about Wyatt all day.

"Your Bonnie — great gal, by the way — patched a call into the lodge radio this afternoon. The FBI agent I have looking into Doherty's past uncovered a murder seventeen years ago in San Diego. The victim was Ginger Doherty."

"His mother?"

"Yes."

"Why wasn't that in his file?"

"Because there is no record of Ginger Doherty having a son. She never filed taxes with his name or Social Security number. In her employment records with King Cruises she stated that she was single, without children, and twenty-nine. She had fake identification and no one who knew her even suspected that she had a child. She listed no next of kin."

"What happened to her?"

"She was stabbed to death. She was living with a man near the beach between cruises."

"So she left her son with an old aunt in Glendale and worked out of San Diego."

"The police had a suspect. A belligerent ex-boyfriend of Ms. Doherty's who was in town at the time of the murders."

"Murders?"

"The current boyfriend was also killed. His throat was slit, he died quickly. Ginger Doherty was stabbed repeatedly. Sixteen times in the chest and abdomen."

"Does that have significance?" Blackstone asked.

"Aaron Doherty turned sixteen the day before. And according to one of his earlier guardians, Annie Erickson, his mother had repeatedly disappointed him on his birthday. Making promises she never kept. Also, the MO matches the Rebecca Oliver crime scene. The man was killed quickly and efficiently, while the female was repeatedly stabbed, most post-mortem."

"How did he find her? Didn't you say the police had a suspect?" Tyler questioned.

"The ex-boyfriend had an alibi, and they couldn't break him. They had to let him go, but they still thought they'd had the right guy even if they didn't have the evidence. They stopped looking."

"So how does that help us now?" Tyler asked. "That he killed his mother and her lover means nothing to me. Right now, he's out there somewhere. I hope he's freezing to death in the middle of the valley. Or maybe he had a destination. SWAT checked out the refuge, but he wasn't there. There are more than a dozen families living in the valley who are still in danger because he's at large."

"Knowing about his mother is important." Hans rose, retrieved the coffeepot, and refilled the mugs while he spoke. "It tells us about his mind-set. It also tells us that he's been a killer for a long, long time. But he's not a traditional serial killer by any means. So far, we *suspect* he killed his mother and her boyfriend, and we *know* he killed five people: Rebecca Oliver and her friend Bruce Lawson; Lincoln Barnes; and today Doug Chapman and Trixie Weber. Each murder was for a purpose."

"What purpose did he have for killing Trixie Weber?" Tyler demanded. "She was a physically handicapped woman with a daughter. She was no threat to him."

"Something has been bothering me about the Sutton murders."

Tyler frowned. Jo didn't need any more tragedy or inquiries into the deaths of her husband and son. "What specifically?"

"How did Lincoln Barnes know where to find Trixie and her daughter?" Hans didn't wait for an answer. "Trixie was an abused woman. Abused women have low self-esteem and often return to their abusers — either because they think they've changed, or they feel they can change them if only they are good."

"You don't think —" Tyler remembered something Jo had said when he had first found her earlier today. When she saw her dead sister's body. "You think Trixie brought Lincoln Barnes to Placerville."

"It's the only thing that makes sense, knowing what we know about Barnes and Trixie."

"He could have tracked her down from mutual friends, maybe an address book with Jo's address in it, any number of ways."

Hans shook his head. "I don't think so. I was reading over the police reports and there was nothing in Lincoln Barnes's possession except a note in his pocket that read, 'Meet Trix at diner on Highway 49 and Main St.'"

"That doesn't mean anything." But Tyler frowned. Did Jo know about this?

"There were also three tickets reserved at the Sacramento Airport; final destination Madison, Wisconsin — where Barnes has family — for Lincoln Barnes, Beatrix Barnes, and Leah Barnes."

"There's no way that Linc could get two people against their will on a plane," Tyler said. Then he said, "Shit. You think Trixie planned to go off with him?"

Hans nodded. "And for whatever reason, something went wrong and Linc snapped. Or maybe he made the reservations, and Trixie just wanted to talk. We'll never know. Abused women have a very difficult time getting away from their abusers. They have a complex psychology. I've known more than one battered woman who went back to her abuser, only to be killed."

"So," Tyler extrapolated, "you think that Doherty killed Trixie because she hurt Jo — by telling Barnes where she was, leading him to the murders of Ken and Timmy Sutton."

"Bingo."

"That doesn't sit well with me." How could he tell Jo something like that? "Jo doesn't need to know," he added.

"Doherty will have told Jo why he killed Trixie," Hans said. "She knows the truth — whatever it is."

Why hadn't she told him? Of course, to protect Trixie's memory. He glanced out the door, though he knew Jo was still with her family.

Blackstone asked, "So what specifically set Doherty off all those years ago that he would kill his own mother?"

Hans paused for a long minute, sipped his coffee, putting together his thoughts. "I think he'd been looking for his mother for a while. Maybe verifying her whereabouts. He found out she worked for King Cruises. He tracked her schedule, found out she was in port. It was his birthday. Certainly she would come visit. She had always promised to see him on his birthday. He would have

441

put aside the fact that she broke most of her promises. This day he was turning sixteen. He hoped she would come."

"And she didn't," Tyler said.

"No. He snapped. I don't know specifically why — maybe he learned that she'd been lying to him, or lying about him. Maybe his aunt said something and he put information together that sent him on a murderous rage. Something happened when he turned sixteen that forever sent him down the wrong path.

"It was shortly after that when he became obsessed with Bridget Hart, a girlfriend in high school. They dated for about a year and she left him. He attacked her, scarred her face. He ended up with six months in juvie and his great-aunt, Dorothy Miles, was granted legal custody when the court couldn't find his mother.

"Shortly after his eighteenth birthday, his aunt died. She was in her eighties and the doctor ruled it as an accidental overdose. She'd had her stomach pumped three times in the preceding four years for taking too much medicine, or mixing them. The first two times happened before Aaron came to live with her, so it could be entirely possible that she did accidentally overdose."

"Or," Tyler said, "Doherty may have

witnessed one of the attempts and thought that was a good way to take her out."

"Possibly. She left him her estate. She lived comfortably so there wasn't a lot of money left, but she had no mortgage and the house was worth a couple hundred thousand back then. She had bought him a car when he turned sixteen. He continued to live there until he killed Rebecca Oliver. Worked at a coffee shop for years. Never made a lot of money, but when you don't have housing expenses, it doesn't matter as much."

"So he killed his mother, may or may not have killed his aunt. Then he killed Rebecca Oliver and her friend Bruce Lawson, and was convicted and put on death row. How does this help us see what he'll do next?"

"With Rebecca, he watched her for a long time. Possibly killed her husband to get him out of the way. He'd died in an apparent car accident a couple of years before the first attack, but the Glendale PD had their suspicions. Doherty was patient. Waited. Befriended her. They had a friendship for years — they were neighbors. Easy to strike up conversation. His fantasy continued to grow in his mind, but for a long time he was able to satisfy himself by keeping his distance. Then something happened, and he attacked her. Sliced up her face in her own house. He never said specifically what had happened, but I would guess it was a way of getting other men to stop looking at her. She was an actress. Her face was part of who she was."

"I read the files you brought," Tyler said. "She identified Doherty and then started putting other information together. That he had been sending her anonymous presents and notes. He would say he was courting her, but he was stalking her. She feared for her life, and rightly so. He disappeared and the police couldn't find him. Then, after her plastic surgery, he broke into her house and killed her."

"You're good at this."

"I wish I didn't have to be," Tyler said. "I still don't see what this has to do with Jo."

"Because Jo rejected him. She turned on him and he isn't going to be able to let her go."

Tyler rubbed his eyes. "He's coming back."

"Yes, I think so," Hans said.

"We'll be ready for him."

"Yes," Hans said. "This time, we will be. But you might want to give Jo a heads-up. He's not going to run away. He's going to try his damnedest to kill Jo."

TWENTY-EIGHT

Later that evening, Tyler knocked on Jo's door.

She opened the door, her face softening when she saw him. Dark circles framed her eyes from lack of sleep and grief. He reached over and lightly touched the bandage on her face. A mixture of relief for her safety and rage toward Doherty battled within him.

She opened the door wider. She wasn't smiling, but her eyes told him she was pleased to see him. "Come in."

He closed the door behind him and put the tray of food Stan had prepared down on her small table before taking Jo into his arms. He held her close to him, breathing in deeply. She'd showered, smelled of soap and water, her hair still damp.

"How are you doing?" he asked, thinking that it was a dumb question after what she'd been through over the last two days. He needed to talk to her, to hold her, to let her know that he was here for her, whatever she wanted.

"Leah wanted me to leave."

"She doesn't blame you, Jo. She's just upset —"

"I know. We had a good talk — as good as

it could be right now while the pain is so unbelievable and raw. She wants to be alone. She's in shock — she cried, but not the way she should. Grandpa is with her. Grandpa . . . I'm so worried about him."

"What can I do?"

"Hold me."

Tyler did, rubbing her back with his hands. Jo's heart beat rapidly against his chest, then slowed as she relaxed. He ran his hand absently through her hair, wishing he could take all her pain for his own.

Jo sighed in contentment, stepped back and gave him a half smile. "How's Mitch?"

"Better. Hans and I spoke with him before I came up here. He says he's going on the search in the morning, but we'll see."

"I've been thinking about that."

"About what?"

"The search. I'm going to go with you."

"No you're not." *Over my dead body.*

"I have to. Wyatt is in the hospital and while Billy Grossman knows the area well, he doesn't know it like I do. I was raised here. Peter Nash can't be back until tomorrow afternoon. You know I can do this."

"You're not a cop, Jo. And —"

"And what?"

"And it's *you* Doherty wants to kill. I can't put you in the middle of another dangerous situation."

"I don't have a death wish. Believe me, I have a lot to live for." She touched the side of his face, her expression full of love even though she'd never told him she loved him.

Time, McBride, give her time.

He wanted her here, under lock and key. On the other hand, she was right: She knew the valley. Her knowledge could help them capture Doherty before he killed anyone else.

He said, "On one condition."

"Anything."

"You stay in the helicopter. Guide the pilot, give orders, I don't care, but stay off the ground."

She wanted to argue, he could tell, then she nodded. "That's fair enough. Maybe I can do more good from the sky."

Tyler kissed her lightly on the lips, then touched the bandage on her face. "Are you really okay?"

"I'm going to be fine."

He skimmed her injured arm. The knife had cut deep through her tendons, rendering Jo's hand useless. The SWAT medic had stitched her up, but didn't know when or if she'd regain feeling and had urged her to see a specialist soon. "What about —"

"I still can't feel my fingers. Don't worry

about me," she said.

"I can't help it!" He ran a hand through his hair.

"I didn't mean —"

"I love you, Jo. I love you. When Doherty had you at gunpoint today, all I could think about was making sure you were safe. That you stayed alive long enough for me to tell you again that I love you. I should never have let Doherty and Chapman leave the lodge with you and Trixie. Maybe Trixie wouldn't be dead if I had followed protocol. Never give in to the demands of terrorists. Never let them take a hostage!"

He turned away, squeezed the bridge of his nose. Getting angry wouldn't help Jo. He'd run through every possible scenario, knew there had been no other way, but still felt like he'd done wrong.

"What were your options? They were going to blow up the lodge, killing everyone inside. Seven children. Leah. Jason. You did the right thing. It was me, I screwed up . . ."

He shook his head. "You got Doherty to come out into the open, enabling us to track the GPS on the Polaris."

"Are they still tracking it?"

"We can't get a signal, haven't for hours."

Jo looked down at her injured hand.

"You did everything you could," he reassured her.

"Did I? I don't know. I keep running over the scene in the kitchen. Over and over. Wondering if I said this or that Trixie might still be alive."

"Stop second-guessing yourself, Jo."

"Then you stop second-guessing yourself. I —" She stopped suddenly, glanced down.

Tyler pushed her chin up and forced her to look at him. "Hans thinks that Doherty had a specific reason for killing Trixie."

"Are you saying she deserved it?"

"Of course not."

"She didn't deserve to die. No matter what mistakes she made in the past, she didn't deserve to be shot to death. She — she — she said she was glad. She wanted to die. Oh, God."

The tears finally came and Tyler hugged Jo tightly, carrying her to the bed. She was so cold. He left her momentarily and turned up the heater, then slid into the bed with Jo, fully clothed.

"You're freezing."

"I don't care. Trixie's dead. I can't be mad at her. I want to be, but I can't because she's dead and she's not coming back. I loved her, and I'm so mad at her."

"I know."

"You know?"

"Yes. Hans — he figured it out. How she led Lincoln Barnes to your house."

"Oh, God, don't tell Leah. Please. I don't want her to know."

"Shh, of course not. No one needs to know, not Karl or Stan or anyone else."

He held her until the tears stopped. It was a long time before her breathing evened out, and she fully relaxed against him, asleep.

Tyler kissed her forehead, holding her close. "I will marry you, Jo. Someday you'll say yes."

TWENTY-NINE

In the distance he saw a single light in the main house. All Aaron knew about the people who lived here was their name: Jorgensen. He didn't know how many lived here, if they were awake or asleep, or if they had guns.

Of course they had guns, living out here in the middle of nowhere.

North of the house was a barn at least ten times larger than the house. What animals needed that much space? But he knew that if there were animals, there was warmth. And Aaron could barely move his fingers.

His fuel was nearly gone — he figured he was running on fumes. A farm like this would have gasoline and he could refuel, leave before dawn — get out before anybody even knew he'd been here.

He didn't want to hurt anyone who didn't deserve it. That had been Doug Chapman's way, and Aaron was glad he'd killed that bastard. No regrets there.

Aaron was nothing like him. He was a good boy. He did what he was told, took care of himself, was polite and respectful. He never caused trouble for anyone. Never hurt anyone that didn't ask for it.

Bridget, for example. She'd hurt him first. She lied to Aaron, said she loved him and then broke up with him because he loved her back. And he'd proven to her that Trevor Keene was an asshole who only wanted a pretty face, hadn't he? Did Bridget thank him? No . . . she made him go to juvie for six months.

And Rebecca had led him on. She practically screamed that she loved him, the way she looked at him, batting her big eyes. She was onstage just for him. She'd hugged him after a performance. She was an angel . . . until she married that asshole. He could never treat her the way she should be treated.

So Aaron killed him.

No one found out. He'd gotten away with

murder. Again.

He didn't want to kill Rebecca, and he wouldn't have if she hadn't sent him away. If she hadn't been with that man. He cut her beautiful face on accident . . . it was just a terrible accident . . .

A flash of Joanna's face crossed his path. He swerved the snowmobile before realizing she wasn't there. But the sensation that she was watching him had Aaron looking this way and that, and back over his shoulder. Was someone following him?

He detoured away from the house, slowing to minimize the noise of his approach. He headed for the barn.

You killed my sister!

Joanna could have been shouting in his ear.

In his mind's eye, like a movie, he saw himself clearly pulling the trigger. The bullet hit Trixie Weber in the chest. Now Aaron felt sick; he dry heaved. He'd killed Joanna's sister. No wonder Joanna turned on him.

But he couldn't ignore the fact that Trixie had deserved it. She may not have cracked the little boy's head open or shot Joanna's husband in the gut, but Trixie had been responsible for their deaths as much as Lincoln Barnes. Linc got the death penalty.

452

Trixie's punishment had been delayed a few years.

Joanna had been shocked at the revelation of Trixie's actions, and then again at Aaron shooting her.

You killed my sister!

She hated him. The pain and fury on her face went deep, he saw it now. She didn't love him. She never had. She was playing games, like Doug said.

Aaron glided the Polaris behind the barn, away from prying eyes in the farmhouse. He grabbed the supplies and the guns, and went into the barn.

Sheep. There were sheep everywhere. At least a hundred smelly animals packed into the barn. How could they live like that?

He knew exactly how they felt. Locked up. Alone. The barn was their prison.

They stared at him. There were a few random bleats, but most just watched with their small, black eyes. The barn was cold, but not as frigid as the outdoors. Four dim lights cast shadows across the flock. A low hum of a generator plus a faint warmth told Aaron that the barn was heated. He wouldn't die.

He should never have left Joanna behind. She was his. But she didn't want to be with him. She ran away. She hated him.

All he had wanted was for her to acknowledge that he was her hero. And yet she'd never even read his letters. She probably threw away the letters Annie sent after learning he was in prison. Garbage. As if *he* were garbage.

He should have shot her like he shot her sister.

Even if she denied reading his letters, she was lying. Hadn't she been lying to him all along?

Joanna lied. She lied like his mother.

It was the day after his sixteenth birthday.

His mother hadn't come. In sixteen years, he only remembered two times when she'd arrived in time for his birthday.

That made fourteen birthdays without his mother. Fourteen birthdays she promised to be there, and wasn't.

The difference between before and now was that he had money. Aunt Dorothy was rich. Her husband had been some big tycoon in Los Angeles and left her with lots of land. She'd been selling off the land over the years to live on, but had never worked a day in her life.

Aunt Dorothy hated him at first. And the feeling was mutual.

But they tolerated each other. She gave him money to keep him away from her, and he took it to keep her away from him.

When his mother left him in Glendale with Aunt Dorothy she told him that she had a job on a cruise ship. "I'll send you postcards from exotic places."

"Why can't I come with you? I don't need a babysitter. I'm almost sixteen."

She laughed and patted his cheek. "Do I look like I have a son almost sixteen years old?" She swished her hips back and forth. "They think I'm twenty-nine. I still look twenty-nine, don't I?"

"You're beautiful, Mama."

She beamed. "I can't very well come on board with practically a grown man as my son. Nosiree, that wouldn't do. I need to find a husband, Aaron. I'll be thirty-five next year. Ticktock. I'm running out of time."

Aaron knew that she'd be turning forty next year, not thirty-five, but he didn't say anything. His mother lied to herself as much as she lied to him and everybody else.

"Mom, I don't like Aunt Dorothy."

"Come on, honey, she's rich. We have an arrangement. I don't tell the tabloids that her husband was gay, and she'll take good care of you. Give me a kiss-kiss."

He kissed her cheek. She smiled as she wiped it off and checked her makeup in a compact mirror.

Just like every kiss he'd ever given her.

Aaron didn't expect that she would send him a postcard. She rarely did. He had all eight cards that she'd sent since he was five. Eight cards. Four birthday cards. Two Christmas cards. A postcard from Disneyland where she'd gone with her boyfriend and *his* two kids — both girls. And a postcard from Florida.

He almost contacted his grandma Sanders, his dad's mom. For years she and Grandfather had written to him, called him, treated him like he mattered, that he was more than an inconvenience. More than a mistake. Then they stopped.

He told his aunt Dorothy he wanted to visit his grandparents for Christmas.

She coughed and cackled. "The Sanderses? Ha!"

"Don't talk about them like that."

"Why do you want to be with them? Preachy people."

"They love me."

She laughed. She *laughed* at him. "Aaron," cough-cough, "you deluded, stupid boy."

He tensed.

"You think they care about you? Why didn't they fight for custody? They have the money. And your mother is such an irresponsible fool, it was a no-brainer they could have gotten custody, especially after —"

She stopped.

"After what?"

"Nothing."

"What?"

She stared at him. "You're nearly sixteen. You should know, I suppose." She sipped her highball, nibbled on an olive. "Your mother left you in her apartment for a three-day weekend while she went off with some guy she'd picked up at the bar. She left you all the time when you were little. She'd put you in your crib, then go out and party. It's not like you could hurt yourself, right? But you were two and she left you for three days. You climbed out of your crib. Lived on cookies and water for three days. Resourceful, you were.

"The Sanderses knew about it. Hell, the three-night-stand boyfriend was the one who turned her in. She cried those big tears and pled that she really thought she'd brought you to the babysitter, she *thought* she had, she was so tired, working two jobs, yada, yada, bullshit. Bullshit is all your mother knows, Aaron, and don't you forget it.

"She didn't need to leave you to work. Half the time she was working on getting a new husband. The woman has been married four times since you've been born. Did you ever meet any of them? Hmm? I think not. She never told them about you. Even Chris Dansen who had two of his own kids from his first wife."

Aaron jumped up. "Stop lying. Leave my mother alone!"

"You're protecting her? After knowing what she's done? She's a selfish bitch, boy. You just forget about her. I'm beginning to like you. You have a core of steel, something that runs in my family. You keep hating her and start thinking about all my money, boy, and I'll take care of you."

Aaron learned to cater to Aunt Dorothy's wishes, even though he hated her so much it burned him from the inside out. But he brought her flowers and lit her cigarettes and learned how to make her martinis just right.

All the while planning how to kill her.

But first . . .

He tracked down his mother. She hadn't lied about getting the job with King Cruises. He tracked her from port to port. She was the activities director.

The day after his sixteenth birthday he borrowed Aunt Dorothy's car and drove to San Diego where his mother had been in port for three days.

Three days that she could have come to Glendale to visit him.

He found out she was living with one of the crew in a beachside apartment. He watched

458

as she practically fucked the guy on the beach before they made it back to the apartment.

He watched from the window. His mother was a slut. She liked screwing around with men instead of being a mother.

Why hadn't she let him live with his grandparents? Why hadn't his grandparents fought for him when she'd abandoned him over and over again?

He hated them. He hated her.

I hate you I hate you I hate you.

What if he'd been a better boy? What if he'd always been clean, always said please and thank you and never spoke unless spoken to? Was it his fault she hated him?

He entered through the unlocked sliding glass door of the beachside apartment where his mother had disappeared with the bastard who was screwing her. The sound of sex came from the bedroom. He had to walk through the kitchen to get there. He didn't even realize he had picked up a butcher knife on the way until he looked down and noticed it in his clenched fist.

He hadn't planned to kill anyone.

Aaron stood in the doorway and watched. She was sucking his dick and making noises as if she enjoyed it as much as her lover did.

He must have made a sound or moved because she opened her eyes and looked at him, the cock still in her mouth. It popped out and the asshole in the bed said, "Don't stop now, baby."

He'd never forget the look on his mother's face when she saw him — total recognition. Then,

"Who are you?"

She blanked her face and stared at him as if he were a stranger. As if, maybe, she'd seen him before but couldn't place him. What did he look like? Did she really not know her own son, or was it all an act? Was that a hint of fear in her eyes . . . or annoyance?

"George, honey, I think we need to —"

"You know who I am," Aaron said.

"Look, son, take whatever you want," George said, starting to get out of the bed, hands up. George was shaking.

The man thought he was a thief? And his mother . . . she looked at him with disdain. A little fear, but that was probably an act for George. Mostly, she looked at him as if she wanted him to scram.

Aaron raised his arm and she saw the knife. She opened her mouth to scream and he slit her throat open so deep her head almost came off.

George picked up a lamp and threw it at Aaron. Aaron ducked, then tripped him. George landed with a thud. Aaron stabbed him twice in the back. He turned back to his mother.

She was dead.

He stabbed her over and over and over . . . he didn't know how many times, he wasn't counting. He hated her.

I hate you I hate you I hate you.

When he looked down and saw what he'd done, he didn't remember doing it. Not completely. He remembered watching them on the beach. Watching them . . . in bed. The knife — where did he get it? It didn't look familiar.

He showered in the dead man's bathroom. Scalding hot water until he'd washed off all the blood. He didn't shower to get rid of evidence. He showered to forget.

He never looked back.

No one ever contacted him about his mother's murder. He never knew why. Hadn't she listed him as the next of kin?

He didn't ask Aunt Dorothy, though the witch probably had found out.

His mother had never wanted him. Why didn't she just abort him? Or give him away? Or drown him in a toilet? Why have him and leave him over and over and over again . . .

In the sheep shed, Aaron cried out, unmindful of the hundred pair of eyes watching him. "You did this! Why did you even have me? I would have been better off dead!

I wish I were dead. I wish I had never been born!"

I'm glad you're dead. I'm glad I killed you. I wish I could kill you again. Kill you over and over as many times as you left me with strangers, as many times as you tore me away from houses where I was just beginning to feel like I belonged . . .

His mother had given birth just to lord him over his father and his grandparents. She'd used him. For money? For attention? Maybe at one point she'd thought that he would get her a husband. But then all he became was a burden.

She'd had a tummy tuck when he was three months old so no one would know she'd given birth.

Married four times without telling him.

Left him with family, friends, and total strangers for days, then weeks, then months at a time.

"I hate you!"

He had a knife in his hand. How did that happen?

A sheep came up to him, baaed.

He slit its throat. Warm blood coated him.

The other sheep started bleating. As if they knew who he was and what he was capable of.

"Shut up!"

He grabbed another by its wooly coat, slit its throat. Pictured his mother: the recognition, the disdain, and then the fear.

The fear.

He killed another. And another. And another.

The bleating became screams, a cacophony that made his head ache.

"Shut up!"

He wielded his knife, slitting one throat, stabbing another. He tripped, fell, rose again.

An hour later he collapsed in the corner, overheated, drenched in blood, so tired and sore he couldn't move.

THIRTY

Jo woke in the middle of the night and Tyler was no longer lying beside her. She'd kicked off the covers, sweating in the hot, stuffy room. She remembered Tyler turning the heater on high earlier.

She rolled over and saw Tyler standing by the window, looking out, shirtless. "You must be blistering hot," she said.

He cocked his head toward her. "It's a little toasty," he said with a half smile. "I didn't want you to be cold."

Jo got up, every muscle in her body sore.

Two days of intense physical activity had taken its toll, and she realized she was no longer a nineteen-year-old who could bounce back quickly. Her bones cracked as she crossed the room to turn off the heater.

"Open the window," she said.

"It's twenty degrees outside."

"Just for a few minutes. I'm boiling." She slipped off the robe and stood in her flannel pajamas.

Tyler cracked open the window and icy air slid in. She breathed in deeply. "Better," she said. She bent down to take off one of the pairs of socks and her back cracked.

"Let me rub your back," Tyler said.

She straightened and looked at him. His rugged face, his hard, broad chest, his flat stomach. She sucked in her breath at the overwhelming masculinity of Tyler McBride. She remembered what it had been like to make love with him. Especially that first time, over Labor Day. Even then she had known she loved him, but she couldn't tell him.

She had missed him. Why had she run away on Thanksgiving?

You were scared. You panicked and were scared because you didn't believe true love could happen twice in a lifetime.

No. That wasn't true. She couldn't deny

her feelings. She knew exactly what it felt like to be in love, and she loved Tyler just like she had loved Ken. The same, but different. Different, but just as wonderful.

"What's wrong?" Tyler caressed her cheek. She leaned into his touch and closed her eyes.

"Nothing."

"Something's bothering you. You're an open book, Jo."

She took Tyler's hand from her face. Rubbed his palm with her thumb. Slowly. She kissed the tips of his fingers and looked directly into his eyes. "I love you."

Tyler's eyes widened, a hint of a smile crossed his face. "You admit it."

"I hid from the truth for a long time because I was scared. I still am."

"Afraid that true love doesn't happen twice?"

She shook her head. "That was my excuse three months ago."

"What then? What are you afraid of?"

"Jason." Her voice cracked and she didn't realize how hard it was to put her feelings into words.

Tyler tensed. Of course, this was his son she was talking about. The most important person in the world to him. She understood that, and greatly admired that he loved his son so deeply. "I don't understand."

"I was scared that Timmy would think I was replacing him with another son."

Tyler said nothing for a long moment. Jo realized how stupid she must have sounded. Her son was gone, and if he were watching from heaven, he'd know her heart and that she would love him forever.

"I'll give you all the time in the world, Jo. All the time you need." Tyler stroked her hair, rubbing his fingers along the nape of her neck.

"Jason isn't Timmy, and he can't replace my son. But I can love him. There's room for him in my life. I want him in my life. He's amazing, Tyler."

"I think so, too."

Tyler pulled her close and she breathed in deeply. Saying it out loud made all the difference in the world. "I love you," she repeated, feeling like the chain that had been restricting her heart had finally broken free.

She kissed his bare chest, first light as a feather, her hands wrapped around his hard, broad back. She'd written about a lot of heroes over the years, but none of her fictional heroes could compare to the real-life man who stood before her tonight.

Her uninjured hand slid down, under the

waistband of his jeans and briefs. He leaned against her, his lips on her ear, breathing heavily.

"You are driving me crazy, Jo. It's been too long since I've made love to you."

Her breath hitched as his words sent shivers down her spine.

"Didn't you promise me a massage?" she asked, teasing.

He smiled down at her, a dark twinkle in his eyes.

"You have strong hands," she said, her voice surprisingly husky. "My muscles are eagerly awaiting your ministrations."

Tyler raised his eyebrows. He took three steps forward, forcing her to walk backward. The back of her knees hit the bed and she thought he was going to keep pushing her back. "Wait here," he said and turned and went into the bathroom.

Wait? She heard drawers opening and closing. What in the world was he doing?

He was back less than thirty seconds later and held up a bottle of lotion. "We'll need this. For your muscles."

She smiled, her heart beating double time.

Tyler kissed her lightly on the lips, then whispered, "Turn around."

She obeyed, the warm and familiar sensation of anticipation vibrating deep within her body.

Tyler grabbed the bottom hem of her pajama top and pulled it over her head.

Then he pulled off her thermal undershirt, leaving her as bare-chested as he. He gently pushed her down to the bed, traced a finger up her spine until she shivered and her lips parted.

"You're not cold, are you?" he asked, though his tone told her he knew exactly what kind of effect his touch had on her.

"No." Her voice cracked. "I'm very, very hot."

Tyler removed the cap from the lotion and the scent of lavender filled the room. She'd never be able to smell lavender again without remembering this exact moment in time, with Tyler kneeling behind her, his jeans unable to mask his own desire. She felt surprisingly vulnerable and powerful all at the same time.

They'd made love before. The slightly awkward first time. The anxious second time. The comfortable follow-up. But this time felt real, permanent, and there was no going back.

He rubbed his hands together to warm the lotion. "Tell me you love me," he said, placing hands on her shoulders and starting to knead her muscles.

"Aw," she moaned, both pain and pleasure assaulting her as he put pressure on her abused muscles.

"What?" he asked.

"I love you," she said.

He leaned over and kissed the back of her neck. "I will never tire of you telling me you love me."

"Life's too short," she said without realizing it.

"Jo." Tyler turned her over, concern on his face. "Are you sure you're okay?"

She nodded, pulled him down to her, kissed him hard on the lips. She'd never get enough of him. Never. Life was too short. But what if he died, just like Ken?

Her breath hitched.

Stop it. You can't live your life fearing the future.

"Jo —" Tyler murmured.

"Make love to me. Now." She kissed him again, didn't give him a chance to argue. Reaching down, she undid his jeans with one hand.

Something was going on with Jo, but Tyler suspected it was the overwhelming emotions of the last couple days and learning exactly what happened four years ago leading to the murders of her husband and son.

Tyler could take away her painful memories for a night. He would take all her pain if he could.

He kissed her, trying to slow down her urgency, but Jo wasn't taking any of his patience.

"It's been too long." She pulled his earlobe into her mouth causing him to lose focus.

It had been too long. He missed her every night he didn't talk to her. He'd been just as stubborn as she had been after Thanksgiving. Why hadn't he just called her? Started over? Made her talk to him about her fears?

Then she pulled his cock out of his pants and he couldn't think at all.

"I need you," she said.

He pulled her pajama bottoms off and tossed them aside. She had her hand wrapped tight around him, guiding him into her.

She was right. It had been too long. He plunged in, held his breath trying to regain control, but Jo kept moving, her hand now fisted in his hair as she kissed him, her tongue mimicking their urgent coupling.

"Jo —"

"Oh, God. Tyler."

She wrapped her legs around his and arched her back. They both were coated in sweat; Jo from rushing to the finish line, Tyler from trying to hold off.

Her voice went up an octave, and Tyler came inside her. They breathed heavily and he didn't move. Then he kissed her, tasting her lust and urgency.

"I promised you a massage," he said.

"You don't —"

"Yes. I do. I want to."

He didn't want to leave the warmth of her body, but he pulled himself out. The bed was a mess, the down comforter on the floor, but neither noticed. "Roll over."

She smiled and complied.

He squirted lotion directly onto her back and she gasped from the cold, slick cream.

"That wasn't nice," she teased.

"It will be," he said as he began rubbing her muscles again. "I'm going to touch every muscle in your body, from your head to your toes. I'm not going to let you rush this time. I'm going to show you I love you and every inch of your fabulous body."

The fast, hot sex was good, but this attention was even better. Jo relaxed, bit by bit, feeling like Jell-O. With the relaxation, a sense of peace washed over her, unlike anything she'd experienced in far too long. She'd been so alone. Even living at the lodge, she had isolated herself from her family. She'd lived in her books, writing faster, writing more, trying to recreate the perfect life she used to enjoy. But every happy ending she wrote reminded her of how deeply sad and lonely she was. That her happy ending had come and gone.

Gone, that is, until Tyler McBride walked into her life.

His hands moved slowly down her right arm, kneading each muscle, starting with the big ones, moving to the small. She couldn't move if she wanted to. And she certainly didn't want to.

She felt his breath in her ear. He kissed her cheek and she tried to roll over to face him, but he said, "I'm not done."

He kissed her shoulder blades, then the small of her back. Then her round bottom, her thighs, the back of her knees. An odd, erotic tingle ran through every nerve ending. She'd never thought the back of her knees could make her so hot and bothered.

Every time Tyler touched her made her yearn for what could be. For what was now becoming her reality.

He rubbed more lotion on his hands, then started rubbing her toes. First the back of her knees, now her feet — her entire body was one big erotic zone when Tyler was in bed with her. His thumbs put pressure on points that heated her simmering desire to boiling, making her shift uncomfortably on the sheets to try to ease the pressure. But moving only made the discomfort more profound as she realized exactly what she wanted him to do. Waiting was torture.

By the time his hands reached her thighs, she thought she was going to spontaneously combust. His breath was only inches from her and every few moments he'd kiss the skin he'd just massaged. The hard fingers and the light, tender kisses made her sigh out loud. It wasn't just her, she realized. Tyler was breathing just as heavily as she.

"Tyler," she whispered, but didn't know what else to say. Her mind went blank. All thought gone, just like that. Her nerves exploded in new sensations, craving more of his touch, more physical contact.

He moved up so that his knees were on either side of her, his penis hard against the small of her back. He kissed her neck and whispered, "I love you, Jo."

Her heart thudded so loud her ears rang.

"Now, Tyler."

"Now what?" His tone teased as he licked the sensitive skin under her chin.

"Make love to me."

He turned her over to face him, as he held

himself above her. He was smiling. "I'm not done."

"I know."

"I haven't massaged this side."

She moaned and he softly laughed, his hands on her shoulders. Putting just the right amount of pressure on her muscles. Moving down to her breasts. Slowly he circled them, moving closer and closer to her nipples. They were hard and tight and she anticipated his touch . . . as soon as he was about to reach them, his mouth clamped down on her right nipple and she arched her back.

Tyler enjoyed Jo's reaction to his attention, then she reached down and squeezed him and he didn't know if he would have a choice but to make love to her again, right then. Blood rushed to his cock and he pulled his lips from her breast in the hopes of regaining control. He stared at her mouth, red and swollen from their earlier embrace. So damn sexy. "Jo —"

He kissed her hard on the lips, pushing his tongue inside, as she opened her mouth for him to go deeper. One hand grabbed her hair at the nape of her neck and held her to him. With his other hand he reached down and touched her hot, wet opening. He moved down so her hand slipped from his cock and took a deep breath. He wanted to move forward, but he didn't want this to be over. He wanted more time to show Jo he loved her.

He kissed her neck, her shoulder, lavender caressing his senses as Jo's fingers caressed his back. She was full of energy, he'd seen it from the day they met on the search-and-rescue a year ago. She didn't stop moving, maybe she couldn't. Her hand fisted in his hair as his tongue found her nipple again while his hand massaged her other breast.

"Tyler," she breathed, a wisp of a sound.

He kissed the underside of her perfect breasts, her stomach, her navel, his tongue trailing a moist path to the hot spot between her legs. When he licked her nub, she gasped, grabbed his hair, and held him an inch away, as if she didn't know whether to push him away or bring him closer to her body.

"I'm on the edge," she whispered.

"I'll push you over."

Jo squirmed, unable to stop herself. She released Tyler and he blew warm breaths between her legs, making her shiver.

Then his mouth sank down and all thoughts fell away. Every nerve in her body tensed, every pore overheated. When his tongue slid inside and he suckled, she exploded, saw nothing but brightness, felt nothing but a huge release of energy.

He kissed her inner thighs as she came down off a high better than any drug. He licked her, lapping her skin, all the way back up to her breasts, to her neck, to her ears, and finally her mouth.

She eagerly kissed him, her arms wrapped around his neck, her legs parted, one draped loosely over his perfect, round ass. She reached down and squeezed it, then reached between them to touch his thick, heavy penis which rested between her legs.

Tyler groaned as she slowly guided him into her. She shook, her opening sensitive from two orgasms, but tingling in anticipation nonetheless. He stopped right after his head entered.

"Don't be a tease," she whispered.

With one thrust, he pushed himself in and she gasped again.

This time, he moved slower. Patiently. At least at first. As they moved together, legs against legs, navel to navel, her hard nipples against his harder chest, their lips and tongues entwined, patience gave way to intensity, to heavy lust coated in love.

He kissed her neck, their bodies slick with sweat. He kissed her earlobe and she moaned. He trailed his tongue from her ear, along the curve of her jaw, across her lips. She claimed his lips, kissing him, and began to move beneath him.

Tyler pulled up, slowly, the exquisite tension building. Then he eased back down, his jaw tight with restraint. Jo stopped moving beneath him and he looked at her face.

Her eyes were closed, head tilted back, golden blonde hair mussed and sexy.

He grabbed her good hand in his, entwined their fingers together, connecting them completely. "Jo," he said. "Jo, look at me."

Her eyes fluttered open, darker than he'd ever seen. From lust or the moonlight filtering through the windows, he didn't know.

Holding her gaze, Tyler eased off her. Almost came out and her chest shuddered, then he pushed all the way back in and she gasped. He loved making her respond, loved that she dripped with passion, their bodies slick and hot together.

Together, they developed a rhythm that wholly satisfied them both. In and out, connected in every way, from hands to eyes to pelvis. Never had Tyler had such powerful emotional and physical sex. Jo's mouth was open as her breathing turned to panting, as her body moved faster with every thrust, urging him on, pushing him harder, until her body tensed and froze beneath him. With a final deep thrust, together they flew over the top, breathless.

He slowly withdrew and pulled Jo into the crook of his arm, while searching with one hand for the down comforter. He found it, pulled it over them, spooning her body into his.

"I love you," she whispered, kissing his arm as her breathing evened out.

To hear her say those three words moved him. He held her tight, until she slept.

THIRTY-ONE

Jane Jorgensen on rolled over and snuggled against her warm husband.

"I don't want to get out of bed," she sighed. "It's probably still below zero."

Bob draped an arm over her, pulling the down comforter tight around them. "I'll feed the sheep if you cook breakfast."

"That's not fair, I burn everything." Jane had tried to learn to cook, but she simply didn't have the touch. Bob, however, could have been a chef in a five-star restaurant.

"How about if we eat fast then I'll go out and help."

"Umm, thanks for the offer, but I'd rather stay in this nice warm bed a little longer

478

and have sex with my husband. Then I'll be ready to brave the arctic chill." She giggled when Bob tickled her.

Thirty minutes later, they were dressed and walking down the stairs. "Wow," Jane said, looking out the large picture window in the breakfast nook to the dramatic Centennial Mountains on the edge of the valley. The early morning sun had turned them pink and purple, the blue sky a brilliant contrast. Low-lying fog wrapped around the base of the mountains, making the snow-covered peaks like majestic islands in the sky.

"I love you, Jane."

She smiled and kissed him. "Make it a hearty breakfast. I've already worked up an appetite."

She pulled on her sweater over her three layers of long-sleeve shirts, then her snowsuit, and finally her boots. She loved winter mornings like today, even if it was still only five degrees. There was no wind, and the drifts created the day before were smooth hills around their property. The white would be blinding when the sun peaked overhead, but now it glistened like cloudy crystal in the still morning.

She pulled on her ski mask and gloves, but the sharp cold still bit into her skin.

The barn was heated, but it still wouldn't be over fifty degrees inside. The sheep they kept over the winter were either too young to make the trip over the mountains, or too old. Some ranchers would slaughter the old, but the Jorgensens took them in from around the valley for another year or two of wool, which was a major income earner for their family.

The birds were out, soaring across the sky. Not all birds went south for the winter, but there were few who could withstand the cold. In summer, more than fifty thousand birds made the nearby wildlife refuge their home. They were spectacular to watch.

She approached the barn and was surprised the sheep weren't baaing at the door. She was fifteen minutes later than usual to feed them. Fear squeezed her heart. Disease could travel so fast in a flock, what if they were sick?

They'd still be bleating she thought as she opened the barn door.

Nothing prepared her for the sight of the blood. Blood everywhere, the smell so horrific that she gagged and turned her head.

All the sheep. Dead.

Killed.

She started to back away when she saw him.

He was standing next to her, naked except for boots and covered in blood. At first she thought he was injured, that he was a victim. Then she looked in his eyes and saw they were calm. Much too calm for what had happened in the barn.

Then she saw the gun pointed at her.

"Do exactly what I say or I will kill you."

THIRTY-TWO

Fog grounded the helicopter until noon, but when it lifted, blue skies and a bright sun shone into the valley. It went from five degrees at dawn to forty-two degrees, and it was still warming. The sun would turn the top layer of snow to slush, making it slick and dangerous.

"Be careful," Jo told Tyler as he mounted an Arctic Cat. "I need you back in one piece."

He kissed her. "You, too." He glanced at Mitch. "Keep an eye on her."

"Yes, Sheriff." Mitch saluted, then draped an arm over Jo's shoulder and squeezed. He had wanted to be on the ground with Tyler and the rest of the team, but Hans Vigo — who outranked him — had said no.

"You're not one hundred percent. You could get yourself killed, or someone else,"

Hans had said. "You can go in the chopper."

Hans was staying at the lodge with two federal agents tasked with guarding Jo's family and Jason McBride. Two agents were at the Nash house in case Doherty backtracked there. Blackstone, Mitch, Jo, and the pilot were in the chopper, and the rest of the team — Tyler, his two deputies, and the remaining four agents — were on snowmobiles with Tyler in command.

They started out together, but would split into three teams. If the chopper saw anything suspicious, one team would check it out. Everyone was in open communication.

The GPS tracker on the Polaris wasn't being picked up by the communications company, but Blackstone thought he might be able to pick it up when they were in close proximity. "Unless Doherty realized he could be tracked and disabled it."

"Or switched sleds somewhere," Mitch said.

"Not likely. Most of the ranches are on the east side of the valley. He was heading west. He could have backtracked, but we would have heard him. Sound travels well here."

"We'll start our sweep where we found Bianchi yesterday," Blackstone told the pilot.

"Yes, sir."

Jo had never flown over the Centennial Valley. The view was breathtaking. They stayed in pattern with the seven snowmobiles below, going ahead, circling around, returning. The valley itself was virtually treeless; on the mountainous slope south of the road, thick woods made it nearly impassable on a snowmobile, unless the rider was a pro. Aaron Doherty was not, and they had no indication that he had moved south.

By the time the riders on the ground reached the point where Mitch had been thrown from his sled, the helicopter pilot had searched a five-mile perimeter. There were several zigzagging lines, and Jo studied the pattern. "I think he was trying to make it hard for us to track him."

"How so?"

"Going in circles. Crossing over his own path. Or he was completely lost. But there's a compass on the sled. He would at least have known what direction he should go in. And he has a map of the valley."

"This same one you gave me?" Blackstone said, holding up the brochure Karl Weber gave to every guest of the Moosehead Lodge.

"Yes."

"What are these lines?"

"Known fences. Mostly ranch property. The thick blue lines are snowmobile trails."

Jo picked up the binoculars Agent Blackstone had given her earlier. The snow sparkled like broken glass under the bright winter sun, the rivets Doherty's snowmobile had made like gouges in the earth. "He's moving northwest," she said.

"How can you tell?" Mitch asked.

"When the snowmobile cuts through the snow it moves the powder to the sides. The faster it goes, the farther out the snow spreads and at more of an angle from your direction. Just like a boat moving through the water."

"What's northwest of here?"

She stared at the map. "A lot of it is the wildlife preserve, some ranches, and the Lima Reservoir. He might think the reservoir is his way to escape. There are two roads leading into it, one on the north, one on the south. They'd be snowed over now, not a lot of traffic, but eventually they merge into more residences and the interstate."

"The Sheriff has the roads closely watched. Every car coming from the valley is being stopped."

"There isn't going to be a lot of traffic now, though this beautiful weather will bring out recreational skiers." She bit the knuckle on her thumb. "And there is a thirty-mile stretch where he could circumvent all roads. The Sheriff's Department can't cover every inch."

Mitch said, "He has patrols on snowmobiles and increased police presence. The surrounding counties have sent in patrols to help."

Jo looked down at the valley. Trixie's killer was down there somewhere. Where? Where would he go?

"Keep going northwest," she said.

"We agreed to follow his wake," Blackstone said.

"He's heading northwest. And those impressions are old. You can see that the wind from last night has already obscured them."

"I can't tell, but I'll take your word for it, Ms. Sutton." Blackstone told the pilot to head northwest direct for the Lima Reservoir, then he radioed Tyler and told the ground search the same thing.

Within two miles, they picked up Doherty's trail again and he was heading straight for the Lima Reservoir. "It's thirty miles from here," Jo said, "and I don't think he had enough fuel, especially since he was moving so fast. There's a natural barrier — a creek — that he would be a fool to try to cross at this point. He'd need to follow it, which will curve around and add another five to ten miles."

The pilot spoke up. "Agent Blackstone, I have a faint signal on the GPS of the suspect."

"Can you track it?"

"I'm trying. Hold."

The pilot adjusted his coordinates. They turned northward, leaving Doherty's trail behind.

The signal became stronger.

"Why would he go north?" Jo asked out loud.

"Maybe he doesn't know how to read the map," Mitch said, looking below with his binoculars.

"If he was planning on leaving the valley through Lima, he'd need to follow the creek southwest, not north . . . it only gets wider there, and with the temperatures rising today there will be melting and make it more difficult to cross."

"Maybe he crossed last night."

"The signal is getting stronger," the pilot said. "About three miles. Stationary."

Jo stared at the map, tried to remember what was out here. They were on the edge of the refuge, flying now over private land. All this was owned by the Jorgensens.

"There's a ranch up ahead. Right at the widest point in the creek. He couldn't have known about it, but if he was following the creek up to North Centennial Road, he would run right into it."

"Are there people there?"

"The Jorgensens. They raise sheep, take them out of the valley every winter, but their son and daughter-in-law stay on and care for the animals too old or sick to make the trip."

Please let them be okay. No more death. No more . . .

Blackstone got on the radio and using Jo's directions, told the team below to proceed with caution to the Jorgensen ranch.

Tyler approached the Jorgensen property cautiously. The pilot reported that the GPS signal was coming from near the barn. They were circling and spotted the Polaris Doherty had stolen on the far side of the barn.

There was no sign of movement.

Tyler split the team in two. Four of them took the barn, the other three the house. "He's armed and dangerous. He may have hostages: a man and woman in their late twenties."

Tyler took the barn with Grossman and

487

two Feds. They rode right up to the main doors, got off the sleds, and drew their guns. The roar of the snowmobiles, in addition to the circling chopper, would have alerted Doherty to their presence, so Tyler didn't bother with stealth.

"Doherty! This is Sheriff McBride. Come out with your hands up."

Nothing.

No sound, but the smell. Blood. A lot of blood.

He held up his fingers. *One. Two. Three.*

He and Grossman went in high, the Feds went in low.

Though Tyler had expected death inside, nothing prepared him for the violence inside the Jorgensens' barn.

There were at least a hundred sheep, their wooly coats stained red. The wet, sickly sweet smell of blood filled the large barn. Blood arced across the walls, the tack, the pillars, and hay.

Some of the sheep had their throats slit. Some sheep had been stabbed. None moved. They were all dead.

Tyler and the cops searched the barn for Doherty; he was nowhere inside. Grossman called to him. "Over here."

Grossman was in a small tack room in the corner. He pointed to a pile of blood-drenched clothes. "Looks like what Doherty was wearing."

"Where did he find a change of clothes?"

They looked toward where the house was. Tyler's gut churned at the thought of two more dead.

Just then one of the Feds said over the walkie-talkie, "We have one unconscious male victim, alive with a strong pulse. No visible sign of injury."

"What about a woman?"

"Nothing. We've searched the entire house."

"Look again," Tyler said, not expecting to find Jane Jorgensen, but wanting to make sure she wasn't hiding somewhere.

Tyler looked around and tried to put himself in Doherty's shoes. Getting in the heads of killers was far from his comfort zone. Agent Hans Vigo seemed much better versed in understanding how psychopathic minds like Doherty's worked.

But Tyler also understood that part of being a good cop was trying to figure out what the criminal planned to do next. He inspected the sheep more closely, hoping for a sign or clue about Doherty's next step.

Many of the animals had only one or two stab wounds. A couple were decimated, shredded to such an extent that they were barely recognizable as sheep. But for the most part, the kills had been relatively clean, the predominant method of murder: a slit throat.

Without a forensic expert, it would be virtually impossible to know where the slaughter started. However, the three over-kills were bunched together. The sheep nearby were repeatedly stabbed, and the sheep closest to the doors — as if they were trying to escape — had slit throats or one or two stab marks. Tyler figured something had triggered Doherty and he blindly killed the first sheep, and then — maybe because he feared the sheep would make noise and wake the ranchers, or maybe out of some sort of sick perversion — he systematically killed the rest, one after the other.

Tyler walked carefully through the carnage. He noticed something oddly similar in the bulk of the sheep. The same type of stab wound on their abdomen.

Tyler examined some of the carcasses more closely. He wasn't an expert in forensics, but since Beaverhead County didn't have a crime scene unit, all the deputies, including himself, had basic forensic training. It appeared that some of the wounds were made postmortem, as if after killing the sheep, Doherty came back and stabbed them once in the abdomen. Why? To make sure they were dead or for some psychotic reason?

Grossman came in. "I got blood outside along with an impression of a snowmobile and tracks leading away from the shed next to the main house."

"So maybe the Polaris wasn't working right and he stole one of the Jorgensens' sleds."

"Jane is missing. They searched the house top to bottom and she's not in there."

"Is Bob still unconscious?"

"Al is working on him."

Tyler left the barn and the dead sheep, relieved. He radioed the chopper. "It's safe to land. Doherty is gone and he has a hostage."

Just as he gave the clearance, he heard a snowmobile in the distance, coming in fast.

"Hold it, Blackstone. There's a sled coming in from the north-northwest."

Blackstone said, "We'll check it out. Stand by."

A couple minutes later Blackstone came back on the radio. "One sled, lone rider, coming straight for you."

"Can you identify the rider?"

"Negative. He or she is wearing a bright yellow helmet and blue ski jacket."

Tyler motioned for his team to take positions. They watched the horizon. Within minutes, the snowmobile was in view, the SWAT helicopter behind it as if urging it forward.

Blackstone's voice came over a speaker system. "This is Agent Blackstone with the Federal Bureau of Investigation. Person on the snowmobile with the yellow helmet: Stop your sled and put your hands up."

The snowmobile didn't stop.

Blackstone issued the warning again. "This is the FBI. You are surrounded. Stop your sled immediately."

The snowmobile slowed, then stopped.

"Rider, remove your helmet and put your hands on top of your head."

The rider complied. Blonde hair fell down the rider's back.

"It's Jane Jorgensen," Tyler said and called to his team, "Hold your fire! It's Jane Jorgensen."

THIRTY-THREE

Jane accepted the cup of hot coffee from Jo and took a sip.

They sat in the living room of the Jorgensen house. All the Feds except for Blackstone and Mitch were outside looking for signs that Doherty would return, though Tyler didn't think it was likely as he listened to Jane's story.

She turned to her husband who was reclining next to her, a bandage covering his head. Some blood had seeped through the back where, according to Jane, he'd been hit with the butt of Doherty's gun.

"Are you sure you're okay?" she asked for the fifth time.

He nodded. He was only semiconscious, with a serious concussion. Sam and Peter Nash had arrived back at the lodge and were coming out to the Jorgensen ranch to tend to Bob and destroy the sheep carcasses.

"Tell us what happened," Tyler said.

Tyler was furious that Doherty had eluded them. That another innocent person had almost been killed.

Jane took a deep breath. "Bob and I didn't hear anything last night. We didn't hear the poor sheep . . ."

Jo took her hand and squeezed. "The barn is north of the house, and the wind was blowing from the south. You couldn't have heard them. And if you did — he may have killed you, too."

Jane nodded. "I went out early to feed the sheep and there was a naked man in the barn. A naked man and a lot of blood. The sheep . . ." She swallowed, looked down, then continued. "He was as surprised to see me, I think, as I was to see him. He had a gun. All I could think of was that he was going to kill me." Her voice hitched.

"I'm so sorry I couldn't protect you," Bob spoke up, his voice full of anguish.

Jane quickly said, "No, don't, Bob. He didn't hurt me. But he grabbed me, made me walk back to the house. Bob came out of the kitchen and the man hit him on the head before I could warn him."

She took a deep breath, seemed to be thinking, and Tyler prompted, "What next?"

"He said he needed clothes. I took him to our room. He told me to sit on the chair and not move or he would shoot me. I believed him. I sat there, watched him get dressed. He didn't really look at me, though when I started fidgeting he turned the gun on me and said 'No Moving.' "

"And then?"

"He told me that he needed to find a way out of the valley. He had a couple ideas, but he needed my help. I remembered Nash calling us a couple days ago about the escaped convicts, and that was the first time I thought that this man was one of them. He brought me back downstairs. Bob was lying there, right in the entry between the kitchen and the living room, and the man didn't even look at him. I didn't know if you were dead, Bob, I was so scared . . ."

Bob wrapped his arms around her and held her. "I'm okay. Thank God you're alive. I don't know what I would have done if he'd hurt you."

Tyler understood this was sensitive and Jane had been through a trauma, but they were rapidly losing daylight. It was already four in the afternoon and the sun was quickly setting. In another hour they wouldn't have the helicopter to search with.

"Where did you take Doherty?" Tyler asked.

"The north side of Lima. He told me that he wouldn't hurt me if I didn't try to trick him. He needed to find a place where he could steal a car and not use the North or South Centennial Road. I knew exactly where — the old logging road that went over the north mountain. It exits out at that 24/7 convenience store over —"

"I know where it is," Tyler said. "And then?"

"He told me to turn around and go home to my husband and not look back. I did."

"What time did you leave?"

"Eight. I didn't go fast — and he didn't seem to mind. I refueled and left him at one. I came back much faster."

"Did he say anything? Like where he was going? His plans?"

"He didn't say anything. I asked him his name, and he didn't even tell me that."

"Did you see what car he stole?"

"He was looking at two. A black Ford 250 with four-wheel drive and an older Chevy, dark green, that I think also had four-wheel drive. I don't know Chevys well; my dad always had Fords."

Tyler wrote down the information, then handed the paper to Grossman. "Find out any stolen vehicles at the store, get the owner's name and license, put an APB out immediately."

"Got it." Grossman stepped out of the living room.

"Anything else you remember?"

She shook her head.

"I just wanted to come back home, see Bob, make sure he was okay."

"I know," Jo said.

Tyler said, "I'll leave Billy and Al here until tomorrow morning, just to make sure that you're safe. Nash should be here soon."

"Thank you, Sheriff."

They left the house and Tyler slammed his fist on the porch. "I can't believe he got away."

"Someone will spot him," Jo said.

Mitch nodded. "Every cop in a hundred-mile radius will be looking for him. He'll be in custody within twenty-four hours."

Mitch was wrong.

Aaron had learned a lot from Doug Chapman. He'd learned to hot-wire a car. He'd learned to swap out stolen cars rapidly, to give the police less chance of tracking them. And he'd figured out how to not be seen on security cameras.

He found his way back to Pocatello and considered just going on. In one of the trucks he'd stolen, he'd found a wallet with eightysome bucks and he paid cash for a cheap-ass motel.

Los Angeles. Ten million people in the county. He'd lived there for more than a decade, he could disappear, start a new life, be free.

Except he didn't have the heart to do it.

He stared at his gun. Bridget had loved him, then didn't. Rebecca had loved him, then didn't. Joanna had loved him, then didn't. He'd lost them all.

You haven't lost Joanna. She's still alive.

He bristled, tightened his grip around the revolver. He wasn't a bad person. Joanna had loved him once. She could love him again.

Love, Tyler.

Had Joanna betrayed him in a far worse way? Had she broken his heart so that she could be with another man? With the Sheriff?

Quiet rage spread through his chest.

They need to have a heart-to-heart.

He flashed back to when he left the lodge with Joanna and her traitorous sister. Joanna and the Sheriff had exchanged glances. They'd looked at each other *that way.*

Aaron would not be used again. He was not garbage. He was important, he was special.

"You're my special little boy. Be good for my friends and I'll be back soon."

He'd always been good. Always. At least he tried. He wasn't pathetic, he wasn't worthless, he was special.

Joanna would know it before he killed her.

THIRTY-FOUR

Four days later

Joanna Margaret Weber, Jo's namesake, was buried in a family plot outside Lakeview. A new headstone nearby read:

BEATRIX "TRIXIE" MAY WEBER
June 1, 1975–February 7, 2008

Beloved mother, sister,
daughter, granddaughter, and friend.

"There are three things that will
endure
— faith, hope, and love —
and the greatest of these is love."
1 CORINTHIANS 13:13

Trixie couldn't be buried until spring. Her body was being kept at the hospital morgue. The ground was frozen. But Jo didn't want to postpone the funeral for two or three months. Her family, especially Leah, needed closure.

The Webers had been long-time residents of the Centennial Valley. This winter would mark their last in Montana.

Her grandfather was closing the lodge. Karl and Stan planned on traveling. "I'm not coming back," he told Jo at Trixie's grave site. "But when I die, I'd like to be buried here."

Jo nodded, looked at the mourners who had come for the quiet outdoor ceremony. Almost everyone who lived year-round in the valley was here, plus Wyatt and a few of their friends who lived in Dillon, Ennis, and other nearby towns. Her parents were on a mission in Africa and unreachable. Jo rarely thought of them anymore — they'd been on missions more than half her life. It angered her that they weren't here for their daughter's funeral, but it didn't surprise her. They hadn't returned home to pay respects to Ken and Timmy.

Tyler came and kissed her on the forehead, but he didn't look at her. He was both worried and angry that they hadn't been able to capture Aaron Doherty.

The FBI had searched by helicopter for two full days, but there was no sign of Doherty. Local police had found cars they suspected he may have stolen, but no sign of him. All local motels had his picture, and the police were widening their search. Two callers in Idaho Falls had reported seeing him, and there was a stolen truck from the area that police were looking for. One caller said he'd seen the truck driving south on I-15 outside Idaho Falls. Away from the valley.

Jo didn't feel one hundred percent safe, but she thought Doherty had left for good. Nothing held him here to the valley — no friends, no family, nothing but violence. Jane Jorgensen had said he seemed depressed and melancholy. Hans Vigo suggested he was suicidal. Mitch Bianchi told Jo and Tyler to keep careful watch — he didn't think Doherty was going to disappear forever.

"He's licking his wounds," Mitch had said, "but I think he'll be back."

When Doherty had been spotted out of state, Mitch and Hans had to return to their respective posts. "Duty calls," Hans had said.

There were two federal agents still at the lodge, and Tyler had a half-dozen deputies on duty at Trixie's funeral.

Aaron Doherty wasn't going to come today. And tomorrow? Tomorrow Jo and Leah were moving in with Tyler and Jason. Tyler hadn't been home since he'd come to the valley a week ago. And until Doherty was caught, he didn't want Jo and Leah out of his sight.

Tyler came up behind her, kissed the top of her head, and caressed the small of her back. She glanced over her shoulder at him. The worry on his face was countered by the love in his eyes.

"Why don't you believe that he's gone?" she asked him.

He didn't say anything for a minute. "It's more the not knowing that is eating me up.

How long is he going to be able to hide? He doesn't have a lot of money, and every time he steals a car the police get that much closer to finding him. I keep thinking I'll get the call any minute, but it doesn't come. And that worries me."

Tyler turned her to face him. "I don't want you to worry, Jo. Not now. Take care of your family."

"You are part of my family."

He ran the tips of his fingers over her cheek. "I don't want you to hurt anymore. I'll do anything to protect you."

"Thank you."

"For what?"

"For being you." She tilted her head up and kissed him. "I love you."

He rubbed her back. "It was a nice service. As nice as funerals can be. Are you doing okay?"

"Yeah."

"And Leah?"

They both looked over to where Jason and Leah were talking, sitting on a fallen tree. Jason had brushed off the snow for Leah. A gentleman, just like his dad.

Your children.

Last week she'd been childless, grieving for her son. Today, she was responsible for raising two kids.

Tyler took her hand, squeezed. "We're going to be good, Jo. Not just okay, but really good."

"Of course we are."

"I'm going to check with my team," Tyler said. "Are you ready to go back to the lodge?"

"When you are."

"Ten minutes." He kissed her again and walked down the slope.

Jo stood next to Trixie's grave. *Beloved mother, sister . . .*

"I love you, Trixie."

Jo glanced over at the kids sitting to the side. Leah saw her, waved. Jo waved back. She walked up the slope twenty feet. Four years ago she had buried two other people on this same hill.

KENNETH RICHARD SUTTON
September 20, 1968 — February 4,
2004
Husband. Father. Friend.
We miss you.

Jo brushed her fingers against the headstone. "Hello, sweetheart."

She turned to Timmy's headstone. She knelt down in the slush. Touched the earth. "Timmy, you're forever in my heart."

She kissed her fingers and placed them on the ground.

Aaron had been compelled to return to the Centennial Valley.

He'd thought he'd won the internal battle. Escape or suicide, he was weighing his options. Escape was hard — always watching over his shoulder, stealing to eat. He couldn't sleep right, he didn't have enough food. He couldn't walk into a restaurant and order a steak; he was dirty and could barely stand the smell of himself.

Suicide had been looking really good. Something flashy. Something that would get Joanna's attention. Like taking people in a bookstore hostage, calling the media, and demanding to talk on the air before turning himself in. He'd never turn himself in, but he'd make sure Joanna Sutton knew it was all her fault when everyone died.

But he only had the one gun left, and two bullets. Not enough to take down anyplace with more than one or two people. How Doug had managed to find them a couple of guns their first day out of Quentin, Aaron would never know. That guy had a sixth sense about some things.

Aaron kind of missed him. He didn't like being alone.

Getting back into the valley had proven more difficult than he'd thought. The main road was blockaded by the cops. Every car searched. The plows had cleared the road from Monida to Lakeview for Trixie's funeral, but still the people from the east side of the valley came on snowmobiles.

The flaw in the protective net was the terrain itself — miles and miles long with many places to cross over into the valley where no one could see him. He'd come early enough that no one had been around; and he'd waited.

He watched from a distance, unable to make out the features of the people gathered below. A calmness wrapped around him. Calm now that he had a plan. It finished taking shape when he saw two figures — two kids — walking toward his hiding place.

Aaron planned to die today. He had two bullets. The first was for Joanna.

"Aunt Jo —" Leah rushed to her, breathless, eyes darting back and forth.

"What's wrong?" Jo stood, looked around. The mourners were all near the tent where there was food and drink. She looked over to where Jason and Leah had been sitting on the log. "Where's Jason?"

"We — we went for a little walk. I know

505

we weren't supposed to leave, but — and — Mr. Miller, I mean Doherty, has Jason!"

Jo's stomach plummeted, her breath stopped. "We have to get Tyler." She looked around, didn't see him. She opened her mouth to call out when Leah said, "No, don't. Jo, he said he'll hurt Jason if you don't come right now. He has a gun. He said I have to bring you back and not tell anyone. I don't want Jason to die."

"Where are they?"

"Behind the rocks." She pointed. About fifty yards up the mountain from where Leah and Jason had been sitting was a plateau. Several huge boulders rested on it.

"Find Tyler now."

"But —"

"Trust me, Leah. Do it."

Leah ran down the hill and Jo went up.

She wasn't going to lose another child.

Jo heard Aaron Doherty's voice before she reached the plateau.

"Where's Leah?"

"I'm not putting her in danger."

"But you'll put the boy in danger?"

She took three more steps and saw Jason. He was on his knees in the slushy snow, hands behind his head. Aaron Doherty stood behind him, a gun to the boy's head.

Oh, God, no. Not again.

Jo swallowed fear so intense that her vision wavered.

"Don't scream," Doherty said. "If you do, I'll kill him. Do you understand that? I will kill him."

"I'm not going to scream. Let Jason go."

"No. No! Where's Leah?"

"I told you. I wouldn't let her come. You don't want to do this."

"You know nothing about me, Joanna."

Something the FBI Agent Hans Vigo said earlier came back to her. Doherty had to believe that he was in control. That she understood him, that she believed in him. She remembered that his mother had left him over and over again, with strangers and friends and relatives, and he never knew when she would return. He had waited so long.

Jo had no sympathy for the man who killed Trixie, but she understood what Agent Vigo had been saying. What had happened in Doherty's past influenced the killer he was today. She needed to stall him, to give Tyler time to arrive. She needed to protect Jason at all costs.

He could have shot her when he killed Trixie, but he hadn't.

"You love me, don't you?" she said. She

glanced at Jason, saw the fear on his face. *Don't look at him. If you do, you'll never be able to do this.*

His eyes widened. "You know I do."

She shook her head. "You never said so."

"In every letter I wrote —"

"I told you I never got any of your letters."

"You've lied to me from the beginning. Why should I believe you now?"

"I'm not lying. I never got your letters." She stepped forward. She had to get between him and Jason.

He stomped his foot. "But she said she mailed them!"

"Annie?"

He stumbled back as if she'd slapped him. His hand fell to his side, gun still in hand. But it was no longer pointed at Jason's head.

Jo took another step forward.

"She talked to the police. Told them everything. She had all your letters and she gave them to the FBI."

"I don't believe you."

"I'm so sorry she betrayed you, Aaron. Every woman you've loved has hurt you. Even your own mother —"

He stepped forward and aimed the gun at her. "Don't talk about her."

Had she misstepped? Where was Tyler?

508

She didn't dare look around for fear Doherty would realize that something was up.

"I don't want to hurt you, Aaron. You're not like Doug Chapman. You're nothing like him."

"He was a vile, pathetic, violent man." Distaste crossed his face. "I'm glad I killed him."

"You protected me from him. When you left me alone at the house, he — he touched me."

"Why didn't you tell me?"

"I was embarrassed."

"You know I would do anything for you." He shook his head back and forth. "But you lied to me. You told me you loved me, then you left me for the Sheriff. My enemy. You broke my heart, Joanna."

She blinked, trying to make sense of what he was saying. Delusional, Agent Vigo had called him. Did that mean he heard voices? Believe something that wasn't true?

On the surface, he seems normal. He can function in society, hold down a job, have normal conversations. But he believes his fantasies, his delusions are real.

She swallowed uneasily and tried to remember the little boy he used to be, the little boy who waited night after night for his mother to come home.

The same mother he killed.

"Aaron, what do you want from me?"

"You really don't know?"

She shook her head, trying not to look at the gun, or at Jason, but concentrating on the sounds around her. Had she heard a footstep in the slush behind her? She didn't dare look.

"I wanted to share my life with you, Joanna. I came here to show you how much I loved you, how I was your hero, like in your books. Your stories showed me what I never had, and I wanted that all — with you. But no longer."

"I'll go with you. Right now. We'll leave."

"I don't believe you. You had your chance, you somehow told that Sheriff where we were."

"I didn't —"

"It's over. For both of us."

"Let Jason go. Don't make him watch this."

"Come here, Joanna."

She crossed the ground that separated them. She reached out and touched Jason on the shoulder. "Get up, Jason, and go."

She saw something out of the corner of her eye and it took every ounce of willpower not to look to her left. Jo put her body

510

between Jason and the gun. "Now Jason."

Doherty nodded. "I don't want to hurt anyone else, Joanna." His eyes were clouded with emotion. Jo didn't look to see if Jason obeyed, but she heard him slide down the slope. Relief washed over her.

Jason's safe.

"I believe you," she whispered.

She opened her arms to show him she wasn't scared, though every cell in her body screamed in terror. She opened her arms to show him she trusted him, when all she wanted was to turn and run.

He said, "That's why I need to kill you and restore balance."

Leah ran into the tent and Tyler instantly knew something was wrong.

"Where's Jason?"

"That man has him! And Jo."

"Where?" Thinking like a father, or a lover, could get the two people Sheriff Tyler McBride loved most in the world killed. He had to think like a cop.

"They're behind the boulders," Leah said.

Wyatt was at his side. "I know a way to get up there without anyone seeing."

Tyler informed his deputies of the situation and followed Wyatt past the new grave. He glimpsed the name *Timothy Kenneth Sut-*

ton and his entire body shook in violent protest.

A flash of an image of *Jason Andrew Mc-Bride* on a similar headstone spurred Tyler forward.

I'm coming, son.

Wyatt was taking him in the opposite direction. Tyler gave him a confused look and Wyatt mouthed "Trust me."

Tyler followed his brother.

The slope was easier from the opposite side, and they ended up above the boulders where Doherty had Jo and Jason. Tyler could see Jason on his knees in the clearing below. Jo had her hands outstretched, talking to Doherty who had a gun aimed at his son.

Tyler wanted to put a bullet in that bastard's head. His hands clenched and he waited. Wyatt motioned that he was going about ten yards over, on the other side. Wyatt was injured himself, his arm in a sling, but he had no problem crossing the cliff, slowly to avoid detection.

Jo walked toward Doherty. *No, Jo, don't.*

She put her hand on Jason's shoulder.

"Get up, Jason, and go," Tyler heard Jo say. She put her body between Jason and Doherty. "Now Jason."

Doherty was letting him go. Less than a

minute later, Jason was behind a boulder, safe.

Tyler missed Doherty's words, then Jo said, "I believe you."

"That's why I need to kill you and restore balance." Doherty raised the gun. Jo was only five feet in front of him. She stepped back.

"Aaron, don't — you don't want —"

"It's the only way we'll find peace."

Tyler was halfway down the slope. He didn't know if Wyatt was in place, but Doherty was going to kill her.

Doherty saw the movement, but didn't seem to care. Jo opened her mouth and screamed.

That surprised Doherty enough that he glanced over at Tyler.

Tyler took a running leap off the boulder at the same time Doherty turned the gun toward him. Tyler tackled him before he could get a shot off. Doherty grunted when he hit the ground, but didn't release the gun. Tyler tried to grab his gun hand and slam it to the ground, but Doherty was moving frantically, and it was all Tyler could do to keep the gun from getting between them.

Wyatt was in the clearing and had pushed Jo aside.

Tyler wrestled with the killer. Doherty had a rock in hand and hit him on the side of the head. Stunned, Tyler held tight to his suspect. Doherty hit him again. Wyatt tried to get the gun from Doherty's grasp. The gun went off, Doherty's finger tight around the trigger.

They struggled in the wet snow, the cold air piercing Tyler's lungs as he fought for breath. He punched Doherty in the stomach, but the ski jacket softened the blow.

Doherty kneed Tyler and moved his gun hand between them.

Jo watched a replay of what happened four years ago. She might as well have been in her warm Placerville kitchen.

The gun went off between the men.

"Tyler!" she screamed. "No!"

Doherty pushed Tyler off him and stood. He stared at Tyler's face.

Tyler pulled a gun out of his holster and fired three shots into Doherty's chest.

He dropped the gun, took a step backward, his mouth moving soundlessly, then collapsed.

Wyatt went over to get Doherty's gun and Jo rushed to Tyler, who lay in the snow.

"No, Tyler, please, please, you can't die."

He shook his head back and forth. "I'm. Not."

He was struggling for breath and Jo saw the burned hole in his jacket where the bullet had entered. She tore open the jacket. "Wyatt, go get help. Get Nash, call Life Flight, get someone!"

"Shh," Tyler said. "I'm okay."

"I can't lose you, too. I love you, Tyler. You've got to hold on."

She pulled open his shirt, felt for where the bullet had entered. Tyler's stomach was hard as a rock.

"I'm wearing a vest." He pulled her down to him. "A bulletproof vest." He swallowed heavily. "Just got the wind knocked out of me."

She started to cry. "I thought — I thought —"

"I know." He kissed her hair. "I know."

"Dad?"

Jo called, "Over here, Jason."

Jason walked over, hesitated, then knelt down and hugged his father and Jo. "You're okay?"

"We're all okay."

Jo touched Jason's face. "I love you, Jason."

Tyler stood and put one arm around his son, the other around Jo, and they walked down the gentle slope on the opposite side of the clearing. Tyler's deputies trudged up the slope and Tyler whispered to Grossman as they passed, "He's dead."

"I'll take care of it."

Leah was standing with Deputy Duncan. She cried out when she saw Jo. They reunited and hugged tightly. "I was so scared, Aunt Jo."

"Me, too." Jo looked at Tyler, saw the love and fear and relief on his face. It mirrored her own. "We're okay," she said, swallowing thickly.

"It's over," Tyler said, pulling Wyatt into their circle. "He's not going to hurt this family again."

Family. Jo looked from Tyler, to his brother, his son, and her niece. She'd lost so much, but she'd also gained much more.

"I'm so lucky to have all of you," she said, her voice catching. She turned to Tyler and took a deep breath. "I — I answered a question wrong that you asked me over Thanksgiving. I hope I can change my mind."

"Nothing would make me prouder, Jo." Tyler kissed her.

We hope you have enjoyed this Large Print book. Other Thorndike, Wheeler, and Chivers Press Large Print books are available at your library or directly from the publishers.

For information about current and upcoming titles, please call or write, without obligation, to:

Publisher
Thorndike Press
295 Kennedy Memorial Drive
Waterville, ME 04901
Tel. (800) 223-1244

or visit our Web site at:

http://gale.cengage.com/thorndike

OR

Chivers Large Print
published by BBC Audiobooks Ltd
St James House, The Square
Lower Bristol Road
Bath BA2 3SB
England
Tel. +44(0) 800 136919
email: bbcaudiobooks@bbc.co.uk
www.bbcaudiobooks.co.uk

All our Large Print titles are designed for easy reading, and all our books are made to last.